Emily Holleman is the author of *Cleopatra's Shadows,* which was long-listed for the HWA Goldsboro Debut Crown. Her essays have appeared in *Elle, Salon,* and *BookPage.* After working as an editor at *Salon,* she has spent the last four years researching and writing about the Ptolemies. Raised in Manhattan, she lives and writes in Brooklyn.

Also by Emily Holleman

Cleopatra's Shadows

THE DROWNING KING

EMILY HOLLEMAN

sphere

SPHERE

First published in the United States in 2017 by Little, Brown and Company
First published in Great Britain in 2017 by Sphere

1 3 5 7 9 10 8 6 4 2

Copyright © Emily Holleman 2017

The moral right of the author has been asserted.

A CIP catalogue record for this book
is available from the British Library.

ISBN 978-0-7515-6018-3

Printed and bound in Great Britain by Clays Ltd, St Ives plc

Papers used by Sphere are from well-managed forests
and other responsible sources.

MIX
Paper from
responsible sources
FSC
www.fsc.org   FSC® C104740

Sphere
An imprint of
Little, Brown Book Group
Carmelite House
50 Victoria Embankment
London EC4Y 0DZ

An Hachette UK Company
www.hachette.co.uk

www.littlebrown.co.uk

For Meg

dear friend, only the gods can never age,
the gods can never die. All else in the world
almighty Time obliterates, crushes all
to nothing. The earth's strength wastes away,
the strength of a man's body wastes and dies—
faith dies, and bad faith comes to life,
and the same wind of friendship cannot blow forever,
holding steady and strong between two friends,
much less between two cities.
For some of us soon, for others later,
joy turns to hate and back again to love.

Sophocles, *Oedipus at Colonus*

THE HOUSE OF PTOLEMY

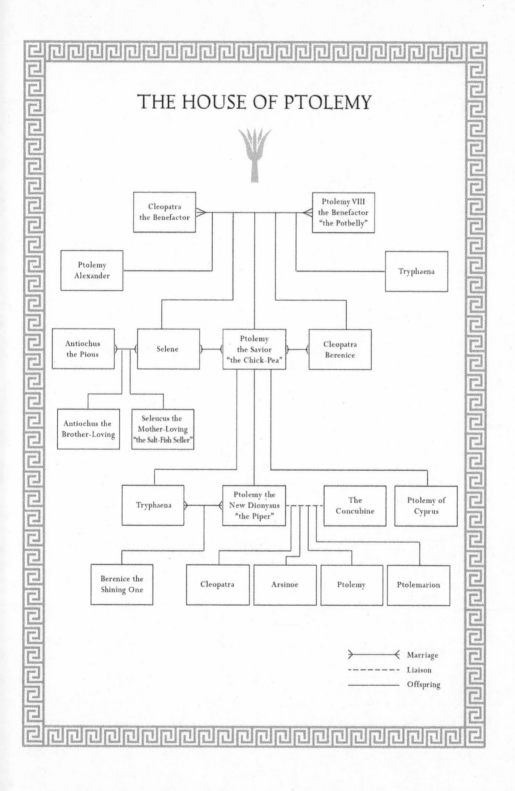

SISTER

Prostrate on his gilded bed, the Piper clung stubbornly to life. The room was dim; the curtains had been drawn throughout the king's illness, and incense had laid the walls thick with grime. Hermaphrodites, breasts and cock unshorn, pined for goat-legged Pan with smoke-blackened eyes. The other paintings—the satyrs drinking and dancing about Dionysus on his jaunty leopard—appeared grotesque, out of place. They no longer belonged here, in this darkened room, this shrine to a shrunken, dying king.

Neither did she. But just as Cleopatra couldn't tear herself away from this vigil, Arsinoe felt compelled to join in the obsession. As though her presence might tug the madness from her sister's mind, banish the moping changeling who slunk about in Cleopatra's form. Scant months ago, her sister had been the toast of the Alexandrian court, impressing bureaucrats with her knowledge of the Nile's whims and charming ambassadors with witticisms in their native tongues. But now, when Egypt needed her most of all, Cleopatra had retreated from public view. Instead, she huddled here beside their father's bed, her dark curls wreathed by her white diadem. And, dutifully, Arsinoe knelt at her side.

Before this shadow of a king, Arsinoe felt ashamed of her old fears. Four years ago, she'd quaked as her father's armies surrounded Alexandria. She'd been eleven then, and everything had frightened her in those girlhood days: first when her sister

Berenice's coup sent the Piper mewling to Rome, and then when Rome's legions brought him back. On his return, Arsinoe fled the palace and disappeared among the street children, hiding from her father's wrath. Dragged back to court, she watched as the Piper ordered his eldest daughter's execution. As he laughed at Berenice's head flopping onto the stone and spat into her empty eye. Fitting, now, that he would join that daughter in death. His *ka* would pass from his body and cross into the next world, where the gods would judge him on these deeds. Perhaps they would look upon him more kindly than did Arsinoe.

The husk before her fluttered and wheezed: the New Dionysus cut down by plebian mortality. Perhaps long ago, when Alexander the Conqueror's blood ran thick through her ancestors' veins, it had been enough to be a Ptolemy, but no more.

With a groan, the man craned his neck. His eyes squinted with determination. His fingers seized and twitched, reached out, past her, to take hold of Cleopatra's hands.

"My dear," he murmured.

Arsinoe's fists tightened at her sides. But, no, this closeness between her father and her sister could not hurt her anymore. She would look on, a stranger indifferent to their bond.

As though he'd heard her thoughts, the king glanced at her, his eyes bright and strangely merry in his sunken face. No matter how the rest of his body strained and atrophied, those eyes belonged to a much younger man. She lifted the corners of her mouth: a small kindness. Her father was dying; she could afford to be generous. To her surprise, he smiled back—grimaced, more; lips straining toward his hollow cheeks—but she recognized the intent. His fingers tugged at the air to draw her in. She couldn't believe it—it wasn't possible, not after the years of slights. But there it was again, that clawing gesture, reeling her in.

Arsinoe leaned forward and reached her hand across the bed. Perhaps she'd been too stubborn all this time, refusing evidence of her father's love. As Cleopatra so often reminded her: the Piper couldn't have known what would befall him and Cleopatra in Rome, just as he never could have guessed what awaited Arsinoe in Alexandria. And so he'd done what kings and gamblers do: he'd split his odds, leaving one daughter and taking the other. Chance, not callousness, had left her, Arsinoe, behind.

Her father coughed, an angry racking of his ribs. She moved to take his hand, but Cleopatra's was already there.

"Leave us, my sweet," her sister whispered. Her tone was gentle, ever apologetic for the Piper's partiality. The pity smarted on Arsinoe's ears.

Her father twitched his fingers again. The movement didn't beckon—she saw that now—it dismissed. A smile, a look, a turn of a wrist—none of it could wipe away the past. He was a dying man, of no use to anyone. She wouldn't—didn't—ache for gestures of love and mercy. As she stalked from his sickroom, she smashed her fist against the ebony doorjamb.

Back in her chambers, Arsinoe stretched on her divan and marveled at her strange quandary. After her days among the urchins, she'd returned half wild to the court, clinging quietly to the name she'd adopted in the alleyways: *Osteodora,* the bone bearer. Only Cleopatra had had patience for her then. Her sister had coddled and humored her, no matter how hard Arsinoe had pulled away. Now the ledgers had reversed: Cleopatra needed Arsinoe's protection. Distracted by their father's illness, her sister was blind to the men jockeying to position their brother as the Piper's heir.

Shouts echoed up from the courtyard, and Arsinoe went to her window to see the cause of the commotion. Across the garden, a horde of Romans had gathered outside her brother's chambers. Her stomach still turned at the sight of these men, though she'd grown accustomed to their presence. In the months after her father's restoration, she'd watched as foreign galleys descended on Alexandria, carrying off the city's grain and gold. That, she'd realized, was the price their father had agreed upon to buy back his throne: ten thousand talents to the Roman general Aulus Gabinius and an unrelenting supply of wheat to the insatiable Republic. The ships had brought a fleet of rats as well as soldiers, sinewy creatures who'd taken up eager residence in the kitchens. The rats at least were easier to get rid of.

A hefty man in a crimson cloak addressed the interlopers. When Arsinoe squinted, she recognized him as her brother's rhetoric tutor, Theodotus, his elephant ears betraying him even at this distance. She studied his lips, and slowly, she managed to work out his words.

"Like his father, Ptolemy recognizes your sacrifices. He knows that without your aid, our city would not have arrived at peace. In recognition of your loyalty, he has ordered that you each receive another five plethra of farmland."

The Romans roared, full-throated and in their mother tongue: *"Ptolemeus rex. Ptolemeus qui rex erit."*

Ptolemy the king. Ptolemy who will be king. The legions loved her brother, and with reason. Every day more fields spilled into Roman hands, all in the name of young Ptolemy's generosity. Theodotus was no fool—he knew rich swaths of land would bind Gabinius's erstwhile officers to his charge over Cleopatra. The soldiers distrusted her sister for what she was: an Eastern woman with an eye for rule. Hadn't they already deposed one of those? *In Rome,* Cleopatra had told her once, slack-jawed with shock, *women are chattel, no more and often less.* Or as Arsinoe had heard more

4

than one centurion sneer after Berenice's death, *In Rome, women know their place*.

The sun's last glimmers had drained from the bruised sky by the time Arsinoe heard her sister creeping up the stairs. Quickly, she wrapped her woolen mantle about her shoulders and skirted out onto the balcony that joined their two sets of rooms. For hours she'd waited, knitting together an argument to convince her sister that she must rejoin the world of the living: Cleopatra needed to acknowledge their brother as a threat. But when she caught sight of her sister—head bowed, eyes red with tears—all her carefully plotted points evaporated.

"Clea." Arsinoe grasped her sister's hands. "What's wrong?"

"What's wrong?" Cleopatra jerked her hands away with an almost maniacal laugh. "'What's wrong,' she asks. *Our father is dying*."

The words cut as intended. "I know," Arsinoe said, firming her resolve, "but you must—"

Her sister pushed past her, prying open the door to her own chambers. Dumbly, Arsinoe followed. Cleopatra collapsed on the first divan in sight, sending Ariadne, the tiger-striped cat she kept, spinning off in mewling protest. The creature didn't run far; she turned back to stare at her weeping mistress, her eyes a pair of unblinking emerald saucers. Tears poured in great rivulets down Cleopatra's cheeks.

"My sweet." Arsinoe knelt at her sister's side. She tried to summon sympathy—but her gentleness had been spent. The image of the courtyard, overrun with Romans, remained fixed in her mind. She could still hear their shouts: *Ptolemy who will be king*. How much longer, she wondered, would it be before Theodotus dispensed with niceties and set her brother firmly on the throne? "My sweet, tomorrow, promise me you'll come to the atrium. The guards, the bureaucrats—they, too, are suffering. Your brave face would give them courage."

Cleopatra snickered again, a cruel echo of her former self, the one who'd always been ready with a smile and a jape. "Why? They see your brave face often enough. Look at you. Untouched and un-burdened. Your eyes and cheeks as bright as ever. As though our father wasn't dying."

"Th-that's not fair." Arsinoe stammered over the paltry words. What else could she say? She couldn't lie to Cleopatra, and she didn't dare speak the truth. Her sister clung to this adoration of their father; it was the last indulgence of their childhood, and Arsinoe wouldn't spoil it—not unless she had no other choice. "Someone has to keep an eye on the goings-on at court."

"That's what Father has advisors for."

"Yes, but you know what those advisors are doing: they're prop-ping up our brother. Every day you spend tucked away in our father's chambers, Theodotus and Pothinus and all the rest are trotting out that boy as their new king."

"Ptolemy is a *child,* Arsinoe. Barely out of changing clothes."

Her sister's blind spots astonished her. Cleopatra was a quick study, able to divine the backstory of each passing diplomat, every official tallying the crops of the Upper Lands. And yet when it came to their brothers, she lacked all sense of proportion. She'd never paid either much mind, never remembered which tutor was assigned to whom; she'd never had to. The favorite, she had been whisked away too often by their father on some adventure. Arsi-noe, on the other hand, had long years of observing behind her. She knew what sort of men backed her brother; she knew how desperately they would clamor for their protégé, no matter how unworthy. Ptolemy might be a boy, but one day he'd grow into a man.

Arsinoe tried once more. "It isn't just Ptolemy you need to worry about. It's his councilors——"

"Trust me to handle a boy and a few thumb twiddlers. I am Father's co-ruler; I am already queen. My name alone appears on the will that Father entrusted to the Sibylline Virgins. You worry too much."

"One of us must."

"I worry *plenty* for the both of us. But I also made a promise to our father. He is dying, Arsinoe, and he is frightened. I won't"——and here her sister's voice trembled——"I won't let him die alone."

A specter of impotence stretched before Arsinoe: Cleopatra locked up in the royal chambers as weeks became months. Who knew how long the king might teeter between life and death? A cruel thought flickered in her mind. If Cleopatra didn't wish to leave the Piper's side until he faded into the next world, perhaps it would be better to quicken his passing.

The idea——unnatural, despicable——riled her. Desperate to push it from her mind, she cast about for a distraction, scouring the walls and corners of the room, all ringed with the dancing nymphs and piping satyrs their father so dearly loved. Here and there, Cleopatra's tastes crept in: a woven map of Alexander's conquered kingdoms; a terra-cotta vase depicting Medea in her dragon-drawn chariot; a delicately carved statuette of the goddess Isis cradling her infant son.

"Arsinoe." Her sister's voice cut soft and sad. "Dear one, I know it hasn't been easy for you."

Cleopatra slid her calves over the edge of the divan and lowered herself to join Arsinoe on the floor. A whiff of Cleopatra's familiar scent——rose tangled with lilacs. As they sat back to back, spines fused as one, Arsinoe felt she might conquer the world. Turn the Romans out and put an end to all her house's shameful indiscretions. The past could be cleansed. Her father's decline was proof of that.

The world sharpened: omens stiffening to fact. The king would die; the only question was when. Visions had haunted her, ever since she was a little girl, and now, each night, it was her father's corpse she came upon in her sleep, stiff and empty eyed. Perhaps, at last, she should embrace her dreams as portents—commands, even. If the gods were determined to make her the harbinger of someone's doom, why *not* her father's? He had abandoned her; he would ruin Cleopatra. With each fleeting hour of the Piper's decline another advisor pinned his hopes on her brother. The king's sickness was a plague on every one of them.

"Theodotus grows bold. Today he handed out new leases of land in the Marshes, reminding the Romans that the king's *son* recalls their service to the crown. Ptolemy may not frighten you now, but his advisors should. They will fight to secure his throne; they'd rather have a malleable boy in whose name they might rule than a sovereign queen."

Arsinoe felt Cleopatra's back tense against her own, but she knew she must press onward. The time had ripened; another moment and it would spoil. And who was to say what their father wanted? He might well embrace death as a blessing, an end to his painful, grating breaths. A darker drive spurred her on as well; she wanted to test her sister's love. It couldn't be as pure as it appeared.

"Our father is suffering, and Egypt too," Arsinoe continued. Her innards tightened. "Perhaps the time has come to hasten..." Her voice caught in her throat. What sort of twisted daughter was she?

Cleopatra shifted away, nearly toppling Arsinoe to the floor, and stared at her with ugly, jagged eyes. As though she was recognizing for the first time the loathing that lurked in Arsinoe's heart.

"And what do you suggest?" Cleopatra spat. "What do you mean by that?"

"I meant nothing," Arsinoe lied. *I meant that we might kill him, you and I.* Did she have the stomach for murder? For patricide? There'd been that boy in the streets of Alexandria, on the eve of her father's return. Her first night outside the palace, she'd hidden in the cata-combs. The boy had cornered her, and something had snapped inside her. She'd grabbed the only weapon in reach: a bone. She could still hear its crack against his skull, still see his body slumped on the ground. But that had been Osteodora's doing, not Arsinoe's.

"No, you meant a great deal by it." Her sister's tone was flat, merciless. *"Perhaps the time has come to hasten . . ."*

"I didn't—I couldn't—I'd never dream—" Arsinoe stuttered through these lies. She *had* dreamt of it; she'd dreamt of so many deaths over the years. Some had come to pass, and some had not—though, she thought wryly, sooner or later they all would. Everyone died, even Ptolemies.

"I know that you have suffered, but let the past remain the past. Surely somewhere in your heart you might find some tenderness for our father . . ." Cleopatra's voice, melancholy, drifted off, as though what saddened her most was that Arsinoe hadn't shared in the Piper's love. Arsinoe bristled. She didn't want her sister's charity.

"My *tenderness* extends beyond our father, Cleopatra, to all of Egypt, to this whole troubled kingdom that one day soon you must rule. A weak king . . ." She stopped herself. She wasn't heartless.

"A weak king reaps a weak kingdom," Cleopatra completed the axiom. "But only fools rely on foolish adages. There will be time for us to right his wrongs. He's tried, and for now that must be enough. He does love you, Arsinoe."

Hollow words.

She shrugged Cleopatra's hand from her shoulder. "His love doesn't change anything. Not for me, and not for Egypt."

That night, Arsinoe's dreams were dark and deranged. The city burned; a vulture, she flew among the flames. She circled lower in her flight to feast upon the corpses. They were but ash and bone, burnt offerings to the gods. Hunger pierced her, and she tried to flee the haunted city, to seek out fish and game along the Nile. But every time she reached the southern gates, the wind turned her; the sky became a labyrinth, a winding maze with no escape. She woke sweating, panicked. A special realm was reserved among the damned for those who killed their kin. What she needed was to blot such thoughts from her head. For the first time in ages, she found herself looking forward to her morning lesson with Ganymedes: at least it might provide some respite from her troubled mind.

But there, too, she was wrong. Amid the sturdy pillars of the library, breathing in the scent of cypress rising off the freshly polished desks, Arsinoe found no solace. Euripides shrieked accusations from the page as she read about Electra's warped tale of matricide, how Agamemnon's daughter was drawn to take revenge upon her mother for her father's murder. Four words ran before her eyes, over and over again. *Electra the wretched prays, Electra the wretched prays, Electra the wretched prays...*

"Arsinoe," her eunuch snapped. "Have you even begun preparing for this exercise?"

"Electra the wretched..." Unwitting, she'd recited the words aloud.

The eunuch cleared his throat. "An *original* speech, Arsinoe. I should hope we were long past the stage where I must test your ability to *read*." Ganymedes scratched at one of his bushy, graying eyebrows. "I've taught ten-year-olds who listen better. You were one of them."

Her anger frayed and snapped. How she had *listened*. She'd always listened. For years she'd soaked in the eunuch's rules, and what good had it done her? Despite his machinations to keep Arsinoe alive throughout Berenice's rule, he hadn't known how to protect her upon the Piper's return. Instead, he'd abandoned her in the agora and hoped that she would—somehow—survive.

"My father's dying, Ganymedes," she hissed. "I should be at his side, as Cleopatra is. But instead I'm here reading about deaths from another age."

The eunuch studied her with narrowed eyes. "You are too old, Arsinoe, for me to have to explain the differences between yourself and Cleopatra. Your father demands your sister's presence; he demands I teach you to the best of my ability. When the day comes that I am released from this duty, you can pass your time howsoever you please."

There was no point, she realized, in arguing. Did she really want to spend another morning by her father's bed? Watching as he clutched Cleopatra's hand, wincing as he spurned her own? And so Arsinoe squinted at the page and tried to force the swimming letters to still. *Electra the wretched prays; year after year her father's blood cries from the ground; but no god hears.*

Her eyes burned. She couldn't read this, not today, and no more could she speak words in Electra's defense. After all, their crimes—Electra's real, hers imagined—were too near. Did Ganymedes suspect her? Why else would he have chosen this particular passage on this particular day? *But I've done nothing; we merely spoke . . .*

"What wretched sights have cursed my eyes!" The howl of some common woman: a barefoot peasant in rough-spun grays wandered about the reading room, weaving demented circles around the scholars' desks. She must have slipped by the guards. "A weak ruler and a weakened land, a pair of Romans ripping apart both land and sea, Egypt come to ruin, drowning and aflame."

Wild-eyed, this rogue prophetess launched herself onto a bench. It wobbled beneath her weight but held. The nearest scholar, a squat, bearded man, furled his scroll and hurried off as though her rages were contagious. The creature hoisted her skirts and, with surprising grace, hopped onto the writing table. Hands tearing at her hair, she cried, "Apollo, lord of light, healer of Delos, guard of the hunt, have pity on your priestess! Let these men, these learned men, hear and heed your warnings!"

Two guards emerged, spiders from the woodwork. But the seer paid them no mind. Arsinoe pitied this creature; they shared the same curse of foresight. *Run,* she mouthed, though she knew the woman couldn't hear her. *Run and hide, for they will find you and they will seize you and they will kill you.*

"Many have already fallen to the Republic that blights our land, to the wolf who nurses traitors at her teat, to the eagle screeching across the sea. And many more shall fall. When a king falls ill, his kingdom falls ill with him. And when the king lingers so long near death—"

Already the soldiers were upon her, toppling chairs as they dragged her from the table. But they couldn't silence her shrieks. And the shrieks, Arsinoe knew, were where her power lay.

"The city burns to the ground, under the warped guidance of an old and dying man! Blood, the blood of babes. Set upon by the Furies, women devour their own young—Oh, Apollo! This is too much to bear—"

A hand sealed the woman's mouth. She flailed and bit like a netted stag. Arsinoe found herself mesmerized by the spectacle; she could not avert her gaze. But she was the only one staring. The scholars busied themselves with their scrolls, looking in any direction save at the woman screaming in their midst. Even the one who'd dashed off in fright had already righted his overturned chair and resumed his study.

"I thought curiosity fitting for learned men," she whispered to Ganymedes. "But these ones barely bat an eye when a prophet spits fire in their faces."

"Perhaps you'll learn something from their focus." The eunuch's tone was severe, but she detected the double meaning in his words.

The liveliest facet of a room was rarely the most informative. Her eyes fixed first on the squat man at the cursed table; she could not make out his notes precisely, but they were of a different character than the ones that had come before. He'd been sketching lines and angles and equations, but now he scrawled row upon row of words. She caught a phrase—*the blood of babes*—among them. His disinterest was feigned. The silence marked not ennui but rapt attention.

A fist thudded on the door. Arsinoe rushed to open it: in the darkened antechamber, her sister looked a fearsome vision. Her hair wild and loose, she might have passed for the morning's prophetess.

"Were you there when it happened?" Cleopatra whispered. Beyond, on the divan in the antechamber, Arsinoe saw her maid lying too still for slumber. She hurried Cleopatra into her room.

"Was I where?"

"In the library, when the soothsayer snuck in from the streets." Moonlight from the window cast Cleopatra in a ghostly haze.

"I was," Arsinoe answered slowly. "I was studying with Ganymedes. What difference does it make?"

"Did you believe her words?"

"Which ones?" Arsinoe forced a laugh, lightness to counter Cleopatra's gravity. "That the city shall burn? Or that women will eat their babes?" Her own dream flickered before her eyes. There, too, Alexandria had been consumed by flame.

"Be serious."

"Why? You surely aren't. You don't even believe in seers." Her nerves grew taut.

"It doesn't matter what I believe. The whole city is buzzing over her predictions. And Father does nothing. He won't listen to me when I tell him that he must." All at once, Cleopatra's toughness faded, and a petulant child stood in her place.

"But what *can* he do?" Arsinoe asked softly. "He's too ill to even leave his chambers."

"We must find a way."

"A way to what?" she echoed, though she knew what Cleopatra had in mind, the idea she herself had planted there.

"Don't play the fool." Cleopatra's eyes, wide and desperate, bored into hers. Arsinoe looked away—she couldn't bear to see the horror she had wrought.

"Fine," her sister went on coldly. "Must I spell it out for you? You were right. It's a dangerous time. Dangerous for all of us. Rome rises each day with a hunger. A weak ruler won't survive, especially not once the people lose faith in him."

Her own words flung back to haunt her. Cleopatra, father-loving Cleopatra . . . even her devotion could be spoiled. Arsinoe felt a great cavern open in her chest. The dark and damaged part of her soul had longed for this cleaving, this shaking free of their father's yoke. To place Cleopatra on the throne, to forget the man who'd allied himself with Rome and murdered Berenice. To bury him.

"There is . . ." Her voice trailed off, and she swallowed. Now, she knew, she must be brave. "You know the way as well as I."

"I want you to say it." Not a request but a command.

"What is it that you drip each morning into his wine?" Arsinoe's voice sounded a thousand stades away.

"Opium to thin the blood and dull the pain."

"And doesn't his doctor sometimes prescribe another drug?" She recalled the physician crushing leaves with a pestle, the bitter stench of poison stinging her nose. "A drug that soothes his limbs?"

"Yes, he does. Father says he feels almost well enough to rise after he has a sprinkle of hemlock." Cleopatra held her gaze.

"It's a delicate plant, hemlock. You must be very careful with the dose."

"I always am."

"For if your hand should slip . . ."

Cleopatra's eyes fell to her feet. Silence spun out between them. Even as they danced about an understanding, Arsinoe felt her sister's disgust congealing into hate. If they sinned in this together, would that loathing ever fade? Arsinoe broke: "I didn't mean—the things I said—"

Her sister stared at her: Delicate eyes sharpened with a newfound strength. A firmness of resolve. "The things you said were right. It should be done at once."

Arsinoe dug her fingernails into her wrists to keep from weeping. Her heart ached for Cleopatra, *the glory of her father*. Cleopatra, whose very name spoke to their differences in the king's eyes.

"I—I could prepare his medicine some nights," Arsinoe said quietly. "You take too much upon yourself . . . You need your rest."

Cleopatra stepped forward and embraced Arsinoe. "No, my dear," her sister whispered, "I must do this. I alone."

By the time Arsinoe put out her lamps and curled into bed, she had begun to wonder if it had all been some twisted dream. Had Cleopatra truly spoken to her of murder? Or had some evil shadow taken on her sister's aspect, a god-sent vision to warn her of the horrors to come? Or perhaps Cleopatra had merely meant to tease her, to make some great joke of the strangeness that had passed between them. Perhaps, in the morning, her sister would laugh. *You believed me, I know you did, Arsinoe!* As she had when they were young. And yet— she'd seen something sinister in her sister's gaze . . .

Arsinoe shut her eyes and pushed away her foolish thoughts. That was the child in her, the one who imagined every corner was full of portents. Ganymedes always told her she should fix her mind instead on the unyielding world, the steady pulse of day-lit truth. And so she would.

BROTHER

S prawled on the grass, Ptolemy reveled in his freedom. New duties had piled up during his father's illness: aside from lessons, he had to hold long, dull audiences with noblemen and bureaucrats. And whenever a spare moment fell to him, his eunuch, Pothinus, would appear and make him sit vigil at the king's bed. This afternoon, though, stretched empty: hours to squander with his friends. At his left, Kyrillos lay winded, cackling and panting to catch his breath. Some paces away stood Ariston, a gold-plated discus in his hand.

Ariston was the oldest of their trio—already twelve before Ptolemy had yet turned eleven—and he looked it too. The boy had spent the flood months on his father's estate in the Upper Lands, and he must have grown half a cubit there. Maybe more. And thick hairs had sprouted along his arms and legs. After their race, Ariston had kept running, his long strides on display. And now he was showing off again: cradling the discus in the crook of his arm. As he drew it back, his triceps flexed like an Olympian's.

Ptolemy flinched when he thought about his own limbs, scrawny and boyish. The body of a child, not a king. A king was broad shouldered and taut with muscles, strong enough to fling a spear through a man's heart. At the very least, he should be able to toss a discus. The saucer sailed onward: five, fifteen, thirty strides before it fell.

"Brilliant," Kyrillos gushed.

"You should get that before someone else snatches it," Ptolemy sniped.

Ariston's face tightened before he raced off to retrieve the discus. How he loved that stupid toy.

"Don't encourage him," Ptolemy told Kyrillos.

"I don't think *my* encouragement makes a whit of difference," his friend replied, cheeks dimpling in a grin. "He has plenty of admirers. He's already lain with a woman."

The knot tightened in Ptolemy's gut. He supposed it could be true. His forefather Ptolemy the Mother-Loving had wed his sister when he was eleven, and rumor had it he'd slept with her not long after.

"You can't believe every rumor you hear," Ptolemy said.

"It's no rumor," Kyrillos protested. "I heard it from the source— Ariston told me everything."

"I don't believe—. That's not possible," he answered. As though his words could amend the past. Maybe they could. Why should the past be other than how he said it was? Soon he'd control the whole kingdom, from the sea down to the Nile's winding cataracts. The thought of his father's death made his heart race. He should be grieved—he *was* grieved, he told himself. He *was*. But excitement lurked beneath the surface.

"Anyway, who would share Ariston's bed?"

"A maid of his," the boy went on, encouraged, "a pretty one who works at his father's farms."

A good lie. Once kindled, hard to stamp out. Ariston's word against some slave's a hundred stades away.

Ptolemy forced a laugh. "Yes, and I've *fucked*"—the word sounded stilted in his mouth—"every maid who ever tended me, from Ligea on down."

"She was your *wet nurse*."

"I *jest*. You'll believe anything you hear," he spat angrily. Ptolemy

17

was sick of both of them: Kyrillos and his awestruck sighs, Ariston with his puffed-up chest. "My seed has value," he added. "I'm a Ptolemy, not some drunken noble's son. I can't afford to sire kids on every willing slave."

Discus clutched at his side, Ariston raced through the cypress grove. As he neared, he slowed to a trot and then a walk. A bead of sweat trickled down his brow. It caught in the crease of his lip before his tongue darted out to lick it away.

Kyrillos made eyes at the older boy as Ariston slumped against a tree. Ptolemy could read the meaning in their glances: *Mind the prince's temper.*

He was supposed to be learning patience. His eunuch always nagged him about that. But instead, his anger tightened on a spring. His whole life required *patience, patience,* and he was sick of it. His first memories were of waiting. Waiting for his father to return to Egypt. Waiting for the Roman legions to crush his eldest sister's wretched coup. Their hideout in Canopus had always smelled of honey. And his mother had filled it with promises too. *You will be a prince again and I a queen, and both of us dressed in gold from head to toe. Just as soon as your father returns from Rome.*

After two long years, his father *did* return. But the waiting stretched on. Back in Alexandria, Ptolemy had to endure lessons on Euripides and Plato before he could ride a horse and learn to shoot an arrow. And now he had to wait until his father's last breath before he could become king.

"You want a try, then?" Ariston asked. He held the discus out. A peace offering. Ptolemy didn't want it.

"Kings don't waste their time with toys," he replied. He saw himself try to fling the piece of metal and fail. He'd look like a fool. It took too long to get good at things, too many years of practice and patience.

"It's not a waste of time. You can use these in battle," the older boy continued earnestly.

"You plan to fight by hurling saucers? Might as well throw stones," Ptolemy scoffed. "Remind me, when the day comes, that Kyrillos should lead my armies. You'll be of no use."

Ariston's back stiffened against the tree trunk. His wide eyes knit together in a scowl. "And what weapon will you use, then?" he hissed. "I don't see you tossing a javelin. Or is that not kingly enough for you either? That's your excuse for everything: why you can't fight, why you can't toss, why you can't fuck."

He could fight and he could fuck. And he would prove it to his friends. Ptolemy eyed the discus; it looked far heavier than the ones they'd tossed on the practice fields. Even Ariston sagged under this one's weight, and the older boy was almost twice his size. It didn't matter. He'd show these boys he wasn't afraid to play some dumb game.

"Give the discus to me." He leapt to his feet and jabbed his hand in Ariston's face. His friend reeled back in surprise, hands tightening on its gilded edges.

"The *discus,* give it. I want it."

"I thought it wasn't *kingly* enough for you," Kyrillos, lazing on the grass, chimed in.

"I changed my mind," Ptolemy said as he seized the discus with both hands. Ariston glowered, but he loosened his grip and begrudgingly let Ptolemy take the toy. His forearms bobbed under the weight of the thing, and he had to clench his fists to stop it from thudding to the grass. He wouldn't be able to throw it far—he might not be able to throw it at all. He took slow, heavy breaths to stretch the seconds out. If he threw and failed—he'd never hear the end of it. Kyrillos cleared his throat in anticipation.

He had no choice. Ptolemy drew back his arm.

"My prince."

A hand clasped his wrist. Ptolemy looked up to find Pothinus staring down at him. Relief flooded his body; he was spared the test.

He groaned, feigning irritation. "What is it, Pothinus?"

"Come with me."

"But I was about to——"

"Now."

Ptolemy thrust the discus back at Ariston. On its release, he felt light and airy, some great burden lifted. The feeling wouldn't last—no doubt the eunuch meant to lead him back to his father's sickbed.

"What is it?" Ptolemy asked again, once they'd emerged from under the crisscrossed branches of the cypress grove.

"Not here, too many prying ears."

The two trod in silence past the rose bushes and the narcissus blooms, past the piping satyr statues and the spouting nymphs. And finally, when they reached his father's favorite olive orchard, Pothinus gestured for him to sit on a lion-footed bench. Ptolemy slumped onto the stone. To his surprise, the eunuch joined him.

"Listen to me carefully," Pothinus said, so softly that Ptolemy had to lean in to catch his words. "I'm about to tell you something important. And when I do, you are to weep."

He glanced about the garden. It was empty. "But no one is watching."

"You are a Ptolemy. You will be a king. Someone is always watching."

He nodded.

"Your father is dead."

Ptolemy blinked rapidly, but the tears refused to flow. He squeezed his eyes shut, pressing at the corners with his fists. Nothing. Finally, he choked out a sob and sunk his face into his hands.

"There, there, my prince." The eunuch stroked his back. An

20

imitation of compassion. "That does for now. By evening, the kingdom will know and fall to mourning. You must play the bereaved son, a reflection of their grief."

His tutor continued, droning on about how his father's body would be anointed and wrapped with white linens, with what solemnity Ptolemy and his siblings would lead the procession to the Sema amidst the throngs of weepers. But Ptolemy had already skipped on to the coronation: the diadem tied about his head and then, farther down the Nile, the double crown in Memphis.

"And when will I be crowned?"

The eunuch's pale eyes narrowed. "Keep such thoughts to yourself. Don't speak, unless it is to show how your voice quakes over your father's death. You are the grieving son. Those should be the only words your subjects can say of you. Do you understand?"

Objections formed in Ptolemy's mouth. He swallowed them. He'd play the bereaved son. He'd wait. Only for a little while longer.

On the steps to his chambers, Ptolemy caught a whiff of a familiar scent, rosewater mixed with myrrh. His mother must be waiting for him; she would have heard the news too. He quickened his pace, taking the stairs two by two, and then he spotted her beneath the archway to his rooms, ageless and perfect, every inch a goddess in mourning: head to toe in black, a golden hair clasp her only adornment. Her eyes, deep and dark, almost ominous, shone in her heart-shaped face.

As a boy in exile under Berenice's rule, he'd built up a glorious picture of his father to match his mother's idol. What a disappointment it had been when he'd seen the king in Alexandria, nothing but a diadem to hint at his divinity. Now the goddess swept toward him, so graceful that she seemed to float above the ground. She wrapped her waif's arms about his waist.

"My sweet one," his mother murmured as she pressed his head to her breast. His anger faded. He might have lingered there forever. Instead, he pulled away.

"Why do I have to wait here?" he demanded. "I should be in the royal atrium, making my mark as king."

His mother cupped his face in her hands. "You will, my dear, in time. But the days after a king's passing are delicate ones."

"I don't see what's delicate. My father is dead; I'm his firstborn son."

Her eyes dimmed. "You know, my sweet, I loved your father, but I've never understood his affections . . ." Her voice drifted off. "I have no wish to cause you pain."

"It's about Cleopatra, isn't it?" he blurted out.

A sad smile spread across her lips. "You're far too clever for me to keep anything hidden from you. Rumors swirl about the will your father sent to Rome."

"What are people saying?"

"That it names your sister as the king's successor." She paused. "Don't fret. Pothinus and I will deal with the gossipmongers; such scheming is beneath you. As long as your name appears as well, nothing else matters. Only a little more waiting, I promise." She kissed his brow. "Tomorrow, at the funeral procession, you will establish yourself. Then you will make your mark as king."

After his mother left, the hours slowed. He waited for a knock to rouse him to some new duties, but none came.

Even Briseis—his favorite maid—had been ordered to leave him alone. When she brought him watered wine and apricots, the girl breathed an apology in his ear. One of her dark curls brushed his cheek. Her breasts lingered against his shoulder. Every hair on his arm stood up in salute. And then she, too, was gone.

Once Ptolemy had sucked the pulp from the last apricot pit, he started to pace. The waiting wore at him. Why were both his eunuch and his own mother so determined to keep him sidelined? But this, too, grew tiresome. Resigned, he flopped down onto his bed.

"Ptolemy." A child's voice. He didn't answer.

"Ptolemy," his younger brother tried again.

"What is it?" Ptolemy mumbled into his pillow.

"Do you want to play a game?" Ptolemarion asked.

"No. I have other things to do."

"You don't look like you're doing other things."

Ptolemy pried his face from the cushion. His brother fidgeted in the doorway, the fingers of his left hand tugging at his right. The eight-year-old wiped his nose with the back of his hand, and Ptolemy noticed his brother's eyes were red.

"Have you been *crying?*"

A twinge of jealousy. He wished he could summon tears. Or even feel pain at their father's death. He should have thrown himself to the ground and spread silt over his face. Like Achilles over Patroclus's murder: *Overpowered in all his power, sprawled in the dust . . . tearing his hair, defiling it with his own hands.* That would be the proper thing— to weep, to mourn. As the heroes did in their great tales.

"No," Ptolemarion protested. "I haven't."

"You have." Ptolemy sprung from his bed and approached the younger boy. He jabbed his finger at Ptolemarion's tear-stained cheeks. His brother drew himself up high, but Ptolemarion's head still only reached to Ptolemy's chin.

"Pothinus told me it was right that I should weep."

That needled him. Pothinus belonged to *him*—why should Pothinus advise his brother? It didn't matter how Ptolemarion behaved. He wouldn't rule. He didn't need to perform for the crowds.

"What does that eunuch know?"

"He's your tutor," the boy objected.

"That doesn't matter. I'm your older brother, and soon I'll be your king." He gave his brother his most withering glare. "What did you come here for anyway?"

"I told you. To play a game." Ptolemarion's voice was small. He opened his fist to reveal a clutch of knucklebones.

"I don't have time for such childishness," he answered coldly, kingly. "I have a thousand important matters to attend."

But after his brother left, Ptolemy felt a pang of regret. Because—of course—he did have time for childishness. He had time for everything. The hours stretched onward until dinner and then into the night.

The next morning, as Briseis marked his face with soot, Ptolemy tried to summon up some emotion. The best he could manage, though, was a slight pang in his stomach. Just as likely indigestion as grief.

The eunuch entered and Briseis scurried away. Pothinus looked him up and down, appraising. "Do you remember that I told you the time would come for you to speak?"

Ptolemy nodded.

"After the will is read, the people will look to you. And no matter *what* is read, you are to say this: *I, the eldest son of King Ptolemy, the New Dionysus, take up my father's mantle and will bring Alexandria to glory.* Can you remember to do that?"

"Of course I can. I'm not a dullard."

But the eunuch still made him repeat the words back a half-dozen times before they set off. When they finally reached the outer courtyard, half of Alexandria had already gathered—a sea of somber mourning clothes and faces black with dirt.

The crowd opened and Pothinus prodded him onward. Ahead, Ptolemy spotted his father's coffin hoisted by four black-tunicked guards. Cut from cedar and inlaid with gold, the coffin boasted a familiar frieze: the king loosed a throng of arrows at a hapless set of Persians. An odd choice, since Ptolemy was sure the king had never fired at an enemy in his life. Before he could ponder further, the eunuch yanked him into another position, then pushed him toward a third. But by the time Pothinus had left and the procession was passing through the palace gates, Ptolemy feared he had drifted into the wrong place. Somehow he and Ptolemarion were *trailing* his two sisters. He was sure the eunuch had said he should be in the lead.

The ranks of professional mourners wailed. They clawed their scarred faces and ripped their thin hair. The veiled dancers, too, had come out in full force. His father had loved these women. Faces shrouded in mystic gauze, they undulated in a despairing wave.

A sniffle broke through the crowd's operatic cries. Ptolemy stole a glance at Ptolemarion. The boy was weeping, again. His own eyes remained dry as sand. Once more he tried—and failed—to muster tears. He surveyed the crowd—no one was watching him anyway. All eyes were drawn to his tear-streaked sisters.

His subjects' attention should be on *him*. He was the heir. The knot of anger tightened in his chest. As the procession crossed the threshold to the Sema, he felt the eyes of his forefathers glaring from their tombs, ashamed. Ahead, Cleopatra approached the altar to anoint their father's body with the last oils and unguents. The high priest chanted his magic words. His sister played her part with grace, her hands steady as she rubbed the corpse and then shaking when she threw herself to the floor in lamentation. And never once did she scrunch her nose at the stink of death. He hated her for that.

Outside, in the columned courtyard among the hordes, the mood had shifted. The plebes no longer bemoaned the passing of their king; instead, they jostled and cheered, solemnity destroyed. Pothinus had been wrong: how could he embody grief that wasn't there?

As the high priest emerged, Ptolemy was surprised to find the man shrunken and weary. Within the Sema he'd seemed like a force of nature. Now he looked like any other old man beleaguered by the light of day.

The priest gestured for Ptolemy and his siblings to gather on the temple steps. With a last burst of energy, he slammed his scepter against the marble until the crowd quieted. A fly buzzed loudly at Ptolemy's ear. He fought the urge to bat it away. He didn't imagine that would look very kinglike.

"There is another matter to attend," the priest announced, his voice steady despite his other frailties. "The reading of the will of King Ptolemy, the New Dionysus, the Father-Loving, Brother-Loving God, who now rests among his illustrious ancestors."

From the folds of his robes, the man produced a scroll. His eyes narrowed and his fingers trembled as he cracked the seal and unfurled its length. But then, regaining his composure, in a booming voice, he read: "On the occasion of my death, it is my decree that the rule of the Kingdom of Egypt will fall to my eldest daughter, Cleopatra—"

The blood pounded in Ptolemy's ears. From every angle, eyes turned on him in disgust.

"—and my eldest son, Ptolemy. May they rule together with a single hand as their father and forefathers did before them."

His shame should recede, but instead it threatened to explode.

"Should any man menace their rule, I lay it at Rome's feet to set such matters right."

Ptolemy scanned the throngs for a friendly face. Someone who might give him a hint of what to do, what to say. At last, he caught his mother's gaze, a black mantle drawn over her head. In some other world, she might have been standing at his side, but his father had kept her in the background, worried a second queen might conspire against him as Berenice's mother had. And so, after all these years, she remained no more than a concubine in the public eye. *As long as your name appears as well,* she mouthed. The order didn't matter. Any fool knew that a king's power outweighed a queen's. Sons ruled, not daughters. He straightened his back. What was it that Pothinus had told him to say? No, the specifics didn't matter—the time had come for him to address his people as their king—

A strident wail pierced the air. Some mourner gone off her cue. He searched the mob for the source, but every mouth was knit shut in shock. And then, not five paces off—there she was: Arsinoe, wild-eyed and hair-torn. Her fingers clawed at her face and then reached for her throat. With a screech, she ripped her tunic to reveal her breasts. Her nails plowed red furrows into her flesh.

SISTER

Arsinoe stood in front of the mirror. Her double—scarred, naked—stared back at her. Welts crisscrossed her breasts and thighs; only her face remained untouched. It thrilled her, the control that lurked beneath the guise of chaos. Even as she had torn her clothes and skin, as she had enacted rage—mourning—outside the Sema and deflected attention from her brother, as she had called upon the Furies themselves, she had heeded Cleopatra's warning: *Don't mark your face. It does no good to destroy the gifts of the gods.*

Already the skin on her chest had begun to mend, scabs receding under freshly woven flesh. Her body's healing was an insult to the growing body of her dead: her nursemaid, Myrrine; her sister Berenice; the Piper. She'd killed them all. By visions or words, by her very thoughts—it made no difference. And while their forms rotted in the earth, her own pulsed with incurable life, her hurts healing in spite of her sins. For a moment, she had been transported—before a crowd of thousands she had wailed and wept and ripped at herself, but more than the sheer pain, it was the weight of so many eyes on her that stuck with her—the lustful, greedy eyes of men.

Clack, clack. A rapping at her door. Arsinoe jumped; quickly she tugged the linen shift over her head. She breathed to soothe the pounding in her chest—her thoughts shamed her. It was no time to dwell on the gazes of commoners.

The knock sounded again. Harder this time, demanding.

Cleopatra stood on the threshold; her eyes bled black with kohl. Depleted, she'd shed her royal regalia—and mourning colors too— for a simple cobalt chiton, and her hair hung loose and lifeless about her face. Arsinoe couldn't remember the last time she'd seen her sister so unkempt.

"Come in, my sweet," she whispered, and Cleopatra stumbled forward. Arsinoe looped an arm beneath her sister's and half walked, half carried Cleopatra to her bed before fetching a cloth and soaking it in the remnants of her morning's bath. As she stroked her sister's forehead, Arsinoe could find no words.

But they spilled from Cleopatra's mouth: "How could we, Arsinoe? How could I? Three nights have passed since our father's death, and I have not slept for even one of them."

"I, too, am grieved," Arsinoe answered.

"Yes, I saw at the funeral how you were overcome. The mob saw too—they delighted in it. I wish I could have clawed away my grief as well. But who am I to weep for him, to tear my hair and beat my breast when I—" Her sister's voice caught. "And now I, his usurper, must try to sleep in his chambers, in the very bed—"

Arsinoe took Cleopatra's hand. It was slick with sweat. "The blame is mine. My words drove you to act as you did, as you had to do."

She needed to draw her sister out, to remind her of all the work that would be required in the days to come. But Cleopatra tossed her head violently back and forth against the pillow.

"You didn't see him, you weren't there. You didn't sprinkle hemlock into his wine. You didn't watch his trusting eyes as he drained the glass. You didn't hear him call you *my beloved nurse* before the poison seized him. And now I am to weep for him. But I can't. I can't, Arsinoe."

"Clea—" Arsinoe traced a rivulet down her sister's cheek.

"I've been crying, yes." She laughed, a harsh and strident sound.

"I can hardly stop. But I don't weep for our father. I weep for myself. And that's the most worthless sort of weeping."

"No one weeps for anyone but herself. That's why we hire mourners."

"Don't be glib. I'm in earnest."

"So am I. And no one cares why you wept, only that you did." Arsinoe cupped Cleopatra's chin and lifted her sister's eyes to meet hers. "What matters now is how you will rule."

That night they shared a bed as children do, cocooned in each other's arms. But Arsinoe awoke to an empty mat; her sister must have risen with the dawn and returned to her own chambers. It was better that way, Arsinoe told herself. The palace needed a strong queen, not the distraught girl who'd curled against her the previous evening.

Still, it was hard to shake the sting of separation. When Arsinoe heard her door creak, she looked up eagerly for a reprieve—but it was not Cleopatra, only Eirene. Her maid plaited her hair with particular care: teasing the tangles from her curls with a silver comb and separating her locks into four equal parts, each twisted into a braid and collected in a clasp at the nape of her neck.

After she'd been dressed and primped to the servant's satisfaction, Arsinoe descended to break her fast. Ever since her father's return, she'd done this in the small lounge nestled beneath the nursery. There she found Ptolemarion perched on the edge of his divan, devouring what looked to be his third custard. As she passed, he smiled up at her with gap teeth. *Spares.* The word rose unbidden and lodged itself in her mind. With the heirs off coaxing nobles to their respective corners, she and Ptolemarion appeared more superfluous than ever. Arsinoe ignored her brother's grin and sat herself as far away as she could.

As the servants went to fetch her food, Arsinoe traced the table's inlay—the white-furred satyr's thigh melted into the flesh of his stomach. Her life felt strangely still and sated. Small. She drummed her fingers against the cypress and waited for the slaves to serve her. If the newfound solitude bothered him, Ptolemarion showed little sign of it. While she pushed her food around her plate, he ate heartily, sopping up the last of his custard and cheese with the crust of a pastry.

The blessing of Ptolemy and Cleopatra's union passed smoothly, with enough panache to satisfy even her father's most dedicated revelers. Elephants dragged enormous wine casks through the streets as men and women swarmed to fill their goblets with the sweet vintage; jugglers and flamethrowers raced on lions along the lines, snatching up the occasional peasant child to join in their fun; the queen and king to be were borne in a golden carriage designed to match the one that Helios helmed to draw the sun across the sky. Dwarfed by these incumbent festivities, the ceremony itself felt somewhat inconsequential. Her sister and her brother echoed the priest's words of duty and divinity, of marriage and rule. They watched dutifully as the heifer's entrails were read, and rose with their hands bound by white ribbon.

At some point during the rites, Alexander appeared and squeezed in beside her. Arsinoe flushed at his nearness. For years he'd been her closest friend, the only one who'd stuck by her throughout Berenice's reign. But here, crushed together in the crowd, she felt acutely aware of his new proportions: he was a man grown, or close enough, with a broad chest and hands that could almost span her waist. She banished those pesky thoughts. Whatever fluttering Alexander ignited was best quashed—if she were to wed, her groom would be some Cappadocian king promising ten thousand archers or a Judean prince pledging access to a new trade route. The bastard son of a local nobleman, Alexander offered no such prizes. She must think of him only as her girlhood companion, never anything more.

Eager for distraction, Arsinoe fixed her eyes on Cleopatra, descending the sanctum steps. She appeared to have set aside whatever demons haunted her and performed her new role with ease. Her gown evoked Isis; her skin glowed like bright copper against the pale linen. Her hair was plaited into a bun; the white diadem of rule swept any remaining strands from her brow. She walked with her chin held high, like a goddess.

"Jealous?" A hot whisper on her neck. Alexander.

"No," she hissed back. "Joyous."

Jealous. The word stuck in her head. *Jealous?* Of Cleopatra? For marrying Ptolemy? Certainly not for *that.* And why should she wish to be queen? She wasn't in love with death nor consumed by a desire to taunt the Fates. She'd witnessed enough bloody ends for enough bloody kings. Far better to sit beside the throne than upon it.

Arsinoe pitied Ptolemy as he trudged alongside the queen. Cleopatra's poise made their brother's fumbling all the more pathetic. He tripped on the final step, and for a moment he looked as though he might fall on his face. His stumble loosed the knot of his diadem, and after that, he kept fussing with it in an attempt to set the ribbon straight. Watching him, one could not help but doubt the gods—how could they have chosen him? It sickened her that—of all the Piper's children—he should be the one to stand at Cleopatra's side, all for that bit of flesh between his legs. She closed her eyes and let such thoughts fade away. It did no good to dwell on them.

As the procession followed the king and queen into the outer courtyard, Alexander stuck close to her, like acacia gum on her skin. It was impossible not to feel his every move, every breath, the way his arms swung as he walked, the way he drummed his pinkie against his thumb. As they climbed down the hill's winding steps, his fingers brushed against her thigh and then sprung away, frightened creatures that they were. She chided herself—she was no better. Her skin tingled where it had met his flesh. Her awareness of his body was excruciating. His very nearness eroded her power of thought.

She could smell the palace before she could see it, the piquant scent of meat wafting on the breeze. There was something tantalizing in the odor's earthiness, nothing like the sickly incense that stank up the temple grounds. The crowd reveled in it too—each face marked by longing for the scrumptious feast that awaited the royal beneficiaries: the partridge and crane and wild boar. A memory flickered: hunger gnawing at her belly, one set of fingers wrapping about a bone as the other reached to steal a handful of nuts. An idea dawned: Cleopatra should offer a feast to the poor.

Determined to catch her sister before the banquet, Arsinoe snuck off from Alexander as they passed into the first courtyard, lit with myrrh to greet the newlyweds on their return. She was halfway across the Sisters' Courtyard before she realized her mistake: Cleopatra had already taken up her father's rooms and residence. That much ran in their favor: despite his weasling, Theodotus hadn't managed to secure Ptolemy that prize.

Arsinoe hurried back toward the royal apartments, where she found some dozen sentinels milling outside. As she moved toward the double doors, a stocky guard blocked her entrance, axe drawn across his chest.

"I am sister to the Father-Loving Goddess," she said, invoking Cleopatra's coronation name. "You will let me pass."

"The queen said to admit no one," he answered in a thick Upper Lander accent.

Arsinoe looked from one dark set of eyes to the next. She

recognized no one until she reached the man at the far end of the group: Apollodorus. Sun-darkened and barrel-chested, he stood half a head higher than any of the others. Something between an advisor and a bodyguard, he had wormed his way deep into Cleopatra's trust.

"Apollodorus," she addressed him. "Tell him to let me pass."

"I can't, my princess. What he says is true."

There was an edge to his tone. He *enjoyed* this, denying her request. As Arsinoe pondered her next move, the doors creaked open, and her sister's Egyptian handmaiden ushered her inside.

The chambers had transformed since her father's death, their spirits somehow revived. The heavy curtains were all cast open and the first antechamber was swathed with white light. The whole apartment gleamed—even the Ariadne fresco looked brighter than ever; the woman's amethyst-cut eyes glinted as readily as real ones. Ariadne the cat, a transplant from her sister's rooms, brushed up against Arsinoe.

"Arsinoe, my sweet." Cleopatra leapt up from the divan. Her face was flushed; the heavy makeup had melted in the afternoon sun, and when she wiped her brow, gobs of it smeared off on her handkerchief. "Tell me, what did you make of the ceremony? You've seen more queens wed than I."

Arsinoe didn't want to recount either of Berenice's marriages— the violent first husband whose death her eldest sister had procured or the second who had been cut down by her father's troops. Those tales would only dampen Cleopatra's mood.

"I would say it was a great success. You heard the crowd roar as clearly as I did. Unless you've grown deaf in your advancing years," she teased.

"They did roar." Her sister smiled, but then she gave a small, sad shrug. "Though they roared for Ptolemy too."

"They were roaring for you, not our brother. He looked like a fool." Arsinoe had lowered her voice. She couldn't be sure who might be listening. The maid readying her sister's bath certainly seemed to be straining her ears.

"No more a fool than I do," Cleopatra replied, gesturing to the diadem, the heavy paint on her cheeks and lips.

"Of course he did. Did you see how he almost lost his ribbon? Theodotus couldn't have been pleased by that."

Cleopatra laughed gaily. Anxiety sated, her sister was in buoyant spirits, pleasing and easy to please.

The handmaiden loosened the golden clasp from Cleopatra's hair. Her braids flopped down with a thud against her shoulders. Up close, Arsinoe could see how slick they were, heavy with oil.

"I know what you're thinking." Cleopatra had assumed a tone of mock gravity.

"What's that, I wonder?"

"You're thinking"—her sister pursed her lips in thought—"that I resemble nothing so much as Medusa."

Arsinoe forced a chuckle. "You looked lovely when you were blessed, and you will look lovely at tonight's feast."

As if on cue, the servant tugged the dressing robe off Cleopatra's shoulder. Standing naked before Arsinoe, she did look formidable. Though Cleopatra was only a few inches taller, there was a solidity to her that Arsinoe herself lacked.

"You flatter me, my sweet. Tell me, why have you come? Not that I don't always welcome your company, but you, too, must dress for the night's festivities." Cleopatra dipped a toe into the silver basin, sending the surface into fleeing spirals.

Arsinoe glanced down at her violet tunic. Dark, it kept her secrets: the sweat and incense stains that came with overuse. Her clothes were fine enough, but their father's richest gifts had always fallen to Cleopatra. Arsinoe couldn't hope to match her sister's costumes in number or in quality. "These robes suit me. I don't need to change them. But you know me too well. There's another matter. I beg a favor."

"What is it, my dear?" Cleopatra lowered herself into the tub, heat billowing off the water in great swirls of steam.

"You should make an offering to mark your rule."

"I believe Serapis has already enjoyed his fair share of my meats. But is there some other deity I've offended?" Cleopatra gave a playful smile as she leaned her back against the silver.

"No, not to the gods—but to the people of Alexandria. All day they've breathed in the enticing scents rising from the palace. Slaughter a few dozen more heifers from the great herd, and let the poor eat and drink to your victory as well. I can't tell you how much it will mean to the small folk of the city." She did not add: *Because I was one of them once.* She didn't speak of her days on the streets: not to Cleopatra, not even to Alexander. Years ago, she'd mentioned Little Ajax, the boy she'd taken under her wing in the catacombs, to Ganymedes, and the eunuch reprimanded her so soundly that she'd never brought it up again.

"That is an idea," her sister said, considering before seizing on the notion. "Why not? I shall do it. But you must promise to go change your clothes. You're beloved sister to the queen! You must dress as befits your status."

"I—I do not know what else I might wear," Arsinoe mumbled.

"It's a good thing, then, that there are others who take care of such matters for you, dear one. Go to your chambers, and you will find something appropriate."

"And you—"

"Yes, and I will accede to your softheartedness and tell Apollodorus to slaughter some thirty heifers to feed the poor meat far richer than they deserve."

"It's not softheartedness—"

"I know it's not." Cleopatra's tone turned serious. "You want my subjects to love me as you do. I'm grateful for that."

Back in her own rooms, Arsinoe found the present: a crimson garment stretched as a drunken lover over the divan. She traced a finger along the golden embroidery of the hemline: the shimmer of Artemis's miniature bow, the jaw of the howling hound.

Eirene cooed over the gift as well, admiring the fineness of the fabric and the size of the stitches. Though Arsinoe had planned to dress quickly, the maid practically insisted on Arsinoe bathing before donning such finery.

"Tell me, Eirene," Arsinoe said as she stepped into the basin, "what did you think of the crowning?"

"I didn't attend, my princess," the servant answered, gaze lowered. "My duties were in the palace."

"Of course," she sighed. "But tell me—what happened here? What did the servants whisper?"

"You'd turn me into quite a gossip if you had your way." Eirene giggled. The maid scoured harder at her shoulder; Arsinoe leaned into the rough scrub of the cloth.

"It isn't gossip if it's the truth."

"I suppose there's little enough harm in telling. A few spoke of how the entrails boded well. And, as ever when a king dies, some are eager for the change."

Eirene was diplomatic; Arsinoe would admire the quality if it weren't so infuriating.

"What sorts of change? What rumors circulate about the end of my father's reign?"

"I haven't heard a breath of rumor here," the serving girl replied. "Merely that he was an old man, and an ill one."

"He was, Eirene," she said, imbuing her voice with as much sadness as she could muster. "He was."

Clad in her new robe, her hair curled and crowned upon her head, her lips and eyes painted in vivid red and black, Arsinoe hurried across the great courtyard. Her preparations had taken longer than she had imagined, and she suspected the feast had already begun. A small part of her admitted that the effort was worth it—if only to see Alexander's eyes drink in her form, listen as his tongue grew muddled when he greeted her. She pushed the thought from her mind—foolishness. The evening belonged to Cleopatra, not to her.

At the entrance to the banquet hall, she paused: each of the tables had been polished until their surfaces shone like mirrors, and the tapestries glistened, basking in the light of the oil lamps, every speck of dust beaten from the cloths. This, she thought, was true power. Cleopatra had willed all this into being: from the rich meats and opulent sauces to the fresh-minted plates. The lesser nobles—a sea of blues and wines and saffrons—had started to arrange themselves about the lower tables, slumping into the couches, licking the juice from chicken giblets off their fingers and helping themselves to trays of Damascus plums.

Set some dozen feet above the fray, the high table—the queen's table—was ringed by a dozen divans of varying sizes, golden legs sprawling from beneath violet cushions. As she approached, Arsinoe recognized the eldest son of Artemon, the patriarch of one of Alexandria's most prominent families—though she couldn't recall the youth's name. She did remember that he was a consummate drunk, though, and his fingers were already twined around his first—or fifth—goblet of wine. No matter how great a lineage, how strong its seed, it still yielded men like him, content to rot away their forefathers' glory.

Two unwelcome faces greeted her as well. One, stern with a closely clipped beard, belonged to Alexander's father. He shared his son's gray-green eyes but little else. Though she'd known Dioscorides since before she could toddle, she'd rarely heard him speak of Alexander—men were peculiar about their baseborn children, even ones they permitted in court—and it always made her wonder what else the man didn't mention in polite company. Now he was engaged in a heated conversation with Theodotus, which died down as she approached.

The rhetoric tutor leaned closer to make out Dioscorides's words and then spun around to stare at her with his left eye; his right, nearly occluded by his bushy brow, drooped off to the side. Such deformities usually left their bearers shunned—*cursed by the gods,* the common folk would mutter freely, and many scholars too, though they'd be loath to admit it. The fact that this unheralded man from Chios had flouted such whispers to rise high in her father's court spoke to admirable talents of persuasion. The very talents that made Arsinoe wary of him.

"My princess," Theodotus said. "What a lovely picture your brother and sister make as king and queen."

"Lovely indeed," she echoed.

Arsinoe chose the divan beside the flushed nobleman, who belched loudly as she settled into her seat. So be it. She'd take the young wastrel over that treacherous pair. And—who knew—her lot could yet improve. Not all of her father's advisors were insufferable. She rather liked Serapion: barely thirty, he was the youngest of the Piper's councillors, and he'd only come to power after Berenice's death. On good days, she felt toward him as she might toward an uncle.

"How does your father?" she asked her dining partner.

"Well enough," he answered too loudly for their close quarters. He was even drunker than she'd thought. "Heartier than you'd expect for a man of his years."

"I'm glad to hear it," she replied, ignoring the bitterness in his voice. Anyone so much as passing through Alexandria knew how keenly he awaited his father's death—and the hefty sum of silver talents it would bring.

She caught sight of Serapion's fiery hair as he made his way toward the high table. Wearing a low-girdled blue tunic cut from fine Chinese silk, he grinned at her as he approached, a welcome change in mood. She was in luck. But Theodotus flagged him down, pulling the younger man into yet another debate over the benefits of an early wheat harvest, the merits of which practice now consumed the court. The Persians, it was said, had applied the method with astounding success, nearly doubling their yield in poorly irrigated seasons.

Weary of those well-trodden arguments, Arsinoe tried to catch snippets of conversations from farther-flung clusters. Perhaps those at a greater distance from the royal dais might be looser with their tongues. The din stymied her—it was too noisy to make out more than a few scattered words, nothing of any use. *Elephant* came up often enough, so evidently the wine-lugging beasts had made an impression. After a time, she gave up. She leaned back on her cushions and let the clamor wash over her, the sounds of half a thousand men clinking goblets and tapping cutlery. As she glanced around, she spotted a few revelers—Romans, she suspected—slipping a bejeweled spoon or another trinket into their satchels. She smiled at the naive thievery—the guests would be sent home with the cutlery and the golden plates pressed with the images of Cleopatra and Ptolemy. Some revelers would even find a slave or two thrown in.

The chatter dimmed, and a few stray phrases broke through: *I'm famished, quiet, the queen.* Her sister stood silhouetted against the central archway. Cleopatra tarried to let the room soak in her presence: her robe shimmered like liquid gold; her arms, her neck, her ears all dripped with pearls and precious gems; the white diadem that cut across her coiffed tresses completed the effect. Somehow her sister managed to appear both older and younger than her eighteen years. Her face retained traces of a girl's roundness, but her eyes sparkled with wisdom and her breasts and hips were lush and full, the body of a woman. The Piper's dying had dragged out for so long that even Arsinoe had forgotten the sheer power, the otherworldly radiance of a hale ruler.

The guests, dumb with awe, erupted into cheers. One man raised his glass and then the whole gallery was stumbling to its feet. "To Cleopatra, the Father-Loving Goddess!" the cry blared.

Only after her sister had quieted the hall and floated across the onyx toward the dais did Arsinoe notice the child trailing in her wake. Eyes darting and mouth pinched, Ptolemy looked bewildered. His clothes equaled Cleopatra's in splendor—his tunic, a pale ivory studded with amethysts to match the violet accent of her gown—but he lacked her showmanship and charisma. Arsinoe hoped he might go utterly unnoticed—but then she saw Theodotus shift on his divan.

Forcefully, the old man cleared his throat and clacked his wooden teeth, banging his silver goblet on the table. "To Ptolemy, our new god and our new king."

Though Theodotus spoke loudly—shouted, almost—few heeded the interruption. The lounge was too ready to bathe in their queen's glories; already the word *goddess* was forming on many a lip. Arsinoe prayed the rhetorician would sink down in defeat. But she should have known better. Instead, he clambered onto the table with the litheness of a much younger man. He stomped his feet and sent a cascade of plates clattering.

"To the new Ptolemy," Theodotus bellowed, as though he'd simply not been heard the first, or third, or eighth time he'd spoken the name. "To our king!"

Obliging, several nobles raised their goblets—Dioscorides among them, though Arsinoe could hardly feign surprise at that. Alexander's father had a peculiar dislike for her sister; Arsinoe had imagined he'd be quick to throw his support behind young Ptolemy. The others looked less swayed by the rhetorician's words than by the invitation to raise a glass. Cut from the typical Alexandrian cloth, they were happy to drink to most anything.

Then the ground roiled. For a chilling instant, Arsinoe feared the gods themselves had intervened—that word of their patricide had reached Mount Olympus and Zeus the Thunderer had set the earth shaking to punish them. Slowly, she realized it was only men pounding on the onyx: the Roman soldiers had taken up the rhetorician's cheer, bashing their spear butts against the ground. *To the great king!* they echoed in Latin: *"Regi magno!"* It shouldn't surprise her—Rome abhorred queens. They didn't even give their daughters distinct names, so little did they esteem members of the female sex. And how many Gabinians had Theodotus recruited for the banquet? Her eyes now caught on red tunics everywhere she turned. The Alexandrians—she hoped, she prayed—would counter. They bore Rome little enough love. Some competing chant in Greek, to remind Pompey's forgotten men that this wasn't their precious *Italia,* that other powers held sway here.

The Galatian guards—the stoic men whose fathers and fathers' fathers had guarded her family's fortune for a hundred years—began to bellow Ptolemy's name as well. Her heart dropped away—the troops rarely chose sides in such matters. Even when her father's cousin Ptolemy Alexander had murdered the woman who was his wife, sister, and mother—the indomitable Berenice Cleopatra— these members of the military elite had kept themselves above the fray. Even when the incensed city folk had stormed the palace and lynched the deranged monarch in turn.

As the voices webbed together in Greek and Latin, and even a word or two of Aramaic, Ptolemy straightened his back and stood taller; his face even took on an expression of nobility. Though Arsinoe knew he remained the same boy of ten, the shouts appeared to bolster him. That was the point, of course. Had Theodotus orchestrated these theatrics? No doubt her brother's eunuch had participated too. The outcry of support from the soldiers was cleverly plotted. The perfect ruse to convince the gathered nobles that there was something behind that pockmarked face, some depth and fortitude that even the boy's own father hadn't seen.

Arsinoe glanced at her sister. Cleopatra had dazzled in her public appearances, but she'd seen the fragility that lurked beneath that confidence. A banquet hall reverberating with cries for Ptolemy— that was enough to sour any mood. Yet Cleopatra appeared unperturbed. Halfway between the entryway and the high table, she stood beaming and bright, as though pride swelled in her breast for her king. As though each turn was playing out precisely as she'd wished.

The pounding grew unbearable; the vibrations thrummed against Arsinoe's bones. She hoped the noise yielded the same disjointed effect on Ptolemy. But the uproar seemed only to embolden him; his chin lifted higher and prouder until she could detect some flicker of resemblance to their vanquished father.

And then Ptolemy's hand began to tremble. At first Arsinoe thought she had imagined it, but the quaking built upon itself until it burst forth in violent spasms, hurling the boy forward, as though the shaking sickness had come upon him. Yet that was impossible—her brother had never suffered from the so-called sacred disease. The thumping calmed as the spectators, noticing the horror, froze one by one. Even Theodotus was caught agape, his false teeth dangling off his gums, staring blankly rather than rushing to his charge's aid. Instead, it was Cleopatra who ran toward the boy and wrapped an arm about his waist to keep his head from bashing against the stone.

"Silence," her voice commanded the surrounding soldiers. "My brother is a sweet child but faint of heart, and only a boy of ten. He is touched and honored by your support, but too much commotion serves only to disturb him."

Foam bubbled at Ptolemy's lips.

"There, there, dear one, no need for fear," Cleopatra cooed as she shooed a lesser noble from the nearest divan and laid their brother down upon the cushions.

The court looked on in stunned silence as Cleopatra called for a physician. Kneeling at the boy's side, she clutched his hand and brushed the stray hairs from his brow. If Arsinoe hadn't known better, she would have thought that her sister sincerely fretted over Ptolemy's fit. Only when—under the doctor's direction—their brother was carried to his chambers did Cleopatra settle into her divan at the high table.

"Your concern is touching," Serapion said softly. "It is good to see such love between a king and queen. It bodes well for their rule."

Arsinoe couldn't tell whether he was mocking—she could have sworn his right eyebrow gave a telltale twitch. But the queen accepted his compliment on its face.

"I'm merely glad that I could offer him some comfort," she answered. "I had thought to warn of his illness, but he performed so admirably at our blessing, I had let myself hope his strength might hold."

The trace of a smile on her lips, Cleopatra glanced toward

Apollodorus, hovering at her left. What secrets, Arsinoe wondered, did those two share?

"We all did," the burly guard agreed. "It's no boon for the city to know the king's true feebleness."

Her brother was many things: childish and spoiled, lazy and a bit of a whiner—much of her house's cockiness with little of its cleverness. But feeble?

Had Cleopatra put something in the boy's drink? Nonsense, she told herself. Her sister would be better off drugging Theodotus—there lay the real danger. The rhetorician was the one who tugged at the strings; Ptolemy was harmless on his own. Arsinoe couldn't take any more familial blood on her hands. For who would be at fault but she? She who had warned Cleopatra about the risks of underestimating Ptolemy.

BROTHER

Ptolemy opened his eyes. His lids felt heavy, like they'd been stitched with lead. Black and red patches blotched his vision. Where was he? He'd been in the banquet hall; men had been chanting his name. He should return to them. Too quickly, he pushed himself up to sit. The walls spun: Orpheus twisted about in circles, fleeing the merrymaking Pan.

His childhood rooms, he realized as he sunk back into the bed. A shadow approached; a blurry face hovered over him. His memory returned: one moment he'd been hailed as king—the next, a writhing monster had seized his body and hurled it to the floor.

"Quiet, quiet," the face whispered as its owner braced a hand against his shoulder.

"Let go of me," he croaked. His throat was scorched.

"Hush, my king."

The face flickered into focus: a bald dome tapering into a sharp, gray beard. *Sophos*. The royal physician.

"I've—I must return to the feast," Ptolemy muttered, straining against the doctor's grasp. His skin was burning beneath woolen blankets. "Get these off me. I have to go back to the banquet hall."

"My king," Sophos said in that same stern tone. "It's best for you to stay here and rest."

Ptolemy was sick of hearing what was best.

"I've rested plenty," he whined. "And it's my feast."

Beyond the curve of the man's pate, Ptolemy could see his inlaid desk had been swept clear of papyri. Now vials of strange-looking unguents cluttered its slate. Such instruments didn't belong here— they belonged to some stinking sickroom. His father's, he recalled with a shudder.

"Your feast has long since finished."

"What—but I—" Ptolemy sputtered. "You're wrong, old man, I just came from there."

"Your fit has left you weak, my king." The physician patted his hand. "You've been in bed for days."

"Days?" Ptolemy groaned. What little strength he'd mustered ebbed, and he shut his eyes to keep the world from twirling off its axis.

The doctor prattled on. "Your sister will be overjoyed to see that you're well. She's scarcely left your bedside, only when duty draws her out."

His heart gave half a flutter. Arsinoe had fretted over him? The scene of their father's funeral played out again: how she'd ripped her tunic to reveal her breasts.

"See," Sophos said as he flicked his eyes toward the door. "She's returned already."

It wasn't his heart-faced sister who stood in the archway. It was the other one. His queen. A familiar uneasiness stirred in his gut. For as long as he could remember, Cleopatra had paid him little mind. On the rare occasions she did glance in his direction, it seemed merely to remind herself that he wasn't worth a second thought. But now her expression had fixed into a mask of concern: her mouth a taut line and her brow knit close to her eyes. She rushed to his side.

"My sweet brother," she whispered. "How worried I've been."

Why? he wondered. Why worry *now?* Of all the times to grow anxious for his health, this one made little sense. Why not when he'd nearly drowned at age six? Or when he'd had that scorching fever when he was eight? Or the time, only last year, he'd nearly split his skull open falling from a horse? His thoughts flopped about fitfully.

"Wh-what happened?" he stammered.

"My dear, don't you remember?" His sister wiped his brow. "You were struck down by the shaking sickness."

Her jaw clenched in concern, and she spoke with such certainty that he almost didn't dare contradict her. He had to summon all his strength to retort: "I don't have the shaking sickness."

He'd seen such saps afflicted in the plazas of the city. With disgust, he recalled how they writhed on the stone as spittle sprayed from their mouths. But he'd never been stricken in that way—if there was one thing he remembered unfailingly, it was humiliation.

"It's never happened before?" His sister's eyes widened as she glanced at the doctor. "Did you know that, Sophos?"

The old man was stoppering up the various vials strewn about the desk; he didn't look up from his work.

"It's not, I'm afraid, quite as strange as it sounds," he answered. "Though the onset usually occurs early in childhood, the illness has been known to manifest itself at any age, even in full-grown men. Your brother's case is not unusual."

His case *was* unusual, though; he was a *Ptolemy* and a king. How was it ordinary for him to be anointed by the gods and struck down by the sacred disease in the same hour?

Cleopatra squeezed his hand. "Soon we'll get you well."

"I missed the feast," he said flatly.

"You mustn't worry about that," she cooed. "You must only promise to regain your strength. Egypt needs you. And when you're better, we shall throw another feast, even greater than the last."

His sister's eyes, ringed in black and gold, swelled like saucers. They widened into mouths that might devour him—the rest of the room too, perhaps the world. And then, just as quickly, the image fragmented. Cleopatra's eyes looked like any others. They even brimmed with tears. He felt his own prickle despite himself. Of everyone—his friends, his advisors, his own mother—only she had cared enough to wait on him.

"I will. I promise."

"That's my brave brother."

"Cleopatra," he began, "where's Pothinus? Where's Theodotus?" He wanted to ask after their mother too, but that would make him sound like a child.

"I've told your tutors of your illness, and Mother as well, but..." The queen steadied herself against his bedpost. "I'm sure they all have many matters to attend in your absence. It is my greatest hope that they shall come to you soon."

He didn't try to form words, only nodded. In one graceful motion, his sister swept down to kiss him on the cheek and then glided from the room. Long after she left, he could feel it tingling. The only cool mark on his burning flesh.

He closed his eyes, but his mind refused to rest. The same images spooled over and over: the Romans banging their spears, the swelling of his heart, and then the fall—

Sophos leaned over him again, pushing a spoonful of some foul-smelling concoction to his lips. Ptolemy didn't want to drink it; it reeked of death.

"I want to get up." He turned his mouth away from the ladle. "I don't need any more curatives."

The doctor scowled. "You promised your queen that you'd be well soon. And you won't get well without rest."

"I've rested plenty; you said yourself I've been asleep for days," Ptolemy answered, stifling another yawn. Sophos seized the opportunity and slopped the liquid into Ptolemy's parted lips. He tried to spit it out, but the doctor poured too fast, and he had to swallow to keep from choking.

"What's the matter with you?" Ptolemy said once he'd stopped hacking. "I could have your head for that."

Sophos appeared unmoved by his threats. "When dealing with a stubborn patient, sometimes desperate measures are needed. I swore an oath, you know."

The doctor sounded unhinged. Perhaps his mind had dimmed in his advancing years, forcing medicines and babbling about oaths. Rumor held that the physician had served the palace for an age— that the man had overseen the birth of Ptolemy's grandfather. Surely that couldn't be true. Ptolemy tried to calculate how many floods must have passed between that day and this, but the numbers refused to sum. His thoughts grew disjointed, and as he tried to follow them, he instead found himself falling yet again.

The next time he woke, Ptolemy found Pothinus squatting at his bedside.

"Do you know how long you've been asleep?" the eunuch scolded.

Whatever relief he might have felt at his tutor's appearance evaporated.

"Not so long," he protested, glancing to the window. The light still poured from the west, just as it had when Cleopatra had come to bid him farewell. "It can't have been more than a few hours."

Pothinus's lips twisted in irritation. Whiskers were in fashion among the court's older set, but the eunuch's cheeks were preternaturally smooth. Their bareness magnified every facial twitch.

"The doctor said I needed sleep," Ptolemy went on firmly. He tried to push himself to sit, but his arms ached at the effort. So maybe he had dreamt another day away. What difference did it make?

"*Cleopatra's* doctor said you needed sleep," the eunuch snapped. "And how much sleep does he prescribe? You've slept through three full days. *Again*. While I'm sure your dear sister prefers you unconscious, the rest of us would like you awake so that you might *rule*."

Three more days had passed? But Cleopatra had been here just moments before—the spot where she'd kissed his forehead still prickled.

"You haven't even come to see me," he said. "What do you know about my illness?"

"Is *that* what your sister told you?" Pothinus let out a harsh bark of a laugh.

"She didn't have to tell me," he snapped. "I haven't seen you until now."

"Short of entering your dreams, I'm not sure how I would have managed an audience. You have, I must remind you, been dead to this world for the greater part of seven days." Pothinus lowered his voice to a murmur. "You can't believe it's an accident that you're laid away in bed while your sisters sneak out of Alexandria."

"What are you talking about? Cleopatra was just here."

"They've sailed to Hermonthis. Cleopatra goes to bless the new Buchis bull—a duty that ought to fall to you. And on her return voyage, I suspect she may well stop in Memphis to be crowned—alone."

His stomach fell away. "She wouldn't dare."

He wanted to be fierce, but he sounded weak instead. What, after all, had ever stopped Cleopatra from daring anything?

"You should get up now, at least." Pothinus sighed. "And stretch your legs."

Ptolemy moved to sit, and black blotches swam across his eyes. Briefly, he feared he'd faint or shake or, worse—vomit. But he didn't. And once he'd paced the room a few times, he began to feel stronger. He even ate heartily when a servant brought a tray of plums and pastries. By the evening, he was tossing knucklebones with a sheepish Ptolemarion. His little brother mumbled an apology for his absence, but Ptolemy brushed off the boy's words. He was eager to overlook the lost week entirely and forget this latest shame.

Within a few days, he was well enough to play outside in the gardens with Ariston and Kyrillos. Though he was sure his friends had witnessed his fit, neither mentioned it. Both boys showed him a shade more deference, now that he was king.

Not that he had much time to enjoy their new dynamic. Mornings belonged to Pothinus, who taught them Pythagoras and Archimedes, Persian and Aramaic. Sometimes the eunuch would throw in a dash of Herodotus, Thucydides, and Polybius. When they broke for their midday meal, Pothinus often tried to pull him aside for private lectures, but these Ptolemy staunchly refused: the eunuch was clearly incapable of relating matters of import. And besides, in the afternoons the boys had to suffer under Theodotus's tutelage through the plays of Sophocles and Euripides and the philosophies of Plato and Aristotle. Ptolemy doubted these dead Athenians could teach him anything useful about rule. Even Theodotus seemed distracted—as distant as his cloudy right eye. And so, mostly, Ptolemy found he spent his time waiting. Waiting for his lessons to end, waiting for Cleopatra to return. In that way, his life as king felt little different from his life before.

The nights, at least, had changed. When Cleopatra had been in residence, the royal banquet hall had overflowed with men: his father's advisors, hopeful emissaries, a fair number of Gabinian soldiers. But in her absence, all the sycophants had vanished—even steely-eyed Dioscorides and jolly Serapion were nowhere to be found. Instead, the lounge fell to him and his friends. Each evening, Ptolemy ordered sweet-voiced lyrists and dancing girls in silks. On the night of Ptolemy's eleventh birthday, Kyrillos got so sauced that he snatched a lyre from one of the musicians and sang a long and bawdy ballad about Patroclus and Achilles. And on another, one of the girls took Ariston's hand and, giggling, guided him behind a scrim. For days the grunting echoed in Ptolemy's head. Something else haunted him as well, something Kyrillos had begun to harp on as they drank: When would he consummate his marriage to Cleopatra? Ariston had already slept with half a dozen women. How was it that he, Ptolemy, hadn't even bedded his bride?

The evenings of carousing ate into his days. Tongue dry and eyes drooping, Ptolemy hardly bothered to feign attention at his lessons. One afternoon, after he'd dozed off during a particularly dull lecture, Pothinus snapped. The eunuch barked at the other boys to leave and dragged Ptolemy back to his chambers.

"There's something I should show you. If you are sober enough to care," the eunuch said. "Here. Take a look at that and tell me that you still trust your sister."

Roughly, Pothinus pressed something small and flat into his hand. When he opened his fingers, he saw it was a coin. A silver tetradrachm, and from its slender face, a single profile stared up at him. Ptolemy turned the trinket over and back again, as though doing so might reveal a different image. But no matter how many times he flipped the piece, Cleopatra's face alone was etched on it.

Ptolemy glanced up to see the eunuch's eyes had tightened into slits, his lips thinned in disappointment. Pothinus wanted to provoke his fury; Ptolemy understood that much. Already the rage was brewing in his gut, but he refused to give in to it.

"And so?" Ptolemy replied. He opened his palm and let the coin fall to the floor. It landed on the onyx with a satisfying clunk.

"I did not expect to have to spell this out for you," the eunuch replied. "What clearer evidence do you need that your sister plans to rule alone?"

His stomach lurched. "I see a coin, that's all."

"Never in your lineage's great history has a *woman*"—the eunuch spat the word with vitriol—"dared to omit her *king* from coinage. You must act—and act now. She's already humiliated you a dozen times, beginning with that feast. You think that bout of illness was a coincidence? It was too well timed for that. It was set up to make you look like a weakling."

"You're supposed to protect my rule," Ptolemy snapped. "If she's made these coins, whose fault is that?"

"It's difficult to protect your kingship when you show such little interest in it. You've made it clear that you'd much prefer to get drunk with your friends than attend to your lessons, let alone mind the actual concerns of rule."

That wasn't fair. No one had ever offered him any hint of how to rule—the eunuch only ever droned on about histories and foreign tongues. And Theodotus was worse. Sometimes Ptolemy wondered if the rhetorician was even trying to teach him anything at all.

"I could face any trouble that came my way," Ptolemy replied.

"How?" the eunuch sneered. "By drinking at it? Are you *determined* to run your dynasty into the ground? To let your pathetic line die with you?"

"No," he fired back. "And when Cleopatra returns, I'll prove it. I'll plant my seed in her at once."

The eunuch laughed. "You think you could do that?"

The shame, the rage, built up in his stomach. His sister's smug face on the coin.

"What *could* you know of such things? My *cock* can harden on its own, you know."

"Ptolemy," the eunuch sighed. "You should know better than to inflict further humiliations on yourself. Think of the story that will spread: the boy king who tried and failed to mount his queen. You can't expect Cleopatra to keep the secrets of your wedding bed."

He was tired of the eunuch's doubts. Of how Pothinus—like the rest—thought he'd never measure up.

"I wouldn't fail!" Ptolemy nearly yelled. "You're just jealous because you can't fuck a woman."

Pothinus studied him for an excruciating moment and then he shrugged.

"You are determined, then."

"I am."

"Very well." The eunuch stood, and the divan jolted forward at the shifted weight. "Briseis!" Pothinus called out.

"What are you doing?" Ptolemy hissed.

Smiling, the maid entered, a half-mended tunic dangling from her hand. Her cheeks flushed prettily in the day's heat.

"I'm giving you the opportunity to prove yourself." There was something cold and hateful in the eunuch's voice. Briseis noticed it too; she tightened her grip on the garment in her fist.

"What does my king need of me?" Her voice faltered slightly.

"He needs you to remove your tunic."

Briseis blushed down to her neckline. She turned a pair of pleading eyes toward Ptolemy. His groin tightened; he thought he might be sick.

"Is—is that what my king wants?"

"Yes. It is." He'd tried to sound fierce and hungry. He *was* fierce and hungry. And his word was law. No matter how Cleopatra tried to wrest power from him.

Briseis took a deep breath; she let her sewing waft to the floor. Trembling, she crossed her arms over her waist. Her fingers pinched the edges of her tunic. Her honey-colored eyes pleaded with him again. She moved slowly as though at any minute he might change his mind. He said nothing. The garment rose, revealing her legs, her thighs, her budding breasts. She shivered naked in the hot, stale air.

"Don't stand there like a fool," Pothinus commanded. "Go to him."

She crossed her arms over her chest and then, deliberately, uncrossed them. As Briseis shuffled toward him, he felt the eunuch's icy gaze on his back. It spurred him to action: Ptolemy stood and straightened himself as tall as he could. He puffed up his chest.

"Stop playing the blushing innocent." He grabbed the maid's hand. It was clammy to the touch, and he yanked her toward him. Like a fish on a line. He felt shy, distant, as though he looked on from above: a sneering eunuch, a naked woman, and a quaking boy. His floating self threatened to vomit.

Her hand reached under his tunic. It ran up his leg until it reached his sex. *His cock*. His heart raced; he began to stiffen, slowly, slowly, beneath her fingers. He could do this—yes. Of course he could. And then, and then—he wilted. Shame flooded his body. *Ptolemy, be a man*. He nearly spoke those words aloud. He willed himself to grow firm, to hold that firmness. He wouldn't be humiliated, not now, not again. Her deft hands turned fast and urgent; one squeezed his testicles and the other wrapped around his fading erection. The motions grew quicker and more desperate. He closed his eyes; he tried to think of her as he did when he was alone. Her breasts beneath his fingers, butterfly kisses on his lips.

"Enough," the eunuch ordered, and the fingers withdrew.

His face burned. And when he opened his eyes, Briseis had already slipped her tunic over her head. She did not meet his gaze.

"Don't speak of this," Pothinus commanded her. "Not to anyone."

Ptolemy pulled his own tunic down, stretching it until it went past his knees. He wished it would stretch down to his toes and swallow him whole.

"Of course. I would—I would never . . ." the girl stammered.

"Leave us," the eunuch said. "You've played your part."

"My king." Her eyes fixed between his feet. And then she was gone.

"When you can fuck your servant girl, you can fuck Cleopatra." Pothinus's tone was matter-of-fact. "Until then, do something of use. Go court Dioscorides, at least. He's no friend of the queen. Or even Serapion. Unless you'd rather waste each night with your pathetic friends until the queen returns and you've lost what little chance you had to gain supporters in her absence."

But when the eunuch left, Ptolemy didn't seek out his father's former advisors. He wasn't even sure where to look, and he had no idea what to say. He couldn't even fuck a serving girl; he was little better than a cuckold king. And, worse, the eunuch was right: in a few short weeks, Cleopatra had turned the court against him. Even in her absence, no one bothered to curry his favor. No one except his foolish friends and the dancing girls—and even they would laugh at him if they knew the truth. He'd enabled Cleopatra's treachery— he'd trusted her. And for what? For a few kind words and a kiss on the brow?

Instead, he walked in listless loops. First, he circled the near gardens, pacing about the satyr fountains and the nymph statues. With each round, he allowed his route to spin outward, until he was strolling through cypress groves and the rose gardens. On his last turn, he spilled out of the eastern gate onto the beach.

The waves crashed angrily against the shore. For years the sea had frightened him; the very sight of it filled him with dread.

With a shudder, he remembered the last time he'd gone into the waves. He'd been five, maybe six. It must have been high summer, not long after Berenice's coup had ended and his mother had brought him and Ptolemarion back to the palace—the day was sticky in his mind. His mother had convinced his father to leave off his boozing and his whores long enough to come down to the sea. Cleopatra and Arsinoe had been sullen—he couldn't recall why. But he'd bubbled over with glee. He'd raced Ptolemarion, tripping over toddling feet, and as he ran, he glanced back to make sure his father followed. The New Dionysus, as he was called, was a stranger. So many years the king had been away in Rome. Ptolemy knew he was supposed to impress him. And when his mother, urging, smiling, mentioned that he'd learned to swim, he was excited to show off his new skill.

He'd splashed through the shallows, as fast as he could manage. Almost at once, a wave washed over his head, and his hands fought helplessly. Water poured into his lungs; he flailed against the surf. He knew now that he'd only struggled for a few moments, but those moments had stretched endless. They haunted him to this day. The taste, the pounding in his head—and then Arsinoe had dragged him from his drowning. He hadn't thanked her for that. Afterward, he'd cried, and his salty tears had confirmed his fears: he'd never be rid of the sea.

There, he realized, lay the root of his cowardice: his terror of the waves. Well, now he'd conquer them and prove himself once and for all. He'd show everyone he was no weakling.

The cool sand caressed his bare feet; his soles sunk deeper with each step, as if the Earth herself tried to hold him back from the madness that drove him. Part of him wanted to die; death would assuage his shame. Besides, the eunuch would be blamed, and Ptolemy took comfort in that. It was Pothinus's fault; he should have kept Cleopatra from seizing so much sway. The eunuch should have come to him with options, not humiliated him before his slave. Eyes welling, his mother would demand who'd last seen her beloved son. The truth would emerge, and she'd strangle his tutor in maternal rage.

In private, Cleopatra would rejoice. She'd wed Ptolemarion and thank the gods for her fortune. What a malleable consort *he'd* make. His little brother was always parroting their sisters' words as though they spouted the wisdom of the gods. Besides, the boy was still young and as unsexed as a eunuch. Cleopatra would like that too.

But a greater part of him felt certain he would prove them wrong. Every nobleman who mocked his rule, every slave who snickered behind his back. Sand turned to mud beneath his soles and the water chilled his ankles, but he forced himself onward. The sea lapped at his thighs. He dragged his legs into its cold embrace; his robes stretched behind him, an indigo train. His progress would be easier if he undressed, but then he'd reach the far shore stripped of all insignia of rule. Or worse, as a corpse, naked and shriveled, nameless and unknown.

The water reached his chest. It would be easy to sink his head under the waves and let the ocean carry him away. How long would drowning take? Would he even mark the time? Or would the waiting stretch on forever? *No.* He wouldn't die. Poseidon would sweep him off to some island, rife with beautiful nymphs and wise centaurs. He'd while away a few years in their company until he was old enough to reign alone. The court would gasp at his return: a grown and handsome man ready for the throne. And why shouldn't the sea god favor him? He was a Ptolemy.

Voices gathered behind him, calling across the water. He glanced back: a dozen or so servants. No one of importance. Each would brag that he'd seen young Ptolemy disappear that fateful day.

"What's come over him?" A bright cry cut through the rest. Arsinoe. As he squinted at the noonday sun, he could make out his two sisters, silhouettes against the sands. They had returned.

This was his moment. His final moment as a failed king, and his first as something greater: a legend.

He plunged his head beneath the waves. Eyes sealed, he kicked his legs and scooped his hands through the water. All at once, fear gripped him, and he tried instead to paddle back to shore. His mouth opened and he swallowed the sea. He begged and clawed at the surf, but each time he neared the shimmering surface, another wave pulled him down again. His lungs ached—he needed air. His arms grew weary of writhing. He waited to be rescued. *Poseidon, Lord of the Seaways . . .*

He was naked—that much he could tell—his bare back and buttocks pressed against something soft. Perhaps he'd stripped his clothes and been swept over to the Greek shore. He would be hailed a hero and worshipped as a god raised from the depths. He kept his eyes closed—he needed to cling to his dream for a little longer. Because in his heart he knew it wasn't sand pressed against his back, but his own bed.

Kings must face the truth, he told himself. *One, two, three,* he counted. He opened his eyes to find Briseis bent over him, wearing her lip away with worry. His mother gripped his hand; tears leaked from her bloodshot eyes.

"He's stirring." Briseis's fingers flew to her mouth.

"Oh, my dear boy." His mother showered him with kisses. He didn't wipe them away. "My sweet, what happened—? Oh, no, I shouldn't trouble you with that now. Sophos said not to upset you with too many questions."

What had happened? He'd prayed to Poseidon; he remembered that bit. And then hands had pulled him from the sea. His mind struck on it: Arsinoe must have saved him. Again. He'd heard her voice and seen her standing on the beach.

"What on earth came over you?" His mother placed a hand on his brow. Perhaps he was running a fever. He felt too happy to care.

"Mama," he asked, "where's Arsinoe?"

"What are you talking about, my dear?" His mother glanced back to Briseis. "Fetch some more smelling salts for the boy, and bring the doctor. He's talking nonsense."

He'd never thanked his sister the first time she'd rescued him, but he would now. Cleopatra had driven a stake between them, but he could change that. He'd mend bridges with Arsinoe.

"I'm not talking nonsense. I want to thank my sister for rescuing me."

His mother's lips folded into a frown. "Oh, my sweet...Arsinoe is still on a barge in the Upper Lands. She and Cleopatra both."

But she was right there, he wanted to protest. His body felt heavy again. His eyes closed and he sunk once more into a deep sleep.

The second time he awoke, it was Pothinus whom he found sitting vigil at his bedside. On the floor lay his little brother, sketching some steed with his stylus. He shut his eyes; he couldn't face the eunuch, not yet, but Ptolemarion caught him out.

"He's awake!" the boy cheered.

It was best, he supposed, for Pothinus to chide and yell and be done with it. He met the eunuch's gaze and waited for the carping to begin. But the lash of words didn't come.

"He's resting, Ptolemarion; no need to yell," the eunuch scolded the younger boy gently before returning to Ptolemy. His tone, for once, stayed soft. "How are you feeling? You frightened us."

"Better now," Ptolemy answered. His tutor bent toward him; the bed creaked under his weight.

"You gave your mother quite a scare," the eunuch whispered in his ear. Ptolemy smelled the familiar rotting on his breath. "But I assured her you were merely being a pigheaded boy who swam out too far. She need never know that there was any more to it than that."

Ptolemy nodded. His tutor was right; no one should know more than that. He couldn't quite explain it himself, what had drawn him to the sea, whether he'd wanted to die or rise to mythic glory.

"I'll leave you to get some rest. I will see you for our lesson tomorrow morning."

"But Pothinus—"

"Ptolemy," the eunuch interrupted. "Perhaps I was too hard on you before. These weeks would not be easy for anyone, even a grown man. But you must promise me something."

"What's that?" This time he kept his voice steady.

"That this is the last of your follies. The Harvest has begun to ripen, and your eleventh birthday has come and gone. You've made your mistakes, and I've made mine. But we must work together now. As men. Can you do that?"

Ptolemy nodded. The time for childishness had passed.

SISTER

Arsinoe pressed her body against the railing, her hip digging into the wood, and drank in the musty river breeze. The air tasted different here, thicker, somehow heavier. A light wind teased through her hair. Aboard the ship, she wore it loose in careless waves. No one dared chide her for it, though Eirene sighed each time Arsinoe rejected her offer to tame the tresses into plaits.

How often her childhood imaginings had carried her up the Nile. Each time her sister departed on the Piper's pleasure barge, Arsinoe would trace the ship's progress along the nursery wall, her finger circling the rhinoceros when the vessel reached Memphis, the Chimera when it passed Thebes. The in between—though this, too, she'd dutifully pictured to foster nearness with her sister—had always seemed far less exciting: the banks of green and yellow, the endless fields of Harvest-ripening barley and wheat. What she'd never envisioned were the crowds: the throngs of natives who lined the banks, strapping men in loincloths and lithe women with baskets balanced on their heads, and little children everywhere, naked and screaming as the day they were born.

Alexandria was full of Upper Landers, but they bore no more relation to these creatures than a tomcat did to a lion. The men who busied themselves along the palace courtyards wore tunics and mantles and bantered in flawless Greek. They even went by names like Antigonos and Pyrrhos and Demetrios, though she knew those weren't the names their mothers had given them. But here men of the same blood looked different, foreign to her eyes, ghosts of some forgotten land. She doubted whether they could even speak her tongue, and she wondered how so many members of her family had ruled without bothering to learn theirs.

"Our people."

Her sister's voice startled her; Arsinoe hadn't heard her approach. Cleopatra walked as surely on the pitching boat as she did on dry land, a skill honed during those many hours spent sailing up and down the great river, even across the wild sea to Rome, where Poseidon's waves would swallow vessels whole. Arsinoe had wobbled when they first set off from Alexandria, though she'd now learned to mask her shaky steps.

"They adore you," Arsinoe said, turning to face her sister, a vision of the goddess Isis. Cleopatra had embraced that role with relish, dressing each day as an incarnation of the mother deity. This far south, her costume had shifted. No longer did she wear the flowing robes of the goddess's Pharos incarnation, a chiton knotted between her breasts; instead, she dressed in a clinging linen sheath, a heavy collar of gold and lapis lazuli about her neck and matching bangles on her upper arms. Rather than the double crown, she wore the horned one, its golden antlers glinting in the sun. *It's best,* she'd explained, *for the common folk to see me match the statues on their altars as closely as I can.*

"It's not me they adore but their god, Menthu. It's him they've come to see."

Cleopatra glanced toward the fortified deckhouse. For once, the bull was silent; perhaps he slept—Arsinoe couldn't blame him. He'd been awake and pacing, snorting through the greater part of the last four nights. The creature confused his daylight and evening hours, and hers had grown confounded too. She couldn't drift off in the darkness and found she dreamt away the mornings. "They want to catch a glimpse as he sails to his seat in Hermonthis."

"I only hope that they'll have better luck than we two."

It felt strange that neither of them had even seen the animal that roused the boat with his stomps and grunts, but the rules dictating his care were exacting. For the forty days between his anointment and his installation, only a select set of priestesses could gaze upon the newly incarnated god. Arsinoe wondered—a heretical thought—how the yearling felt about the arrangement, whether he would have preferred to stay with his mother, grazing in some overlooked pasture.

Spurred by a mysterious impulse, Cleopatra stretched her arms out to either side in the gesture of blessing. A few days prior, the action—its suddenness—would have alarmed Arsinoe, but she'd grown accustomed to such behavior, though she couldn't divine what inspired it. As ever, the spectators responded with enthusiasm—the crowd roared, or so she had to assume. Their voices couldn't carry across the spread of the Nile, but their mouths gaped and stretched with animation. Had they screamed this way for her father? Had they mourned his death? She doubted it; where the Alexandrians concerned themselves altogether too much with who ruled the city, the people of the Upper Lands cared merely that a king—any king—stood as their god, to bless their crops and ensure the river's rise. One Macedonian slipped into the skin of the last. What difference could it make to these farmers, breathing and plowing and dying four thousand stades away?

Cleopatra had returned her hands to her sides, but she kept her eyes fixed on the shore. "The harvest has been adequate, and so today they love me well. I should relish it while I can. It won't last. By next year's Inundation, they'll have forgotten that they credited

65

me with this one. If it is low, they'll curse my name, and if the Nile swells too high and drowns their crops . . ."

"They'll rise up and retake Memphis in revolt?" Arsinoe teased. She could jest about rebellions in the Upper Lands—those didn't worry her. It was the Romans back in Alexandria who roused her concerns. She hadn't forgotten how they'd chanted for Ptolemy, spears crashing on the onyx.

"Just because the past forty years have been quiet doesn't mean the next forty will be, Arsinoe," Cleopatra answered. "Our house has spilled much blood to keep the Upper Landers in check. You mustn't forget that."

Arsinoe said nothing. The time hadn't come to discuss their homecoming—she should wait until after the ceremony, when Cleopatra discarded the guises of Isis and Horus both. Away from the roaring throngs, her sister would be more receptive to advice, and she'd recognize where the real danger lay.

From the corner of her eye, Arsinoe noticed Apollodorus climbing onto the deck, his skin gleaming in the molten sun. He'd shorn his inky hair short against his scalp in the style of the Romans. She disliked the look—and all its implications—but despite her reservations, she had to admit the cut became him. In the heat of the Upper Lands, he wore a short tunic belted at his hips. His sinewy thighs strained at the fabric, and his shoulders bulged from the openings, threatening to bust the seams. Color flamed her cheeks—she found herself looking at men, appraising, far more often than she should. At least Apollodorus wouldn't notice her gaze—he viewed her as an annoyance, nothing more. He had eyes only for her sister.

"My queen." He greeted Cleopatra with a slight incline of his head. "We've nearly arrived at Hermonthis, and the priests are ready for the ceremony."

"How wonderful," her sister exclaimed, offering a bright smile for his pains. "I am anxious to begin my transformation."

"Princess," Apollodorus addressed Arsinoe curtly. "It is time for you to disembark. For the revelation of the bull, only the priests and the Horus incarnate are permitted on the ship."

She'd known this moment would come, and yet she'd dreaded it all the same. Another division between her and Cleopatra. And she didn't trust these clerics of the Upper Lands. They saw her sister and her forefathers as paltry imitations of the gods—good enough to fool the people but of little other use. Just as Cleopatra could be changed from Isis to Horus in an instant, one ruler could easily stand in for the next.

Tucked away in some vacated priest's chambers with only a bare cot, a half-inked copy of the Book of the Dead, and a few Galatian guards for company, Arsinoe peered out the window over Hermonthis. It was a small city, hardly worthy of that designation. Outside of the great limestone complex that housed the bull and his attendants, the town comprised perhaps two dozen brick buildings on the far side of the river and twice as many scattered wooden huts with thatched roofs. The pleasure barge, which in Alexandria had seemed too small to hold even their meager entourage, loomed large, dwarfing the edifices on either bank.

As the boat swanned toward the shore, the mob roared. With no distance to dull the noise, the sound was deafening—and incomprehensible. Her Egyptian was no more than passable on good days and only when she listened to a single suppliant speaking slowly. Here, amidst a thousand tongues, she could scarcely snatch any individuated words.

She had wanted to watch from the docks, among its men and beasts, but Apollodorus had insisted otherwise. *It's too dangerous for the queen's sister to lurk among the common folk,* he'd told her. She'd heard the disdain, heavy in his voice—he imagined her as some fainting flower, unable to fend for herself. If only he'd seen her in her urchin days, when she'd stalked the alleyways of Alexandria, a bone clutched between her fingers. In a final, desperate ploy, Ganymedes had left her to fend for herself, and so she had. Name and family ripped away, she'd faced the hostile, war-torn streets and struck down the first boy who'd tried to steal from her. Those days served as a talisman, a reminder of her fortitude. After that, what harm could come to her in Hermonthis or anywhere? Besides, she trusted these cheering peasants. Their cries, unlike those of the priests, ached with sincerity. These were not the troubled days of yesteryear when her forefathers faced a rebellion at each disappointing flood. The region had lain quiet ever since her grandfather had destroyed Thebes, razing the great city to rubble.

Two priests wobbled onto the gangplank, their shorn heads shimmering with sweat. Impervious to the heat, their robes gleamed a brilliant white. She wondered how they managed that. Her own clothes were stained with mortality, creased and damp with sweat.

Below, a changed Cleopatra alighted on the docks. All Isis insignia had vanished and been replaced by the trappings of her son, Horus, the proper escort for the reincarnated war god. Dressed as the great goddess, Cleopatra had looked the idyll of beauty and fertility, but now, in the pleated linen skirt of Horus, she transcended gender. Though she didn't wear the customary beard of kings, her regalia otherwise matched their father's: the white crown nestled in the crimson one, the gold-and-onyx collar at her throat.

A few words floated up from the onlookers—*Horus* and *Isis,* and *nsw* and *mwt.* Arsinoe recognized those local words: *king, mother.* Definitions grew loose here, one entity flowing freely into the other. She wondered that it didn't confuse the peasantry—she'd always been taught that the common folk were able to hold only a scant few concepts in their minds. And yet now they seemed to acknowledge her sister in all her sundry forms, praising her as a male god and a female, as Egypt's king and mother.

The horde surged upward, a thousand rising to their toes to catch a clearer view. Arsinoe, too, wanted to witness the Buchis bull reborn. Leaning out the window, she gazed at the blackened doorway of the deckhouse. For a moment, it appeared empty, but then his face emerged, so dark that it was hard to parse where the void ended and the creature began. His snout and brow were black as night, his eyes a pair of onyx stars visible only in the gleam of the sun. Next came a glistening white foot, and then a second—the same hooves whose stomping had shaken her cot these past few nights. In stark contrast to his sable head, the yearling's body glowed a luxurious ivory.

Untethered, the bull followed her sister through the throngs, his great muscles tensing with each step. Despite his commanding heft, his gait was steady, his demeanor subdued. What had happened to that formidable creature of the deckhouse, snorting up a storm? She wasn't the only one who wondered—the mob grew so quiet that Arsinoe could hear the clack of the animal's hooves, the river's steady slosh, the breathing of the royal guards. Something felt wrong. The beast matched the appearance but not the spirit of Menthu, the fearsome god of war. His incarnation should bellow and writhe and buck, not walk with a woman's serenity. Ahead, Cleopatra floated on, unperturbed, but Arsinoe caught two of the priests trading a worried glance.

Then, to the procession's left, she saw a flash of movement—a figure darted out behind the bull. A boy, she guessed, from his size, but his white tunic marked him as a member of the priesthood. He grasped something in his hand; she squinted to see that it was a wooden pipe. Slowly, he brought the instrument to his lips. She heard nothing—no peep of music—but then the bull snorted and transformed: he pawed the ground fiercely; his nostrils flared. Tossing his head, he emitted a sound so strident that Arsinoe had to cover her ears. And then the beast charged her sister.

"Clea!" she shouted, despite herself. If her sister couldn't hear the raging yearling, how could she possibly hear her cry?

The bull bore down on the queen, the crowd scattering in his wake. Her heart thudded in her ears. For the second time she would stand by helpless as a sister was slaughtered. Berenice's head, tongue lulling, rocking on a plate. Wherever she went death perched, a carrion bird on her shoulder. *Turn, Clea,* she shrieked inside her head, as though she might instead be able to reach her sister there. Often enough, she would have sworn Cleopatra could read her thoughts— *Why not this one?* And then, slowly, in one graceful motion, the queen spun toward the animal—but it was too late. The beast was already nearly upon her. Her hands flew up, not to protect her face but to reach for his. The bull bellowed, enraged at the provocation. Arsinoe fought the urge to close her eyes—if these were Cleopatra's final moments, she would bear witness to them.

Hooves screeched against the stone, and the bull ground his body to a halt. He leaned forward to sniff her sister's fingertips. Cleopatra whispered in the beast's ear and stroked his neck and nose. She grasped the creature behind his horns and leaned forward to kiss him on his forehead. With the touch of her lips, the bull bent his front legs into a bow.

The roar that exploded from the mob sounded both more and less than human, as though those gathered had tapped into some primordial sentiment. The shouts shrilled and pierced, crested and fell and crested again. Throngs collapsed in on one another, each man pushing and elbowing to get closer to the god and the queen. In the swell of colors, the whites and ochres and earthy greens, she tried to pick out the small priest, but he was nowhere to be found. What had his intentions been? Had he meant to aid Cleopatra or kill her?

After the ceremony had ended and their entourage had returned to the pearl-encrusted barge, Arsinoe sought out her sister. The boy and his wooden flute, the charging bull and Cleopatra's soothing hands—had it all been part of some secret plan to impress the locals? Or did it speak to some rebellion brewing in the Upper Lands? She wasn't sure whether any queen—or king, for that matter—could head off both the natives and Rome. Concerns badgered her. Yet when she reached the royal berth, she found Cleopatra reclining in her bath. Her face was tranquil, without a trace of worry.

"Did you know?" Arsinoe asked. She hung back in the entryway. All at once, she felt unwelcome in the cavernous hold with its enormous silk-draped bed bolted to the cedar, its Dionysian carvings flecked in gold along the rounded walls.

"Did I know what?" her sister said with a smile. "You know how I hate when you speak in riddles. It reminds me of that eunuch of yours."

"Did you know what the priests were planning with the bull?"

Her sister cocked her head to one side, as she often did when amused or perplexed. For some reason, the look reminded Arsinoe of the one the bull had given Cleopatra. "What do you mean?"

"That priest, the little one," Arsinoe went on. "He did something to the creature to make him charge."

"That's impossible." Cleopatra sunk deeper into the basin, the ends of her hair floating about her head like a crown. "You must have imagined it."

"I was watching, Clea, and the beast was completely calm, almost sedated, until the little priest, the one who looks a boy . . . He spat something at the bull."

"Spat something?" Cleopatra laughed. "Don't be ridiculous, Arsinoe. The Buchis bull always charges when he's led to his new temple; that's no surprise. Though I didn't realize he'd charge so very close to me."

"I see," Arsinoe replied, though she felt sure her sister was hiding something.

Cleopatra straightened in her bath and lifted the emerald-encrusted looking glass at the edge of the tub. Fixedly, she stared at her reflection, turning the mirror to examine every angle. She'd grown vain these past few weeks, but Arsinoe could forgive that. In her sister's position, under the exacting and admiring eye of the double kingdoms, she would have grown vain as well.

"We should return to Alexandria. We've been gone too long," Arsinoe blurted out, shattering her sister's reverie. She'd planned to give Cleopatra another day to revel in her triumph.

"It's been but a few short weeks." Cleopatra batted away the idea with a flick of the mirror. "A queen must rule her entire kingdom and fulfill her duties to all her people, not merely the Alexandrians."

"Of course she must. And your people adore you, but Ptolemy..." Arsinoe chose her words carefully, remembering the foam rippling on her brother's lips. "Ptolemy is only a child; his advisors will grapple hard for power in your absence. They will be breathing venom against you in every nobleman's ear."

"Ptolemy has his snakes and I have mine. I've taken precautions in Alexandria. I know every move those men make. And as for our dear brother? He has barely left his bed."

The truth unfurled with blinding clarity: Cleopatra had poisoned their brother; in her absence, she poisoned him still. Enough to weaken, not to kill. Arsinoe swallowed the lump in her throat—her sister did no more than what was needed. In Cleopatra lay strength, she reminded herself, hope for Egypt: this willingness to do what only the gods dared. Timidity served no ruler, least of all in the face of Rome.

"I suspect, my sweet, another reason makes you anxious to sail home. Perhaps you miss a certain someone there?"

Arsinoe could only pray her sun-darkened skin wouldn't betray the blood rushing to her cheeks. Of course she missed Alexander—but she certainly wouldn't admit it.

"Don't fret," her sister teased. "I'm sure he pines after you night and day. You're a Ptolemy, after all, and he's nothing but Dioscorides's by-blow."

"That isn't—" she began to object, but she couldn't precisely name what it wasn't.

"He will never be worthy of you." Cleopatra softened her tone. "I know that is a hard truth. You worry too much. All is well. The sun is bright. And we're sailing on the grandest barge on the grandest river in the wide world. Enjoy yourself."

She tried. She did. That night, and on the nights that followed, she drank and feasted and reveled. The time they whiled away with tender harpists and skilled mimics and lissome dancers recalled the early, easy days of their dynasty, when Ptolemy, the Father-Loving God, rained opulence upon the double kingdom.

And as Arsinoe drank down the watered wine and barley beer of the Upper Lands and devoured rich game hen and honeyed goat, she did her best to forget her worries, the gnawing hunger in her heart and the heretical musings of her mind. It was not her place to judge her sister's acts, to wonder whether it might be better to coopt Ptolemy than sicken him. But even when she stumbled drunk onto the deck and gazed up at the stars and listened to the soldiers rutting slave girls in their chambers, she felt somehow set apart. Watching, listening, observing. From the royal entourage, but never of it.

Cleopatra stood apart as well, but for reasons quite divorced from her own. Swathed in the robes of a fresh Isis incarnation each evening, her sister appeared at once untouchable and irresistible. Arsinoe noticed the way the men aboard looked at the queen, a tangle of yearning and awe. Even Cleopatra's own advisors lusted after her, which made Arsinoe mistrust them all the more. She missed Ganymedes back in Alexandria, who—for all his faults—could never dream of taking her to bed. But her sister didn't keep even a single eunuch in her train. Most of the men were far too ancient—and too pragmatic—to believe they might actually come to share Cleopatra's bed, but Apollodorus seemed to have more serious ambitions. Thirty, or perhaps younger, he was handsome, jealous, and Cleopatra's indisputable favorite.

"Clea," Arsinoe asked one day, reclining on one of the violet divans that had been set up along the barge's portside deck. "What is your measure of Apollodorus?"

Her sister smiled almost to herself as she glanced toward her counselor. He was never far, her pet, eager to lend a hand. A half-dozen paces off, he chatted with several members of the royal guards.

"I think he is a man I can trust," her sister answered.

"That's not what I mean."

"I know."

"Do you see the way he looks at you?"

At each lull in his conversation, Apollodorus would cast an eye toward them. Cleopatra looked particularly lovely that day, having at last shed her Egyptian linens and returned to an indigo-and-crimson chiton knotted at her shoulder.

"I do see it, yes," she replied. That, at least, marked a bit of progress. She didn't often concede men's lusts, as though queenship had elevated her to a plane above such pesky yearnings.

"And do you look at him in the same way?" Arsinoe prodded.

"It doesn't matter how I look at him, or he at me," Cleopatra answered sharply. "He's of lesser birth than that bull we escorted. And I am a woman wed."

"To Ptolemy?" Arsinoe laughed. "There's a fact you rarely own. And besides—you two have never shared a bed unless perhaps when we were very small, as brothers and sisters do."

"As brothers and sisters do? And what, pray tell, does that mean for our dynasty?" Cleopatra grinned.

"The boy's scarcely eleven," Arsinoe pointed out, fighting back a giggle.

"It's no laughing matter." Cleopatra became abruptly serious, her voice dropping to a whisper. "Do you think I'd take Apollodorus to my bed? And waste the goodwill between me and our dear brother? Apollodorus is no one. A useful voice, perhaps, and a pair of hands, that's all. What would I gain by sleeping with him? A bastard in my belly, at best."

The words stung. Arsinoe heard them for what they were: a rebuke of her and Alexander. For, in her heart, she had considered it. For pleasure, and pleasure alone. At night, alone in her bed, she thought about it often, how his lips would feel on hers, his hands firm on her hips, and firm on other places too. A fool's reverie. At most, Alexander could be to her what Apollodorus was to her sister: an advisor and an admirer. Nothing more.

For the rest of the journey, Arsinoe kept her distance. Her sister's mockery had cut deeper than she dared admit. From among the crowds, she watched her sister's Memphis coronation. The queen, dressed in bright white linens, bent before the shave-pated Psenptais, who murmured Ptah's blessings and placed the double crown upon her head. The ancient regalia somehow suited Cleopatra: although the black beaded wig lent some harshness to her face, she wore it well. Again, Alexander's accusation echoed: *Jealous*. No, she told herself firmly. She would not let her love for her sister be tainted by that.

As the ship neared Alexandria, her dreams turned strange. A falcon beset by eagles, she watched as crocodiles devoured their young and shed crocodile tears. The city was on fire; a thousand years of knowledge seared away. Though the smoke simmered, she could not find corpses anywhere, only a mob murmuring of wolves and gladiators. The Great Theater turned into a death ring, and she, transmuted too, slithered through it with her teeth bared.

Gladiators and wolves—these were portents of Rome. She half expected to find the city besieged by ships and the great library burned to ash. But when they arrived, Alexandria appeared as peaceful as ever. There was no doom and no destruction. Perhaps her nightmares were merely relics of more tumultuous days. Now that Cleopatra ruled, she might hope the menace of those visions would fade.

BROTHER

His sisters returned, and for weeks the court was yammering about how Cleopatra had tamed some bull. No one even mentioned what else had happened: that Cleopatra had added several dozen Upper Landers to her entourage, and twice as many mercenaries too. But every time he brought *that* up, the room went quiet and grown men began picking at their nails. So, instead, he watched in silence as these new recruits were folded into the Galatian guards. *Turncoats,* he thought. Those same soldiers had cheered him the loudest at his blessing feast. They and the Gabinians, and he couldn't tell which set of troops was more fickle in their loyalties.

Whatever spark of opportunity had flickered in Cleopatra's absence was quickly stamped out. Even the dining lounges—the place where he'd held makeshift court with Ariston and Kyrillos—were seized by his sister. Again these halls filled up with men, bristling for the queen's attention. Redheaded Serapion, who'd scarcely entered the palace while the queen was gone, caused a stir among the more conservative set by bringing his new wife to royal dinners. A dark-featured beauty of Persian parentage, she was not much older than Ptolemy himself, but she showed none of the shyness expected from a girl her age. Despite her heavily accented Greek, she would carry on about every topic from farm techniques to naval tactics, a quality that endeared her to Cleopatra. Dioscorides, stern and steely as ever, looked decidedly less pleased by the fresh-faced foreigner, but even the eldest of the New Dionysus's advisors didn't dare speak out against one of the queen's favorites.

The worst part was that Ptolemy couldn't even blame these men for pandering to his sister. The whole court had seen how he'd squandered his time alone in Alexandria; nearly half of Cleopatra's absence he'd been laid up in bed. An echo of his father's dying days. If the priests were to be believed and each king was some incarnation of the last, perhaps it was fitting that the Piper's waning fell to him. Cleopatra had always taken the better parts. As he'd caroused in the palace, she'd tightened her grip on power: She'd enchanted the devout Upper Landers with her blessing of their bull and swayed the coastal merchants with coins pressed in her honor. She'd even persuaded the prophet at Memphis to crown her rule. And here in Alexandria, she had a fleet of fresh soldiers at her disposal, ready to slay any man who spoke against her. And whom did Ptolemy have in his corner? Theodotus and Pothinus. He wasn't sure the eunuch could wield a sword.

At times, Ptolemy let himself hope that rebellion might spring from the land herself. That the gods would intervene and nature would cast off this queen masquerading as a king. But here, too, he was disappointed. Time carried on much as it always did. The olive trees blossomed, and torchlit processions came to guide Serapis's return from the underworld. After a particularly noisome lesson about Plato, which involved figures in shadows and how they reflected the light, Ptolemy stayed to watch the march from one of the windows of the great library. The other boys grew bored and left, but Ptolemy remained, transfixed. The final figure struck him: a priest stumbling in a jackal-headed costume. Arsinoe had explained the meaning to him once—some legend about Anubis and that old Egyptian god Osiris—but Ptolemy couldn't keep the details straight.

He only noticed now how lonesome the man seemed, abandoned by the other celebrants and left to carry on some old tradition long since forgotten.

These festivities bled into the Greater Dionysia, a favorite among the Greek and the native Egyptian populations alike, and rowdy revelers flooded the streets, enormous wooden cocks belted to their groins. For days after, the city stank of slaughtered hog. It was Cleopatra who presided over these celebrations—appearing before the plebeians in various guises of gods and holding court before the nobles' feasts in the royal halls. Ptolemy sat off to the side of the dais, with his little brother for company. He watched; he waited. With Cleopatra's coterie of soldiers guarding every corner, he didn't dare try to do anything else.

Theodotus appeared the most affected by the developments; he seemed to take the Gabinians' cleaving to Cleopatra as a personal defeat. Ptolemy supposed it was. The rhetorician had aggressively courted the Roman soldiers, deeding them plethron upon plethron of farmland in the Marshes. And for nothing. In a fit of pique, Theodotus turned his energies to teaching. His once-reserved style became frenzied, his lessons no longer opportunities to sink into daydreams. To make up for his wooly one, his good eye roamed wildly about the library as he lectured, catching out any hint of distraction among his pupils. After class, he had taken to holding Ptolemy back to clarify a particular argument or reveal some shred of news he'd heard from some undisclosed informant. Ptolemy wasn't sure what to make of his tutor's transformation—whether he should rejoice, as his mother counseled, in Theodotus's renewed interest in his education or resent the fact that he had to memorize whole swaths of Plato's dialogues.

As usual, Pothinus proved no help at all, taking a positively cheery view of matters. "Bide your time," the eunuch instructed.

"Don't let on to Cleopatra that you see through her antics. Let her think that you're still in her thrall." What happened, Ptolemy wondered, to acting together *as men?*

Harvest stretched into Inundation, and turbulent news arrived from the Upper Lands: both the wheat and spelt harvests yielded low. Much of the vegetable crop in the Marshes, Theodotus reported, had been destroyed by some blight that caused the half-sprouted pods to shrivel. Starving peasants, the rhetoric tutor went on in a euphoric vein, had descended on Memphis, and the priests of Ptah had sent word to Alexandria warning the unrest might brew to rebellion.

Ptolemy clung to these tidings: his glint of hope. He began to look forward to his lessons, rushing to the library with a spring in his step and hungering for news from the unsteady south. But within a few weeks, all hints of an uprising faded. Cleopatra dispatched two legions of Gabinians to keep the peace, and despite another low flood, by the beginning of Emergence, tempers cooled and there was no more talk of revolt. Ptolemy slunk back into his routine: Herodotus, Archimedes, Plato, Homer. The only thing worse than waiting for *something* was waiting for nothing at all.

It was his mother who comforted him through those disheartening months, though he knew better than to admit that to anyone. Almost every evening, she would join him either for supper or afterward while he soaked in his bath. Some nights, she dismissed Briseis, and washed his hands and hair herself. "You have another sister," she reminded him, "who might rule with you." The first time she mentioned this, Ptolemy blushed so deeply that he had to bury his face in his palms. The idea of sharing his bed with Arsinoe set a strange twitching in his gut. But his mother—thankfully—took no notice of his embarrassment. Instead, as she massaged the oil deeper into his roots, she talked about his fore-fathers, how his great-grandfather wed his sister and his stepdaughter, and how his grandfather had married both his sisters. When Ptolemy worked up the courage to ask about Arsinoe's loyalty to Cleopatra, his mother laughed. "Sisterly love is cheap when weighed against the draw of rule." He tried to guard himself against false optimism, but the idea proved too sweet to resist. He could spend whole hours picturing how he might rule if only Arsinoe were at his side.

At night, he had different sorts of dreams. Ones that left his sheets sticky and his body aching from pleasure and shame. Dreams whose images drifted back at inopportune moments throughout the day—Briseis's lips on his, Arsinoe tearing open her tunic—only to leave him stiff and reddening in the middle of his lessons. These imaginings convinced him of another truth: that soon he would indeed be able to plant a seed in his sister's womb.

As the weather grew warm and the fields ripened, the dynamic of the court shifted: Cleopatra began to request his presence for certain public occasions. Theodotus was convinced the change had to do with the nearing of his twelfth birthday—"She can't expect to rule alone forever," the rhetorician gloated, "not when you're so close to becoming a man." Ptolemy felt less sanguine; more likely, the queen meant to humiliate him by seating him at her left, or she'd grown so confident that she didn't even see him as a threat. Most of the time, those days proved dull enough: an endless string of complaints about taxation in the Upper Lands. The Harvest looked to be another paltry one—perhaps the queen meant to string him up as the goat to blame?

His favorite escape came in the form of jousting lessons. His mother had at last enlisted a tutor to teach him military tactics: a Greek general fresh from fighting the Parthians. Broad-shouldered and with a head of tousled chestnut hair, Achillas looked and swaggered like a king's advisor. His iron armor wasn't the gleaming stuff of city processions; it was scratched and rusted from use. Even his *name* was worthy of a royal councilor—so near to that of Achilles, the *best of the Achaeans*. Sometimes the commander would toss out a careless reference to a battle he'd fought or a barbarian he'd sliced from nose to nape. Here, at last, was a man who could teach him something of worth: how to act and fight and kill.

On the best days, Ptolemy would get to train on horseback. While his friends were stuck reading Thucydides, he'd go down to the stables and watch the grooms prepare his great gray steed. Perched behind Aethon's withers, Ptolemy felt the full measure of any king: he could forget his clumsiness and fold into the stallion's grace. As one, they galloped across the practice fields; as one, they mowed down the straw-sack soldiers. And when the javelin pierced the wooden shield of the mocked-up enemy, he felt sure he could face off against any man. Or any woman.

One morning, a few days before his name day, Ptolemy arrived in the royal atrium before the hour Cleopatra had appointed. Except for a half-dozen Galatians standing guard, the room was empty—but it clearly had been prepared for esteemed guests. The coat of Dionysus's leopard gleamed a freshly buffed gold, and the great pillars had been polished so assiduously that he could glimpse his reflection in the purple stone. The dais had been set with two thrones: his sister's, the proper one, with lions roaring from its golden legs and red Chinese silk stitched along its seat, and his own, diminutive by comparison, shrunk smaller still by its placement off to the side. Not long ago he might have rushed to take Cleopatra's chair. But he saw now that would be a child's move. *The greatest victories come when our enemies least expect them.* That was what Achillas said. So he sat at his intended place.

The chair was painful, its cushion too thin to soften the goldwork underneath. No matter how he shifted, he couldn't find a comfortable position. Just as Ptolemy was beginning to wonder whether his sister meant to keep him waiting, the guards around the periphery stilled. A dozen helms shifted toward the grandest archway, and there stood the queen. Crowned with the white diadem, Cleopatra almost glided on gem-encrusted sandals. A finely spun golden mantle drifted over her purple chiton. The rest of her body had been dipped in gold as well, from her fingertips down to her ankles and up to her throat. She gazed at him with liquid eyes, and he felt a familiar roiling in his stomach. It was the same calculated look she'd given him on his sickbed: love and worry spiked with a hint of lust. Despite so many months of sidelining, she still thought he was dull enough to fall for it. He focused on her flaws: the bump in her hooked nose and the mean cut of her cheeks.

"My dear brother and king," she said with a smile. "How good of you to join me in greeting our important guests. The sons of Marcus Calpurnius Bibulus have come all the way from Antioch."

Whoever Bibulus was—he could almost hear the eunuch badgering that he really *ought* to know—his sons did not cut very impressive figures. One was of skinny, sickly stock, a scarlet cloak draped over his mop of flaxen hair; the other was more compact, a stocky man with a sizable paunch. Though they both wore the tunics of Rome, they looked more dilettantes than centurions. Their skin was too smooth, untouched by scars or sun. And they had another strike against them: each was casting wistful eyes at Cleopatra. *Dolts*.

The plumper one, Gaius—the herald had announced him—bent his knee in supplication, but the other, Marcus the Younger, only tugged his head covering down onto his shoulders. Ptolemy had noticed this strange custom among the Gabinians—though they covered their heads before their gods, they bared their hair before their betters. He wasn't surprised: Romans who hadn't spent time in Alexandria—he'd been told—were often reluctant to give royals their proper due. He glanced at his sister to see how she weathered the insult. Her face was fixed in the same simpering smile. The sycophancy sickened him, and so he cleared his throat in disapproval. One of them ought to be brave enough to make their displeasure known. The moment the sound escaped, Cleopatra was on her feet and then at his side, bending over him so quickly that he jerked back in surprise. Undeterred, she placed her palm firmly on his forehead.

"Are you quite well?" she asked, her face a veneer of sisterly affection. "Have I urged too much on you? You need your rest, my dear."

His face grew hot at the humiliation. Even now, Cleopatra thought he was too dumb to see through her games.

"I don't need rest," he snapped. "I just got here."

"Of course you don't," she cooed. "I only meant—you see." She looked back to the Romans, the kneeling one and his stubbornly standing brother. "He is so very brave, my dear king, despite his fits, and sometimes he taxes himself."

The two men exchanged a knowing look—as though they'd already heard about his "disease" at length and had formed their own dismal impressions of his bravery.

No matter how he answered, she'd find some way to twist his words and make him look like a child. He held his objections—they'd only add to her fodder—and fixed his eyes on the petitioners.

"My thanks for your gracious attentions," began Marcus. "My brother and I have come bearing greetings from our father, Marcus Calpurnius Bibulus, governor of Syria, and from Gnaeus Pompey the Great of Rome, who hopes his kindness and generosity to your family has not been forgotten."

Pompey, Ptolemy recalled dully, had been somehow instrumental in his father's restoration. Had the Roman sent Gabinius and his legions in the first place? Or perhaps the connection had been shakier—

"Such debts are never forgotten," Cleopatra answered. He hated her quickness. Somehow she always claimed the best words before he'd even had a chance to think them.

"We are glad to hear it," Marcus answered, glancing disdainfully at his brother, still kneeling on the onyx. The stocky Gaius scrambled to his feet. "We would expect no less from you. The House of Ptolemy is famed for its generosity."

From the corner of his eye, Ptolemy watched Cleopatra nodding her assent. He tried to understand the ways she exerted her influence: how she managed to make herself agreeable to everyone and at the same time get her way.

"We appreciate your kind words," his sister replied, "but I can't imagine you have traveled so far merely to praise us. Tell me, how may we assist you and your father?"

Gaius shifted in his sandals. He tugged at the hem of his tunic; it had risen too high on his thigh.

"There were several legions," Marcus went on, "legions led by the erstwhile governor of Syria, Aulus Gabinius, who remained in Alexandria after the late king's triumphant return. We offer our condolences—and Rome's—for his passing."

"I thank you for your kindness. His death has been difficult." Cleopatra paused to dab at her eyes with the edge of her mantle, though Ptolemy could see that she wasn't actually crying at all. "But Egypt, as always, does prevail. The legions you mention have helped maintain that peace."

Marcus preened at that, as though he'd fought those battles with his own sword.

"We are glad our men have been of use to you in these intervening years," he continued, "but the time has come for them to return to Roman service. As you know, my father fights the Parthians—in Syria, he stands as the last barrier between those boors and the civilized world."

Ptolemy thought he detected a shadow pass over his sister's face. After all, without the Gabinians, who would hold the Upper Lands in check? But her expression flowered into a smile, one so convincing that he wondered if he'd imagined the darkening altogether.

"An admirable mission, I have no doubt. The men are free to return to Rome," she replied. "I make no claim on them. Egypt is strong and at peace. We no longer need those legions in our streets."

"I thank you for your kindness." Marcus paused, his lips pursed in concern. A tension ran between Cleopatra and this Roman, but Ptolemy wasn't sure why. As far as he could tell, she'd given the man precisely what he wanted. "I fear, though, that this might not be enough."

"What do you mean?" she asked, all lightness.

"My brother is trying to speak delicately," Gaius blurted out, "but we've heard that these Romans are quite content here. Their years in Alexandria have made them soft."

Cleopatra glanced from one man to the other. Her brow arched beneath her diadem. "And I am supposed to harden them?"

Gaius laughed heartily at the joke, but Ptolemy cringed. She shouldn't speak like that, jesting as baldly as a man.

"My brother"—the tall one cut in—"merely means that we're concerned they might not wish to leave. Many have settled in Egypt, taken wives and families."

"Don't men take wives wherever they go?" Cleopatra shrugged. There it was again, the gentle goading, the massaging to her way of mind. And how easily these grown men bent to her will, blind to how she tugged at their strings.

"They do, indeed," Marcus conceded, "but we would appreciate some reassurance from you that should they prove reluctant..."

His voice drifted off, as though he realized he'd said something shameful. Perhaps he had—after all, wasn't it strange they were requesting these troops from Cleopatra to begin with? If these legions were sworn to Rome, why not address the men directly?

Cleopatra picked up the line. "That I should what? Execute them? Banish them from Alexandria? Kill their wives and bash in the heads of their squalling babes? Surely you jape, my friends," she said with a laugh. "You can't mean to imply that you need *my* help convincing your own men to return to Roman service."

"I don't know what nonsense came over us, my queen," Marcus replied. "I'm sure we'll have no trouble bringing these troops back into the fold."

SISTER

F lush with wine and the ribald songs of Cleopatra's guards, Arsinoe wandered back to her rooms. The celebrations for Serapion's name day had run late into the night; troupes of veiled dancers were hired for the occasion, and Serapion's wife had even persuaded several of the bolder ladies to join her in their undulating dance. The effort soon collapsed into laughter, but a raucous mood had seized the party.

By the time the sun had set, the man of honor had sunk deep in his cups, and when Cleopatra had asked what gift he wished from the crown, he'd sent peals of laughter through the party by declaring he ought to be named governor of Upper Egypt. Despite the debauchery—or perhaps because of it—Arsinoe recognized the festivities' import: Her sister was right to keep their father's advisors close, and Serapion was by far the most amenable of that set. Dioscorides would sooner have put his sword through his breast than allow his wife to attend such celebrations—far better to cleave to a man who embraced the court's new dynamic, with its smattering of ladies among the high tables.

So, out of some sense of duty, Arsinoe had lingered into the small hours, calling out ballad suggestions to the singers and bawdy remarks to the veiled dancers. These she found endeared her to the men of the company, as though she might shed her gender by her tongue. And, loath as she was to admit it, she discovered that she'd developed a taste for drink. She knew she should be wary; after all, wine had exacerbated the Piper's weaknesses, shifting his eyes from rule and toward the next pretty girl—or boy—who struck his fancy. But *she* didn't seek out orgies—she merely enjoyed a few more rounds after her evening meals. Where was the harm in that?

And how alive—how generous—the wine made her feel. She didn't fret over her father's death or the uprisings in the Upper Lands or what her dreams meant. And wasn't that what Cleopatra was always telling her? *Not* to fret? After she'd drained her glass to dregs, she spun her way through the Sisters' Courtyard, past her namesake's fountain, whose spouting water glittered in the moonlight, and up the well-worn steps to her chambers.

Arsinoe hiccupped as she slipped inside, and giggled. Perhaps she was just slightly drunk—Cleopatra had teased her as she left, *Remember, to cross the courtyard, you must walk in a* straight *line.* She leaned against the door as she shut it behind her, humming to herself. A tune stuck in her mind—some phrase the harpist had plucked.

When she glanced up, she gasped to find Alexander perched on one of her divans. Idly, he passed an unlit oil lamp from palm to palm. She covered her gaping mouth and hiccupped again. To stop her head spinning, she tried to remember the last time he'd been in her rooms. When they were small, she would sneak him in from time to time, thrilling at their subterfuge. They'd lie on her bed, giggling and sharing confidences. But years had sprouted and stripped away that innocence. Now, as her eyes adjusted to the light, she noticed he was wearing the red-bordered tunic of a Roman officer.

"I believe Anubis is the more traditional character to invoke for the Serapia," she teased.

If her friend heard her mockery, it didn't deflate him. Instead, he leapt up to stand. His sandals scratched against the onyx as he scrambled to her side.

"I have wonderful news."

"What is it?" Her heart thudded in her ears.

Alexander's eyes brightened; he seized both her hands in his and squeezed. "I have joined the Third Legion of the Gabinians."

She stared at him, disbelieving. The red-bordered tunic, his shorn hair—still, it was impossible. He couldn't have joined—he must be playing some elaborate joke.

"You jest," she answered flatly. "You must be——"

"I'm not!" he exclaimed, plowing over her protests. "When I heard that Bibulus's sons arrived to call them back to Syria, I joined at once—I'm to go fight the Parthians!"

"You're not serious." Arsinoë shook her head slowly, surely. "You can't mean to fight for *Rome*."

"I have to fight for someone, Arsinoe." He laughed, his mood too blithe to be dulled by her reaction. "And there's no one for me to fight here."

"But why do you have to fight at all?" Of the myriad horrors that haunted her nights—the beheadings and the poisonings, the invasions and the library in flames—she'd never imagined this: Alexander abandoning her. Even as they grew older and distance cropped up between them, even when she shied and shivered at his touch, he was supposed to remain here and hers. What was the point of visions if they didn't warn of the worst treacheries to come?

Alexander let go of her hands and dropped his own to his sides. They had grown large and calloused. She watched as he drummed his pinkie against his thumb. She could feel his gaze searching for hers, but she stared stubbornly at his hands instead.

"Because I am a man, Arsinoe, and that is what men do. I am eighteen years old, and I have nothing to show for it. No family, no trade, no fortune."

"You have me," she whispered. She glanced up and regretted it. His eyes bored into hers. Their gray-green turned almost milky, and she feared he might cry.

"You can't have thought I'd live idly in the palace, knitting with the womenfolk, and waiting, waiting . . ."

Arsinoe pressed her fingers to her temples. This wasn't happening; she'd drunk too much, her mind had lapsed into a dream. A moment would pass, and Alexander would dissolve into a lion or a snake, and she'd open her eyes and be alone—and see this as no more than another frightful imagining.

"My namesake was not much older than I am now when he conquered the world," Alexander went on.

"Your namesake," she remarked, more cruelly than she meant, "was a Macedonian prince."

"I know," Alexander answered. "I know what he was and what I am: a nobleman's bastard. You think I don't remember my place? Dioscorides secured me a spot among your companions, where I might learn from the best tutors in the land. He won't give me any more favors. Not while his wife lives, at least. And so I must make my own way, Arsinoe. They say a man of ambition can earn a name for himself in Rome's army, that those with births far lower than my own have risen high. . . . There's even a phrase for it. They call them *novi viri.*"

New men. New or old, they all dreamt of death. As in the epics, they rushed to battle, to the blood and the goring, yearning to prove their manhood. But once at war, what they longed for—Odysseus and Hector and even poor ill-starred Agamemnon—was to return to their homes, to their shunted wives and cold marriage beds: *Look at them now, like green, defenseless boys or widowed women whimpering to each other, wailing to journey back.*

"You're a fool if you think you'll see battle with that legion. The

Gabinians will refuse to leave Alexandria," she told him. "That's what the sons of Bibulus feared, and they're *right*."

She'd heard rumors to that effect, though she couldn't vouch for their truth. Unrest mounted in the streets—brawls around the barracks and holdups at the ports. Frictions crackled: civilians tutting over whether the legions would stay or go, soldiers draining their last casks of wine.

"You're lying. Roman legionaries are the bravest men alive—every officer I've spoken to is itching to fight the Parthians."

"The bravest men alive? *Listen* to yourself. A regular Roman polemicist."

She wanted to scream, to shake him—anything to make him see reason. He couldn't have forgotten what Rome was to her, to Alexandria—to Cleopatra. The Republic had devoured every dynasty from Carthage to Pontus. Its men had already stolen Cyprus; how long before Rome lay claim to Egypt's shores?

"What else would you have me do?" He gazed at her with those aching eyes. Was he testing her somehow? Did he want her to convince him not to go?

"If you must join an army, enlist in ours," she pleaded, the idea gathering momentum as she spoke. "Join Cleopatra's guard. My sister needs men, good fighting men, to defend her. The more so now that the Gabinians are leaving."

"Defend her from what?" Alexander laughed. "Cleopatra defends herself. Generations have passed since Egypt's great wars. The Seleucids are dead; the Upper Landers might grumble among themselves, but it won't come to anything. It never does. I don't mean to join the army because I'm bored—so I can grow fat off the land in the Marshes. I want to make something of myself. And the only way to do that is through Rome."

She should have foreseen this much—for years the boys had

goggled over the Gabinian men, dressing in their style, cutting their hair above their ears.

"So we are nothing to you, then. The House of Ptolemy, the last and greatest of your *namesake's* kingdoms—we are but ants beneath your tread." Her voice quaked. "We're not even worth defending from the Roman horde. Oh, no, you'd rather join the wolf's twins and fight against barbarians alongside those no better than barbarians themselves. What has Rome brought to the world? What contributions has that city made? It is a pestilence that sweeps across these lands, and you—fool that you are—*you* want to embrace it."

"I should have known you wouldn't understand," Alexander said through gritted teeth.

"In that, at least, you were right," she snapped. "I would *never* understand a man who wed himself to Rome."

Arsinoe turned toward the westward windows, the flicker of Pharos gleaming in the distance. She couldn't look at him, this changeling Alexander, this man in soldier's garb with the shorn hair of a Roman. He was nothing to her.

"Arsinoe." His palm cupped her shoulder.

"Don't touch me. You've no right to touch me. *Centurion*."

The hand receded. And so he, too, would leave her. Just as her father and Cleopatra had left her for Rome, her mother and her brothers for Canopus. Even as Ganymedes had left her in the agora those wayward years ago.

"I suppose I should go, then. I only came to say good-bye."

His boots pounded toward the door. In a moment, he would be gone from her, and when he returned—if he returned—it would be as someone else.

"Alexander," she said. Perhaps there was one last way. She ran to him. "Wait."

Crazed, desperate, she flung her arms about him. He trembled, but he didn't shrink away. She stroked the place where his cropped hair met his neck, and his skin bristled under her nails. Her body shook too—and she couldn't tell whether it was with his fears or her own. She loved him fiercely. The very smell of him intoxicated, that mix of sweat and soap and starch, and something else, something utterly specific to *him*. She would not lose him; she would not let him leave. His hands held her waist, tight and steady, keeping her soles planted on the stone.

An inch, two inches, she pulled back and looked into his eyes. His gaze was split, fierce and frightened all at once. His lips parted, a scant hairsbreadth, and their parting made her bold. She stood on tiptoe to kiss him. At first, it felt chaste, like the times they'd played at kissing when they were small. Two pairs of lips pressed shut, neither sure what to do. And so they'd count to ten—or twenty when they were feeling brave—and then fall away, shy and giggling. For a moment, she thought it would be the same now. And then something changed—Alexander's grip tightened on her hips, and his mouth opened on her own. His tongue met hers, and it felt odd at first, invasive even, and then somehow pleasant, yearning. Her skin tingled and her heart raced; something hard pressed up against her stomach, and she scarcely blushed when she realized what it was.

"Don't go," she whispered as they pulled apart. "Don't leave me here."

"It's not enough, Arsinoe," he said, blinking back tears. "It can't be enough."

He bent to kiss her a second time, but she stepped away. "What do you mean? What do you mean it's not enough?" At first she'd whispered, and then she nearly shouted, striking her hands against his chest. "What's not enough?"

"What would you have me do, Arsinoe? Wait here in Alexandria until you're wed to some worthier man? I'm not Apollodorus, do you hear?" His voice grew cold. "Even you can't ask that of me."

"Get out," she hissed. "Go and join your Romans. The next I see of you, I expect it'll be on the battlefield. With you leading legions against my own."

She didn't mean those words, but she didn't regret them either, not even when he had stormed off, the double doors slamming in his wake, and she was curled up on the floor. She'd offered him everything—she'd kissed him and pressed her body to his—and it wasn't enough. The water welled in her eyes, but she refused to set it free. She'd murdered her father, unnatural creature that she was, and that hadn't made her weep. She wouldn't cry over Alexander. Over some nobleman's by-blow.

Arsinoe couldn't say how long she rocked herself against the cold stone before Eirene found her. It might have been hours; it felt like days. In her head, the time had spooled on endlessly, but when she glanced at the window, she saw that the sun still hadn't begun to rise.

"My princess." The maid knelt at her side, stroking her back gently as she might a child's. "Are you unwell?"

"I was feeling a little sick." She kept her voice steady and slid her knees beneath herself to sit.

"Should I call for a doctor?"

"No, I feel much better now."

"Permit me to help you to your bed. Let me do that, at least."

"No, Eirene." Arsinoe got to her feet too quickly, and black blots scored her sight. A serpent curled in the corner of her vision. "I don't need your help."

Eirene sighed. "I merely—I saw Alexander leaving here. He looked upset. I thought you might have quarreled. I know what great friends you've always been."

"Well, we aren't anymore."

Even that denial didn't cure her shame. As she lay in bed and waited for dawn to break, the same question haunted her: why did she have to kiss him? That was the worst of it. If only she'd sent him off and finished with it there. At least then she wouldn't have to live with the humiliation of having tried with every fiber and failed. Failed to seduce Dioscorides's bastard—and she, a Ptolemy.

In the days that followed, Arsinoe did her best to forget about Alexander. She tried instead to fill her time, begging a bewildered Ganymedes for extra lessons to perfect her Aramaic and attending Cleopatra's audience sessions at all hours of the day and night. But the world conspired against her: the model sentences the eunuch taught her were all rooted in military terms, and the court was seized with talk of the Gabinians' rebellious stirrings. Finally, one afternoon, after she'd stumbled into the royal atrium to find Dioscorides debating—idly, as though his own son hadn't joined their cause—whether the lost legions would return to Rome or not, Arsinoe gave up. She returned to her chambers and had Eirene draw her a bath.

Eyes sealed, Arsinoe let the waters soothe her. In this dark cocoon, she could become a little girl again. She might imagine Myrrine—not Eirene—untangling her hair. *The Fates don't often send friends such as that.* Her nurse had been right, those years ago, and still she'd somehow pushed Alexander away. If Myrrine were here, she'd know what to say. If Myrrine were here . . . But Myrrine wasn't here and could never be again—and Arsinoe herself was to blame. Her father's wasn't the only death she'd brought to Alexandria. Under Berenice's rule, she'd dreamt of her nursemaid's murder, and done nothing. Another black mark against her. Now the woman rose in Arsinoe's mind: she looked a thousand years older than she'd been in life; her lips drooped and her wrinkled skin had taken on a bluish sheen. When Myrrine's spirit, her *ka,* whispered, it sounded muffled, as if it spoke from beneath the waves: *I suffered for you, child. How I suffered...* The figure drew closer; the ghost hands reached for her shoulders, and as they did, they sprouted claws. Arsinoe's eyes sprung open.

A crone had come to steal away her youth, but it wasn't Myrrine. Another face loomed: the same heart shape as her own with deep-set eyes to match, though crow's feet stretched from their creases. Close at hand, her mother's appearance alarmed her—it was too much like looking at her own reflection aged two dozen years. As Arsinoe sat up and drew her arms across her breasts, she peered around the room for Eirene.

"I sent away your maid," her mother said coyly as she settled onto the vacated stool. "What I have to say isn't fit for slaves to overhear."

"I see," Arsinoe replied. She was still flush with reproach—she didn't trust herself with idle conversation. But she knew better than to dismiss her mother. The woman held Ptolemy's ear—she'd always had it, pampering him since his infancy—and she might let some detail slip of his advisors' plans. Arsinoe knew as well as anyone that the Gabinians' revolt gave her brother an opening. Despite Alexander's starry-eyed delirium, the rank and file muttered more about mutiny than a return to Rome.

Her mother's presence wasn't merely unnerving; it felt positively unnatural. Arsinoe could hardly imagine the last time they had been alone together. Surely there had been some afternoon, some meal—but in each memory lurked an extraneous figure: one of her brothers playing in the background, or else a fussing nurse, or three. She sifted back to earlier times, when it had been only her and Cleopatra—but her mother had barely looked in on them then. The woman's interest in the nursery was piqued only when it swelled with boys.

Arsinoe grew impatient, waiting for her mother to go on. "What is it?" she asked. "What's this matter unfit for servants' ears?"

"I worry for you, my dear. I heard your friend Alexander is leaving us."

"He does what he likes." She forced her voice to remain light. "It makes no matter to me." Beneath the tub's waters, she dug her nails into her palm.

"It does a mother good to hear that. Your love of that boy has kept me awake more nights than I can count. I'm glad you'll waste no more time with a man who could never match you in birth or ambition."

What was her mother jabbing at? The woman never spoke a careless word. She'd clawed her way from concubine to royal wife—she wasn't one to waste breath.

"You're right," Arsinoe agreed stonily. "I had been foolish."

"Why must there be such coldness between us?" Her mother reached into the basin and cradled Arsinoe's hand in hers. "You were such a sweet child. Cleopatra always cared more for your father. But you, you loved me once."

Arsinoe bit her lip and said nothing. She'd endure this too; she'd endure this for her sister, nearer to her than either parent had ever been. Her mother's taunting couldn't touch her, no more than a fly might change the path of a lioness. All she had to do was listen: wait until the woman revealed some hint of how her brother's advisors meant to proceed.

"I wept, you know, when you were born," her mother whispered. "When the midwives handed you over, all wrapped and soft and clean."

"Women often cry in childbirth, I hear." Her own voice sounded far away.

"So perfect, I thought, as I gazed down at your eyes and fingers. So perfect, except for one thing."

The tub had turned cold. A chill ran down her spine. *Why tell me this?* Arsinoe wanted to yell. *Why tell me what I've always known?* But she stayed as still as the water buoying her body.

"You were a girl," her mother went on in a singsong voice, almost like a lullaby. "I'd already borne the New Dionysus, Lord of the Two Lands, one daughter. What was I to do with a second? Sons, those were what I'd promised him. 'My love,' I whispered in his ears, 'take me as your wife and I'll give you what Tryphaena's failed to do for all these long years: boys.' What use was another girl? To him, to me, to Egypt?"

Her mother paused, awaiting a response. But Arsinoe had fled; she watched the scene from her corner, in soiled garbs, as her mother spoke to some older girl—a woman, really—whose breasts and hips and painted eyes she didn't recognize.

"Those were four long years, your first four years of life, though I can't imagine you remember them. Four years of hoping and wishing and praying for a son, and four years of bleeding away your father's seed each month. I had worked so hard, Arsinoe, harder than you can ever imagine, to become your father's wife. You're a *Ptolemy!*" She spat the word. "You've never had to work for anything. But I was born merely another aristocrat's daughter, and now all that, all the years of flirting and planning and fucking . . . Only to fail at *this:* I was no more able to carry the New Dionysus's son than Tryphaena had been. And every time I looked at you, it was another bitter reminder of my failure. When at last my womb quickened again, I sent you from my sight. You and Cleopatra both. 'Girls long for sisters,' the midwives say, and I wouldn't have you two polluting my third, my best."

Ptolemy. Her best. The words plummeted Arsinoe back into her body, and her tongue lashed out. "Why are you telling me all this, Mother?"

"Because I need you to understand something else." The woman's lips curled into an unnerving smile, a parody of Arsinoe's own. "I was wrong. I needed you then, my dear, just as I need you now. Sons are nothing without their mothers, and one day I will be gone. Cleopatra will never guide Ptolemy's hand; she cares only for herself, her own glory. She doesn't care for Egypt. Ever since your father took her to Rome, she's been polluted by it. Why else would she agree to send away the Gabinians? She is more concerned with the Republic than with the double land."

"Any queen who rules Egypt must concern herself with Rome. She'd be a fool to do otherwise."

Arsinoe knew how bleak her sister's options had been: allow the legions to return to their masters or give the Romans an excuse for war. Besides, the Gabinians' loyalties were suspect; though they'd quieted, the men had first declared themselves for Ptolemy.

"Perhaps you're right. Cleopatra had little choice," her mother continued. The woman picked up the comb Eirene had discarded; gently, she worked it through Arsinoe's hair. Arsinoe recoiled at the touch. "But a queen must also balance her people's needs. What will happen now that the Gabinians have turned against Cleopatra? They already have begun to riot in the streets. You've seen Alexandria in times of strife . . ."

In Rome, Cleopatra had told her once, they had their slaves bait bears in a great ring, poking at the beasts until the poor creatures lurched forward to their deaths. Arsinoe refused to reel.

"I'll say no more for now, my sweet," her mother whispered, drawing her mouth near to Arsinoe's ear. "But remember, there's another way. You could wed Ptolemy and rule Egypt through him. Men are easily ruled. And your brother . . . he loves you well."

The next morning at dawn, Arsinoe woke shaking. In her dreams she'd been a snake turned against its own kind. Her twin had laid eggs of speckled gold and she herself had devoured the brood. The meaning was stark: the twin stood in for Cleopatra and—*No*. These dreams—these hauntings—they hadn't served her well.

Somewhere below, she heard the crush of boots. Not a solitary guard or two but what sounded like an entire phalanx. At first, she thought she'd fallen asleep again—the palace should be quiet at this hour, only the kitchens beginning to stir. Yet as she roused herself to listen, the sound didn't dim. Instead, the boots grew louder, her heart skidding with each thud. She had to warn Cleopatra. Arsinoe slipped from her bed and draped yesterday's mantle over her night tunic. That would cover her enough. On silent toes she crept through the antechamber; she needn't have worried, though. Eirene was enjoying some man's bed that night, and her other handmaidens slept soundly still.

Outside, the colonnade purpled in the first shimmer of wolf light. The marble skin of Arsinoe and her nymphs was cast in rose, and the water that poured into the fountain might have been the honeyed ambrosia of the gods. As Arsinoe passed through the Sisters' Courtyard to the royal one, she caught sight of the offending guards. Not a phalanx but at least four dozen sentinels patrolling the inner and outer colonnades. When she reached the entrance to the queen's apartments, the guards made no effort to stop her. In fact, one smirked conspiratorially at the other, as though they'd been laying bets on when she might arrive. Once she'd climbed the stairs and reached the antechamber, she saw the reason: Cleopatra was already awake—and furious.

Pacing back and forth across the first antechamber, the queen tore at her hair and cursed. In the far corner, hunched between the embossed writing table and the wall, shrank the object of her sister's rage: Apollodorus.

"They *killed* them," Cleopatra exclaimed, though Arsinoe

couldn't tell if her sister was addressing her, the unhappy advisor, or the gods themselves. "*Killed* them."

"Yes, my queen," Apollodorus answered with the resigned tone of a man who'd already confirmed the same information several times.

Her sister spun on her heel and plowed the length of the room again. "*Both* of them?"

"Yes," Cleopatra's councilor answered steadily, as though his steadiness might soothe the queen. "Both sons of Bibulus are dead."

Despite her sister's rage—despite the chaos in the courtyard below—in mockery of every reasonable fiber in her body, Arsinoe felt a prick of hope. With Bibulus's sons dead, Rome's legions could not follow them to Syria. Alexander would remain in the city—at least for the time being. Perhaps he'd even be barred from joining another Roman legion, now that he was tainted by association with a rebellious one.

"A Roman governor sends his two sons to ask for troops, and they turn against him. What am I to do with that? I have four legions of Roman soldiers, lapsed Roman soldiers, murderous, mutinous Roman soldiers, within my city walls. What am I supposed to *do* with them?"

"You don't need to do anything," Arsinoe offered quickly, before Apollodorus had a chance to speak. "The Romans are always turning on one another. Even now two of their acclaimed generals are readying armies against one another. They're savages."

Cleopatra gazed at her with blank eyes, washed of kohl, void of recognition. She seemed to look through Arsinoe. And then her face cracked, her lips widened into a flat, mirthless smile, and she laughed. "Yes, *do nothing*. What a brilliant idea."

The reaction was alarming; an unrestrained wildness lurked in Cleopatra—the torn hair, the unmade face, the mad cackling. Arsinoe searched for ways to calm her sister, to read sense into the murders and situate them on some spectrum of perspective. She floated outside her body, above the room, above the palace, and watched the full picture unfold: the Parthians attacking Syria, the Romans defeating the Gauls, and the Gabinians rioting in Alexandria.

"Their deaths aren't your fault," Arsinoe said softly. "You gave those two men what they asked for: an audience with the troops their father's predecessor had left behind."

"The Senate will not blame me?" Her sister laughed again, brash and cruel. "What a lovely world you must live in, Sister, where Romans dole out blame only where blame is due."

All at once, Arsinoe recognized the mood—the caprice laced with rage—though she hadn't seen it manifest in ages. When they were children, she had caught glimmers of it, but not once in the five years since her sister had returned from Rome. She'd hoped that the staid city had cured Cleopatra of the changeability, but perhaps instead the trait had built up beneath her sturdy facade, waiting for this very crack in its smooth veneer.

"Yes," her sister went on, "you're right. I gave them what they wanted—and now they are dead. Two sons are dead, and their father—the governor of Syria, no less—will search for vengeance. Rome already has her wolf eyes set on Egypt. All the Senate must do is read this as a provocation . . ."

"And do what? The Romans already have too many wars on their hands. If they are begging for Gabinius's legions, they must be desperate."

Though she'd met the men herself, Arsinoe felt no pang of sorrow over their deaths. She wondered if that made her heartless. The two soft noblemen with their virgin hands had irked her. Their manner had been far too easy around Cleopatra, how eagerly they'd sworn themselves bosom friends. Even when asking for favors, they hadn't paid her sister the respect owed a queen. *It's not their fault.* Cleopatra had smiled sweetly. *They're Roman. They don't understand what it means to bow before a queen—we must teach them.*

"Today Rome is weak," her sister began, "but we have seen Rome weak before, and she always rises again. Under Sulla's disastrous reign, many men thought the Republic would corrode, but Pompey crushed Mithradates just the same. The *great* Mithradates. And now he grapples with another Roman general. Whatever the end, nothing changes. The Republic will rekindle her strength—and if I don't act, she'll turn her greedy eyes to the double kingdom once more. Just as Cato did."

But why couldn't Rome break? The Seleucids had fallen; so had the Carthaginians—perhaps it didn't matter so much that they had fallen to Rome but that they had fallen at all. An idea came to her— at once audacious and obvious. If they could convince the legions to fight for Alexandria, and if they recalled the resting armies from the Upper Lands at once and began training all the settlers' sons in the arts of war, perhaps they could face down the Republic. Or at least keep her claws from stretching toward the Nile.

"But we could be ready for them," Arsinoe pressed on. "Ally yourself with these troops and tie them to Egypt's cause. They have wives and children here; they'd rather fight for Alexandria. And then—"

"Arsinoe," her sister cut her off. "One day, I promise, we will fight Rome and we will win. But that day is far off, and until then we must be cautious. We must give the Republic what she thinks she wants."

Cleopatra's eyes had steadied, and her tone was final. That frenzied energy washed off her in great waves until she was still. Whatever reason had won over Cleopatra, Arsinoe didn't approve of its conclusion. In the corner of her eye, she noticed Apollodorus.

The advisor had relaxed his stance, and he was leaning almost idly against the frieze, his head resting on the satyr's lyre. The only tension left was in his face, his russet eyes set in fawning, yearning focus on Cleopatra. He would never abandon his queen's side, Arsinoe knew; unlike Alexander, he would content himself with what crumbs Cleopatra allowed him.

"Apollodorus," Cleopatra said, calling him from his reverie. He started forward, almost stumbling to respond to his name.

"Yes, my queen?" Already he was at her side.

"Who is responsible for these murders?"

"All the companies agreed to them, but it is said that Marius Sura and Appius Camillus each wielded a knife."

Cleopatra pursed her lips. "Bring them to me. And gather the rest of the legions as well. They should all hear my judgment."

BROTHER

The Great Theater ran Roman red. Soldiers overflowed from their benches and onto the stairs, clotting the aisles with their sandaled feet. Ptolemy knew, of course, that there were four legions in the city, but he hadn't considered what that meant. The manpower those numbers punched. Only in the higher rows did the colors ease into an amalgam of blues and greens, pinks and violets, where ordinary Alexandrians had packed in to see what Cleopatra intended to do with the soldiers.

The Gabinians had grown ragged. The crimson borders of their tunics still stood out, but many of their bright whites had faded to a murky gray. Everywhere Ptolemy looked, men jostled one another, cursing and roiling up their comrades. And yet these same soldiers had once formed the methodical troops that had restored his father. His memory of those days was hazy, cobbled together from oft-recited stories and a few disparate images frozen in his mind. When his mother had received tidings that the Roman army neared, she had carried him onto the roof of their safe house to watch. As he remembered it, he hadn't been outside in weeks. The sea smelled so strongly of salt it stung his tongue. At the sight of the relentless stream of soldiers marching beneath the eagle standards, he began to cry. His mother bent to whisper in his ear, *Don't fret, my sweet, your father rides behind. They've come to restore your throne.*

At the time, he hadn't understood those words—he'd never had a throne. He'd known the palace only through his mother's descriptions of its luxuries: how water came bubbling from the tap on every story, how the frescoes glimmered with real gold, how servants tended to all their wants.

Once his father had returned, that phrase—*your throne*—had grown more tantalizing with each passing year. In the theater's royal box, he sat squarely in his father's place. Of all the city's royal stalls, he liked this one best—it was set high enough for him to look down on every player in the arena. From this perch, Ptolemy would tower over even Great Ajax himself if he strutted across the stage.

Cleopatra's presence marred the effect, of course. Her very nearness was a rebuke, a reminder of all the wretched mistakes he'd already made. At his left, she sat a full head taller than him, even when he stretched his spine so straight that his back ached.

His sister stood—voiding his efforts—and raised her arms above her head. All around the nattering died away and thousands of eyes fixed on Cleopatra. Ptolemy watched her too—her rich purple gown studded with pearls, her piled tresses wisped about her white diadem. He wondered how she managed it. What about her transformed these Roman warriors into docile dolls? He knew it wasn't beauty—or not beauty alone. Arsinoe had the lovelier face; her features were softer, her eyes more delicately drawn. But there was little fearsome about *that* sister. In Cleopatra's expression lurked some other attribute—something hard and captivating.

"Bring out the murderers," she commanded.

A pair of guards emerged from the wings; between them they dragged an old man, his hands and feet fettered in iron. Wearing the rough-woven tunic of a slave, the prisoner was bald save for a few tufts of gray hair behind his ears. One of his eyes was swollen shut, the other wide with terror. He had served as centurion once—but he'd given up all pretense of that office. Ptolemy spared no pity for him.

The second prisoner was more interesting. Though outfitted in a similar fashion—the same chains bound his limbs—this one kept a shred of dignity. He held his head high, and his close-cropped hair shone a reddish-gold when the sun hit it, almost like a crown. His face was clean-shaven and smooth; Ptolemy pegged him as no more than twenty, a mere boy when Aulus Gabinius and the New Dionysus had seized the city. At the sight of this captive, a murmur of protest rippled through the stalls.

Ignoring the whispers, Cleopatra continued. "These creatures have broken the rules of gods and men. The sons of Bibulus ate your food and drank your wine and then these two killers cut their throats. Your guests, your own countrymen. And for what crime?"

This time, instead of muttering, it was silence that pulsed in Ptolemy's ears. Quiet laced with fury. Did Cleopatra recognize the muffled rage?

"For the crime of asking you to fight for your fatherland. It seems these men have turned so craven that they'd prefer to break the laws of *Jupiter*"—Ptolemy flinched at the harsh sound of the Latin name— "than do battle."

Objections simmered once again. Not twenty feet from the royal box, a curly-haired youth leaned in to his companions. When the group glanced up, Ptolemy could feel the anger in their gaze.

"But it is not my duty to discipline your ranks. That joy lies with your generals. As queen of these lands, I merely dole out punishment for our two murderers. I will send them to Syria. Let the bereaved father, Bibulus, decide the fate of these cowards."

Another wave of murmurs undercut the silence. The calm threatened to shatter but then held. What a *fool* Cleopatra had been, gathering these soldiers together only to provoke them. If it had been up to him, Ptolemy would have sent the Roman traitors off to Syria in the dark of night. Why tempt the Fates by shoving the disgrace down their comrades' gullets?

A voice rose from the stage. "And what of your cowardice?" Though scarcely louder than a whisper, the words commanded the attention of a shout. They'd been spoken, Ptolemy realized, by the auburn-haired prisoner. On either side, his guards stood dumbly, too stunned to rebuke their captive.

"What of your cowardice, my queen?" the man repeated.

Cleopatra trembled. Her fingers tightened on the cedar rail that hemmed in the royal seats. Ptolemy recognized the signs of fury; that little, at least, they shared.

"For five years, five *long* years," the prisoner railed on, "we've protected your father's reign and yours. And *this* is how you repay us? To send us back to Rome rather than upset the Senate? As children, we heard tales of Egypt in her glory—look at what you've made of her now."

One of the guards recovered his senses and clocked the man's face with the butt of his spear. The Roman collapsed to his knees, blood dripping from his jaw, but he managed to keep talking.

"What fools we were to build our lives here in Alexandria, a weak land ruled by a weak queen."

The guard kicked the prisoner in the head. Spots of crimson flecked the stone. Again and again, the boot slammed against the youth's face until his mouth collapsed into a bloody pit. Bile rose in Ptolemy's throat, but he couldn't look away.

Like a chorus in a play, commotion poured in from all corners. The Romans stomped their feet so hard that the stadium began to quake. Shouts pierced the air in Greek and Latin—Ptolemy couldn't tease sense from the deluge. His eyes remained fixed on the bloodied youth. The guard no longer touched him, but still the boy didn't move.

The thud of boots, the sputter of spears on flesh, but Ptolemy remained stuck in his seat. Cleopatra's voice cut through the madness, shrieking curses and commands: *"I will not run in fear,"* she shouted. He heard her repeat those words half a dozen times amid the crushing sound of bodies jostling one another. The action spread onto the stage; the broken prisoner was swallowed by a sea of red and gray.

A pair of hands grabbed his shoulders. The world slowed as though submerged in water. Dully, Ptolemy realized someone must be attacking him.

"Ptolemy." The voice hissing in his ear sounded familiar. He didn't think it belonged to an enemy. "Ptolemy."

A finger snapped against a thumb inches from his eyes. He stared at the hand gripping his shoulder. It was doughy and pale, not the hardened, sun-dark grip of a soldier. The eunuch had come for him.

"Get up, my king. We must get you away."

"But—but there are a thousand centurions blocking the exits."

Pothinus smiled, his lip curled above his snaggletooth. "I know another route."

Ptolemy tried to stand, but his legs buckled. In a single sweep, the eunuch hoisted him over a shoulder. His pride splintered, but he didn't struggle; he only prayed that no one would glance his way. That everyone was too distracted by the madness unfolding below. More guards had—finally—poured into the theater; one set had formed a ring around the two captives. Others grappled with clumps of Gabinians on the risers.

Catching glimpses past the eunuch's ear, Ptolemy looked for

Cleopatra. He could see no sign of his sister's violet robe. Had she run in fear in the end? Or been cut down by some Roman blade? He shouldn't dare hope for that.

Once they'd reached the bottom of the steps, Pothinus set him on the ground and guided him into the actors' wings. Here, half-repainted theater friezes melted into one another: the Furies' grove where Oedipus took refuge became a scene of bludgeoned Troy. Some two dozen masks hung in various spasms of humor: a bearded face cackled while a doe-eyed one wept enormous tears. Gathering dust on the ground below were the staff that Creon carried to mark himself as king and the cloak by which Electra identified her brother. Up close, the props looked cheap and flimsy—nothing like the potent symbols they appeared to be when the actors clutched them onstage.

Slowly, the sounds of struggle died down, but he found the quiet somehow unnerving too. He didn't like this place with all its strewn bits of magic stripped away. Even as the ceiling sloped upward to match the stands rising above, everything seemed to shrink around him. It was as though he had slipped backstage in his own life, and he could see just how tightly circumscribed were all his moves.

They'd traveled so far into the building's underbelly that Ptolemy could no longer tell which direction was which. Undeterred, the eunuch plowed on, even as they headed—as far as Ptolemy could figure—directly toward a wall. An enormous flat leaned against the marble; perhaps twenty cubits high, it was painted to resemble a great and gnarled oak. Ptolemy tried to place what play it belonged to—something to do with the spinning Fates?

Pothinus heaved the set piece aside to reveal a small wooden door. At first, Ptolemy assumed it was another prop, or maybe a false entrance to fool the spirits, like the ones the ancients had put on tombs. But then the eunuch shoved his shoulder against the wood and the door sprung ajar.

"Hurry." Pothinus pointed at the opening. "Go on."

Ptolemy hesitated. The hole in the false oak opened into a pitch-black abyss. The eunuch shoved him into the darkness. The hinges creaked as Pothinus shut the door behind them, cutting off what little light had crept into the passageway. Unnerved, Ptolemy felt for the wall with his fingers.

He heard the eunuch at his side, the rustling of his tunic. Then the dull, familiar blaze of an oil lamp flickered in Pothinus's hand. Did his tutor keep one hidden on his person?

"What is this?" Ptolemy asked, gesturing around the banished darkness. He kept his voice low; it felt like the sort of place where he should whisper. The dust lay heavy on the floor and the cobwebs grew thick in the corners, as though no one had passed through in decades or more.

"The palace has many entrances. You can't imagine you are the first king who's had to flee an angry mob."

The eunuch walked at an assured clip even though the ground was uneven, the rough-hewn tiles rising and then falling again without warning. More than once, Ptolemy stubbed his toe on a half-uprooted stone, and he had to scramble to keep up.

"Why are you in such a bright mood, Pothinus?" he asked sulkily after he'd jammed his big toe for the fifth time.

"The better question is why you aren't, my king. Cleopatra's missteps play out rather well for you."

"I fled from the Great Theater, flung like a sack of grain over my eunuch's shoulder. I don't think I won many admirers."

"Gabinius's legions were angry and ashamed. They couldn't distinguish one Ptolemy from another under such circumstances," the eunuch replied. "But when their senses return, they will remember who humiliated them after years of loyal service. It was not their king who sold them out to Bibulus, who branded them as cowards, who sent two of their comrades to their deaths. It was Cleopatra."

Ptolemy tried to ignore his mother's pacing. He leaned back on the lip of the fountain; he craned his neck to stare at the round-faced Arsinoe, who looked nothing like his sister; he ogled her two bare-breasted nymphs. But nothing he did could erase the scratch of sandals back and forth against the stone. The sound irked him. It reminded him that he should be pacing too. Or doing something to distract himself from the ignominy of having to wait.

Five days or so after the debacle in the Great Theater, his mother had brought him the news. He couldn't remember the last time he'd seen her in such high spirits. She was practically shaking with excitement as she told him: *Dioscorides seeks an audience*. He understood her glee, though he couldn't quite share in it. Like the rest of his father's advisors, Dioscorides had all but declared himself for Cleopatra. He'd attended her council sessions and dined with her most nights. And yet—after the queen's blunder with the Gabinians—the man might be ready to shift allegiances.

But the audience had proved difficult to organize. First Dioscorides had agreed to wait on Ptolemy in a formal setting, but at the last minute he'd reneged and insisted on meeting in a private courtyard instead, far from prying eyes. And now Dioscorides was late. After all the concessions Ptolemy had been forced to make, he—the *king*—was left waiting for some lowly functionary. The rendezvous had been set for the fourth hour, and Ptolemy could see from the shortening shadows that it was already nearer noon. *The justice hour*, Arsinoe called it, though he couldn't recall why. Under the circumstances, the name alone was taunting enough.

"He'll come," his mother soothed. At last, the woman had given up her pacing and settled down beside him. He could see the paint cracking around her eyes. "I'm sure he's merely been delayed. He'll be here soon."

"I am king. Men should wait on my leisure. Not the other way around."

Doubts kept nagging at him. His mother and Dioscorides had sworn him to secrecy, and that worried him too. Perhaps he shouldn't have listened to her—and how often had the eunuch warned against following her advice? She was a woman, not even born of royal blood. Whatever power she wielded over Dioscorides clearly didn't hold in the bright light of day.

"Mother," he said firmly, stretching his legs to stand. "I've sat here long enough."

Besides, the longer he waited, the flimsier the plan appeared. Dioscorides was father to Arsinoe's dearest friend—he wouldn't turn against Cleopatra so lightly. More likely, Ptolemy had snared himself in some trick of his sister's.

His mother grasped his hand. "A few moments longer."

Unless Arsinoe had already decided to abandon the queen. Maybe his sister wouldn't be content to prop up Cleopatra's rule forever. She, too, was a Ptolemy, as his mother reminded him. Surely Arsinoe harbored dreams—as he did.

"Did my sister plan this?" Ptolemy asked.

His mother laughed. It was a delicate sound, like notes strummed from a harp. "My sweet, the queen doesn't want you to meet with your father's advisors. Surely I don't have to tell you that."

"Not Cleopatra, Mother, my other sister."

His words wiped the mirth from his mother's face. Her lips thinned to a red gash.

"It's not the time for such thoughts. Put them aside."

His mother's speech had grown clipped, as it always did when she was cross. Or when there was something she wanted to hide.

"You *said* you'd speak with her," he insisted. "Why should I put that from my mind?"

"I merely meant that this is not the *wisest* time to grow distracted by such desires——"

"What do you know of *wise*, Mother?" His anger at her——at waiting, at Arsinoe——boiled over. He stared at this ordinary woman his father had mounted. A vessel to bear the king's seed. His own children would be full-fledged members of the dynasty. No aspersion would ever be cast on their lineage. "You're no one. You're not even a Ptolemy."

"Hush, my child. Not now." Rising from the fountain's edge, she reached for him, but he jerked away. Her touch was tainted.

"I'm not a child, and you can't dictate when I hush and when I don't. And if you can't treat me with the respect due to your god and king——"

"My sweet——" His mother tried to cut in, reaching for his hand.

"I'm not your sweet. I wish I weren't your son. You made my father weak——" The accusations poured forth easily and he savored each one. "It's your fault he didn't love me. Because you polluted our blood."

Footsteps slapped against the marble walk, but Ptolemy could barely hear them over the din of his rage. For too long, he'd nursed all his fury inward. His mother's mouth had widened with horror; paired with her painted eyes and lips, her expression worthy of a tragic mask.

"You offer up one lie after another. Like I'm a child who will be easily distracted by a new bauble. Who knows if you even spoke to Dioscorides? It's just another one of your desperate ploys——"

"My king," a deep voice interrupted.

Ptolemy spun around to find himself eyes-to-chest with the man himself. There were some men whose heights he hoped to one day reach, but Dioscorides was not among them. A good head taller than most members of the court, he positively towered over Ptolemy.

"I apologize for my delay," Dioscorides said softly. "I was waiting on an important message."

"You kept your king waiting so that you might receive a letter?" Ptolemy asked spitefully. Already the man had slighted him— Pothinus was right: he never should have trusted his mother to handle such affairs.

"Begging your pardon, my king, but it was no personal correspondence. I would never be late on my own account," Dioscorides replied deftly. "It's a matter that may be of some interest to you. I've received word from Bibulus, that unlucky governor of Syria whose two sons met their deaths here in our dear city."

Ptolemy held his tongue. His interest was piqued.

"As a friend, he writes to say that Queen Cleopatra ought to leave the punishment of Roman soldiers to the appropriate authority: the Senate in Rome. He has sent a similar rebuke to your sister. Though his sons are dead, he expresses himself with remarkable stoicism. The Gabinians, on the other hand, still fester at her treatment of their comrades. The queen's allies grow scarce." Dioscorides paused, a conspiratorial smile spreading across his lips. "And so the question becomes: How do we turn that to your advantage?"

Ptolemy didn't dare speak. Too often, he knew, he said the wrong things. Silence was better, some said even golden. Dioscorides's eyes darted to his mother, and doubt festered in his gut once more. How did it come to pass that *his mother* should have been such a convincing advocate? Why hadn't Pothinus or Theodotus brought Dioscorides into the fold?

An image sprung to his mind unbidden: his mother, naked and screeching as one of the Bacchae, her legs spread open on a mat, and

Dioscorides on top of her. A mutt pounding into a bitch in heat. He drew his hand to his mouth; he feared he would be sick all over his royal garb.

His mother grabbed his elbow, but he pulled away.

"Don't touch me," he hissed. "Don't ever touch me."

Nonplussed, Dioscorides stood, his eyes glinting between mother and son.

"Perhaps," the man suggested, "we should discuss this another time."

"No," Ptolemy said firmly. He had to compose himself. There were words to right this moment, ones that would prove a salve even now. They twisted in his mind, just out of reach, but he stumbled forward as best he could.

"For many years, you advised my father well. I would be honored if you would serve me in the same manner. Tell me, Dioscorides." He stared at the man fixedly, fearing what new mirages might arise if he glanced at his mother. "What must I do now?"

"Your first step, as I see it, remains rather clear. The Gabinians are displeased with your sister. And the Romans abroad are no more eager to come to her aid. But what keeps them in line? What are they waiting for, do you think, my boy?"

He was *not* this man's boy. His fury stirred at the insinuation, but he let it subside. Dioscorides already had proved himself useful. What was it that Theodotus said about useful men? *Even a king must flatter such as these.*

"You have seen many years at court." The words, for once, sounded right as he spoke them. "I trust your wisdom. Perhaps it is obvious to you, but I am yet unschooled in the ways of diplomacy. Please, what are the Gabinians waiting for?"

"They are waiting to see if another Ptolemy might show the mettle to rule Egypt in her stead."

If. The word echoed in his ears. These Romans who'd lived in the city for years, who'd watched him grow into a king. They still weren't sure of him. Like the rest of the world, they imagined him weak. Could he blame them? After all, what images had they seen? A boy fainting after his blessing, a child fleeing from the Great Theater. The memories sickened him, and he wanted to lash out, to shriek at Dioscorides that he was wrong, that the Romans would already be hungry to embrace his rule. He did none of that. Instead, he formed careful, self-effacing phrases in his mind.

"And so I must prove myself to them." Ptolemy enunciated each humble syllable with care. "I must show them that I shall be the sort of ruler who remembers his friends and crushes his enemies."

"It will not be difficult, my king. They are predisposed to you. Don't you remember how they cheered you at your banquet?" Dioscorides smiled. "All you need is to show them that they were right. 'He may be young,' I've told them, 'but he is as brave and bold as the son of Lagus, Ptolemy the Savior, who fought beside Alexander. He will make his forefathers proud.'"

SISTER

The summer winds twisted through the palace grounds in willful ignorance, as though the world had not spun from its axis, as though the Gabinians didn't clash with the royal guard in the theater and in the streets. These breezes were the last talismans of normalcy, the final bulwarks against the splintering chaos. Soon they, too, would fade. Even the library had been shorn of life, the scholars preferring to hole up in the dormitories rather than brave the route to the reading rooms. At least Ganymedes allowed her to take her lessons out of doors. She couldn't bear the stillness beneath the Medusa-headed columns, the ghost of the prophetess clambering over desks and chairs. Not that she could focus among the laurels of the Sisters' Courtyard either. All she could think of was Cleopatra—worried, overwrought with Roman tempers—while she sat about with her eunuch, pretending all was well.

Ganymedes glared at her and Arsinoe returned her gaze to the blank papyrus stretched over the bench. She sucked on the end of her reed pen and tried to draw an adequate comparison between Alexander of Macedonia and Mithradates of Pontus. Her thoughts refused to cooperate, meandering instead toward her sister, toward that other Alexander, whose name scraped at her heart. Only superficial points of similarity sprung to mind: *Both men were lauded by their contemporaries and successors as "the Great."* But that epithet had grown cheap; the Roman general Pompey had been granted that title for doing little more than defeating a few pirates. Perhaps her Macedonian forefather had heralded the degradation of greatness. Once these later men were crowned by the epithet, its luster tarnished. After all, Alexander had swallowed the world whole, only turning back when his army rebelled against his strength. The Pontic king earned the moniker merely by providing a token resistance to Rome. Soon anyone—any man, at least—would be able to lay claim to *greatness*. Perhaps that could be the theme of her composition—the diminution of grandeur from that day to this.

As she dipped the tip of her pen into the inkwell and prepared to write at least a phrase or two, shouts pierced the air. Fear coursed through her. Nestled behind the great square, the Sisters' Courtyard was buried within the palace complex, many stades from the street. The blows—even of a great battle in the streets—should not echo here.

The eunuch placed a gentle hand on her wrist. "Calm yourself, Arsinoe," Ganymedes said. "It's a child's cries. Nothing more. Your brother Ptolemarion enjoying the good weather."

She heard that now—the boy calling after his playmate: "I'll catch you yet!"

"Yes, of course," she murmured. "We wouldn't be lazing about over verses if something more sinister were afoot."

"Watch your pen, Arsinoe," the eunuch warned.

She glanced down at the instrument. A great blob of ink bubbled at its point. Slowly, the dollop plopped onto her papyrus.

"I'll need a new sheet," she said.

She would take this moment to slip away from the eunuch's grasp and listen outside the audience hall. Rumor whispered that her brother and his advisors—Dioscorides now among them, damn him—met with the Gabinians almost every day. Perhaps she might carry some breath of news to Cleopatra.

"No, Arsinoe, that won't be necessary." The eunuch's hand tightened on her arm; apparently her excuse had been too feeble to fool him. "You'll make do with what supplies you have."

A sallow boy with a mess of inky hair screeched into the courtyard, a wooden sword clutched in his hand. Moments later, a breathless Ptolemarion followed. She couldn't help but smile at their antics—it was good to see her youngest brother racing about at boyish games. More often than not, he withdrew from the world, devoting hours to sketching serpents and lions, phoenixes and sphinxes. In another era, such behavior might have suited a Ptolemy—the son of Lagus himself had written the long-winded biography of Alexander the Great that Ganymedes had insisted she read. But the sheen of the double crown had dimmed, just as the luminaries of the library had faded. Her dynasty demanded warriors now, not intellectuals or artists.

Ptolemarion backed his friend against the stone lip of Arsinoe's fountain, poking at him with the edge of his false lance. "That'll show you, you filthy Gaul!"

Arsinoe held back a sigh. Another set playing at the Republic's wars. It seemed Alexander's passion for all things Roman was catching.

"It's like a sickness," Ganymedes whispered, as though he could pluck the thoughts from her head. "The Roman obsession that plagues our dear Alexandria."

"It shall pass, as all such manias do," Arsinoe replied with more certainty than she felt. Her brother's friend had toppled backward into the fountain, and Ptolemarion unlaced his sandals to follow. The two boys splashed at one another, swords and feigned battles forgotten.

"No more than that? I did not imagine you so impassive. Are you so anxious for the wolves to destroy this city's wonders? For them to turn its theaters into gladiatorial death rings, its library into a garrison?"

"You know I'm not impassive." Arsinoe kept her voice quiet. "I won't stand by idly as Rome ruins everything my family has built."

The eunuch pursed his lips. With his cheeks flushed red with sun, he made an absurd picture. Like some desperate concubine past her prime. Arsinoe looked away to stop herself from laughing.

"Then you need to consider, very carefully, where you stand," Ganymedes said.

Watching the two boys playing, gleeful and guileless in the water, she turned the eunuch's words over in her mind. They were meant to inflame her, to suggest her allegiances flickered in the wind. She forced a cool response: "I know where my loyalties lie."

"Your loyalties," Ganymedes replied, "yes, indeed. Those lie with Egypt, or so I believed, and with your dynasty. With protecting this land from Rome."

"And who better to do that than Cleopatra?" she retorted. "Ptolemy is a child, ruled by ambitious advisors. You know as well as I do that he doesn't stand a chance against the Republic."

"Nor does your sister. Her goodwill is spent: she's angered the Gabinians and angered the Roman governor of Syria besides. A revolution is brewing in the streets. It's only a matter of time before it engulfs the palace. And when it does—"

"And when it does," Arsinoe hissed back, "I will be on my way to gather an army with Cleopatra."

"Or you could remain here," the eunuch suggested, toying with the edge of his tunic, careful not to meet her eye, "and do what must be done to save Egypt: marry Ptolemy."

Her stomach roiled at the thought. "Have you lost your mind?"

"I should hope not," Ganymedes quipped. "It is my sole asset of value. You recognize the truth in my words—don't deny it;

that's why they upset you. Loyalty is a fine quality, Arsinoe, fine for orderlies and soldiers. But it is not the most important one, not for a Ptolemy. If you remain in Alexandria and wed the boy, you will be the one who rules the double kingdoms. Your brother is taken with you; he always has been. It will be far easier for you to manipulate—"

"Enough," she interrupted, raising her palm to stop his spew. "I won't betray Cleopatra. Besides, I've no reason to believe that Ptolemy would bend so easily to my will. As a child, he fawned over me, but his sentiments have muted. And his advisors would know well enough to steer him from me."

"He also has a mother who is desperate to stay in favor with her king. You might be familiar with her." The eunuch's wry smile revealed his blackened teeth. "She is your mother too."

Did Ganymedes know that the woman had already sought her out to propose such a scheme? The two had long been enemies of sorts, each clutching at fraying threads of influence. And yet Arsinoe could imagine her tutor forging such an alliance. He was—above all else— a pragmatist.

"No more talk of this, Ganymedes."

But it was too late. Treacheries descended on her mind, like the winged afflictions from Pandora's box, screeching and cawing for her attention. The same thoughts every Ptolemy nursed from the cradle, sucking at his fostering mother's teat, visions of reconquering his forefathers' lands, of unfurling the empire across the great expanse of Asia just as Alexander had.

The breeze had ebbed, and the boys had quieted their game, leaving her no distraction from the turmoil in her chest. The stagnant air was suffocating; even the great pillars of the colonnade appeared to close in around her. The world had coalesced in a singular determination to spur her toward betrayal. She needed to escape the cloying reach of her mother and her eunuch. Hands shaking, she set her reed pen down and stood.

"Arsinoe." The eunuch's voice had sharpened. "Where are you going?"

"I need a moment, Ganymedes. I need to be alone."

Without willing it, Arsinoe broke into a run—faster and faster, as though she might outpace deceit. The Piper, at least, she'd never loved, so that could not stain her soul as a treachery. And when she'd whispered poison in Cleopatra's ear, she'd never dreamt that her sister would embrace the idea. Yet she had—and so Arsinoe had curdled Cleopatra's love.

As she sprinted through the gardens, past the cypress groves and rose bushes where she and Alexander had so often played, she yearned for her childhood companion. He alone knew how she'd suffered for her loyalties. Or, better still, she wanted Cerberus and Little Ajax; she wanted to disappear again into the alleys of Alexandria, to become a street rat and take on another name: *Osteodora*. The bone bearer, leading her merry set of urchins. But however much she wanted to fade away, in her heart of hearts, she also longed for something else. She longed to rule: queenly and undying, rebellious and strong.

"No!" she chided herself.

To shake this desire from her mind, she tossed her head fiercely from side to side as she ran, her braids loosening as she sprinted. She darted through the last of the new gardens and out through the eastern gate. Had ambition sprung on Berenice in this same way? Like a fever rising in her cheeks? Her eldest sister—the dead one, whose severed head haunted her dreams—had dared to envision an Alexandria without Rome; perhaps she was the bravest daughter of all three. Arsinoe's sandals thwacked against the sand as she sped onward toward the waves.

Her shoes sank into the mud, slowing down her steps, and the skirt of her gown splayed in crimson petals around her hips. Waist-deep in the waves, she stopped. A thousand times she'd stood like this, gazing out over the wine-dark sea and praying for some return. Now she didn't ask for anything.

"Arsinoe."

Her mother's voice.

"What do you want from me?" She knew the answer. She'd always known: to sacrifice herself to her brother, to sublimate her desires to his. To abandon Cleopatra. To rule.

"Come out of there. You are too old for such nonsense."

She did not move.

"One day you will understand," the breeze cried out. "One day you, too, will pray for boys."

"It will not matter whether I bear boys," she answered. "I am not the queen."

"Your day has ripened. You must only reach out and pluck it from the tree."

The day had ripened. She needed to face her mother, to helm her own destiny. There was no time left for fear, for shame.

"Very well," she said softly as she turned, "I will wed Ptolemy."

But there was no one there. No one wading behind her in the waves or waiting on the sands. Her mother hadn't followed her, would never deign to beg so brazenly for aid. Merely the wind, playing at his tricks.

Broken, Arsinoe sank to her knees. The water climbed up to her ears and her robes floated about her shoulders. She could hardly keep her mouth above the waves. She didn't care. They washed over her in crashing wails. She didn't mind that either. The air she gasped in bits and blasts—that was enough. More than she deserved.

The tide ebbed, and Arsinoe watched the sea slip away. Soaked to the bone, she shivered as the water receded below her breasts, her waist. The evening cooled the air, but Arsinoe made no move to leave. She'd lost the will to comfort herself, to seek out the warmth of her chambers.

Later, Eirene found her, head and hands and knees pressed in the damp sand. Her maid, so often talkative, fell as quiet as the day they'd met: the mute servant of Berenice's rule returned. In silence, she led Arsinoe from the sea.

Back in her rooms, her wet clothes clung to her skin, and when Eirene stripped them away Arsinoe couldn't stop quaking, not even when she'd slipped into the steaming bath. She'd been foolish; she knew that. As she gazed up at the muses, Kaliope with her lute and eyes refurbished with lapis lazuli, she started to wonder whether the whole afternoon had been some sort of fever dream. She'd given her visions too much sway for far too long—it was no wonder that her imaginings had begun to steal into the daylight too. No more.

"What have you heard of these Gabinians?" Arsinoe asked as the maid massaged oil into her hair. "Of the trouble they're stirring in the city?"

"Soldiers always stir trouble, my princess, even in the best of moods," the girl said softly, "and now they are angry. My sister works in a tavern, and she says they talk all sorts of treason, that they've raised a guard around the palace to block the queen's escape. She worries for Queen Cleopatra. As do we all."

"As do we all," Arsinoe echoed.

"But the Romans are a fickle breed; not long ago they sung the queen's praises. They might change their tune again."

There was the rub. Ptolemy favored Rome, or at least his advisors did. But could she claim that Cleopatra was any different? Her sister played the Republic as deftly as she could, just as her brother's councilors did. And for the time being, the latter had emerged victorious.

"Tell me, Eirene, to whom do we owe our loyalty: the living or the dead?"

Eirene gave her a curious look. "The living, my queen. The dead have already abandoned us."

A leaden sleep fell on Arsinoe that night. She dreamt of cold scales and the taste of iron blood on her tongue. She dreamt of papyrus in flames and corpses belched from the sea. She dreamt of Cassandra's unheeded prophecies and Oedipus's empty eyes. And when she woke, for the first time in months, perhaps since her father's death, she knew what she must do.

The path from her rooms to the royal apartments, so well trodden during the Piper's illness, felt much longer than she remembered. The Sisters' Courtyard seemed to double in size, and the distance she traveled through the great courtyard to reach the royal one stretched as a boundless stream of pebbled dolphins dipping amid the browning grass. Dread swelled in her throat; each breath became a battle. A trio of ibises—Thoth's birds of wisdom—pecked at the ground along the far end of the royal courtyard. The temptation clawed at her—to divine some sort of meaning, mark this as yet another *sign*. But she'd finished with puzzling over dreams and portents. They'd only brought her confusion and grief.

Outside the queen's rooms, two sentinels stood watch, tall and stern, with the sun-darkened skin of the Upper Lands. That was a relief—at least Cleopatra no longer employed Roman guards. The younger of the two, a round-faced man with a crooked nose, moved to block Arsinoe's way. The other made no attempt to stop her, acknowledging her presence with only a slight tilt of his helmed head. When had her sister's men grown so suspicious of her? Had it always been so—and she only noticed now, when she arrived laden with guilt?

"I am here to see my sister, the queen." The words formed strangely on her tongue, as though someone else had spoken them. The title *queen* still sang of Berenice's rule, the horrors of its aftermath.

But the phrasing made no difference. The first guard squared his shoulders and braced his stance, as though he half expected her to charge him like some maddened harpy. Perhaps she would.

"Let me pass," she told him firmly. "It's what Queen Cleopatra would want."

The other sentinel nodded his approval. Reluctantly, the disapproving soldier stepped aside. The double doors screeched open to reveal the refurbished royal chambers. In place of the Dionysian scenes the Piper had had carved and painted on every edge, Cleopatra had installed gold-flecked mosaics of Isis and the Horus babe. The windows were cast open, and the rooms rustled with a lively breeze.

The private audience chamber confirmed Arsinoe's suspicions. On the blue-stitched divan sat Cleopatra and Apollodorus, huddled together as close as galley slaves on a rig. He cradled her hands, gingerly, as though he feared his grasp might break her fingers. Cleopatra's hair hung loose past her shoulders, and she wore only a linen shift, so light that Arsinoe could almost make out the dark rings of her nipples beneath. Were they lovers, already? Or did Cleopatra merely taunt him? A pang of jealousy dug into her side.

"My queen," Arsinoe announced herself.

Before her sister looked up, Arsinoe dropped to her knees, her eyes set on the satyr that piped on the floor in front of her. She heard the creak of the divan as Cleopatra stood, the gentle footfalls pressing nearer on the onyx.

"Why so formal, my sweet?" Cleopatra hovered over her. Soft fingers wrapped around her upper arms, urging her to stand. She kept her body heavy, like the cat Ariadne when she refused to be lifted from a sunny spot.

"I beg you, my queen, forgive me," Arsinoe muttered. She brought the hem of Cleopatra's gown to her lips.

"For what must I forgive you?"

In the manner of a suppliant, she clasped her sister's knees. "The Gabinians plot against you and plan to secure Ptolemy alone on the throne."

"I know they do, my sweet. That's what we were discussing when you surprised us. But, pray tell, for what must I forgive *you?*"

The scene of her confession didn't measure up to her imagining. There, she'd pictured Cleopatra alone, unhampered by guards and advisors. Perhaps she'd been naive—to think they might ever share such private moments now that her sister ruled. Cleopatra's legs tensed against her cheeks; she had to press on.

"I suspected for days, weeks. I should have been at your side," Arsinoe choked out.

"And so why weren't you?" A coldness had entered Cleopatra's voice.

Arsinoe had wanted to tell her sister everything: to address the distance that yawned between them, to air her agony over how Apollodorus had usurped her place. To confess that she had no notion of how to right matters between them after their father's—. *After their father's.* She couldn't complete the sentence. Not even silently, to herself.

She burst forth with half-truths. "I thought you shunned me. That you no longer valued my confidences."

Head buried in Cleopatra's skirt, Arsinoe couldn't make out the room beyond the colored cloth that shrouded her eyes. But she could picture it: The queen motioning to Apollodorus. Mouthing that he needed to free her from this clutching creature. Her sister's calves strained against her arms until, defeated, she released her grasp. But then, to Arsinoe's surprise, Cleopatra didn't flee—instead, she knelt and joined Arsinoe on the stone.

"Is that the only reason?" Her sister's dark gaze bored into hers.

"No, it isn't," Arsinoe answered honestly. She couldn't help herself now. "I thought you were too close to Rome; I feared that you would be no different from our father."

Cleopatra let out a harsh laugh. "Did I ever tell you what happened in Rhodes?" she asked. "When Father and I left?"

Arsinoe shook her head. Neither of them had spoken much of the time they'd spent divided under Berenice's reign. Perhaps that had been the moment the seed first germinated: their distance, her yearning for rule.

"It was the first stop Father and I made, after we fled Alexandria. The first time I had left our kingdom's shores. And we had gone to seek a Roman. A man named Marcus Porcius Cato, you may remember, the very man who'd stolen Cyprus from our late uncle."

Arsinoe nodded.

"And Father sought an audience with this man, this Roman. To beg for his restoration to the throne. For this alone, I was appalled—Father was the divine New Dionysus; I couldn't imagine him begging anything from anyone. But Cato saw things differently. Each day he found some reason to be indisposed." Her sister's voice grew hoarse with anger. "And finally, on the fifth day, when he agreed to see Father, his slaves led us to his privy chamber. While our father—the Lord of the Two Lands, the son of Horus, the heir of Alexander—came to plead for his crown, Cato sat smirking on his toilet, groaning over an enormous shit."

Cleopatra's eyes tightened at the recollection. Shame twisted in Arsinoe's gut, just as it must have in her sister's those years ago.

"So if you think I am too easy on the Romans, or that I do not know what sort of creatures they are, you are mistaken. No one hates Rome as I do, Arsinoe. And I promise you this: When the moment comes—and it will come—that we can spit on the Republic, I will be the first to spit. I will be the first to avenge the disgrace descended on our father and on our house. I will be the first to watch them roll in their own excrement."

Arsinoe grabbed Cleopatra's hands and brought them to her lips. This was the sister she adored, even worshipped. The fear that Cleopatra had been subsumed by the tedium of politics and rule lifted from her heart. Here was the queen Egypt ached for: pugnacious and enflamed.

"I know you will," Arsinoe whispered. "I am sorry that I ever doubted you."

A guttural voice cleared its phlegm. Her spinning joy had wiped Apollodorus from her thoughts, but now she looked to him. Dark stubble dusted his high cheekbones and his chin. His cracked lips thinned in disappointment.

"I hate to interrupt this display of sisterly affection, but I must remind you, my queen, that we need to set upon a plan of action. The Romans patrol every exit."

Arsinoe smiled slyly.

"I know an escape that won't be blocked," she said.

Tensions surged between the Gabinians and Alexandrians, fueling the sisters' preparations: the secret midnight rendezvous to map their route, where Cleopatra traced her ochre-tinted nail over the Nile's winding path, and the letters smuggled to send word to various sympathizers from Memphis all the way to Tarsus. Meanwhile, Arsinoe's lessons with Ganymedes went from irritating to interminable. To her surprise, the eunuch was determined to flee with her. "I won't leave you, not in your hour of need," he told her.

EMILY HOLLEMAN

"Even if your hour of need springs from your foolish insistence on

following Cleopatra to the ends of the Earth." But he insisted on

keeping up appearances. "Remember," he explained to Arsinoe for

the umpteenth time over Plato's dialogue on Courage, "everything must retain the guise of normalcy."

When the appointed day arrived, the odd foursome—she and Cleopatra, Apollodorus and Ganymedes—dined together in the royal apartments. Arsinoe watched the eunuch fondly as he dug his blackened teeth into the tender game hen, the juices dripping down his jowls. He was no Apollodorus, and no Alexander, but he was still hers.

She bit into another piece of wild boar and the flavors exploded in her mouth, as though her taste buds suspected they would soon face a stint of deprivation. Though Cleopatra ordered many casks of wine, they hardly touched any, mixing only a pittance with the water. Instead, her sister offered it up to "our most noble friends and guards," allowing the sentinels to drain through some of the finest Macedon vintages.

When their guards railed and then quieted outside the chambers—Arsinoe suspected Apollodorus had laced the grapes with something stronger—their set crept through a secret door in the private dining lounge. From there, they made their way to the scholars' lodgings, the familiar path along the satyr-lined colonnades and out across the starlit shore. She recalled that other escape with Ganymedes, when he'd snuck her out of the palace those many years ago. How frightened she'd been, how little she'd understood. *It was too dangerous for anyone to know of your whereabouts,* the eunuch had told her, years later, *even me.*

The dormitory itself was not nearly as intimidating as Arsinoe remembered it, a simple brick-laid building bereft of palace opulence. The corridors and stairways were dull with dust. When they reached the top floor, where the grimy muses still lurked on the walls, it was not Kleon the Argive who greeted them. No doubt the ancient scholar with his whitened eyes was long since dead. But, still, she was startled to see a bull-shouldered Syrian in his place.

The man looked not in the least surprised to find the queen and her entourage planning an escape through his cabinet. He ushered them in, and once he shut the door, he sat back at his desk and returned to his studies. And he paid no more heed to them than he might a spider creeping across the floor.

Armed with oil lamps, they descended—first Apollodorus, crumpling his enormous frame to fit into the crawl space, and then Cleopatra, graceful, delicate, and finally Ganymedes with Arsinoe in tow. When her eyes adjusted to the darkness, she saw that what lay before them was an ordinary wooden staircase—far from the ominous steps hewn of skulls and femur bones that she'd long pictured here. Even the strongest childhood memories wizened with time.

As she climbed down the stairs, Arsinoe realized that for all her planning, she had no idea where they were going. Would her sister take them to her worshippers in the Upper Lands? Or cut out toward the Judean kingdoms in the East? She wanted to ask, to pester, but she fought the urge. She'd promised to lead Cleopatra from the palace—the rest she would entrust to the queen.

BROTHER

P tolemy woke to sticky sheets and a sticky web of half-forgotten dreams. He'd been sprawled out in the grass, basking in the sweet scent of rose. Arsinoe had stumbled upon his idyll. She lay down at his side and curled into him. Her lips kissed his mouth and then slipped down to his throat. He trembled at the memory. He shut his eyes and tried to retreat into the vision. She'd tasted so very sweet...

"My king." A whisper in his ear. "My king."

Someone was bent over him; a few stray wisps of hair tickled at his nose.

"Arsinoe?" he murmured, opening his eyes.

In dawn's first light, he had to squint to make out the details of the face: Briseis. Of course. A breeze danced over his chest, and all at once, he realized he was naked. Shamed, he snatched up the bed-clothes to cover himself. Not that his slave took any note. She still saw him as a boy, as everyone did. Even though he'd seen twelve summers. Even though he was called king.

"No," his maid whispered. "It's the queen."

His thoughts swam through silt. He tried to parse what Cleopatra could have done now, at this early hour, for the maid to wake him. No small part of him wanted to seal his eyes against golden-haired Orpheus's lament and reknit the threads of sleep. Instead, he pressed the most basic question from his lips:

"What about Cleopatra?"

"She's gone. Snuck from the palace in the night."

The sleepiness evaporated as quickly as dew in noonday heat. He sat up with a start—Briseis reared back to keep his forehead from slamming into hers.

"What!" he yelped, wincing at the high pitch of his own voice. "Gone where?"

"I—I don't know. The eunuch said to fetch you. That you're needed in the royal atrium at once."

Forgetting all modesty, Ptolemy threw off his blankets and stood. His vision blotted, and he blinked the splotches clear. As Briseis rushed to prepare his costume, his heart steadied. This—this was the ineffable thing that he'd been waiting for: the queen had fled in fear, and the tides flowed in his favor.

With his silken tunic girdled by a jewel-studded belt and the white diadem bound tightly about his head, Ptolemy did his best to bear himself as king: the embodiment of strength. Beneath that calm, another hope flickered—so delicate he didn't dare dwell on it too long. But despite his efforts, the dream swelled from the corners of his mind until it occupied its center: he would wed Arsinoe. No one could object—Cleopatra had forsaken the city, and in her stead, his other sister must emerge as queen. Their union would be of a different ilk—he was old enough to marry not only in name but in rights as well.

What was it that Achillas was always telling him? *Women are there for the taking, in your case even more so than in that of ordinary men.* Cleopatra's time had waned, and there was nothing now to hold him back from his pleasures and his rule. The imaginings came one upon the next: Arsinoe in the bright white garb of the ancients, her luscious hair pinned up beneath a straightened wig. Later, a shy smile as they stood joined before Serapis's altar. And then the fantasy lingered onward, sweeter, as the two retired to his chambers, as she slipped her chiton from her shoulder . . .

The griffon-handled doors of the royal atrium parted, and the stink that greeted him brought him back to earth. No perfumes were present here—evidently his advisors had been drawn so hastily from their beds they'd had no time for ablutions. In the far corner of the room, they clustered like vultures over a diminutive scribe. The whole company looked worse for wear. The servant—still wearing a stained night tunic as he hunched over his scroll—appeared utterly despondent to have been yanked from his dormitory. Dioscorides, usually fastidious and clean-shaven, had a blanket of stubble along his jawline, and Theodotus's good eye was so rheumy that it was hard to distinguish it from his bad. Only Pothinus had bothered to scent himself, and as Ptolemy crossed further into the atrium, he found the air polluted with the sour odors better suited to a city inn.

A figure pried itself from one of the columns, and Ptolemy started at the movement. It was only Achillas, his hair gleaming copper in the morning light. As usual, the commander set himself apart: unlike his half-dressed compatriots, he was fully clothed, breastplate and all. As though the general knew that he—a man of action—should not associate too closely with these mere traffickers of talk.

"My king," the general said.

"Where is the queen?" Ptolemy asked in a great voice, loud enough to draw the room to him. The other three glanced up from their bickering—Ptolemy caught some guilty looks in their eyes. Though he'd only just been roused, he felt sure his advisors had known of Cleopatra's flight for hours. After all, here they were, already preparing some decree for him to sign.

"The truth, I'm afraid, is that we don't know," Theodotus replied. "That is why we didn't—"

"They sail up the Nile, to Memphis or perhaps another town in the Upper Lands," Achillas interrupted. "No doubt your sisters mean to raise an army of their own."

Sisters. Not one, but two. A splinter caught in his chest. The eunuch added something else about the Upper Lands, but Ptolemy didn't register it.

"Achillas." He kept his voice steady. "Do you mean to say both my sisters have left the palace?"

The general's handsome face pinched; his left eyebrow twitched above a squinted eye. Almost imperceptibly, the man shook his head, as if to warn Ptolemy away from some outburst. Ptolemy fortified his efforts to remain aloof.

"Yes, my king," Achillas confirmed. "Cleopatra and Arsinoe have both fled."

Stupid, Arsinoe, stupid. She might have been his queen, but in casting her lot with Cleopatra she'd spoiled everything. Arsinoe preferred their sister's shadow to his throne.

Another voice, a shrill one; he couldn't parse the words. Then Pothinus repeated: "My king, my king. What say you?"

He wished he'd heard what had come before. He was no child; crushed dreams wielded no power over him. He wouldn't let them. Instead, he said mildly: "Very well. What must now be done? Shall we send our army after the traitors?"

To that, all councilors fell dumb. A riddle sprang into his mind: *What both loosens tongues and mutes them? An execution.* He'd witnessed that other sister, Berenice, beheaded. He'd seen her head thump across the floor and watched her body writhe before falling still. How would it feel to watch Arsinoe and Cleopatra meet that end? Would he revel in it?

Dioscorides spoke for the first time, palms planted on the cedar tabletop. "A military response is not the answer." His voice rang at the same low timbre as ever, but its effect had eroded. By remaining in Alexandria, Ptolemy realized, the man had chosen sides, and chosen *his*. And yet with Cleopatra gone, Dioscorides's importance waned. His lands, his titles, his very life—all these were gifts of the crown. Ones that might just as easily be revoked.

Oblivious to his reduced stature, Dioscorides went on. "Such a move grants too much credence to your sister's influence. Besides, whom would our soldiers fight? Two adolescent girls and a handful of foolhardy loyalists? Few will be attracted to such a hopeless cause."

The taunt was too easy for Ptolemy to resist.

"Your son might, Dioscorides," he replied. "Your Alexander. He positively dotes on Arsinoe, if I recall."

The man's face reddened. Even at his advanced age, he cut a formidable figure; Ptolemy could see the veins bulging in his neck as the excuses spewed from his lips. How the boy had joined the Gabinians and how Alexander meant to protect the king.

The very mention of the Roman soldiers sent his mind reeling again. Without a single legion, or the slightest prayer of victory, Arsinoe had chosen Cleopatra—she preferred exile, even death, to sharing a throne with him. What wrong had he committed to deserve such treatment? He'd done nothing but love his sister—not in Ptolemarion's fawning fashion, but in his own, quieter way. It was his mother's fault, he realized. She'd ruined this for him, despite her promises to convince Arsinoe to his side. Another lie. Just like the ones she used to tell about his father's love.

Ptolemy tried to listen to Theodotus's nattering about low harvest yields. And then to Pothinus, who was discussing some decree directing grain storage. They circled about him, each trying to push him in a particular direction. He could feel that it was a coordinated attack—every one of them prodding him toward some common goal. But what, precisely, they proposed to do to combat his sisters' efforts he couldn't follow.

"Go on, just tell me," he said, exasperated. "You've already decided what's best. Tell me what it is."

The eunuch sighed. "As I said, my king, the best option is to starve the natives. That way they won't be able to shelter her."

"Look," Dioscorides offered, snatching the scroll the scribe had lately been poring over. "We've already drawn up an edict to ensure that levied crops reach Alexandria."

Slowly, Ptolemy examined the papyrus. It was exhaustive in its details: it not only stipulated that all grain be sent directly for storage in Alexandria but promised death to anyone who disobeyed, a penalty extended even to those who had knowledge of any such criminal acts. The phrasing ended with a familiar construction: *By order of the King and the Queen.*

"Why?" he asked, his finger pointing at the word *queen.* "Why is *she* referenced here?"

Glances were exchanged, as though this chorus had already been staged. It likely had. The eunuch took it upon himself to answer. "This way, when she comes begging, they'll fault her as well as you. Cleopatra began this mess, and so she should enjoy the blame for it."

He pictured Arsinoe, bone-skinny and begging for her supper. It served her right—he only wished their mother might share in the punishment. For too long that woman had poisoned his mind with lies, false claims of his sister's love.

"So be it," he said. "We will starve them for now. And when the time comes, we will fight."

To his relief, his voice held firm. It had taken to cracking at unfortunate times, especially when his emotions ran high. Sometimes his whole body seemed resolved to betray him. Though he'd gained some height, he'd added just as many inches across his girth. While his legs and underarms sprouted tufts of thick black hair, no beginnings of a proper beard marked his chin and his chest remained stubbornly smooth.

Theodotus removed the pearl-embossed seal box from its hide-away beneath the throne, and Pothinus took the key from about his neck to wrest open the lock. There it lay: the ring of the reed and the bee, the joined symbols of the Upper and the Lower Lands. The emblem was too precious for even Cleopatra to steal. The eunuch furled the papyrus and a slave dolloped out a bit of fired wax. Ptolemy slipped the ring onto his finger, pressed its face into the heat. Such a small motion—yet it was done, the document sealed with the insignia of a king: his first death warrant and his first decree.

But that wasn't enough to staunch his mood. After he'd dismissed his advisors—no doubt back to their beds—he headed toward his mother's apartments. Already he sensed that news of his sister's flight had spread—the regard once reserved for her was now bestowed on him, and everywhere he looked, men bowed their heads and parted for his train. The guards didn't question him at the threshold; they stepped aside and allowed him entry.

Within the bejeweled antechamber, his anger tightened. Perhaps if his mother had spent more time courting Arsinoe and less appointing her own rooms with gold-stoppered perfumes, she might have met with greater success. What need had she for such finery: pearl-stitched divans and brightly polished silver mirrors? She'd done nothing to be worthy of it. Perhaps the eunuch was right: he should banish her from these queenly apartments. Remind her where true power lay.

As he crossed over the bucolic mosaic, Ptolemy made sure to grind his heel into the fawn's bright eyes. The woman had rendered him—from the time he was a suckling babe—the object of Arsinoe's loathing. How could his sister help but resent him when his mother chose him first, again and again? From the corner of his eye, a black shadow rushed toward him, and then a solid form crashed into his shoulder.

"My king." The slave girl stumbled forward, her soap-roughened hands grasping at his robes. "Your mother is bathing. Please wait and I will fetch her for you."

Repulsed, he slapped away the maid's fingers. She had no right to forbid him anything.

"Please, my king, she'll only be a minute." The girl reached for him, and he pushed her aside, harder than he meant. He heard her body thud onto the stone behind him, but he was already shoving open the door to the bedchamber.

Stark naked, his mother stood silhouetted against the evening sun. Droplets of water trailed down her veiny legs and her sagging breasts. He remembered when they were pert and full, and Ptolemarion would suckle at them. Perhaps this was why Dioscorides treated her with such scorn—her power waned with her tits as his own waxed to fruition. Then, slowly, he realized she was not alone.

A nude and oiled Adonis lay on the gold-buttressed bed. Ptolemy could count ten different muscles rippling in his torso. But more frightening still was the enormous member that sprouted between his legs. In length and girth, it more resembled a tree trunk than the sapling between his own thighs. Embarrassed, Ptolemy wanted to look away, but he could not. In the bathhouses and the gymnasium he'd seen many men naked, but never like *this*. All at once, he understood why Pothinus had shamed him rather than let him try to bed Cleopatra. How could he measure up to such competition?

"Ptolemy." His mother's voice summoned him from his trance. Anxious to forget what he had seen, he looked to her—but that was little better. Her body still had a startling effect, even weighted with age.

141

"Now, my child," she continued, "it's not polite to stare. Step outside and let me dress in peace."

Eager to be gone, he returned to the antechamber and sank onto the divan. He let his head fall into his hands; he'd lost all claims on dignity. Through his fingers, he could see the maid staring at him. Rage should have pulsed through his veins, stronger than the first wave, but he didn't have the will to harness it. Instead, unbound, the anger dissipated and his heart swelled with a child's desperation for his mother's, his nearest sister's, love.

"Wine, my king?" the girl sputtered, hands quaking. The terra-cotta pitcher trembled precariously in the air.

He nodded as she poured the dark elixir into a bejeweled goblet. He downed a large gulp. It might steel his nerves for the man's reappearance. Stubborn tears gathered in his eyes.

"It's my fault. I should have done a better job of warning you," the maid whispered. She was around his age, perhaps a year older. Her face was sweet and open, her hazel eyes wide set and kind. He wished he hadn't shoved her.

"It's not your fault. I wouldn't have listened." A few salty droplets escaped down his cheeks. He turned away and drained the rest of his cup. *You should be more careful with your drink,* Pothinus would chide. It didn't matter—now, of all times, he deserved the dulling pall of wine.

The minutes stretched on until his mother entered. Donning a silk chiton studded with pearls, she had hidden the traces of decay. Her face, too, had been pressed to perfection. The kohl and coral drew attention to her eyes and lips, not the lines that ringed them. Behind her, without a shred of shame, came her lover, clothed in the simple white tunic of a servant. That mark of low birth curdled Ptolemy's fury once more. But his mother didn't notice—she even gave the man a lingering kiss before he disappeared. And then she came to sit next to Ptolemy, to take his hands in hers, filthy with sex and gold.

"If you insist on drinking so fast, you must at least wipe your mouth," she scolded as she wet a handkerchief with her tongue and dabbed it over his upper lip. Ptolemy wrenched away from her touch.

"Don't treat me like a child."

"How else should I treat you, then? You certainly behaved like a child, bursting into my chambers unannounced. That's no way for a boy of twelve to act. And Pothinus tells me you've been distracted both in your audiences and in your lessons." Her eyes narrowed. "Cleopatra may have left the city, but you can't afford to be careless. I'd hoped you'd have learned that by now."

"You can't scold me, Mother, not when you sell yourself as a common whore. What wonder is it that the court still calls you a concubine behind your back?" he spat. "You disgrace me."

"Do you think that I care what they call me? I've been called names worse than concubine. My children sit upon the world's last great throne. Those gossipmongers are jealous peasants. And if they repeat those words before the wrong ears, they will be dead peasants. I don't concern myself with slurs, and neither should you."

Even in his anger, he heard the truth in her words. But someone had to pay for Arsinoe's abandonment, and it would not be him.

"You disgust me, Mother. I should have listened to Pothinus long ago and banished you from court."

"When it comes to humiliation, I would worry more about your behavior than—"

He spoke over her, plowing toward the crux of his rage: "And you've broken your promise. You've ruined everything. It's your fault that Arsinoe—"

To his horror, his mother laughed. As she did, she looked as though a dozen years had slipped away. She sounded—even looked—like Arsinoe. When she met his accusing eyes, she clasped her palm over her mouth. Yet her shoulders continued to shake.

"What is so amusing?" he hissed.

"Oh, my child, Arsinoe's loss brought you here? It brings you storming through the corridors and slinging insults? It is far worse than I feared, then—"

"It's not because of Arsinoe. It's because—"

"Hush, my boy. Don't fret over your sister." His mother squeezed his shoulder; her voice grew serious. "Today she betrays you. And you have every right to be upset. But soon—very soon—she will realize that you are a much better ally than Cleopatra. I promise you that."

Her words soothed him, though he didn't want to admit it.

"It doesn't matter." He shrugged, but he didn't pull away when she stroked his cheek. "That's not why I'm here."

"If you say so, my love." She smiled brightly. Her eyes gleamed.

"But—but how can you know?" he asked.

She kissed him gently on the brow. "A mother always knows."

SISTER

Their flight from Alexandria unfurled as a legend: two sister-goddesses fleeing their evil brother. Nephthys and Isis seeking out the scattered bits of Osiris's body to magic him to life again. Though, Arsinoe supposed, there was no hope for the corpse Cleopatra might wish to drag back from the undergloom. Like those divine sisters, they sailed up the Nile flanked by banks of virgin wheat. She could only pray that it would ripen gold, untouched by blight. So much of their fate depended on the yields of crops, the river's rise.

Their single-masted riverboat lent credence to the myth. Though the quarters were cramped for their set of four, there was a romance to their reduced circumstances. Ganymedes grew green and taciturn at the gentle milling of the skiff, but Apollodorus for once proved his worth. The colossal man revealed unexpected nautical skills, rowing and steering the round-bottomed boat with ease. Arsinoe felt as weightless as their vessel; they'd freed themselves of Ptolemy and Rome. The heat of Inundation had given way to the cooler breezes of Emergence, and the mornings were bright but bearable. The sun shone flush with hope.

Despite the drabness of their craft, the small folk of the valley sensed Cleopatra's presence on board. Each morning Arsinoe would wake to find the shores lined with sunbaked farmers cheering for their queen. Even in retreat, her sister clung to the trappings of rule. Once outside the palace, she'd shrugged off her rough-spun cloak to reveal the garb of Isis underneath. With the horned crown on her head and a shimmering chiton knotted between her breasts, Cleopatra looked every inch a goddess. But her power emanated from some deeper source: in her bearing; the way she cried out in the native language, whole batteries of phrases that Arsinoe could scarcely follow. She wasn't sure whether the locals caught her sister's every word, but perhaps it didn't matter—they needed only know that Cleopatra, like any true deity, could address them in their own tongue.

By the time Apollodorus steered their skiff to the quay, news of their arrival had reached Memphis, and a crowd had gathered there to greet the queen. First among them was Psenptais, arms outstretched in welcome. Though he was dressed in the same white linens as ever, his appearance jarred with Arsinoe's memory. Not much more than a year had passed since she had seen him at her sister's crowning, but the priest seemed to have aged a decade in that time: crevices were etched about his eyes, a few purple veins twined along his shaven neck. Legend told that he'd been a mere boy of fourteen at her father's coronation, and all her life she'd imbued him with that faded youth. But thirty long floods had ebbed and flowed since the Piper's ascent to the throne, and those years no longer rested so easily on Psenptais.

As he offered the customary blessings, Arsinoe noticed a slight tremble in his hands and words. She tried to climb into the same gilded litter as the priest and the queen, but Psenptais insisted on riding alone with Cleopatra. In the carriage she shared with Ganymedes and Apollodorus, she had no chance of overhearing the priest's whispers.

The warm welcome extended through their first nights at the red granite palace. Even in exile the queen managed to summon displays of opulence impressive enough to wow the local noblemen. The trade routes to the north and across the sea were blocked by Ptolemy's men, so Cleopatra demanded honey from Ptah's temple and filled the cellars with barley beers from outside Thebes. Bereft of the singers and dancers who usually accompanied the royal entourage, Cleopatra provided the entertainment herself, reciting tongue-in-cheek monologues from satyr plays and plucking out a few verses on a harp. And her sister's efforts paid off: soon Cleopatra had cultivated a small but loyal set of natives. Word spread, and a stream of Upper Landers flowed into the city, offering arms in support of Cleopatra against their brother.

As the weeks drew on, Arsinoe spotted cracks beneath the surface of hospitality. Psenptais visited far too often, taking stock of the amount of food consumed and oil burned. And one afternoon, the priest exploded at Apollodorus over their expenses. "The king orders that all grain must go to Alexandria, while the queen burns through supplies faster than ten quartered legions. What do you think the people will do when they start to starve?" When Arsinoe asked Cleopatra about the upset, the queen shrugged away her worries. "He's a priest, and priests grumble."

By the time the Rural Dionysia began, the mood in the city had taken a turn. Rioting broke out on the final day of the festival, and their newfound guard had to buttress the palace gates against the frenzied crowd. From high in her palace room, Arsinoe watched. She recognized the anger—the hunger—in the peasants' eyes. Ptolemy's advisors had played this round well: they were the ones who stole the commoners' wheat, but Cleopatra would be the one to pay for it.

The queen alone remained reluctant to depart. Cleopatra's attachment to the town, the meeting of the Upper and the Lower Lands, was strong. Strong, Arsinoe feared, to the point of foolishness. First

Psenptais and later Apollodorus pleaded with the queen to quit the city and gather her troops in Syria, where Ptolemy and his decrees would hold no sway at all—but she ignored their arguments. Only when Cleopatra's own litter was attacked did she agree to travel east. Though Arsinoe wouldn't admit it to her sister, these setbacks hewed her closer to the cause. Her heart still sung with heroes' songs, with tales of woe and wonder, Odysseus tossed and turned by cruel Poseidon across the seas—such champions forged their marks by overcoming the myriad obstacles in their paths. It boded well that their journey should follow that familiar arc.

The next night, holed up like paupers in some forsaken inn in the dusty backwater of Bubastis, Cleopatra cursed the priests and aristocrats alike. Arsinoe smiled at her language—the coarse words pinched from her sister's many months aboard ships sounded comic on the queen's tongue.

Even with the disappointments met in Memphis, their train had swelled. When they had left the city—again at night, by river— it had been on a larger boat with a far more impressive number of men. Arsinoe was prepared to remind Cleopatra of that fact the next time her sister sunk into one of her moods. These, at least, the queen managed to hide from the rest of their company—it was Arsinoe, her sister's cabinmate and confidant, who bore their brunt. The worst sulks—the ones that terrified Arsinoe—struck Cleopatra silent. For hours the queen would crouch on the edge of her mat and stare into the darkness, her gaze hardening with resentment. The unfairness of that struck Arsinoe sharply. What claim could Cleopatra lay to bitterness?

In those dismal days, Apollodorus kept them on course, prodding their company farther north and east until they reached the mud-brick garrison of Pelusium. Here, finally, Ganymedes sprung into action: milking connections forged in his youth, he hired a set of seagoing vessels on the sly. Rather than flaunt Cleopatra's divinity, the eunuch insisted they pay their way in coin, and Arsinoe found herself digging through what few possessions she had brought to find jewels to trade for passage.

Ascalon proved as amenable as Apollodorus had promised. The whitewashed streets of the bustling port town whirled with jockeying crowds: a procession of flame jugglers and strumming harpists, elaborate zebra-drawn carriages and wine carts, greeted their arrival. As they were carried, litter-lofted by slaves, Arsinoe noticed a turquoise pond beyond a great temple, whose golden doors and pillars were decorated with sea creatures.

"Is that the temple to Astarte?" she murmured to Ganymedes, solid and stoic at her side. She didn't want her sister to hear her ignorance.

"It is indeed. The mermaid goddess. The reason no one in the city will offer us a bite of fish."

Arsinoe nodded. She'd heard that tale before, how the goddess, from shame of sleeping with a mortal, hurled herself into the glistening pool. Rather than drown, her body transmuted into a fish. It was a harsh fate for a city so near the sea—to be forever forbidden from feasting on Poseidon's gifts. Her own punishments—the dreams that taunted her—seemed slight in comparison.

Cleopatra brightened with each lurch of the litter. She grew talkative, pestering Apollodorus with questions about the details of the city and its constructions, questions—Arsinoe suspected—that the man had no more business answering than she herself did. Arsinoe knew she should rejoice at their reception, at each man who prostrated himself at the sight of the carriage, at every reveler stumbling through the streets, but instead her insides calcified. *Jealous of her sister?* No. She would not grant Alexander that. As the great gymnasium mushroomed from a faint shadow to a mass of purple marble, Cleopatra emerged from their enclosure to greet the crowd. Apollodorus followed, cleaving to her side. For once, Arsinoe was relieved to be left alone with only the stalwart Ganymedes.

"Why do the crowds love her so?" she asked as she peered through the curtains. Men and children tossed roses at her sister's feet.

"And why not you?"

Arsinoe sighed. The eunuch was always eager to stir up trouble where there was none. Hadn't she put aside whatever faint blossoming of pride had tormented her in Alexandria? There was no place for it now.

"I didn't mean that," she told him. "I meant why *here*. What interest do these people have in whether Cleopatra or Ptolemy rules?"

A chuckle escaped her tutor's rotten teeth. "With all your feigned sophistication, I sometimes forget how very provincial you Ptolemies are. Egypt's influence does not end at its borders. More importantly, neither does Rome's."

"But Ascalon is allied to Rome," she answered, almost by rote. In those middling years of childhood, between Berenice's fall and Cleopatra's rise, the eunuch had forced her to memorize every city along the eastern coast and their ever-changing pacts and allegiances.

"Yes, but an *independent* city allied to Rome, and one with strong ties to your family."

The past washed over her, all the dates and battles from her lessons soldering together. The connection, she remembered, sprung from her forefather Ptolemy the Benefactor. Generations past, that illustrious ancestor had defeated the Seleucids and stolen half their lands. In the decades that followed, her family had controlled this territory. That was before her progenitors' seed had corroded to nothing.

The earth itself still felt far more foreign than any patch of Egypt.

Here, the worship of the usual gods, like Isis and Serapis, flourished alongside that of unfamiliar oriental ones. The sort carried west by caravan and slowly staking their claim in this new, fertile ground. Even the customary deities emerged as strange iterations of themselves; their worshippers were seized by violent urges. She'd heard stories of how men would castrate themselves in worship of the god simply called Bel, cutting off their genitalia and flinging them into the throngs. Those thoughts she kept to herself—they might strike too close a nerve. From the hints the eunuch had dropped over the years, she'd pieced together an image of his early life: how he'd weaseled his way from singing as a lowly, traveling castrato to climbing the palace hierarchy. Yet she had never discovered how he'd lost his sex.

"Don't forget," Ganymedes interrupted her musings, "Rome has grown weak. The elites turn against one another, and the longer Pompey and Caesar build up their armies in Spain and Gaul, the closer the She-Wolf grows to gnawing off her own tail."

The procession wound deeper into the town's heart, and Arsinoe began to wonder at their destination. The finer houses lay near the sea, and yet their destination appeared to be in the opposite direction, amidst the workshops and factories of the city's crowded core. The alleys grew narrow and so packed with men that the litter bearers were forced to halt every five paces or so. Arsinoe grew weary of the glacial pace, and the next time the carriage jerked to a stop she leapt from the vehicle.

On the street, the mob rang louder, as though her ears had been plugged with beeswax before the sirens and only now were cleared. *So they sent their ravishing voices out across the air and the heart inside me throbbed to listen longer.* Unlike Odysseus, Arsinoe could listen as long as she liked. As Cleopatra marched onward, Arsinoe noted how her sister's head seemed to swell with each wave of cries.

The queen would need that confidence, Arsinoe reminded herself, to battle Ptolemy's men and—most of all—to rule in the face of Rome. Gradually, another noise joined the cacophony: the thump of hammers striking in unison.

Ahead, the road widened to reveal an enormous edifice, which dwarfed the nearby mills and foundries. A small man with a wispy beard appeared between the building's two central columns. Hands clasped at his chest, he bowed to Cleopatra. His palms opened like a flower to reveal a silver mound of coins. Coins, Arsinoe realized, minted with her sister's face.

As soon as Arsinoe and Cleopatra entered the factory, it became clear that this unimposing, shrewish man held some important position in the city. He guided the sisters through the minting plant with an air of ownership, showing off the city's silver reserves and its deftly crafted hammers, which pounded Cleopatra's profile—wide-eyed, hook-nosed—onto one side and the emblem of an eagle on the other.

Azmelqart—as he was called—had whipped the town into a frenzy over Cleopatra's arrival. "You've rescued us," he explained during their journey by yet another litter from the factory to his home. "For years we've suffered low crops and low rains, but the moment you headed east from Egypt, the gods smiled and opened up the skies." Something in his smirk made Arsinoe mistrustful—she didn't believe that he bought into such notions about gods and higher grains, but he'd twisted the tale to her sister's advantage nonetheless. As they entered his villa, she was quick to note the porphyry-pillared colonnade and the gold-tipped frescoes. Whoever this Azmelqart was, he certainly had a knack for amassing wealth.

When they stepped into the great dining lounge, a dozen harpists plucked out their arrival. Cleopatra's hips swayed ever so slightly in time with the rhythm. A bright soprano cut through the strings, spinning a tale of Jason when his ship first left Thessaly. At her side, Ganymedes bristled, and when she looked closer, she saw the reason: a moonfaced youth whose balls had been sacrificed to provide them with this sweet entertainment.

The next few feasts ripened with promises of men and arms and ships to mount a full-scale attack on Alexandria. But despite the lavish celebrations, Arsinoe noticed that not all their hosts were pleased with their arrival. As the days stretched and talk of war droned on, the nervous tics—the dart of an eye, the twitch of a lip—grew more pronounced. Their boisterous reception of Cleopatra was mingled with fear—fear of what bloodshed she might bring to their walls. Almost imperceptibly, the discussion shifted. No longer did the nobles speak of launching an assault from Ascalon but rather of sending them to Petra first. "A stronger town by far, fortified by cliffs—and protected from the sea." The promised soldiers dwindled from ten thousand to five thousand to two, and by the time their caravan was packing for the desert, a scant thousand infantry were set to accompany them and only a tenth so many on horse. To her eye, Cleopatra seemed content, basking in their praise. If her sister had worries, she only shared them with Apollodorus.

By the time the Harvest had been shucked and the far-off Nile began its rise once more, their band found itself moving on. As Arsinoe watched the slaves load the packhorses and camels with bulging skins of water and wine, she caught a glimpse of Ganymedes. Leaning against a well-worn wooden pillar, his left hand resting on a bale of hay, her eunuch looked decidedly incongruous in his palace silks. Arsinoe sidled up to him.

"Ensuring that no one steals our wine?" she asked by way of greeting.

"It is no laughing matter, Arsinoe. Supplies run thin in the desert."

"You're in a mood, I see. Are you so reluctant to leave Ascalon and her comforts?"

She'd grown weary of the city, of its men whose lies spilled forth more readily than truths. Of how thirstily Cleopatra drank in those same falsehoods.

"I doubt that Petra will bring any of us what we're looking for. Your sister least of all."

A scrawny slave tripped over a wagon spoke; he broke his fall on a burlap sack, and barley sprayed across the dirt. A ruddy overseer pounced, screeching obscenities.

"What makes you say that?"

The overseer tugged off his girdle, flipped it back to strike.

"Only that the desert tribes have simpler, less bloody ways to gain their gold. Far easier to tax those silk-bearing caravans from the East. What your sister needs—what you need—is someone who knows Ptolemy's plans."

The slave master's leather flicked against the cowering man's skin. Arsinoe winced at the noise.

"Send me back to Alexandria, Arsinoe." Ganymedes seized her hand suddenly. "Let me advocate for you there."

His beady eyes brightened with intensity. He had changed. His face was gaunter than she'd ever seen it; she could almost make out the line of his cheekbones. She had misjudged him—perhaps he did not long to waste away in luxury.

"Cleopatra would—"

"Cleopatra needn't know. Tell her I fell ill and remained in Ascalon. Your sister has her secrets. It's high time you invested in some of your own."

The childish part of her wanted to beg him to stay. To follow her to the Earth's ends. Even if Cleopatra didn't fret over Ptolemy's plans, Arsinoe knew better: they needed allies in Alexandria. And who would be more convincing than Ganymedes?

The midmorning sun had burned off the last hint of cool. The heat would scorch their pathetic caravan all the more ferociously as Harvest drew on. The soldiers Ascalon had provided were under-trained and overarmed for the desert temperatures. Equipped in the Parthian style, they wore helms that fully covered their faces and iron plates clamped to their arms and legs and chests. She wondered how they would withstand the punishing heat, the withering winds.

By late afternoon, their company had fallen into an uneasy silence. Even Apollodorus could not keep up his steady commentary on the dunes that served as the route's only markers. The more fertile land that cloaked the coast had given way to endless, gusting sands. Every ounce of energy she had went into staying on her horse, a sturdy strider whose step had begun to strain. That night, when they made camp, she hardly had the energy to keep her eyes propped open long enough to find her mat and curl up next to Cleopatra. Sleep claimed her at once, empty and dreamless.

The following morning, Arsinoe woke to find her whole body aching so fiercely that she could barely launch herself into the saddle. Worse, nearly a quarter of their water supply was lost when two pack carts collided. Arsinoe had already suspected they'd been too liberal with it the previous day, and so she swore off even a sip now. Her head spun in the dust, and her throat stuck when she tried to swallow. By midday, when the sun burned at its apex, two soldiers—burdened by their bulky armor, the heat trapped against their skin—fell down dead, and several others collapsed in solidarity with their lost comrades. Cleopatra ordered that the remaining men remove the greater part of their armor and pack it onto camels.

The queen kept them marching through the twilight until Arsinoe was no longer sure how her horse—a sorrel mare, another gift from Azmelqart—managed to put one hoof in front of the next. The darker the path grew, the more the soldiers' formation broke down, the third line running into the second and the distinctions between ranks blurring. Arsinoe heard the men's grumblings intensify with each step. Her Aramaic was rusty, but she caught more than one crude epithet hurled at the queen. When at last they stopped for the night, Arsinoe realized why Cleopatra had spurred them on: she heard the gentle rushing of the river long before she saw it the following morning. They'd reached an oasis in the sands.

"Cleopatra," Arsinoe whispered that night in their tent. "What are we doing here?"

"We're raising an army," Cleopatra replied. Her voice sounded dry.

"But why in Petra? What good do we expect to find there?"

Cleopatra laughed and ran her fingers through Arsinoe's hair.

"We're not going to Petra," she confided. "Apollodorus thought it best not to reveal our plans before those flatterers in Ascalon. We're raising an army right here. We'll train and winter by the river—and come spring, we will march on Pelusium."

Ganymedes was right. Cleopatra did have her secrets.

BROTHER

No one laughed at him now. Instead, the whole palace quieted at his step. Kyrillos and Ariston shrank in his presence, and even his own mother had grown careful with her criticisms. And why shouldn't they fear him? Long months had passed since he had sent his sisters fleeing from the Upper Lands, paupers and nobodies. While they begged for armies in far-flung Ascalon, he had turned thirteen and sprouted inches through his spine. He ruled—in all matters—as king.

And so he was all the more irked to witness the frenzied reaction of his advisors to this latest news. Pompey the Great, it seemed, had sent his son Gnaeus to beg for troops from Alexandria, and from the reaction of Theodotus, Ptolemy might have imagined the petitioner was Zeus himself. At least he'd ordered Pothinus off to deal with the treacherous priest in Memphis; otherwise, the eunuch would no doubt be dancing about on tiptoe as well.

"This is an opportunity," the rhetorician intoned, hovering at the edge of the dais. "Your cooperation will secure your rule in the eyes of Rome."

Would Ptolemy never hear the end of Rome? Even before this young Pompey had landed on his shore, his advisors could speak of little but these battles across the sea. A convenient excuse to put him off from the *actual* war he longed to wage against Cleopatra. It wasn't enough to drive her from Egypt—he wanted her dead.

"Enough of *Rome's* battles. We should worry about our own."

He looked to Dioscorides, who—along with his arms master, Achillas—managed to maintain a respectful cubit's distance from the dais.

"An excellent point, my king," Dioscorides answered. "We can hardly offer aid when we've not yet quashed Cleopatra."

His father's advisor hewed closely to his opinions these days—perhaps the man had sensed his own tenuous status.

"I wish that I could agree," Achillas interrupted, "yet I fear we are already caught up in Rome's wars. These are no ordinary Romans who battle against one another. Pompey is the finest general Rome has had in a century, and this Caesar, perhaps the finest general the world has seen since Alexander. One of them will emerge as the victorious leader of the Republic. We can't sit by and do nothing."

Ptolemy had become attached to the Gabinians, and even more so to the notion of having Roman legions under his control. He had no desire to see them go.

"What would you suggest, then?" he asked.

"Pompey has the right to those men. Our natural allegiances lie with him. He was a loyal friend to your father. Besides, he has the greater force of soldiers." Achillas paused. "And I do not trust this Caesar."

How could Ptolemy trust either of these Romans? A pair of narcissists, each as eager as the other to gobble up the double kingdom. But if he had to throw in his lot with one, why not Caesar? Even Achillas acknowledged him the better commander.

"Pompey might have been my father's friend," Ptolemy replied haughtily, "but he's no friend of mine."

Theodotus snapped the gnarled knuckles of his left hand against his palm. Each crack grated on Ptolemy's ear. He recognized the habit: the rhetorician would employ it to draw attention to what he planned to say when he intended to amaze the room.

"My king," Dioscorides cut in before Theodotus had the chance to speak, "you are quite right. You must choose your own friends. But there are other considerations as well. What message will it send to your allies if you refuse Pompey in his hour of need? Many will feel they have little to gain from supporting so . . . fickle a monarch."

Fickle. A rich insult coming from a man who'd taken his sweet time deciding which of the Piper's children to back.

"You accuse *me* of fickleness?"

"Oh, never, my king. I only wish to warn you of the accusations others might fling," his father's advisor answered.

Fury clogged his throat and threatened to escape. Ptolemy slipped his hand under his thigh and pinched himself. He needed to maintain his cool. These men still viewed his rages as a relic of childhood. But he was a man now. And his advisors would come to recognize that and fear him just as Kyrillos and Ariston had.

"If I should *lend* these legions out, tell me, what men shall I lead against my sister, the traitor?"

"That is simple, my king. There are thousands who wish to follow you," Achillas replied. "We summon mercenaries from across the sea and the clerics settled in the Upper Lands. We raise an army that is loyal to you, and you alone. You are king. You needn't feed off Rome's leftovers."

He *did* deserve his own army. That much was true.

When Gnaeus Pompey came to make his suit, Ptolemy found himself disappointed. This high-ranking Roman didn't look so different from other men: a creature of medium build, with sunken eyes and slightly fleshy cheeks. He was dressed in military garb—though he'd abandoned his weapons at the door and removed his helmet in the Roman gesture of respect.

"King Ptolemy," he said. "I offer greetings from my father."

"I offer my greetings in return," Ptolemy replied and then cleared his throat so that Gnaeus would meet his eye.

"I heard your sister attended such meetings as this," Gnaeus blurted out, craning his neck down and to the left as though the queen might be hiding beneath the dais. "Where is she?"

That was his game, then. Ptolemy felt the anger mount in his throat, but Theodotus spoke before he had time to snipe back.

"You've heard much of Cleopatra in Rome," the rhetorician replied drily. "No doubt she is a great curiosity to you—a woman who rules. It is a happy day, then, that Rome should discover that Alexandria no longer splits her allegiances. King Ptolemy now reigns alone."

His advisor's voice had left no room for question—though Ptolemy noticed the Roman scarcely looked pleased by the news.

"I—I meant no offense, King Ptolemy," Gnaeus stammered. "It would be—be a curiosity, as you said. That is all. Please accept my apologies."

Ptolemy forced a slight tilt of his head.

"As you know," the general's son went on, periodically reaching out of habit for the empty hilt at his side, "my father was a great friend of yours, one who always helped the New Dionysus in his times of need. When the Senate wanted to let the king rot, it was Pompey the Great who supplied troops to Aulus Gabinius and saw that your father was restored."

Ptolemy puzzled over this man—clearly he belonged fully to his father's cause, but for what reason? Even if Pompey the Elder conquered the whole of Rome, his son would inherit nothing but some sacks of gold and heaps of stone. Strange how little certain lives were worth. It was only when Theodotus cleared his throat that Ptolemy remembered he was expected to answer.

"I am aware of the services your father paid mine."

How many Romans, Ptolemy wondered, would try to make good on the Piper's debts?

"Then I might ask you for a favor in return: The upstart Caesar has broken all laws of decency and attacked Rome herself. My father is the only hope the Republic has left. Give us back the Gabinian legions and let us extend the friendship between the Ptolemies and the Pompeys into the next generation."

Boldly, Gnaeus stepped toward the dais, hand outstretched. Ptolemy had no wish to spare his legions—after all, they were the ones who'd driven his sister from Alexandria in fear. But he knew better than to make an enemy of this man's father. Surely there was some other path. And then it dawned on him: What was it that Cleopatra had told the sons of Bibulus when they'd arrived on a similar mission?

"I make no claim on them," Ptolemy said, standing and reaching to take Gnaeus's hand in his. "The men are yours. As they have always been."

The play did not work as Ptolemy had hoped: Pompey, it seemed, was a far more appealing leader than the Syrian governor had been. By morning, two of the legions had agreed to sail to Spain to join up with the great general. Ptolemy's only consolation came, perversely, in the form of Pothinus's return: the eunuch brought nearly a thousand clerics with him, men recruited back into the service from their farms in the Marshes. Some part of Achillas's plan—at least—bore fruit.

All across the kingdom, golden wheat was husked to clear the fields for leeks and radishes and cabbage. One day, he swore, he would sail up the Nile as his father often had done at this time of year, before the waters began to rise once more. He remembered the searing jealousy he'd felt over Cleopatra's voyages. Voyages that should have fallen to him. Then, he'd wished nothing more than to dab his chin with acacia gum and don a false beard alongside his father. *Next year,* his mother had comforted him. *Cleopatra is the eldest, but you are the son. Soon he'll take you in her stead.* Another of his mother's thousand lies.

Back in the fading days of their father's rule, Arsinoe had offered a terser explanation. She'd come upon him weeping once. He couldn't remember how old he'd been—seven, maybe eight. One look at him, and she'd known what the matter was. Some claimed—his own father among them—that Cleopatra could read a man's mind, but he'd never seen any evidence of that. It was his other sister who time and again read his. On this occasion, she stroked his hair and kissed his brow. *No one matches Cleopatra in Father's esteem. You are our mother's favorite; take comfort in that.* And even at the time, he'd heard the words she left unsaid: *And I am no one's.* He'd longed to tell her *I love you most of all,* but he'd been too shy.

Would that have made a difference? If he'd told her how he loved her—how he'd always been the one who loved her, ever since he was a babe lying in his crib? Maybe then she would have chosen him over Cleopatra. Ptolemy pushed those thoughts away. Regret couldn't change the past.

The sweet odor of hay mixed with manure washed over him as he neared the stables. With soldiers and mercenaries flocking to Alexandria, Achillas attended to his military training with new vigor. Most afternoons Ptolemy now spent on horseback, practicing his jousting skills and marksmanship.

The barn itself was nearly empty; the cavalry mounts were all housed in the larger stable closer to the barracks. Only two young horse hands disturbed the peace, calling loudly across the aisle to one another as they mucked manure into a cart. The smaller one, a pimply youth with ears too large for his face, spotted Ptolemy first. He fell quiet and stared pointedly at his pigeon-toed feet.

"I asked ya what ya though' of them dancers. Are ya deaf?" the other shouted, oblivious, dumping shit from his shovel as he turned. His gaunt cheeks went white when he caught sight of his king.

Ptolemy suppressed a laugh and ordered the boys to fetch his horse. He looked on with satisfaction as the hands snapped into action.

His steed was tacked and groomed, his dapples gleaming in the late afternoon sun. The saddle glistened too, oiled for battle. Ptolemy took the reins from the smooth-faced groom and scratched Aethon below the withers. As he led the horse along the patch-stoned corridor and out onto the grass, the stallion quickened his pace, nearly treading on Ptolemy's heels. The charger knew their destination: the large boulder outside the barn. Despite his best efforts, Ptolemy still couldn't mount from the ground on his own. His leg would never fling high enough, no matter how many times he bounced to propel it over, and he hated asking his guards for help. In his father's failing months, the Piper had proved unequal to the same task, and Ptolemy remembered the snickers all too well.

Once on horseback, Ptolemy urged the stallion to a trot. Not that Aethon needed much encouragement. The charger yanked his head eagerly against the reins. Each time the pair passed the mares' stables, Ptolemy felt the beast's muscles tense as the horse nickered and gathered his pace. "I understand," he whispered as he scratched beneath the horse's mane, "but now's no time for that." A stiff breeze blustered off the sea, but the exercise, the nearness to another living body, kept him warm. Only after they'd galloped three times about the exercise ground did Ptolemy begin to wonder at Achillas's absence.

Reluctantly, he sat back and reined the stallion in. Aethon tugged against his grasp, and Ptolemy pulled back until they slowed to a walk. The shadows of the trees stretched, and his worry flamed into anger. Kings shouldn't be kept waiting.

"You there," he called out to the pigeon-toed stable boy, who now struggled to balance two pails of water. Someone—Arsinoe? Cleopatra? His mother?—was always urging him to learn the servants' names, but he didn't see the point of it. They changed often enough with the seasons. "Tell Achillas I have gone for a ride. He can wait for my return."

He kicked Aethon back into a gallop, anxious to leave his guards spitting in his dust. Perhaps it was foolish to rush off on his own, but what harm could befall him? The gates were watched by his men, the barracks, filled with his soldiers—he hardly needed to be tracked inside the grounds.

Over the untouched sand, horse and rider sailed as one. A cool breeze teased Ptolemy's hair. If he closed his eyes, he could picture himself as Alexander the Conqueror, riding off to war and women and glory. No one would dare refuse him, not once he'd emerged victorious over the traitors in his midst—not even Arsinoe, not even Cleopatra. And why, after all, should he have to choose the one or the other? His grandfather, Ptolemy the Savior, had married both his sisters, and the niece his brother had fathered on his eldest sister besides. The ancients Theodotus was always harping about had taken as many wives and concubines as they liked, the way they did in Persia as recently as Darius's day. Why not embrace those practices? His father had married first his sister and then the woman who pleased him. Perhaps it was better, Ptolemy thought, to do the both at once.

Farther out, near where the fortifications bent into the sea, a shadow crept along the beach. His heart raced; the reins were slick against his sweaty palms. Though more than half a year had passed since his sister's flight, Theodotus's warning still rang in his ears: *Cleopatra will never stop trying to spy on Alexandria.*

Ptolemy laughed at his own fears. To enter here, an intruder would have to either scale the highest portion of the wall or risk taking a small craft across a wild bit of sea with no docks or ropes waiting on the other side. But, a nagging voice answered, that might be *precisely* what a spy would do. He could turn back now—gallop to the stables and tell his guards what he'd seen.

But what *had* he seen? It might be nothing, some stray dog that had wandered the wrong way. And then how they'd all snicker, how they'd laugh. *Ptolemy the Coward,* they'd call him, *afraid of his own shadow.* Only recently had he shed those whisperings—and he knew his position was still unsteady. One false move and he'd fall back, a buffoon once more.

Ptolemy squinted, and the silhouette solidified into a man on horseback. A full-grown man whose nag looked as though her knees might buckle beneath his weight. The sort of man who would defeat him in an open fight. In any fight. Dully, he thought to spin Aethon around, but he remained frozen. This creature—no doubt one of Cleopatra's underlings—would be as quick to kill him as to look at him. And toss his ill-spent body out to sea.

"What are you doing?" Ptolemy shouted with all the courage he could muster. "This is the king's land."

And I am the king, he was tempted to add, but he bit back the words. If the trespasser was too daft to realize his identity, Ptolemy knew better than to enlighten him. Clucking, he urged Aethon on, and Aethon—reckless, brilliant Aethon—showed no fear at all.

"My king." The intruder's voice cut a high treble through the ocean air. "Take pity on a poor and pathetic servant of your family."

The disparate parts came together: the high voice, the sagging skin of a once-plump man, the knowledge of the palace's secrets. This was no common assassin. This was Arsinoe's tutor. There was only one explanation for the eunuch's appearance: subterfuge.

Ptolemy summoned his surest voice. "Ganymedes, one word from me, and my guards will shoot you down. Stay back if you want to live."

Reining in his weary nag, the eunuch unbuckled his girdle to show he was unarmed.

"My life is rather dear to me, my king, and yours is too. I mean you no harm, I assure you," Ganymedes called out, eyes lowered in deference. "Please accept my humblest apologies for frightening you."

"I'm not frightened of some eunuch," Ptolemy hissed. "I was merely warning you. Ten soldiers are at my heels."

"Quite right, my king. I misspoke; I merely meant that my appearance"—he gestured to the filthy rags that clung to his skin—"is rather frightful in and of itself."

"It's not your clothes I'd be worrying about if I were you. You're a traitor now, and you're on the king's land."

"A traitor!" Ganymedes's laughter revealed his rotting teeth. Ptolemy's skin crawled. The eunuch held some power over him—it wasn't fair. "An odd word, that. I wouldn't be so quick to apply it to one who carries the news as I do."

Ptolemy swallowed, hard, and tried to shunt all excitement from his tone. "And what news is that?"

His voice had squeaked. He'd failed, and badly. Ganymedes smoothed his mount's tangled mane and pretended not to notice any difference.

"It would be best," the eunuch replied, "if we retire to discuss such matters away from prying ears."

166

"What ears? There's no one—" Ptolemy cut himself off, but it was already too late; a grin had spread over Ganymedes's face.

"Why, your guards, of course," the eunuch chimed. "The ones who are likely to kill me on sight, my king. It's the rare ruler who can trust the men who watch his life with his secrets."

"I see your point," Ptolemy ceded. He spun Aethon back toward the stables.

To his surprise, the eunuch kicked his horse into a clomping canter, spurring her on until she caught up with the stallion. Her fortitude impressed Ptolemy: the nag was a small, spindly thing. He hadn't imagined she could match his courser's pace.

For a long while they rode quietly, the eunuch studying him and Ptolemy trying his hardest to ignore the impertinence. Poor Aethon bore the brunt of his irritation; Ptolemy's fists tightened on the reins and more than once the horse jerked his head against the bit in frustration at the unjust punishment.

"You're very like your sister," the eunuch said when they were already in sight of the eastern gate.

"What do you mean?" Ptolemy asked, his curiosity winning out.

"Neither of you likes to admit when you're wrong."

"Arsinoe *never* admits she's wrong."

"On that point," the eunuch answered, "she may surprise you yet."

Petulantly, Ptolemy paced the royal chambers. He walked past the shimmering statue of Isis with Horus suckling at her teat. He walked past the wall of nymphs performing ancient rites, past the tapestry he'd had hung of red-plumed Jason regurgitated from the dragon's jaws, the golden ram's skin hovering among the apples. Past Dioscorides reclining on the silver-stitched divan and Theodotus practically squatting at the edge of his, his filmy eye cast off as always to the middle distance. Past Achillas standing sentry by the door. None of his advisors spoke. He wondered if they thought him utterly mad.

And with reason: How was it that *he* was waiting for Arsinoe's eunuch? *He,* who had just treated with Pompey the Younger, had become a child in the face of his sister's tutor. But Ganymedes had insisted that the royal apartments were the only safe place for them to talk. On the beach, the idea had seemed to hold water, but now, as he waited, he wondered at the request's true purpose. Did the eunuch think he would glean secrets from his rooms?

At least he could savor Ganymedes's other demand: that Pothinus be excluded from the proceedings. Since his return from Memphis, the eunuch had grown insufferable, trumpeting his regency from the ramparts and proclaiming his successes in reclaiming troops to the cause. His tutor would be furious to discover that a matter of consequence had been discussed in his absence. Ptolemy could picture the look on Pothinus's face: the tight-lipped grimace, the squinting brow.

Not that he much preferred his other advisors at the moment. Even though Achillas had apologized for his lateness—a misfired javelin had wounded a man on the exercise fields—Ptolemy was still angry with the commander for nearly missing their lesson, and the collective reaction to his news had been dispiriting at best. When he demanded why not one of them was shocked by Ganymedes's appearance, Dioscorides had scoffed. *Your sister Arsinoe picked the losing side.* He'd smiled. *Why wouldn't she send an emissary?*

At last, Ganymedes was shepherded into the room, and Ptolemy felt a flood of irritation mixed with relief. Though the eunuch had retained his impish grin and blackened teeth, he appeared otherwise transformed. The haggard creature from the beach had vanished: his skin had been scrubbed free of grime, his hair clipped, and

168

he'd somehow managed to acquire a cobalt tunic stitched with gold thread. Ptolemy even caught a whiff of frankincense mixed with rose water, an echo of the perfume Arsinoe often wore.

"My king," the eunuch began. "I thank you for your kindnesses. I cannot imagine my face proves a welcome one in these bitter times. But I always told Arsinoe you would be a great man, and a great king."

Theodotus cut in hastily, his lazy eye cast even farther afield than usual. "You've kept us waiting long enough. Stop sniveling and get to the point."

Ganymedes yawned in theatrical defiance but then continued: "When Cleopatra first fled, she headed toward Memphis. She harbored hopes of building an army with the aid of the disaffected kings of Judea and the rabble of the Upper Lands."

"See, my king." Theodotus smirked, determined as ever to demonstrate that no one's knowledge could match his own. "The eunuch's information is outdated, as I suspected. We know the girls have long been in Ascalon."

"There you are wrong," Ganymedes interrupted. "Cleopatra has left the city. The Asian rulers wanted nothing to do with her. They know how much the people adore you."

Ptolemy felt the color rise in his cheeks. His people loved *him*. Though his father had been plagued by a strange love for Cleopatra, her influence didn't stretch beyond his death.

"Cleopatra plans to build her army in the Syrian desert," Arsinoe's tutor continued. "They are largely unprotected, but soon a force from Antioch will join them. Such might would frighten me, but you, surely, are much braver."

Ptolemy did his best to read the room. To his left, Dioscorides remained quiet, reclining on his pillows, one eyebrow cocked upward, an expression somewhere between derision and interest. Achillas stood at full attention, tense from his chinked breastplate to his sandal leathers. And Theodotus, good eye roving, looked all too ready to attack.

"Tell us, Ganymedes," the rhetoric master said, "now that we've broached the subject of your courage. Let's recall how you've come by this useful knowledge. Did you not flee in the night with a pair of traitors?"

"I did indeed. I feared for my life just as my mistress feared for hers."

Arsinoe had been afraid—of him? *That* was why she'd left. Hope churned in his stomach. He could grow accustomed to this new role: purveyor rather than possessor of fear. "Why should Arsinoe have been afraid? Before she left, I was quite ready to take her as queen."

"An excellent question, my king." The eunuch's eyes gleamed.

In the corner of his vision, Ptolemy could see Theodotus slowly shaking his head. Had he already revealed too much and played into Ganymedes's hand? Was this another test that he'd failed before he'd hardly begun? He shook away the thought. Enough time with Pothinus would make even the bravest man paranoid.

"Surely she was wrong to fear you, my king," Ganymedes continued. "But Cleopatra has long painted you a monster."

Ptolemy nodded; this much he knew to be true. His mother had planted jealousies; Cleopatra had tended them.

"But," Ganymedes mused, "in her heart of hearts, Arsinoe longs for reconciliation. She knows you have the better claim."

"Strange, then, that she should run off with Cleopatra," Theodotus scoffed. With each rejoinder, the old man crept closer to the edge of his couch, as though preparing to pounce at the slightest provocation. "Very strange indeed."

"Let our guest speak," Ptolemy snapped. He turned to

Ganymedes. His head swam; his tongue stumbled. "And so does Arsinoe have a proposal for me? An alliance?"

The eunuch twisted the cameo ring about his index finger: an agate portrait of another Arsinoe and Ptolemy, the sibling-loving gods.

"Not yet," Ganymedes hedged.

His heart sunk; a leaden weight lodged itself in the pit of his stomach. "But—but—" Ptolemy stammered. "She does know you're here. She did send you?"

"My king." The eunuch sounded wounded. "What sort of advisor do you think I am?"

Ganymedes had cast a strange pall across the palace. Ptolemy had him followed day and night, and no one could figure out what precisely he did with his time. As far as the guards could tell, he rarely left his chambers and sent no letters—but that could hardly be believed. More than the rest, Pothinus occupied himself with the other eunuch's movements, and so Ptolemy did his best to focus on more pressing matters.

The Nile rose and fell, and Ptolemy grew weary of waiting, weary of the drama between the eunuchs and of wondering whether Arsinoe truly wished to change sides. After all, even he could see that the eunuch had ample reason to lie. One morning Ptolemy woke with a plan all his own: it was time to go to Pelusium. If Cleopatra built an army in Syria, that was the city she'd strike first. Why idle in the capital? He should show the kingdom what sort of king they had. And once he set his mind to something, it came to pass. On the eve of his fourteenth birthday, he sailed at the head of a hundred-ship armada.

Dioscorides was left to tend to business in Alexandria, along with young Serapion. Neither would be much use in battle planning.

Only Achillas, he suspected, would be of help there. And, on his orders, his mother and his brother stayed behind as well. To Ptolemy's surprise, Ptolemarion had put up the bigger fight, pleading to accompany him as his second, his squire, his *anything*. Ptolemy was touched: he'd never thought his peaceful little brother would have been so eager to wage war. His mother had barely spoken when he'd told her of the plan. She'd merely stared at him with liquid eyes and shaken her head slowly from side to side. As though to say: *You, too, after all these years, have set me aside.*

From a distance, Pelusium looked promising enough: red limestone walls rising four stories above the desert sands, punctuated by garrison turrets every few hundred cubits. But within the walls, the city was dispiriting indeed. The town was small—he could have crossed its length by foot in a quarter watch—and its fortress bleak. Except for a few rooms occupied by an almost forgotten garrison, old men with teeth swallowed by their gums, the place had stood empty for decades.

It took several days before the royal apartments were aired out enough for occupancy, and so the first nights Ptolemy spent sleeping among his officers in the largest banquet hall. Initially he'd dreaded the prospect—he was very particular about his space—but he found himself enjoying the company. The soldiers grew raucous late into the night, relating tall tales of the men they'd killed, the women they'd bedded. Better still, they embraced him, guffawing over his jokes and encouraging his own stories of debauchery. He developed a knack for inventing these tales—after all, there were only so many times he could reenact the occasion in which Kyrillos got so drunk he nearly vomited in the double crown before the story grew stale.

Late on the third night, when the men were already deep in their cups and Ptolemy was preparing to bed down on one of the divans, Pothinus came to tell him his chambers were at last fit for use. The eunuch gave him a dirty sort of look, as if to say he didn't quite approve of his current state: his tunic stained with wine, his skin grimy with dirt. Ptolemy didn't care; he'd bonded with his army. Been with them and of them—not that the eunuch could understand such things.

Hours dwindled before he bothered to return to the refurbished royal chambers, bloated with boar and wine and confidence. A bleary-eyed Briseis greeted him with a steaming bath. She must have been waiting for him all that time, heating and reheating the water. He didn't care. Her small fingers untangled his girdle, slipped the greasy tunic over his head. As he stepped into the bath, his head spun. His body pulsed with wine.

"I've not seen my king so happy in months. It is good to see your smile again," Briseis said, fighting back a yawn. "What brings about this welcome change?"

He *had* undergone a change. Pelusium made him bold; he boasted and drank among his men, and soon he would go out onto the battlefields and kill with them. He was a man, and finally he felt it to his bones. As he looked at Briseis—her white tunic tight against her breasts—he wondered why he'd waited so long to become one. The frightened boy, the one Pothinus had shamed, was long gone.

Briseis rubbed his shoulders, his back, his chest, and he felt that familiar stirring between his legs. He grabbed her hand and dragged it into the water, forcing her fingers around his hardening.

"My king." She giggled and stole her hand away. "You are too young. Pothinus said—"

"I am fourteen years old. Don't repeat that eunuch's fool words to me. Don't pretend you've never done it before."

Briseis whispered, "Yes, my king."

And when he placed her hand between his legs a second time, she did not pull away.

SISTER

The sand thickened in her lungs. She woke in the sumptuous tent she shared with Cleopatra to find it caked over her eyes and lips. Staffs of bamboo sprung from the ground like so many pillars in a colonnade, a rich stretch of purple silk draped over their pikes. If she overlooked the sand, she might imagine herself in a boudoir on her father's pleasure barge. She wondered if the Ascalon contingent had gifted this particular tent as a taunt—too rich, too luxurious for the scrappy business of making war.

In her heart, Arsinoe had begun to fear their cause a folly. Even if they marched on Pelusium, they'd never take the city from her brother's men. Throughout the cooler months, her hand had tired from penning pleas—letters to Petra, Antioch, even Jerusalem, begging for men. Though Cleopatra insisted, clinging to some hint of hope, Arsinoe could scarcely see the point. If the petty kings of Judea and Syria declined to treat with them in Ascalon, she didn't imagine they'd change their minds now that Cleopatra was bent on taking Pelusium with so few soldiers at her command.

But still, despite Arsinoe's worries, their entourage had started to swell after the dark solstice turned. First to arrive had been a small contingent of Upper Landers. Only fifteen hundred men, but she would never forget how her sister's eyes brightened at the sight. A dark sweep of figures across the horizon—archers with glinting breastplates fastened flat against sun-dark skin and light cavalry mounted on the swift-footed horses of the south. Garrisons of Arabs followed—tribesmen from the lands flanking Petra along with a small number of Judeans. These infantrymen wore newfangled breastplates wrought from a thousand tiny pieces of iron knit together as neat as wool.

Priests were courted and heifers slain and libations offered in the names of all the gods of men so that a date might be set to launch their attack. She knew Cleopatra didn't believe in such superstitions, but Apollodorus had suggested it—and the queen hewed so closely to his advice that his word might as well be law. Though Arsinoe knew she should be pleased when the army at last set off, she felt a sharp sting of solitude. Often her thoughts would wander to Ganymedes, wondering why she hadn't heard from the eunuch since he'd left for Alexandria. Was he dead, imprisoned? Or had he simply given up on their plight?

And then, stubborn and unbidden, her mind would turn to Alexander. In her loneliness, she ached for him as she'd never ached for him before. There was an edge to her longing, sharp and deep beneath her ribs. After they made camp each night, safe within her tent as Cleopatra plotted with Apollodorus, she snuck her fingers beneath the sheets and thought of his lips pressing against hers. If the maidservant who helped Arsinoe into her riding clothes each morning heard her gasps, she never said a word.

As their party neared Pelusium, her dreams returned to her, black and bloodied. She was neither snake nor vulture now but some strange amalgam of myth: an eagle's wings, a leopard's claws, a lizard's tail. Sometimes she'd be blind, her eyes pecked out as she opened them, or destroyed so long ago that at night she could no longer remember when or whether she'd ever seen. These empty dreams scared her most of all, because she feared they weren't visions but some darker vestiges come to haunt her from a more primordial world. She could not help but fear they foretold nothing but death for her and Cleopatra.

Dust-covered and ragged, their entourage reached the Nile's easternmost mouth. Apollodorus and Cleopatra had decided to pitch camp a dozen stades down the coast, and the slaves hurried to stab the ground with pikes and transform the flattened tarps into war tents once more. When Apollodorus had suggested the place, Arsinoe hadn't seen any particular benefit to it, but now that they'd arrived, she felt a wash of relief. Her thighs chafed and her knees were calloused from so many days on horseback. She needed rest, and this spot, a fertile oasis not far from Pelusium, promised that.

The soldiers looked the worse for wear. They were green boys, for the most part, not battle-hardened Roman legionaries. Though she couldn't understand their whispers as they struggled with the tarps, she could see the exhaustion in their eyes: the crusty look they had about them, these youths of only thirteen, fifteen years, exhausted by the interminable marches that had brought them first to the Syrian desert and now to the edges of Pelusium. A journey that for many would end only with death.

In the days that followed, more tarps sprung up, and as battle neared, the kings of Asia grew bolder with their men. They did not shun the prospect of war as Arsinoe had feared—instead, they appeared eager to hedge bets on the Egyptian army, once its fangs were poised to devour its tail. For the first time, Arsinoe found herself doubting the virtue of their fight, wondering whether a united Egypt—even united with the likes of Ptolemy—might be a stronger one. She pushed the irksome idea from her mind.

With a few carefully placed compliments to one of the vainer of Cleopatra's guards, Arsinoe weaseled her way into her sister's military meeting that night. At the center of the gathering, Cleopatra pored over an intricately sketched map; bright cobalt tokens marked their troops amid a sea of Ptolemy's crimson ones. Apollodorus's voice echoed loudly, almost cheerily, through the air as he pointed out the weak points of the city's walls. Though Arsinoe couldn't say she liked the man, he did make a strong impression: standing nearly a head taller than all but the largest Upper Landers, his presence commanded an immediate respect.

While he carried on about how to breach the eastern gate, Arsinoe felt herself becoming a little girl again. Though no one spoke of it, every man in that room remembered the last time Pelusium had been seized. The news had come from Ganymedes—she and Alexander had been quarreling over who'd won a game of knuckle-bones when the terse-tongued eunuch had arrived. He'd tsked at her muddied tunic and dragged her back to her chambers. She should have recognized his desperation then, his halting speech, the way his hands twitched as he paced. Half mad, he'd seemed, muttering to himself about what to do with her now that *That damned Gabinius has taken Pelusium from Berenice without the slightest fight*. Perhaps, she reflected, if she'd paid more attention then, she would have understood better what all had happened next.

Trumpets blared, cutting short Arsinoe's memories. Outside, a horse snorted, a wagon wheel squealed—and then the sound of hooves pounded toward their tent.

A slight man entered. Arsinoe could see why he made a good spy, light on horseback and ordinary looking. Aside from a hairline scar above his right eye, there was nothing to distinguish him from a thousand other youths. His origins were opaque as well: his skin neither fair nor dark, but that same coppery tone could belong to any man from Greece or Italy, the Lower Lands or the nearer parts of Asia. Even his gender appeared indeterminate, his finely cut features veering toward the effeminate. A brush of kohl along his eyes, a veil over his head—he might have changed himself into a woman. She envied that: the ability to vanish into whatever identity would suit.

As the youth made his way through the gathered soldiers, Arsinoe followed. The air was sour at the center of the tent, where the men clustered together; breezes couldn't penetrate that sweat.

"My queen," the spy said, dropping to his knees in supplication. "Your brother has sent troops out of his garrison. His general, Achillas, brings the Roman legions and fifteen thousand mercenaries besides. They patrol the other side of the Nile's easternmost mouth."

Apollodorus's lips tightened into a grimace; his whole face looked overgaunt—his nose bony and pronounced, his eyebrows leaping toward his hairline. Ghoulish somehow, a tragic mask's mockery of fear. Despite herself, Arsinoe felt oddly vindicated. For all his handsome blustering, she had long pegged him as craven. Her sister, she observed, had undergone the opposite transformation; in the breathless tarp, Cleopatra—white diadem cut across her tightly wound hair—seemed to grow taller, more majestic with the news.

"A battle, then, and soon," her sister said.

Her admiration for Cleopatra—fallen dormant in the desert sands—bloomed fresh. The queen didn't shy away from her fate, from the threat of their brother with his battle-tested legions.

"My queen—" Apollodorus started, but Arsinoe cut him off.

"Cleopatra is right." She'd used her sister's name rather than her title, cleaving to that precedent of closeness. "These Roman legions have turned soft; they wouldn't even fight for their own people. Our brother might pay them well, but gold coin can't make cowards into men."

Cleopatra looked at her. Her eyes overwhelmed her face: painted as her own were, with rich greens around the upper and lower lids, and black framing the eye itself, protection from the glaring sun. They exchanged a brief smile, and Arsinoe felt that familiar warmth, that primal bond she'd never tethered to either parent, the one that tied her solely, irrevocably to her sister. And in that moment, all her other worries crumbled to dust.

Pelusium, the city of mud. An apt name. Her sorrel mare was soiled up to the chest in muck; her own boots were soaked through with it. There was no respite from the filth; they dined in mud, they slept in mud, the soldiers and the camp followers fucked in mud. On the other side of the Nile's mouth, Ptolemy and his men did the same, mirroring their army's steps, their feints north and south along the river's banks.

Each day, the Nile rose and the sludge thickened. When they'd first arrived, it had been Harvest still, and the swamps around the basin were damp but not intractable. Now that Inundation had begun, Arsinoe had grown accustomed to waking to the water rising beneath her mat. All her clothes had been sacrificed in one form or another, cloaks and chitons seized to stem the tide. It did no good. Her bedding and tunics were soaked; sometimes she thought her hair, her skin would never be dry again.

Urging on her horse, Arsinoe looked over the weary faces of the soldiers: the Upper Landers, whose deep brown skin had taken on a grayish hue; the fairer men sent by Asian kings, whose skin had burned and crisped and hardened into a deep, unnatural red. None of them, she feared, had slept in weeks—and still they hadn't seen a single battle. Worse, she knew her brother's legionaries had an easier time. Scouts reported that his soldiers circled in and out of commission—returning to Pelusium every few weeks for sleep, gorging themselves on the rich food that a port city afforded.

The tributary that divided the two armies narrowed to a stream in places, and in such close quarters, their enemy was no cipher.

She could not help but compare the Romans' orderly camp construction to the haphazard base set up by Cleopatra's troops. Some evenings the queen joined her, relying on Arsinoe's sharp eyes to point out details: the sea-goat standard that marked the Second Legion, the purple cloak that Achillas wore in pale imitation of the great Alexander. When Arsinoe squinted, she could even distinguish a few other familiar faces: Ariston, for instance, one of her brother's childhood companions. Only once did she catch sight of Ptolemy himself, raised high above his men in a gold-plated litter. Most of his time, Arsinoe suspected, was spent at the fortress in Pelusium. On these rare occasions, he was trotted out like a talisman, but real command lay with his underlings. In that, at least, Cleopatra emerged the victor: the soldiers knew and lived and breathed their queen.

Shadowing—that, she learned, was the military term for what they did. She understood now why the *Iliad* opened only in the Trojan War's final days: the first ten years had been like this. Dull and miserable, two half-starved armies daring the other to advance day after day, night after night. On occasion, their side would offer battle—and then only because Cleopatra was convinced that they must fight before the soldiers lost all faith in them.

In her heart, Arsinoe wondered if it was already too late to forestall that. As she made her rounds to the dining tent each morning— a great sheath of canvas long since muddied into brown—she heard more than a fair share of grumbling. The Galatians and the Upper Landers muttered in their own tongues, incomprehensible to her. They only slipped into Greek on the rare occasions they found to address each other: a fresh-faced boy from outside Hermopolis asking a stern Galatian guardsman to pass a pot of gruel across the flame; a patch-eyed soldier grudgingly sharing a few battle tips with a new recruit. The Syrians, at least, she could understand when they murmured among themselves in Aramaic: *Who knew it could be so scalding hot at the same time it's so fucking damp?*

One dawn, without warning, without the usual clatter that preceded a call to battle, the horns blared their triplets at daybreak. Arsinoe sat stock-still on her mat; the damp, for once, had not yet soaked through, and except for a trickle of sweat forming on her brow, she felt very nearly dry.

Cleopatra was already dressed, in the Greek guise of Isis, a thin linen sheath of gold beneath a red chiton knotted between her breasts. On her head, the white diadem had drifted too far back in her hair. Arsinoe slipped off the mat to adjust her sister's costume. As she got closer, she noticed that it wasn't just the ribbon that had gone askew—one of her sister's carefully clasped braids had untangled from the others and lay limply down her back. Arsinoe had come to cherish these quiet moments, the only times she saw Cleopatra away from Apollodorus.

"My sweet," she murmured as she unwound her sister's errant bun. Days on horseback sent her own hair into ruin, and she'd made a practice of watching how the servants managed to tame it. "What happened here? The sun's barely up."

"I was called away in the middle of the night."

Arsinoe smoothed the braids over her sister's shoulder blades, gathering them together in her fist like so many snakes. For the first time in ages, she thought of Medusa, of the cursed beauty transmuted into a monster.

"News from across the sea. Pompey and Caesar meet one another for the first time since both men were in Italy. The seers say it will be decided there, in Pharsalus."

Arsinoe's hands shook. Months had passed since she'd considered the Roman war; she'd been too preoccupied with her own. She

closed her eyes to recall where the various legions were stationed—
Spain, Greece, and of course in nearby Libya.

"You think the victor will come here," Arsinoe said quietly.

"At least to Africa. If Pompey wins, he will need to rejoin his
troops—the greater part of the Senate is camped with Cato in Utica.
And if Caesar does, he must face his enemy's legions one day or the
next."

"And what will you do?" Arsinoe asked. "Surely you will not bend
before Rome."

Cleopatra turned, wrenching the strands of her hair from Arsinoe's grasp. Her eyes were smudged with black and green. For a
moment her lips tightened, a bow flattening into a thin line. But then
the tension in her brow eased and a smile spread over her face. She
wrapped her arms about Arsinoe and whispered in her ear. "No, I
will never bend to Rome, never in my heart."

BROTHER

Briseis slept heavily; her cheekbone dug into his chest. Ptolemy matched his breath to hers, letting his ribs fall with each warm exhale. He envied her—he wished he could sink into such easy slumber. At night, his restlessness was almost unbearable, an army of ants teeming through his veins.

As gently as he could, he slid his slave's head onto a pillow. She stirred and murmured to herself before quieting. Relieved, he slipped out from beneath the sweaty sheets and moved quickly toward the fortress's window. He crept to the ledge and gazed into the darkness.

An unfamiliar night stared back at him. Unlike Alexandria, Pelusium sat some dozen stades from the shoreline, and a muddied expanse stretched out from the fortifications toward the sea. In recent days, the land had swelled with barefoot laborers, sowing flaxseeds as their backs baked in the sun. At night, though, without the light of Pharos, he could hardly distinguish muck from river from wave. But he could see the stars well enough, and the bright grin of the crescent moon. He cursed each individually, the stars and the moon herself. They were to blame, after all. For somewhere in the midst of that wine-dark sea the Roman general thanked the selfsame stars, his guiding lights to Pelusium. And these stars—these hangings of the thankless gods—would ruin everything.

The injustice stoked him—he'd wanted to avoid affairs with Rome. When he'd lent legions to Pompey's cause, he'd already had his reservations. For decades, his father had circled about that city like a desolate moth, but even the Piper's fawning hadn't been enough—Cato had still taken Cyprus. Ptolemy didn't remember the island's fall, but his life had been shaped by the aftermath. The ugly days he'd spent hidden beneath the teeming streets of Canopus. His brother's wails for his wet nurse tapering into moans as he gnawed at their mother's empty teats. Those were his first, his sharpest, memories.

And still his father had crawled on his knees to the Senate, mewling before Cato and pleading before Pompey. Begging any Roman who would listen. *Please, an army, please, ten thousand talents for an army.* And what good had that done? Years swept by before the Piper had managed to muster ranks and retake Alexandria. Ptolemy had hoped Rome's war would be a boon: that her legions would devour one another as he waged his own battles. He didn't want them on his shores or at his gates. Not when he'd finally convinced Achillas to lead his men against Cleopatra.

But the elder Pompey's arrival jettisoned that plan. His sister's ragtag army might have melted into the mud for all his advisors mentioned it now. From the instant the rumor reached Pelusium, they'd talked of nothing else. Pothinus and Theodotus had spoken over one another, as they always did, arguing over whether to embrace Pompey or betray him. It was Achillas's council Ptolemy was more likely to heed, but his general had stood by in thin-lipped silence. When at last he'd weighed in, he'd taken a different tack: *Pompey was your father's constant friend, and you have broken bread with his son. If Egypt doesn't stand with her friends, she won't have any left.* Theodotus had laughed, his good eye rolling into the back of his head. He'd only stopped when he realized Achillas was in earnest. *The only friend we need is Caesar. And his rival should know better than to seek sanctuary here.* The rhetorician had smiled. *Best to execute him on sight.*

Ptolemy could not remember a time when he hadn't dreamt of his first kill: the angle of his blade as it plunged into a man's throat; the slice of his javelin as it pierced the gap between a soldier's breastplate and his armpit; the shrieks of a legionary trampled beneath his charger's hooves. What he'd never imagined was that it would come not on a sword but at a word. There was no glory in ordering death, only in dealing it.

After the victory in Pharsalus, no one—not even Achillas—could deny that Caesar's army was impregnable. And if Ptolemy did offer refuge to Pompey, what good would that do any of them? Surely Caesar wouldn't allow his sworn enemy a peaceful retirement in Egypt. And harboring Rome's fugitive would mark Alexandria as the next target in Caesar's war. Ptolemy was not ready to die. He wanted to rule.

His gaze wandered back to Briseis. Dark curls cascading over her shoulders, she looked like a dryad, some creature too perfect for mortal life. Even now, he might rouse her. He'd done it before, that very night. She never seemed to mind. Yet it wouldn't change anything. A sweet release that would offer no reprieve. And so he stared back out at the night, until the dark gave way to a red and unforgiving dawn.

Ptolemy had hardly broken his fast that morning when word came that a lookout sought his audience. "Fresh tidings from the shore." Whisked by Pothinus to the throne room, Ptolemy waited for the messenger to speak and wondered at the fuss. He knew, after all, what the boy would tell him: that Pompey had arrived. Yet despite this surety, Achillas couldn't keep from pacing back and forth along the pebble-mosaic floor. The eunuch and Theodotus were still more agitated, hovering near Ptolemy like a pair of flustered owls.

"They've been spotted, my king," the messenger announced once he'd caught his breath. He was a diminutive, delicate creature and, from what Ptolemy could tell, capable of speaking only in roiling bursts. "The ships, some twenty stades away."

"How many ships?" Theodotus demanded.

"Three, I think, my lord. Or perhaps four . . ." The boy's voice trailed off.

"Well, which was it? Three or four?"

"I only saw three. But Hermias swore that he spotted a fourth on the horizon."

"Who has sharper eyes: you or Hermias?" the rhetorician growled.

"I do, my lord."

"And so how many ships were there?"

"Th-three, my lord."

"Very good."

Ptolemy leaned forward to duck the stinging rays of sun that cut through the room's solitary window. "You may go now," he told the messenger, and the boy scurried away. Murmuring broke out as soon as the guards shut the ironwork gates behind him.

"My king," Achillas said, stepping forward into the light. "The time has come to show your true colors—"

"What our general means to say," Theodotus sneered, "is that the time has come for you to die. Because sheltering Pompey would bring your death, of that you can be sure."

"Indeed, my king, why not murder all your allies? No better way to win men to your cause. The rhetorician has no more honor than a eunuch."

"My king, you must listen to reason. Achillas's vaunted honor won't defeat Caesar's legions. Even the general admits that much. But perhaps he plays a double game."

"How dare you of all men question my loyalty!"

Ptolemy tried to speak, but the feuding men talked over him. Their words piled on one another, *wisdom* and *honor* and *prudence*. The syllables broke down, beating on his ears; they became letters, divorced from any meaning. All he wanted, needed, was silence. He coughed into his hand, but his councilors were too consumed by their bickering to notice. *War* and *Cleopatra, loyalty* and *vengeance*. Ptolemy's resolve threatened to snap. Finally his fury boiled over and a shout burst from his chest as he stood: "Enough!"

The voices quieted; two sets of ordinary eyes, and the rhetorician's unmatched ones, fixed on him.

"I've reached a decision," Ptolemy declared, daring any of them to protest. "Pompey must be executed before he sets foot on Egyptian soil."

Theodotus clapped his hands together. An ugly, squelching sound. The man's gloating was sickening. Ptolemy wasn't a boy—he was a king. He didn't need a tutor's approval.

"Do you think this makes you brave?" Pothinus asked.

Ptolemy's skin crawled beneath the eunuch's rheumy stare.

"Perhaps you do, though I doubt Achillas taught you that this would count as courage."

His rage flashed and fluttered. He saw the eunuch's game: Pothinus thought he could bend loyalties and emotions with ease. Ptolemy refused to be snared by such obvious bait.

The eunuch pressed on: "What's worse is that you betray a fundamental misconception of Rome. Do you think Pompey's slaughter will win Caesar's friendship?"

"I do," he answered, clinging to his new position. If nothing else, a king must keep his word. "I'm delivering Caesar his enemy's head. What man would not be pleased by such treatment?"

The eunuch laughed. "How simple matters are when you put it that way. I suppose you've forgotten Pompey's late wife."

"Why should I care what hole he stuck his cock in?" Ptolemy snapped.

"Why do we ever care about our enemies? So that we might understand them better." The eunuch continued, casting a searing glance at the rhetorician. "Theodotus prefers to ignore such matters, but I hope you won't learn from his example. Pompey was once wed to Caesar's beloved daughter, Julia. And if you kill him, you'll be slaying Caesar's former son-in-law."

The rhetorician straightened in his chair; the purple vein that crossed over his weak eye bulged.

"Ah, yes, your knowledge of Roman entanglements is impressive, Pothinus," the rhetorician replied, voice dripping with irony. "Do pass it off as insight. But you know as well as I that Caesar would love to see Pompey dead. Why berate the king for his boldness? As his tutor and regent, you should support him."

"As his tutor, I must urge him toward wisdom. And as his regent, I must protect him until he reaches the age when he might rule alone. Why not capture Pompey and send word to Caesar?"

"And build an alliance in which Ptolemy serves as Caesar's errand boy," Theodotus shot back. His bad eye slipped so far to the right that for a moment all Ptolemy could see was its milky, empty white. "Is that what you want, my king?"

No, it wasn't. He didn't want to turn into his father, to beg Rome for troops each time low floods stoked rebellions.

Theodotus growled, "Of course you don't. Why would any man want to kneel before Caesar as a suppliant when he could instead meet him as an equal? But how could a eunuch understand such distinctions."

"I am no eunuch," Achillas said softly, "but I don't support this plan. Hospitality once had meaning in this land. The god of hosts does not look kindly on those who murder guests in their beds."

"Oh, here we are again with your sense of *honor,* your pleas to Zeus." The rhetorician scoffed. "Do you want to see the boy deposed—beheaded? In your heart, do you yearn for Cleopatra's restoration?"

As Theodotus railed, Ptolemy glanced out the high slatted window that opened toward the sea. From there, he caught a glimpse of white, bobbing at the edge of the horizon: the sails of Pompey's ships. If he squinted, he could make out their prows—mermaids crashing over and under the waves—but perhaps that was a trick of the light. The ships might not be helmed by mermaids at all but by some other gruesome creature: a gorgon or a siren or Scylla. Seamen knew no end of horrid women beasts.

"Hear reason," Pothinus was saying. The eunuch placed a palm on his shoulder. He neither bent to it nor shrugged it away. Out there, a scant twenty stades away, breathed the first man who would die by his command. "Caesar is a proud creature. He'll want to deal with Pompey himself. Imagine if you were at war with Kyrillos—or, better yet, Ptolemarion. Would you rather some far-flung ally murder him or bring him to justice yourself?"

"Caesar's more than welcome to kill Cleopatra," he answered.

A chuckle answered his gibe. It belonged to Theodotus, of course, not Achillas. When the general laughed, the sound came from his belly, a deep, sonorous tone. Ptolemy realized then that the commander was right: he shouldn't joke about such matters. A man's life hung in the balance. He hoped his own death would be plotted in more considerate terms.

"That's the spirit, my boy," the rhetorician said. "The others are afraid, but remember: if you embrace Pompey and call him a friend, he will not be so easy to dispose of. Dead men don't bite."

The thick walls seemed to close in around him, clogging his nose and throat with stagnant air. He couldn't simply wait here in comfort; he had to go down to the shore. He had to watch the ships. The unlucky Pompey deserved that much, at least. And, at once, Ptolemy was on his feet, racing toward the stables.

Galloping his stallion toward the tangle of soldiers on the shore, Ptolemy couldn't shake Theodotus's phrase from his mind. There was a logic to it. A simplicity. *Dead men don't bite.*

Ahead, the knot split into individuated men, several dozen helmed against the cool sky. The larger barges were beached, and a small boat had been readied to meet Pompey's ship.

Ptolemy tossed his reins to a nearby slave as he dismounted and braced himself to address these soldiers. He found his fingers twisting at his tunic, and he flattened them to his sides. Speaking before legionaries always made him nervous; they were Romans, and for some reason that made him all the more fearful that they might see through his bravado. Hooves tramped behind, and Ptolemy looked up to find Achillas mounted on his bay.

"I'm not going to change my mind," he told the general sharply.

"I know, my king," he said. "Whatever your directives, I am here to carry them out."

Achillas slid his right leg over the horse and landed in the sand with a soft thud. With the general at his side, Ptolemy's confidence grew. He approached the guards—the remaining Romans who'd once served under Gabinius. Before that, he knew, many had fought beneath Pompey's standard. That was the most brilliant aspect of the rhetorician's plan: to have the man's own legionaries sail out to meet their fallen general. Surely Pompey would prove too pompous to doubt their loyalties.

"You there," Ptolemy said, addressing the tallest of the Romans. A grimace spread across his sun-worn face and his grasp tightened on his blood-dulled spear. "What general did you serve before Gabinius?"

"Pompey the Great." The man's tone was curt. Ptolemy cleared his throat, loudly; these officers needed to learn some modicum of respect.

"My king," the soldier added with the same stubborn absence of enthusiasm. Ptolemy supposed it would have to do.

"And how long did you serve under Pompey?"

Anger flickered in the man's eyes, but he answered in the same implacable voice: "Ten years, my king."

"And now you greet him on Pelusium's shores," Ptolemy taunted, circling his prey. "Will you kill him?"

"If the king wishes," the centurion replied through gritted teeth. Ptolemy grinned up at him.

"Even though he comes here in peace, fleeing Caesar and begging for his life?"

The soldier barked a wheezing laugh. "I'm a mercenary, my king. I've never pretended to be anything else."

Horns sounded. Ptolemy glanced out over the waves; the ships had drawn near, mere stades away. Near enough to send an emissary. Suddenly, desperately, he wanted to ask—once more—for Achillas's advice. To see if there was some way to shirk this particular first, to shift the burden of murder to another's soul. But there was no time for that. The signal must come, and it must come from him.

"Kill him."

The words thrilled his ears. For a brief moment, even the cocksure mercenary gazed at his king in awe.

Time ached on as the ships crept nearer, as his men pushed their rowboats to the sea, as Pompey waved them aboard and the traitor took his hand, as the great man clutched his blood-blossomed cloak and heaved his final breaths, as the wife gasped and shrieked and wept.

SISTER

Soaked in the cold sweat of a colder dream, Arsinoe stirred from troubled sleep. She threw off her damp coverlet. The remnants of a dream darted through her mind. Chased by something—someone—her wings spread in frantic flight. Or had she been the pursuer? Ah, yes. She was the hunter, her tongue flicking at the air, though her quarry could overpower her with ease. An image of it formed and corroded, a monstrous creature with an eagle's head and a leopard's paws. The avian face with its hooked beak somehow resembled her sister's. She reached out to shake Cleopatra from her slumber, but her fingers met with only empty sheets. Her sister had fled.

No. Impossible. She refused to fall prey to such imaginings. Almost a year had gone by, longer, since she'd had a dream that came to pass.

It must be later than she'd thought, nothing more. That would explain why her sister had already risen. Her vivid vision had stolen her hours, sucking away her energy through the early light. Cleopatra, no doubt, was already breaking her fast among her soldiers. Her sister excelled at that—communing with the common folk. She'd be busy charming the Arabs and the Upper Landers as the armies waited to engage, fluidly switching from one tongue to the next. Arsinoe rose and flung a light cloak over her chiton before stepping into the morning air.

Outside, she realized that she'd been wrong about the hour: it couldn't be much past dawn. The sun was young, barely over the horizon; the men were safe and snug with their whores. Days had elapsed since they'd last caught sight of Ptolemy's army—and many suspected that Achillas had drawn his legions to retreat. No wonder the soldiers had grown comfortable. She envied them their ease. When she reached the main bonfire, she found it, too, forsaken. The coals simmered, red and warm and crackling, but no one tended them.

A lone bird—an eagle—soared across the brightening sky. Was that what she had chased through the night? What sort of vulture pursues an eagle? "Cleopatra has not abandoned you," she whispered. "The cold morning stirs strange thoughts, nothing more." She refused to succumb to the madness of dreams. Cleopatra would be with Apollodorus as she always was, and so Arsinoe cut a path toward the man's tent.

Among the largest in the camp, the tent with its red-dyed tarp was easy to spot. As she neared, she slowed her pace, sharpening her ears for voices gusting from its skins. She might even overhear something of use—though they slept side by side, Cleopatra had grown stingy with talk of what she plotted next. They could not shadow Ptolemy's men up and down the Nile forever—sooner or later they'd have to attack Pelusium or pull back. Arsinoe paused before the tent's flap and placed her ear against the fabric, but she couldn't hear a peep from within.

A new fear seized her: her sister had been snatched away by force. Their brother's army had dissipated only to surround their own—to steal Cleopatra from their midst. The notion was deranged, she told herself. She was a light sleeper; surely she would have heard sounds of a struggle. Wherever Cleopatra had gone, it had been of her own volition.

"Apollodorus," Arsinoe called out softly.

The only answer came from the river birds, squawking at the dawn.

"Apollodorus," she tried again, more forcefully this time. And still, despite her unwavering voice, she felt like the same frightened child crying out as her sister sailed across the great sea all those years ago: *Cleopatra! I had the strangest—*

Perhaps her sister's advisor slept soundly. Or—more likely— he was busy relishing the company of some bed warmer. And why should she care if she happened upon him with some whore? He'd merely grin and shrug his broad shoulders. As for the woman—well, she could only imagine such humiliations were common enough. She tore aside the tent's flap.

What she found was far more troubling than any orgiastic scene: The tent was empty. The interior had been stripped bare, cleared of furs, belongings, food. Arsinoe was surprised the tarp itself hadn't been torn down.

Abandoned, once again. Only this time not in Alexandria but far off in the marshes of the eastern Delta. No Ganymedes, no Alexander, no Myrrine. Surrounded by an army that revered her sister as a queen and saw her as nothing.

She knew she shouldn't be surprised—after all, what else could Cleopatra have learned from their father other than to flee at the slightest sign of trouble? Arsinoe waited for the shock to set in, the pang of a fresh betrayal, but none came.

Instead, her mind turned to practicalities: Who else knew of her sister's desertion? The camp lay quiet, so it was unlikely the news had been sown. And so Cleopatra had left her that as well, to clean up the mess as she ran off to do what? Seduce Pompey? Treat with Ptolemy? Wed one of the Judean kings?

She could run too. Snatch a horse and steal away into the east,

195

back to the desert, past Petra and into the heart of Asia. She could still become the Ptolemy who disappeared, but what then? She was no longer a girl of eleven, able to blend seamlessly among the street rats, but a grown woman of eighteen. Her older, wiser self asked: *What hope do you have with your cursed name, your divine claims?*

"Apollodorus."

A man's voice disturbed her thoughts: she had to choose a course and fast. Arsinoe steadied herself before she turned to the speaker. A pair of wind-worn eyes looked her up and down. *Bolis*—the name came to her as she examined his leathery face, his pate burned the color of ochre and ringed with a sparse crown of hair, the raised scar that cut along the length of his left cheek. Culled from the ranks of the Galatians, he had come to serve as Apollodorus's second. If he didn't know of the man's absence, no one did.

"My princess," he greeted her, mustering more respect than Apollodorus's soldiers often showed. "What are you doing here?"

"I might ask the same of you," she replied. Her mind raced—she needed to put him on the defensive. "Does Apollodorus know that you regularly enter his tent unannounced?"

"I am sure he'd be happier to find me doing so than you," the soldier sneered. His right hand tapped idly at his sword's hilt, a reminder of how quickly her circumstances might sour. Shorn of Cleopatra's protection, she was at any man's mercy. If her sister's disappearance came to light, the army would disperse—to Ptolemy or whatever other king might pay their dues. How would these mercenaries see her then? As leverage against lost wages, at best.

"The queen herself asked me to fetch maps from here," Arsinoe answered haughtily. "I doubt you can make that claim."

Bolis studied her, his eyes narrowing to slits, but didn't object.

"I merely sought out Apollodorus," he said gently, cowed. "His advice is needed—"

"Apollodorus has more pressing matters to handle," Arsinoe lied fluidly. The path before her solidified: she had to establish herself as Cleopatra's intermediary, the conduit to power. "You may pose your question to me instead. He has left me instructions on the army's movements."

"Ptolemy's troops have retreated."

"Tell me something I haven't already heard." Knowledge was a potent shield. She'd cloak herself in it.

"Does *Apollodorus* want us to cross the river in pursuit?" Bolis stressed the general's name as a taunt, a reminder that he would not respect the babbling advice of some woman.

"No," Arsinoe answered sharply. The army couldn't break camp; Cleopatra's absence would be discovered at once. Feverishly, she spun out fictions. "More forces gather to us by the day. We should wait before we attack."

Bolis had begun to examine the tent's interior, taking in the stripped bedding and emptied chests.

"Where *is* Apollodorus?" he demanded.

Arsinoe weighed her options. Apollodorus's absence might be explained, but Cleopatra's could not. The soldiers needed to believe that their queen—their Horus incarnate—would never leave on the eve of battle.

"Apollodorus said I could trust you with this information. And only you. I hope that his faith in you is not misplaced."

Bolis took the bait; he stepped toward her.

"My sister has fallen ill. The general has gone to Pelusium to seek the cure."

"You're lying."

"I am telling you what the men must know." Arsinoe lowered her voice to a whisper. "Apollodorus has left us in charge. Do you want a mutiny on our hands or to keep order until your superior returns?"

197

"Very well," he answered warily. "I'll inform the men."

To her relief, Bolis was as good as his word: by noon, news of her sister's sickness had spread through the camp. There would be no uprising that day.

Arsinoe's fury, though, coalesced into something darker, grittier. The next morning she woke with a leaden pit lodged in her stomach, which grew tighter as each hour wore on without word from the queen. She'd been a fool to think this venture would end any other way—it was right, natural, that she should be abandoned, as she'd been at every other juncture of her life. Not even her sister, on whose promises of shared destiny she'd been weaned, could be trusted. The selfsame sister who'd comforted her as a sick and frightened child, who'd rescued her from Alexandria's streets, who'd cleaved to her even when she bucked and shied away.

The men grew restless; her lies grew thin. "The queen grows stronger by the hour," she found herself saying one minute to pacify the fretting Upper Landers, who feared Cleopatra's looming death, only to turn to the Galatian troops the next and claim that her sister was most certainly *not* well enough to meet with them. And so her first false report birthed others, sowing suspicion in their wake. Gossip invaded the camp like so many tenacious weeds. "The queen was never sick," the rumors went. "Her sister lies to cover some worse treachery." Others claimed Cleopatra was already dead. "Burnt and buried." Why else wouldn't she have emerged after so many days?

Arsinoe didn't blame the soldiers for their speculations or their flickering morale. She didn't know what to tell them about their queen; she had no plausible explanation for where Cleopatra could have gone. At first, Arsinoe had suspected a secret truce with Ptolemy, but if that were the case, tidings of it would have already arrived from Pelusium. So she had to imagine Cleopatra had instead sought aid from somewhere farther afield. Perhaps she'd returned to the Upper Lands or decided to try her luck in Petra after all. Worrisome, too, was that the store of silver coins her sister had left behind had already begun to dwindle. One day soon her mercenaries would decide to cast their lots with her brother's army, and her mirage of authority would vanish into the ether.

She knew what Ganymedes would counsel. *Cleopatra has forsaken you,* she could hear the eunuch's voice breathing in her ear. *Take this army from her, and have them declare for you.* She recognized the wisdom in those words, and in her angrier moments she allowed herself to weigh them seriously. Would turning against Cleopatra now even qualify as a betrayal? Her sister had left her without warning and still she could not bring herself to act.

The days slid by. Time, when she most longed for it to slow its paces, emerged as her most tenacious enemy. The longer she failed to act, the more impossible it became to do so. Even in the sunlit hours, she'd hole herself up in her tent—as though her own scarceness would lend credence to Cleopatra's. But her canvas cocoon couldn't protect her; there, too, she was haunted by whispers. At times she couldn't tell which were real, which imagined—her waking and sleeping lives skated seamlessly together. Her dreams had taken strange turns; in them, she was no longer snake or vulture, merely hapless human, tormented by manifestations of her deepest fears. *Cleopatra has rejoined her brother, Ptolemy, and wages war against her sister,* the dream folk claimed. Or, worse still, *The queen has signed a treaty with Rome—she will serve as the Republic's vassal over the province of Egypt.*

Dark news—when it came—arrived in the form of a gaggle of recruits from Memphis. She called the youngest before her, a fresh-faced Upper Lander who spoke passingly good Greek. He'd overheard the tale at a tavern—he seemed most nervous to tell her that bit, as though she might be shocked by the nature of the place—where a few Arab traders were resting, fresh from Pelusium. They'd been laughing about a horrific spectacle they'd witnessed. And here the young man stumbled: "They said—they said that the young king murdered Pompey." The tidings stole away her breath and stirred her from her impotence. News of the death could be contained for only so long now. And if Ptolemy had already allied himself with Caesar, what chance did Cleopatra stand? Arsinoe had to address the soldiers.

Since her sister's disappearance, Arsinoe had ignored the overtures of her new handmaiden, a meek creature from the Upper Lands, preferring to remain untended and coiled on her mat. But on this morning she called for the skittish woman to tidy her. Trembling, the slave drew one ordinary robe from her chest after another. Each selection proved more disappointing than the last—and Arsinoe had to bite her tongue not to snap in anger. She didn't need a plainly cut linen chiton but something far finer—a robe that reminded the men of her status as Cleopatra's sister and surrogate. As a divine Ptolemy in her own right. Something that evoked the gods themselves. Otherwise, no matter how rousing her words, the soldiers would shrug off their wisdom.

At last, Arsinoe ordered the slave to root through Cleopatra's trunks. Though the woman's frail fingers quaked at the order—as though the queen, even absent, loomed, awe-inspiring as ever—she did as she was commanded. Arsinoe stroked each option, inspecting its stitching and color. Finally, she settled on a deep violet robe with a gold-stitched border of tiny ibises. She ordered the chiton knotted between her breasts, revealing the translucent sheath she wore beneath. The gold-horned diadem that Cleopatra wore in her Isis guise pressed hard against Arsinoe's brow. For a moment, she let herself imagine it as the double crown. Once her eyes were lined with kohl and etched with green, her lips darkened with crushed kermes, she looked the part. No mere woman stared back at her but a goddess. A queen.

Slowly, Arsinoe emerged from the tent; the sun beat down on her. Already sweat pooled behind her knees, beneath her breasts. Her blood thrummed in her temple; her heart weighed heavy in her chest—it would surely fail the judgment of the feather. But she wasn't descending to the undergloom; she wouldn't have to face the dead, only her sister's abandoned men.

Though she didn't fully trust him, she'd enlisted Bolis to put out word of a speech. To her relief, she saw that he'd done his duty. The neighboring canvases were cleared away to make room for the gathering. Some ten thousand men filled the void, jockeying for a position nearer her person. Arab tribesmen and Upper Landers with their breastplates fastened against their bare skin stood shoulder to shoulder, some still hunched over their clay bowls of gruel, others downing mugs either of wine or of that honeyed brew preferred by Nubians and the southern villagers.

She was on her own, with only her wits to protect her. That knowledge soothed her. She remembered this world, the old, dark days under Berenice, when she'd had to figure out what to say, whom to trust, without the help of anyone—not Ganymedes, and certainly not her sister Cleopatra. She stretched her neck and held her chin high. They would yield to her focus—*Some men are born to follow*. The clanking of spoons ceased; the slurping sounds died down.

"A stench of slander lingers over this camp," she started softly. "Lies and rumors about my sister abound. You wonder whether Cleopatra will ever return to lead you in glorious battle. You wonder whether you would have been better served by joining with my brother's forces, or perhaps by signing on for Caesar's next war."

Her voice grew stronger as she went on. The soldiers' silence held; they listened with interest.

"Perhaps you feel abandoned. Perhaps you wonder why you should remain when Cleopatra has fled. The gods know such doubts have clouded my mind. And so I put the question to you: Should I continue? Or should I lay down my arms and sneak back to my brother Ptolemy? Perhaps he would take me on as some lesser wife. And maybe he would allow you all to serve him in some lowly segment of the palace guard . . ."

The air was so taut her breath sent tremors through it.

"That would be the easy route. Wouldn't it? To assume my sister has forsaken you as so many rulers, so many generals, have before her."

She reveled in the thousand eyes begging her for answers. As though she held the balm for all their woes. It was a powerful feeling—more intoxicating than wine.

"But you misjudge her. Because the reason Cleopatra has left the camp," and here she paused. Her life boiled down to this moment: either they would believe her or they would rise in mutiny. "The real reason Cleopatra has left is not because she disdains your lives and your sacrifices, but because she values them."

She could hear the mutters, the hisses—the quiet tattering.

"She goes to join Pompey's son, Gnaeus, rife with rage over his father's murder. She will weld our forces to his and retake the throne in exchange for Egypt's aid in Gnaeus's war against Caesar. Ptolemy doesn't care whether his men live or die in battle, but Cleopatra does. Cleopatra is a mother to all her subjects—and to all those in her pay." She addressed this last part to the Arabs who'd joined her sister's cause, though she didn't know if they could follow her Greek. She repeated the phrase, this time in Aramaic, to make sure they would understand.

The murmuring crested, loud and threatening, but then just as quickly it ebbed. They didn't believe her; she saw the echoes of mistrust in their darting glances. But they yearned to. And that was enough to soothe them for another day.

BROTHER

Expect my ship in Alexandria.

For days the Roman's missive had jockeyed about his mind. Pompey's ships—robbed of their master—had scarcely dotted into the horizon when the order had arrived. Ptolemy recognized the message for what it was, for the effect it yielded on his councilors. Their preparations to abandon Pelusium had been swift, almost gleeful—Cleopatra's army had diminished to a mere distraction. Achillas had stayed behind to guard the city; with a small coterie of soldiers, Ptolemy and the rest of his advisors had set off for Alexandria.

Returned to the capital, Ptolemy braced himself for this first meeting with the Roman. But as he neared the banquet hall, his thoughts were scattered, unkempt after too many sleepless nights. Every time he closed his eyes, he heard that widow's shrieks. Even when Briseis offered comfort, he couldn't jettison the weeping from his ears. Now his terrors blistered in the daylight. They were absurd, unbearably so. How could he have even heard her cries? She'd stood—collapsed—on a trireme stades away. He had barely seen her, so why did her tear-spattered face hover in his dreams? He only knew that he woke, shouting. *Leave me, leave me be!*

Expect my ship in Alexandria.

The words chafed. Short, sharp, perfunctory. The gall was sickening—that Julius Caesar thought he had the right to summon him. And worse still, that he'd come as called, a beaten dog beckoned by his master.

His knees were wobbly, his nerves taut, even though by then he should have felt prepared to meet the man: he'd spent the better part of his waking hours listening to Pothinus drone on about the Republic. Ptolemy was so bloated with facts about Rome and Caesar that he half expected them to start bleeding from his ears. *The Helvetti and the Belgae, Ilerda and Pharsalus*—the names of the battles and the vanquished grew muddled.

And Caesar's victories off the battlefield loomed more daunting still. From Asia to Gaul to Spain, the man was painted a great seducer of women. Rumor had it that in Rome herself there was scarcely a senator whose wife Caesar hadn't bedded. Here was a man who knew how to speak to women, and how to fuck them. Ptolemy felt a surge of gratitude that both his sisters had fled.

Expect my ship in Alexandria.

The banquet hall gleamed. Every inch had been scrubbed, from satyrs' flutes to the ebony doorjambs to the golden platters on the cypress tabletops. The bejeweled eyes of the muses dancing along the wall glimmered with life. Ptolemy couldn't recall the last time he'd seen the place laid out with such splendor, more dazzling even than at his wedding to Cleopatra—not since his father's feasts had the palace looked so lavish. He wasn't sure whether to be heartened or discomfited by that.

He'd *liked* this plan, Ptolemy reminded himself. Best to greet the Roman with opulence, awe his war-weary men with wine and roasted lamb. Magnanimity bespoke strength—even as Caesar enraged the city, marching his staff-bearing lictors along the Boulevard Argeus, past the Sema and Pan's winding hilltop chapel. The crowd, he'd heard, had hissed and booed. A few had gone so far as to chuck rotten fruit at these new, unruly Romans.

His advisors were already gathered about the royal dais—Theodotus had secured the seat to the right of the throne while Dioscorides reclined to the left. Pothinus had drawn a poorer lot: a small table far from the action. Romans didn't approve of eunuchs. As Ptolemy took his father's place—his own now—he banished comparisons from his mind. His eye fell to the glinting wine. Theodotus cleared his throat and tried to stay Ptolemy's hand, but he ignored the rhetorician. He gripped the goblet's stem and drained its contents. Purple spattered on gold. He snapped his fingers to summon more. He needed something to bolster his courage if he was expected to treat with Julius Caesar.

At the far end of the hall, the gold-wrought doors opened, splitting Alexander's stallion, hind from head. The selfsame lines of lictors entered—the ones who'd sent the city spinning into a rage—lion-faced wooden staffs hoisted high. A familiar fire seared his gut, but before he could translate it into words and curse the Romans for heralding Caesar with undue pomp, Pothinus was summoning the guards. As though emerging from the frescoed walls, the vulture-helmed Galatians sprung to life.

Already their short swords were drawn, the sharpened iron glinting in the waning light. The tension bristled between the lictors and his men. Even among well-trained soldiers the slightest slip could incite a battle. Ptolemy braced himself, but suddenly the frictions faded—the man they'd been waiting for materialized in the archway.

Crowned with a wreath of laurels, Julius Caesar cut an impressive figure. He looked like a man born for greatness. No, that wasn't it precisely. Though there was something kingly in his appearance, it was his *bearing* that distinguished him. After all, the Caesar who stood before Ptolemy was no perfect specimen. His stomach bulged beneath his tunic and his hair thinned with age. Yet his step, his gaze, sang of power. He was clad in a crimson cloak to mark his rank, and the tunic he wore beneath had a deep purple border but otherwise might have been cut from the same cloth as those worn by his lictors. Ptolemy's own opulent, gold-threaded robes itched his skin—the attire of a layabout, not a warrior.

With a single glance from their general, the lictors melted to either side, leaving Ptolemy's Galatians foolishly brandishing their naked blades.

"Many thanks for your warm welcome," Caesar began. His voice was rich and sonorous, the sort of voice that cast men under its spell. Ptolemy was half drunk on it himself.

"The pleasure is mine, commander of Rome." Ptolemy didn't sputter; his voice held. The words, for once, came easily. Before Caesar, he felt—oddly—that he might speak of any topic with grace.

"I should like to think of us as friends," the Roman went on. "Good friends."

Ptolemy nodded his agreement. He wondered whether the general knew. Had word spread of how he'd killed Pompey? Surely it had, for why else would the Roman greet him so amicably?

"Excellent. And, as friends, I hope we may do away with courtly courtesies and call each other by our given names." From any other man, such words would be an affront, but something in the general's gaze softened Ptolemy to the request. A glint of closeness and respect.

"I shall call you Julius, then?"

"Please."

"Then, yes, you may call me Ptolemy, Julius."

He didn't look to his advisors for confirmation. Real rulers knew when to trust their instincts.

"As a small token of our thanks for your generosity, Ptolemy, I would like to present you with a gift."

The wine had settled in his stomach, branching out into his

veins and cooling his tremors. Everything was progressing as he'd hoped. Caesar had taken a liking to him, of that Ptolemy was certain. Strange how troubled he'd been before their meeting. How sure he was he would foul it, as he feared he'd somehow fouled Pompey's execution. After all, what other reason could there be for that weeping woman haunting his nights?

"Lucius and Quintus." Caesar had addressed two of his attendants. "Bring forward the present for the young king."

"Aye, I hope he's old enough to recognize her worth," one cracked, a stubby-looking man with a gray and grizzled beard. Ptolemy waited for Caesar to reprimand the soldier's insolence, but to his surprise, Julius guffawed as loudly as any of his lictors.

And then, with a grin, the Roman added, "I expect the king has much experience with worldly pleasures."

A pair of slaves passed through the archway, bearing an embroidered pillow suspended between them. On it stood a lifelike statue of Aphrodite, emerging from the foaming sea, all lips and breasts and hips. Her eyes were two glinting sapphires; her hair twisted with real gold. It wasn't carved by a Roman artisan—even Ptolemy's untrained eye could see that; the craftsmanship was far too fine. Somewhere near Pharsalus, a looted temple lacked a deity. A fitting present from a Roman, though. Petty and stolen.

"A kind offering," Ptolemy proclaimed. It pleased him to be the greater party, at least in this—the one providing a gift of real worth. With a glance, he motioned to Dioscorides to give up his seat. "Come, Julius, sit by my side. Feast with me in celebration of your arrival."

"My men are tired, and grateful for your accommodations," the general told him, a smile twitching on his face. "They are a little dumbstruck by your luxuries. As am I. We are but simple soldiers. Rare has been the day when we've eaten as well as this."

The words puzzled Ptolemy. As far as he could tell, the general sought out opportunities to raze divisions between himself and his men. This leveling ran contrary to everything Ptolemy had ever been taught of power. And yet—the more Caesar declared himself a common soldier, the more his soldiers seemed to adore him.

Caesar settled onto Dioscorides's vacated divan and his men sought out their own seats. Each of them looked up eagerly as the first servants entered, bearing tray upon tray of pheasant dumplings and crabmeat sausages, cumin-spiced pumpkin and fluffy Alexandrian bread. They attacked the platters set before them, some eschewing gold ware entirely and shoveling up the food with their hands.

"What they lack in manners they make up for in enthusiasm," Caesar commented, gesturing to the soldiers.

Ptolemy nodded. At arm's length, the general's presence had been comforting, but now that they sat side by side, Ptolemy felt unsure of himself, of what to say, of how to conduct a casual, rather than official, conversation. Which of his stories could hold a candle to the ones the general might tell? And a doubt rubbed at him: what if the eunuch had been right and Caesar wasn't grateful for the gift of Pompey's head? The general, exuding both authority and self-effacement, was nothing like what Ptolemy had expected.

Theodotus leeched onto Caesar, pestering him about the winds along his passage and what aspects of Alexandria he found most striking. Ptolemy felt at once grateful and vexed by Theodotus's loquaciousness—it spared him the stress of marshaling the conversation, but at the same time he was jealous of the general's diverted attention.

The rich scent of roast boar rose to fill his nostrils. The servants had arrived with the second course. With an orange in its mouth and its tusks laced with garnish, the largest and most fearsome specimen arrived at their table. Caesar leaned forward to carve the meat, his knife slicing through the flesh with a butcher's ease. Ptolemy could readily picture his dinner companion cutting through an enemy's chest.

Caesar inhaled the meat, the juices flowing freely down his chin. "This is among the finest boar I've tasted," he avowed between mouthfuls.

"You'll never eat better than you do in Alexandria," Theodotus answered. A white bit of fat had missed his mouth and was stuck in his beard. Ptolemy hid a smirk; he enjoyed witnessing the rhetorician's missteps.

"Hear, hear." Julius pumped his fist against the cypress tabletop and raised his goblet. "To Alexandria!"

"And to Rome," Ptolemy chimed in hastily. He'd allowed the conversation to meander long enough—his quiet, he feared, smacked too much of deference. As each man drained his cup, Ptolemy realized the time had come. Why wait for the hour Theodotus had appointed?

"In fact"—Ptolemy heard his voice crack on the second syllable, and a blush rose to his cheeks—"there is a special gift we'd like to present to you as proof of our friendship."

Caesar patted Ptolemy's back heartily, as though he'd hiccupped rather than squeaked. "No need for that. You've already humbled us with your generosity. Let's eat and drink. That's more than gift enough."

Pothinus—Ptolemy couldn't say how or when; sometime after the toasting had ended—had come to stand behind him, breathing poison in his ear. "My king, this is not the moment."

Ptolemy shrugged away the unwelcome words. What was done was done. No point delaying it. With a curt nod, he sent the serving boy scampering to deliver his message: *Bring out the final gift*. Loudly, he pounded a fist on the table. The general was the first to quiet, his left eyebrow cocked in surprise.

"Hear, hear," Ptolemy bellowed. "It's my great pleasure to present to you: Pompey the Great."

A murmur stirred among the Roman soldiers; at the nearby table, he saw several reaching for phantom swords before they remembered that they'd been forced to abandon their weapons outside the banquet hall. *What does he mean?* He saw the question form on more than one set of lips.

Ptolemy had pictured this scene a dozen times; alone at night, he'd conjured it to frighten away the ghosts. The imagining recalled Berenice's execution: his sister's pate spinning, his father's crooning delight. But when a servant emerged bearing the old man's head, his stomach sickened: the hair—what little remained—was stiff and frayed; the skin dragged and peeled in places. He'd never seen his sister thus. The beheaded Berenice remained the enemy she was in life, or as his young mind cast her: fierce and vital, not mottled by death.

With mounting dread, he looked to Caesar. The man stared, disbelieving, at his countryman's face. Perhaps it was that he couldn't recognize Pompey in his disfigurement. Ptolemy wished that someone—*Pothinus*—would lean in to explain, but before he could hiss some direction at the eunuch, the general's expression drew pinched. And a tear, a single tear, blossomed in the corner of Caesar's eye.

And yet the servant daftly carried the plate ever closer. Ptolemy wanted to shoo the bearer away, but he was frozen in his seat. His breaths were tight, defeat heavy in his chest. *Dead men don't bite.* No, Ptolemy thought coldly, instead they turn the living bitter.

When Ptolemy woke the next morning, the fear writhing in his stomach had been replaced by sturdy determination. Things had gotten off to a rocky start, but that wasn't his fault. The blame lay with Theodotus and Pothinus and Dioscorides and even with Achillas. He refused to be cowed by Caesar's weeping.

He wasn't some Rome-indebted monarch, ruling in name alone. If Caesar resented his gift for whatever strange reason—was it pride, as Pothinus had suggested?—so be it. He would simply have to find another way to set matters right. To succeed in all the sundry ways his father had failed. The Piper had been wrong to throw his lot in with Pompey, just as he'd been wrong in everything.

After Briseis helped him into one of his simpler tunics and knotted the white diadem about his head, Ptolemy sent word to Caesar: *The king requests your audience in the royal menagerie.* If nothing else, he knew he needed to wipe the previous day's impressions clean. What better place than the menagerie? With its collection of mythic beasts and majestic trees, the island looked like no other place in Egypt, perhaps like no other place on Gaia's Earth. Even Caesar would marvel at its collection of beasts.

And yet, once the well-muscled slave had docked the skiff in the island's small bay, Ptolemy found himself disappointed. He hadn't visited since his father's death, and the place looked diminished. Where a herd of four or five giraffes once ranged, only a lonesome cow remained, munching on acacia leaves. Years ago he'd come here with Arsinoe—had Ptolemarion tagged along as well? His shouts of glee had scattered the group; he'd watched their slow, loping strides in awe.

"Greetings."

Caesar's voice startled him and he spun around. The man was dressed even more humbly than he had been the day before—not even a garland to mark his brow and hide his baldness. And yet somehow this didn't mar his appearance. Sword girdled at his waist, this Roman represented everything Ptolemy longed to be: strong, calm, commanding. And perhaps he could be that way if he made up for his missteps. Here was his chance to discredit Cleopatra's claims once and for all.

"Julius," he said lightly, pretending his future didn't rest on this moment. "I am so delighted that you've joined me here."

"These walks are famous for their loveliness. I was grateful for the occasion to enjoy them."

The strained formality tormented him. Where was the man so eager to befriend him, to call him by his given name? Had the presentation of Pompey's head spoiled everything? He hadn't *known* it would look so foul, that the stench would linger in the hall.

"You can wander them as much as you like," he answered. *Too young, too eager.* "You are my guest, and you are welcome to all my kingdom has to offer."

Caesar allowed a slight smile. That, at least, was something. An opening, or near enough.

"You are kind," the Roman offered. "And I can't tell you how I wish I might remain here. What man hasn't dreamt of whiling away hours along the Nile, exploring the birthplaces of the gods?"

Ptolemy tried to work some deeper meaning from that riddle, but he could not. Perhaps he'd grown too accustomed to the intrigues of the Alexandrian court—maybe the general meant his phrases as innocently as they sounded. For surely Caesar had more fearsome weapons to deploy than words.

"But you're no child, despite your youth," Julius continued, walking now at Ptolemy's side. "I sense some spark of greatness in you. A perceptiveness that belies your years. You know what it means to be a leader of men. It's not so simple as some would believe."

"No," Ptolemy agreed. "It is not."

He thought of all the things he'd given up to rule. The friendships he could never have, the games he could never play, the intimacies he could never share. Not with anyone, not even his brother. Being king wasn't all glory—it carried a heavy dose of sacrifice.

"It takes years for many men to realize that. Men who might have been great but instead drink away their power. Men who entrust their fates to the wrong advisors," the Roman went on. "There are so many moments when we might fail. So many faithful friends who reveal themselves to be power-hungry thieves."

That, too, rang true. None of his advisors was trustworthy. It was their fault that he'd made such blunders and fallen to temptations. They were commoners. They could never match his greatness, and in their greed, they tainted it.

"I thought—I worried that you were angry with me," he stammered.

"Angry?"

"Because . . . of Pompey."

Caesar stopped midstride and faced Ptolemy. He placed his worn hands on Ptolemy's shoulders and looked at him with a dark, piercing gaze. In it, Ptolemy saw not only strength but also kindness.

"You did what you thought you should. What those councilors of yours convinced you that you must. Many an older ruler than you has been deceived. Perhaps you feared you had no other choice but to listen to them. But now, Ptolemy, you do."

"I do?" Ptolemy asked dumbly.

"Yes. You have me as your ally. Our positions are aligned, and when I look into your eyes, I see not only a friend but the sort of"—his voice cut out, as though the words were painful to speak—"the sort of son I've wished I had."

Ptolemy's heart cleaved to that phrase. Julius Caesar, the mightiest general since Alexander, recognized his true self: inheritor not of the Piper's legacy but of a return to greatness. That night, he swore to himself, he would host the most sumptuous feast Alexandria had ever seen.

They would celebrate the birth of a new world, a new beginning for Rome and Egypt. For Ptolemy, the Father-Loving God.

That night's banquet indeed rivaled those of the Piper. Dancers in gossamer veils invoked the three goddesses, pawing over Paris's golden apple. A raconteur crooned the tales of Odysseus, the great tactician bound by his men, beseeching before the sirens' song. By the time the actors took the makeshift stage, Ptolemy was so drunk he could hardly follow the plot of the rowdy satyr play. It didn't matter, though—Caesar's centurions laughed raucously, stamping their feet and banging their goblets against their stands. Ptolemy's head spun with wine—and when Caesar, steady despite his cups, went off to bed, Ptolemy soon followed. Briseis eased off his tunic and stripped away his diadem, but he lacked the vigor for anything else. He fell asleep almost at once, arms and legs wrapped about his maid.

A terrible pounding shook his room—his head, the bed, perhaps even the palace itself. Ptolemy squinted his eyes open. Briseis sat bolt upright, clutching the coverlet over her naked breasts. She looked so tender and vulnerable that his heart threatened to snap. Without thinking, he told her to hide under the bed. As soon as the words were out of his mouth, he recognized their absurdity: whoever came banging at his door wasn't there for his slave.

"Who disturbs the king?" He'd pitched his voice low. This had become easier in recent months. Whole octaves opened up to him.

Ptolemy peeled himself out of bed and rummaged around for his tunic. Without a servant to help, he was all head and limbs. The neck opening seemed far too small, his arms incapable of bending at such angles. For one ignominious moment, he thought he'd have to re-call Briseis from her hiding place—but with another twist, his hands rooted out their paths through the sea of fabric.

"Let me in, my sweet." His mother.

He'd avoided her since he'd returned from Pelusium—her company tainted him, casting him back to his childhood self. Better she stay in the nursery, tending to Ptolemarion and his simpler needs.

Ptolemy struggled to knot the diadem behind his head. He knew he was making a mess of it, but he wanted to remind his mother of what he was: a king who'd raised armies and treated with Caesar. In no way her little boy.

He wrested the bolt and pulled the door open. The threshold dwarfed his mother's frame, but it didn't dint her glamour. Wrapped in a clinging chiton laced with pearls and dripping with gold-set jewels, she was dressed to play the part of queen. Her face, too, had been painted with extraordinary care—the kohl that lined her eyes was thick along the edges and her cheeks were burnished a healthy bronze. Her expression, though, ruined the mirage—her mouth was pinched and narrow; anger flamed in her pupils.

"You should come when I summon you. Not before," he told her coldly as he slipped into the antechamber. Her eyes widened and watered at the slight.

"I understand, my king."

It was the first time she'd called him that, and somehow it made him feel both vindicated and betrayed. Gently, she reached her fingers to his cheek.

"But I have news you must hear: your sister has bested you."

Ptolemy grabbed her wrist and yanked her hand from his face. Her skin felt papyrus-thin under his grasp, the bone as flimsy as a twig. His mother had shrunken in his absence, just as he'd grown. He loosened his grip and let her hand drop to the side. Instead of raging, he spoke quietly. He knew he'd already won.

"Inventing lies won't endear you to me, Mother." Caesar and his

216

promises echoed fresh and glorious in his mind. Father and son. "Cleopatra has no chance. I have *Rome* on my side."

But his words didn't have the intended effect. His mother tossed back her head and cackled cruelly.

When she finished, she said in a hiss: "*You,* my son, *you* have Rome on your side?"

"Is that such a surprise? Julius and I have made our peace. He is my friend and ally."

"You need me, Ptolemy. You may fuck your serving girl, but you are still a child."

His face burned and betrayed him. How did she know? How did she always know?

"I ruled well without you in Pelusium, and I rule well here. I'm not a child."

"If you rule so well here, my son, how did Cleopatra find her way into the palace? You are not the only one who pays court to Caesar. And in this respect, my son, your sister has certain advantages you lack."

It wasn't possible—there was no way. He refused to believe it; his mother made up stories, nothing more. To steady himself, he stared off at the far wall, where he'd hung a tapestry of Jason. The hero reached for the glimmering Fleece dangling from Ares's majestic oak. *Don't touch it,* he wanted to whisper. *It will only bring you pain.* Ptolemy blinked; he took hold of himself.

"That's not——. She couldn't have."

Through his denials, the idea wormed itself into his mind. Ganymedes had snuck onto the grounds undetected; had Cleopatra followed a similar path? *No.* He would know if she had—her presence would reverberate throughout the palace.

"No," Ptolemy repeated aloud.

His eyes focused on his mother. As he'd fretted, she'd gone to recline on one of the red silken divans. Her ornamented arm draped over the back of the couch as though she hadn't a care in the world.

"It's true," she mused. "You think we women are useless—refuse for you to toss aside. As you've done with me. But we know these things. We mind the comings and goings of servants, the flow and foibles of domestic life that escape your sharp-eyed advisors. That— it appears—escape your royal person too."

She'd never been so cold to him—so distant. The very air around her seemed to bristle. "But surely the Roman has already told you this. He is, after all, your dear, dear friend."

His mother toyed with one of her bracelets, a golden snake de- vouring its own tail. Another suspect talisman. She was merely a lying woman, just like Arsinoe, forever feinting toward him, then away. Besides, surely Caesar, vaunted among the wisest of men, knew better than to fall for Cleopatra's tricks. A man of his years would temper his passions better than that.

"She's with him now," his mother prodded, gaze fixed on her jewels. "Go and see if you don't believe me."

Already part of him was running down the cedar stairs, across the courtyard, and into Caesar's apartment. He longed to fight the urge and save face—he didn't want to cry wolf over another ruse. But his curiosity—his dread—got the better of him.

"Fine, I'll go and put an end to this." He made to dart toward the door, but his mother grabbed his wrist as he passed. She gave him a pleading look.

"My son—I didn't mean—. Don't go in anger. Not like this."

He wiped away her fingers roughly. See, he told himself, she'd gone too far—and now she wanted to cover her lies. Once he'd seen Julius, the whole matter would be laid to rest. Spinning out the door, down the steps, he heard her footsteps—light as a girl's—chasing him, her pleas that he be *reasonable*. He'd had his fill of *reasonable*.

She should have thought of *reasonable* before prodding him into this corner.

Ptolemy quickened his pace, his confidence waxing with each step. Yes, she was jealous as ever, inventing this story to turn him against Julius.

Two men flanked the entry to the apartment he'd provided for his guest. The taller of the pair leered menacingly. The other, a short fellow with an easy smile, looked more approachable.

"My lord," the smaller soldier said. That form of address irked Ptolemy. The Gabinians knew enough to call him *king*, but *lord* was the best he managed to get from Caesar's men. "How may I be of service?"

"I need to see your master. At once." He eyed the door for hints of recent entry. He saw none—the ebony was firmly sealed. The dust unmolested. No sign that Cleopatra had come here.

"The hour is quite early, and the general is still asleep, my lord. But I will tell him of your visit. I am sure he will come to you as soon as he wakes."

Ptolemy scanned the guard's face for some tell, but the man's expression remained steady. Perhaps he spoke the truth: that Julius still slept. But Ptolemy was king—and if he had to rouse his guest to prove his mother wrong, he would.

"I need to see him *now,*" Ptolemy ordered as he took a step toward the threshold. The blunt side of the man's spear blocked his path.

"My lord," the soldier repeated, "I told you he's indisposed."

"I am the *king*. This is my palace. Admit me."

"My lord, I mean no disrespect, but I've had my orders." The sentry kept his spear set across the door.

Dark images swam through Ptolemy's mind: Cleopatra sneaking through the palace, seducing her way into the Roman's chambers . . .

"Julius!" Ptolemy shouted at the top of his lungs. "Julius!"

His suspicions clawed at him, growing grotesque in mockery. His sister mounting the general, arching, screaming, *I am the queen.* He yelled to drown out the vulgar Cleopatra in his mind and stomped his feet against the onyx. He couldn't fight his way in, but he could create such a ruckus that Julius would be forced to come out.

And then, as though the gods for once were listening, the door creaked open to reveal the Roman. Scratching at his forehead, he stared at Ptolemy dumbly.

"What's happened?" Julius asked, his brow knit in concern.

"My mother——" He cut himself off. Before Caesar, magnanimous even when woken by his shouts, his worries revealed themselves for what they were: paranoia. "I wanted——" He stalled for time, spinning his story from the ether. "You went to bed early last night. I wanted to make sure the banquet was to your liking."

The general rubbed remnants of sleep from his eyes. "Very much so. With dancing girls and everything a war-weary man could want."

The knot in Ptolemy's stomach loosened. "Good, good. I only—— I want you to know how much your friendship means to Egypt. How much it means to me," he added shyly.

Behind Julius, a shadow crept through the darkness. Nothing, he reassured himself. He had Briseis; a man of Julius's stature would have his concubines.

"And I yours," the Roman answered.

A figure coalesced beside the general and slipped a slender arm about his waist. What sort of whore would dare——? The woman took another step forward: two orb-like eyes suspended in the darkness. The morning light spilled onto her face—and, horrified, he recognized her.

"I see my dear brother has been so good as to join us," Cleopatra said. Holding Ptolemy's gaze, she kissed Julius beneath the ear.

Bile rose in his throat. Julius had betrayed him. Julius who'd called him *son* and promised friendship. A single glance from Cleopatra had reduced those words to dust. He swallowed, hard, against the burning liquid in his mouth. It wasn't enough—he was never enough. He spun on his heel to leave—why humiliate himself further? He wouldn't give his sister that satisfaction. In stormy silence, he fled down the steps and through the great courtyard and past Alexander's shrine. He ran to the edge of the complex, to the great looming gates of gold. And then he screamed and screamed and screamed for all the world to hear.

SISTER

Bolis stepped into the tent, a bundle of taut and trembling nerves. Arsinoe watched him pace its length five times before she insisted that he sit. But even seated, he fidgeted relentlessly, picking at his cuticles and shifting his weight on his stool. He looked like a boy who hadn't learned his verses for that day's lesson. The comparison made her smile—with his bald pate and scarred left eye, the commander bore little other resemblance to a child. She shook the amusing thoughts from her head. Whatever fretted Bolis would surely fret her as well.

"The men grow restless," he said, speaking as much to his feet as to her. The words didn't alarm her—they were the same ones with which he greeted her each morning. It was his tone that betrayed his anxiety. Perhaps her speech had yielded more harm than good. Maybe she should have stayed quiet, allowed more soldiers to abscond into the night. Now they lingered, restless and loyal to her—if they were loyal to anyone—and she had no idea what to do with an army, of where or against whom to lead them.

"So nothing has changed," she gibed cheerily, though her attempt at humor had no effect on Bolis's mood. With a sigh, she pulled her chair closer to the spindly table. It overflowed with papers—much as it had under Cleopatra's auspices—but she was no longer sure of their purpose. Each morning she and Bolis would review the maps, marking where the army stood and discussing what moves they might make. Yet with all their talk they did nothing. The scene had grown familiar with its repetition: their call-and-response, the plotting as a means of distraction. The routine was comforting, almost intimate. The sort of unspoken understanding, she imagined, that passed between lovers.

Arsinoe blushed at the thought. Though she bore no passion for poor scarred Bolis, she did feel a creeping tenderness for him. He'd belonged to Apollodorus just as surely as she'd belonged to Cleopatra, and their losses yoked them together.

"I don't know how much longer we can hold them here." Bolis glanced up at her. His left eyelid drooped a little more each day, as though the recent uncertainty weighed particularly heavy on it. "The Galatians mutter about the gold coin they've missed out on from the Romans, the Arab tribes have begun fighting among themselves, and even the Upper Landers are growing eager to return home to sow their crops."

He was right; tempers had soured in the camp. During her morning tour, she'd heard as many grumbles as greetings. The mercenaries ranked worst among the whiners—the picture of politeness in her presence only to breathe poison once her back had turned.

Bolis studied her with weary eyes. "What do you mean to do with them?"

"What does anyone ever intend to do with an army?" She forced herself to laugh, though there was little to laugh over. One way or another, she'd have to send them somewhere, and soon. The waiting for Cleopatra had stretched on long enough—wherever her sister had gone, she had no plans to return here. The answer sprouted, ripened, in her mind: they must go home. "We will march on Alexandria."

Bolis started with surprise, bracing his feet against the ground. But he did not object. Perhaps he'd toyed with the idea too: if they went to the capital, they might meet with Cleopatra. Or perhaps her sister had mimicked their father and already fled to Rome. Either way, the journey to Alexandria would set them directly against her brother and his troops. She hoped that was enough.

Outside, a voice pitched against the tent. An address to her sentinels, and at once her thoughts leapt to mutiny. She listened for other hints—a few pairs of feet scuffling in the dirt were all she heard. Her heart settled in her chest—the sounds of a small confrontation, perhaps two men addressing the dozen who guarded her person.

"Go," she commanded, "see what the trouble is."

"My queen." Bolis bowed his head and disappeared beyond the tent's flap. His baritone cut through the noise outside—men listened to him. The talk grew angry; harsh tones beat against the tarp, though she couldn't parse the words. But the sniping didn't taint her newfound calm. The decision to march to Alexandria spread like a balm over her nerves. She should have plotted that course the day Cleopatra left rather than fretting over what instructions the queen might send. Waiting, always waiting, on her sister.

And for what? Half her life she'd wasted, worrying over Cleopatra and wondering what she wanted, praying and pleading for her return. Any moment—every moment—when Cleopatra had needed her, she'd been there, desperate to please. Who had warned her sister to flee Ptolemy and the Gabinians? And who had soothed the queen when Memphis turned them out? And, yes, even when their father clutched at his fading light while Egypt crumbled around them—who had taken the sin of his death upon herself, spoke the harsh and necessary truth? All that, and for what? To be abandoned with strangers in the desert, cast aside for the mooning Apollodorus.

The leather flap lifted, allowing a blinding flash of sun into the tent. Bolis's bulky form blocked it; bowing his shoulders, he squeezed through the opening. Behind him followed another, slighter figure. She narrowed her eyes at this newcomer—a gangly youth. As he straightened, his fingers stroked the first sprigs of beard on his chin. The vanity made her smile.

"My princess," he said, "I bear tidings from Queen Cleopatra, the Father-Loving Goddess."

Though she had heard that epithet a thousand times, she'd never recognized its cruelty before. *Father-Loving*. Had Cleopatra chosen that coronation name to mock her? To widen the chasm between them? The murder that neither dared name . . . No. It was her sister's penance, nothing more.

"What news?"

"She has sent me to inform you, her dearest sister, that she has won Julius Caesar to her cause. The Roman swears to restore her rule."

Julius Caesar? At first, she thought the boy misspoke, and she waited for him to correct his error. For of course Cleopatra would look to Pompey's son, not his enemy. The speech Arsinoe had spun to the army had been a lie, but one she had believed held at least a grain of truth. After all, Pompey had restored their father to power, and now the Piper's ungrateful son had murdered him. Who would make for a better ally against Ptolemy than the young, dashing Gnaeus Pompey? But, Arsinoe supposed coldly, when had her sister cared for loyalty when a greater prize lay in play?

A pit hardened in her stomach. Arsinoe knew she should be grateful. Her sister hadn't forgotten her—she'd even thought to send a messenger. And Arsinoe had served Cleopatra's purpose: She'd held the army at bay while her sister bent before Rome. She'd performed her role and the drama had drawn to a close. So where was that sweet rush of relief?

Quietly, she thanked the messenger and told her guards—*hers or Cleopatra's?*—to escort him to the dining tent. She felt an acute need to be alone, but Bolis lingered stubbornly, worrying away his nails with a knife.

"Are you sure this is wise?" he asked at last, scarcely looking up. "To let him sit among our soldiers?"

Arsinoe shrugged.

"They'll find out soon enough," she said. "Let them rejoice over my sister's victory—they deserve something to celebrate after these long weeks."

And celebrate they did, loud and late, until the stars began to dim against the dawn. Seething beneath her blankets, Arsinoe listened to their revelry. For as long as she could stomach, she'd remained among them, feigning all the motions of joy. Until the moon had glistened high overhead and the men had fallen too deep into their cups to note the whereabouts of the queen's sister.

Outside, the shouting crested; a band of merrymakers stumbled by her tent.

"T' Cleop'tra," a voice slurred, piercing the skins.

"Yes," another echoed. "To Rome's beloved whore."

She let the words slide off her. Soldiers, she'd learned by now, gossiped as ardently as spinsters did. No amount of scolding and punishment would alter their elemental nature. After those weeks bereft of news, Cleopatra's seduction of Caesar was far too tempting a tale to forbid talk of. Disguised as a sack of grain—no, of laundry—wrapped in a Turkish carpet, dressed as a beggar, appearing before Caesar in the guise of a goddess. Already Arsinoe had heard half a dozen iterations of the story, each peppered with more creative flourishes than the last. And those were the more flattering ones—she supposed that now she had gone to bed, the less savory details would be trotted out. Casting aspersions on Cleopatra's honor was easier for the men than accepting the truth: that their rag-tag army could never have beaten Ptolemy.

"Why d'you cheer?" a wine-thickened voice cut in. "It's the Piper all o'er again. Her father suckled at Rome's teat, and the girl sucks at its cock."

A few guffaws crackled.

"Come off it, Antiochos. The boy'd be worse. This un's fierce. She'll hold her own."

Antiochos. She marked that name. As she'd always marked the names of those who might prove disloyal to her sister.

"Or at least better than you can hold your wine," another voice howled. Whistles and chortles greeted the third speaker. After a time, the men passed on, their tones receding into the general merriment. Laughter and murmurs, the sultry moans of camp followers and the earthier grunts of rutting men. Her eyes grew heavy, her limbs light. Soon she would soar—

The scrape of footsteps outside sent her skittering back to earth. She listened keenly to the paces—their author must be close. She could hear the steady rise and fall of his breath, and yet her guards didn't stir. Bolis had sworn up and down that he'd set his most loyal men outside her tent: *Soldiers who'd lay down their lives before joining the revelry.* But this revelry, it seemed, had proved too tempting.

Arsinoe wrapped the furs tightly around her, trapping the sweat against her skin. She wasn't sure what difference it would make—furs or no, she lay vulnerable, exposed. She slipped her hand beneath her mattress and felt for her dagger. Her fingers closed around its hilt and she drew it out. It comforted her, even though she saw it now for what it was: the weapon of a child. But it was the only weapon she had. The only one she had ever used. Except for the blunt side of a bone, but that was another life, belonging to another girl, named Osteodora.

"Arsinoe."

The sound of her name returned her to the sticky tent, to the woman she was now.

"Arsinoe," the voice tried again.

She stayed silent.

"Arsinoe, please."

The words sounded wrong together, ill paired.

Dry leather crackled, and the figure entered, lamp in hand. She sprang up and rushed the intruder. Her dagger pressed against his neck. She could now see from his eagle helm and bordered tunic that he was Roman.

"Don't take another step."

"Arsinoe," he repeated dumbly. "Don't you recognize me?"

She stole a glance at his face. The familiar gray-green eyes, the nick of a scar under his chin. She'd been there when he'd earned that mark: headlong into the lip of her namesake's fountain, blood curling in crimson swirls. No. It couldn't be.

"Alexander?" She'd tried to keep her voice steady. She didn't loosen her fingers on the blade's hilt.

"I see all this time spent with soldiers has taught you to arm yourself well."

"I can't say as much for you. It's a military camp you've entered, not some lady's boudoir. You should guard yourself with greater care." She'd kept her voice light and teasing, as though months of absence hadn't passed between them. Under her gaze, he grew into something recognizable, adjacent to the Alexander she'd known but no longer that same boy.

"I suppose I expected to be greeted with something sweeter than a sword."

He smiled and she forced one in return. Grudgingly, she lowered her blade so it no longer nicked at his skin. Late at night, when she'd dreamt of this moment, her heart had nearly burst with joy. In those imaginings, she'd embraced Alexander and pressed her hungry lips to his.

But she didn't float light and airy as she'd imagined. Instead, she felt defeated. More alone, somehow, than she had been before. The bond that had yoked her to her childhood friend had crumbled into dust. She didn't know *this* Alexander any more than he knew her. The familiarity had been stripped away and replaced with something else entirely: desire, a hint of fear.

The air crackled between them.

"Arsinoe." Her hands shrunk beneath his as he peeled away her dagger. "You're shaking."

"The nights get so chilly here—" She hiccupped a laugh. "It never used to bother me. I don't know what's changed."

Gingerly, as though she were a horse he was afraid to spook, Alexander bent down and placed the lamp on the ground between them. From below, the light struck him strangely, his scar a white dash amid his stubble, a few unscrubbed blemishes burned bright. He wrapped his arms around her, but her shivers only grew more violent. Rubbing his calloused fingers up and down her arms, he tried to warm her. It did no good. And then, at last, he dropped his hands to his sides. Blankly, he stared at her, as though he didn't recognize her either.

"Strange, I've pictured this meeting so many times, and yet in each imagining you were pleased to see me."

An accusation, blame cast onto her.

"Alexander." She spat the name like venom. "You abandoned *me*. You needed to prove yourself, join an army—well, we raised one here. Where were you then, Alexander? When we were fleeing through Upper Egypt, desperately searching for men?"

"I wanted to join you as soon as I learned you'd left Alexandria.

The Gabinians were folded among Achillas's troops—it wasn't easy to slip away."

"But I suppose it was easy to switch allegiances now that Cleopatra has seduced Caesar and the battle's done."

"You think that's why I've come? To play favor with the victors?"

She ignored the hurt in his voice. She wouldn't be weakened by it. "Isn't it? What else would bring you here?"

His fists clenched at his sides. Perhaps he would lose control of his passions. She longed for that; she wanted to say something—anything—that would snap his resolve and reveal what sort of man this new Alexander was. That would make him slap her hard across the face. But when he answered, his words remained cool and calm as ever. Practiced.

"Arsinoe," he began. He shifted from one foot to the other, a stance that mirrored that of his boyhood recitations. Tenderness threatened her resolve. She beat it back. "You know why I've come. I've come because I love you, and I've always loved you, for as long as I can remember. Even when we were two foolish children running through Berenice's court. I loved you then as I love you now. And so I've come to you. To pledge allegiance to Egypt's queen."

She fixed her gaze downward, staring into the flickering lamp. "You've run a fool's errand, then. Cleopatra is long gone."

"I don't mean Cleopatra." He dropped to his knees, a suppliant. "There's only one Ptolemy I trust to rule, and she stands right here before me."

There they hung, exposed: her secret, treasonous yearnings. A pang of betrayal pierced her innards, and she yanked Alexander to his feet.

"Don't say such things." She glanced about the tent as though spies might have stolen in with the muck. It was one thing for her to think it, but it was entirely another for someone else to voice her perfidy.

"There's no one here but us," he whispered.

His tone was soft, soothing, and yet it frightened her all the more. She grew conscious of her lips—half a dozen times she'd licked them moist. Her breasts turned tender beneath her tunic; even her gaze felt lustful. This last she could conceal, and so she forced her eyes down to the oil lamp again.

"You can't be moved by those loyalties still. She's—"

"She's done what's best for Egypt. I'd expect no less." Her voice trembled despite her attempts to keep it firm.

"I didn't mean to upset you—I only meant . . . We needn't talk of Cleopatra. There are other things . . ." He reached to stroke her hair and then suddenly withdrew his hand. His face flushed, his desires and insecurities writ plain.

"What other things?" Arsinoe teased. His shyness put her at ease. She knew this boy, though he was playing at a lover, at a man.

Alexander blushed darker, but he held her gaze.

"If you don't know what I mean"—his voice was hoarse as he bent over her—"I'll show you."

His lips met hers; this boldness sent her pulse racing. She'd only had one real kiss. The one they'd shared in Alexandria those years ago. But she could tell he'd experienced many others between then and now. She supposed he must have known his share of camp followers and city whores.

His fingers fumbled as he tried to stretch her tunic over her head, unsure how to free her arms as he did so. Impatiently, she grabbed the edges and lifted it away herself. As she let the fabric fall at her side, she felt more naked than she'd ever been. And as Alexander's eyes devoured her form, his boyishness vanished. He kissed her in earnest, hard and rough. Teeth nipped at her neck, calloused hands explored her breasts, a cock stiffened against her leg.

Lifting her as he might a doll, he laid her down on the furs. Somehow he'd shed sword and scabbard and tunic, and she was trapped between his arms. Her trembling began again, and she tried to remember anything she'd heard about lying with a man. Eirene had spoken on occasion of the men who took her to bed, but never in great detail. Alexander slipped a hand between her legs, and a wetness soaked the sheet. Her face lit with shame.

"Alexander—"

He stroked her hair and kissed away her words. He pressed his palm flat and hard between her breasts.

"Your heart's racing. Have I frightened the fearless Arsinoe?"

"Never." She forced a defiant smile.

"I'll be gentle. It will hurt only a bit." His voice softened, and his eyes did as well. "Or we can stop now, if you're too scared."

The talk made him sheepish, and she kissed him fiercely to restore the other Alexander. It was better this way than to succumb for the first time once she'd been sold into marriage. She'd seen how Seleucus had rendered Berenice weak and frightened. That would not be her fate. Cleopatra had shed her maidenhood to Caesar, and Arsinoe would not be far behind.

His cock tore into her. She gasped and dug her nails into his thick shoulders. The pain seared between her legs, but she didn't cry out.

At first, he kept his word. His body lowered, slowly, gently into hers. It was his gaze that frightened her: how his eyes devoured her with such intensity. His thrusting quickened; his breath heaved. He writhed inside her, and his grip tightened on her waist.

"Arsinoe," he groaned as he collapsed on top of her. For a long moment—so long she wondered whether it was over or not—he smothered her with his full weight. Her ribs compressed and she gasped for air until finally he rolled off to the side and clutched her to his heaving chest. Soon his breathing settled into a rhythm, his body twitched, and he fell into an easy sleep. A child's sleep. But she found no rest that night; she tossed and turned and listened to the drunken men stumble back to their furs until dawn's prying fingers slid through the tent's cracks.

BROTHER

Rage came to define his days. It was his boon companion. Each morning he woke to its familiar clenching in his gut. As the hours passed, he nursed the sentiment, most of all when he caught earfuls of the Alexandrians screeching in the streets. Inflamed by Caesar's presence, they shared in Ptolemy's anger. And every night as he lay down beside Briseis, the fury sunk its talons into his chest. For years he'd thought—he'd *known*—that he hated Cleopatra. For her ease, her wit and charm, for the fact that everybody—even Arsinoe—loved her best.

But he hadn't known what loathing was then. Not as he did now. His heart gathered every sin of his sister's, turning over everything she had destroyed. Before, he'd blamed her for conniving a path to the throne, but that, he realized, scarcely scratched the surface of her deceit. Her treachery hadn't begun at the Piper's death—oh, no, it had sprouted at the moment of his own birth. From that day onward, Cleopatra had devoted herself to worming her way into his father's heart, sapping an already weak man by poisoning him against his sons.

Of course Caesar had been taken in by her. Ptolemy had thought the general impervious to such pettiness. He'd been wrong. No one could resist his sister's scheming. Cleopatra was the rotting core that threatened to bring the world collapsing in on itself.

Ptolemy's own advisors were blind to her corrosiveness—or,

more likely, party to it. With Achillas still in Pelusium, he knew there was not one of them he could trust. Circling him like vultures above a corpse, the rest tried to pass their poison off as wisdom. *Put your faith in Julius. He promises you joint rule.* As though *joint rule* was anything more than another of Cleopatra's ruses.

These scavengers suffocated him—crowding into his antechamber each morning. The public halls were overwhelmed with Caesar and Cleopatra's fawning, and so they were forced to meet in his rooms instead. Theodotus had grown quiet in defeat, simmering and twisting at his beard. Pothinus perched on a lion-headed footrest—the eunuch was ever watchful of what the other men said. Dioscorides alone looked comfortable, lolling on his silk divan as though he'd transferred all his nerves to young Serapion, who was now pacing incessantly. At the window, the redheaded man paused and flicked his eyes back to Dioscorides, who straightened and prepared himself to speak.

"My king," Dioscorides began. "Julius makes you a generous offer."

Ptolemy's fury flared at that word. *Generous.*

"He asks only that you rule alongside your sister, as your great father intended."

That word as well. *Great.*

"What he wants—what all of us want—" Dioscorides crossed to Ptolemy and put a firm hand on his shoulder. Ptolemy stared at it. *Filth.* "Is for Egypt to be strong and stable, secure."

Secure. Ptolemy exploded.

"Secure?" he echoed, his voice taut and uncracking at last. He jumped to his feet—he recognized Dioscorides's game. "Secure under Cleopatra's thumb, perhaps. Secure as Rome's client kingdom, bowing down to the greater power across the sea. Don't you remember how he entered our city—parading his lictors through the streets like he'd already conquered Egypt?"

"You didn't seem so averse to Rome a few days ago, my king."

"That was before——" Ptolemy caught himself. *That was before Caesar forsook me. That was before he tossed me aside as my own father did, as my own sister did, as all of you plan to do in time.* But he held his tongue: he had no desire to detail his own humiliations.

"Tell me, my king," Dioscorides went on, his tone treacly with condescension. "Are you familiar with the works of Polybius?"

"Of course," he spat back. And he was. The name sounded familiar, at the very least. He could place Polybius among the historians—what was his topic? Wars, of course—whose wasn't? Yes, the wars with Hannibal. That was it. "Hannibal fought Rome and lost. I can't see what there is to learn from that."

Dioscorides cast a withering glance at Theodotus and Pothinus before he continued. "Your father and I both would have hoped your tutors taught you what might be learned from the past, especially from past failures."

The rhetorician looked up from picking at his beard. "The boy—the king—is well versed in Polybius, in all the details of the histories."

Ptolemy waited for the eunuch to chime in, to defend his own teaching methods. But to his surprise Pothinus said nothing. It worried him—for all his annoyance with the eunuch, Pothinus had long been his staunch defender. Had the eunuch given up on him too? His bowels clenched; his throat tightened.

"And the king knows the history of Egypt too," his rhetoric tutor continued. "And how much stronger she is when a brother and sister put aside their petty differences and rule together."

"Petty differences?" Ptolemy scoffed, straightening his back and puffing up his chest as he'd seen Ariston do on many occasions. "Cleopatra doesn't respect my right to rule first and foremost. As king. As her brother and her husband."

Dioscorides exchanged a meaningful look with Serapion, who was leaning against the window frame. Some plot, Ptolemy felt sure, had passed between them. After all, they'd had long hours to conspire while he'd chased Cleopatra to Pelusium. Then the moment lapsed and the older man returned his focus to Ptolemy.

"So what, then, do you propose, my king? How will you wrest Caesar from your sister's clutches? Or do you intend to face the great general in hand-to-hand combat, or to pit your wits against his?"

"Why not? Why shouldn't I fight him?" he asked, even though he knew it was a foolish question, one that didn't merit an answer. But he was king—at least for a little while longer, at least before these men if not before Caesar, if not before Egypt—and he would demand a response. As he looked from Serapion's open face to Theodotus's half-ruined one, from Pothinus's glum scowl to Dioscorides's glinting eyes, he saw what united them: desperation. For too long they'd sworn themselves to him, and now they were tainted by association. Cleopatra would not accept them into her fold. They had no other choice but to follow him.

"You cannot fight Caesar," the eunuch said at last, "because we do not have the men."

"He brought only three legions with him," Ptolemy pointed out, digging into his position, shaky though it might be.

"His three *fittest* legions," Theodotus replied. Unlike Ptolemy's eunuch, who had the decency to appear punctured by his falling fortunes, the rhetoric master seemed to revel in them. "His personal guard chock-full of men whose loyalties are above reproach. Men who can't be bought with gold or silk or cunts."

"There are no such men."

"There are, and they are called Romans. These are not mere mercenaries you can purchase at some Rhodian bidding block. Loyalty courses through their veins."

Ptolemy studied the rhetorician for a moment. The same man had advised him to murder Pompey, promising that would win Caesar to his side—and look what good that counsel had wrought.

"I know what Romans are like as well as you do." His voice grew shrill and strident, and so he had steadied it. It was Caesar's voice he thought of as he composed his tone. The calm tenor that could sway even the most implacable of men. "But we have an army too, an army that was prepared to fight Cleopatra. An army that might march back from Pelusium in a few days' time. An army loyal to me, and me alone."

"Yes, you have men. But, as you said, their loyalty might be easily bought."

There was a knowingness in Theodotus's tone that hinted at some deeper betrayal. Had Achillas turned against him too?

"We'll offer them twice what the Romans would." Ptolemy found himself casting about for relief. Dioscorides remained stubbornly silent—he never was much use in military discussions. Desperate, Ptolemy looked to Serapion, but the man had folded his hands over his belly and fixed his gaze on his cuticles.

"It doesn't matter if you offer these men ten times what Caesar would pay," Theodotus sneered. "The question is whether they believe anyone will be around to pay out at day's end."

"We'll pay them up front," he replied sharply. Why did no one else offer any solutions? Could his advisors be as daft as they seemed? Or was it some mask they donned, a way to play the odds against him?

"Pay them up front?" Theodotus smirked at the idea. "And have them desert the moment their lives are threatened? No, my king, that's no way to deal with mercenaries."

"Are you an expert on mercenaries? On fighting men?" he shot back, and Theodotus looked uncharacteristically surprised. Ptolemy then turned to Serapion, who at least had fought among the men who restored the Piper. "You know the ways of soldiers. What say you?"

Serapion peered up from his fingers. He lacked his customary jolliness, and he looked old, suddenly, and tired, as though he'd aged ten years while Ptolemy had been away.

"Theodotus has a point, my king. It won't be easy to convince mercenaries to lay down their lives for a losing cause. After all, even the lowliest of men gets only one, and coin does little good when it belongs to a corpse."

He wouldn't just roll over and accept defeat. "B-but—" he sputtered. "There must be another way . . . You can't—you can't think I could rule with Cleopatra. Or rather sink into the background as Cleopatra rules. Not you too."

His gaze danced around, skipping off Theodotus's furrowed brow and onto Dioscorides's gray eyes, usually so bright but now dull and resigned. Even Pothinus, who could always find the most inopportune moments to grin, shared their gloomy aspect. They were weak, old men, and they preferred to sink with the floundering ship rather than struggle to right it.

"Get out," he hissed. "Get out, all of you."

There were the typical sounds of affront, the snorts and sighs of disbelief, but he didn't look up to match the noises to the faces. None of them deserved that courtesy. He fixed his eyes on the floor mosaic; a raven-haired satyr smirked back at him.

Someone cleared his throat, nearly in his ear. It was the eunuch; he caught Pothinus's smell, the dainty dabs of frankincense he rubbed behind his ears.

"Get out," he said icily.

"My king, there is another way," the eunuch whispered, so softly that at first Ptolemy thought he'd misheard.

His fury tightened. "Why didn't you say so earlier?"

Pothinus's hooded eyes glinted toward the doors.

"I wanted to wait until we were alone. Theodotus has grown watchful, paranoid, after his failure with Pompey. And Dioscorides...one can never say where his loyalties lie. My plan requires secrecy, not a single misplaced word."

"And what of Achillas?" Ptolemy asked, teetering between dread and hope. "Our army in Pelusium? Will they march?"

"Of Achillas's loyalties, I am sure." The eunuch's face softened. "I have sent word to him to keep heart and prepare to come to Alexandria."

The knot in Ptolemy's stomach loosened. Tears of relief threatened in his eyes, but he squeezed them away. He'd judged the general correctly—despite all his gnawing doubts, he could still trust in that.

"Two choices lie before you," the eunuch went on. "One will enrage the Alexandrian horde, and the other will endear you to their cause. Which will it be, Ptolemy?"

He started at his name—he couldn't recall the last time the eunuch had addressed him as Ptolemy rather than as *my king*. And yet the form comforted him, recalling some closeness between them.

"You know what I choose. I need the city on my side if I am to rule."

"Very well, then, my king. You are a braver man than most." The eunuch paused and then leaned close. "The Roman must die."

Ptolemy didn't gasp. He didn't even feel surprised. Somewhere in the dark recesses of his mind, he'd been turning over this possibility. Though he hadn't admitted it to himself, he'd pushed for it, goading his advisors until one dared to speak his desire aloud. The thought should thrill him: the murder of another Roman, the greatest Roman of them all. Yet instead, he felt a softness caving inside him. His rage swelled to counter it. *There is no other way.*

"How?" The question slipped from his lips. And with that word, they were agreed. From the look in the eunuch's eye, Ptolemy saw that a plan had already been spun and set in motion. For a moment, his heart ached for Julius, for the heralded general who would die without a son and heir. "But the man has faithful guards, surrounding him day and night."

Pothinus shrugged. "If there are guards, one can always be persuaded. It's the nature of men."

Ptolemy nodded, though the thought disturbed him. If even Caesar, the most beloved of leaders, had sentinels who would slit his throat in an instant, what chance did he himself stand?

And once it was decided, the pieces fell all too readily into place. Poison emerged as the chosen method, though Ptolemy pleaded for a less womanly means. The eunuch scoffed: "That's the point. If his men blame Cleopatra, so much the better." Caesar drank heavily in Alexandria, embracing any excuse for excess. In this, fate sat on their side: Cleopatra's birthday neared, and the celebrations promised to be lavish. At that banquet, the Roman surely would sink deep into his cups.

A dear friend, his barber, was easily bribed. At first, he denied their entreaties—a move Ptolemy suspected was largely to save face—but he changed his tune readily enough. And why not? For a hefty weight of gold, the man merely had to slip a pinch of poison into Caesar's goblet.

The sun fell on another day, but Ptolemy knew better than to hope for rest. He could scarcely remember the last time he'd slept. His body was weary, but his mind refused to settle. For his whole life, he had taken sleep for granted, certain it would come whenever he needed it. Another childhood folly.

The night that stretched ahead of him was the worst of all. The last before the world would change forever. Six days had shrunk to four, to two, to now: tomorrow. At his side, Briseis stirred.

"What's wrong, my love, my king?" she asked, and his agitation melted away. She called him that now, when they lay together in his bed. The phrases forever paired. *My love, my king.* Alone, either would have chafed him. He was more than her king, more than her love. Sometimes it surprised him, how well she understood him, this slave, this nobody plucked from Judea or from whatever land she hailed.

Part of him yearned to breathe secrets to her as he might to a wife. He bit his lip against that inclination. Beneath the sheets, Briseis found his hand and clutched it to her breast. She kissed each of his fingers gently in turn.

"You needn't tell me," she whispered, "but I know it will all turn out for you."

Her voice ached with sincerity. Of all the world, she alone believed in him. He gazed into her eyes, wide saucers lit by the moon, and saw himself reflected as a god.

"We . . ." He stopped himself. What good would confessing to Briseis bring? She loved him, yes; he was sure of that. Deeply, without reservation, in a way not even his mother, who was always needling him for something, ever had. Her fragile frame trembled at his side; a cool breeze teased through the shutters. He wrapped his body around hers; she felt small in his arms. He'd grown again these past few months, sprouting inches he'd feared he never would. His body hadn't hardened, but it stretched over a larger scaffold. And when he stood straight, he was taller than Pothinus and his hair tickled at Achillas's nose.

"What, my love, my king?" She curled into his chest.

"You can't tell anyone." He inhaled the sweet smell of her hair.

"Who would I tell? I hardly speak to anyone but you." Her fingers teased along his clavicle. His hairs, the dozen or so that had sprouted around his nipples, stood on end. "It worries me that you toss and turn every night. Perhaps I no longer please you?"

"That's not possible." He laughed. "It's only—I am anxious for tomorrow. It will be a great day."

"I am sure the queen will be pleased by the festivities," she said solemnly.

"But there's more than that," he whispered, clutching her tightly. "It will bring the end of Rome."

"The end of Rome?" She gasped. "But—how . . ."

His heart leapt and hammered in his chest. The plan that had caused him such worry, such consternation, sent thrills through his veins. Her awe revived his confidence—no matter what means he used to murder Caesar, and no matter how he might pity the man, his doing so would prove his power. For years to come, the world would praise him: the king who killed both of Rome's greatest generals.

"When he puts his goblet to his lips, late in the night, he'll drink not only wine but aconite." *The poison is hardly detectable, and it will act quickly,* Pothinus had assured him again and again. *It's a mercy—far better than whatever fate he'd someday meet at Cleopatra's hand.*

"But, my love, my king," Briseis said, her face a mask of concern, "he's surrounded by loyal men . . . Surely it's too—" She cut herself off. "Forgive my impertinence. You know better than I ever could. My concern for you makes me say things I shouldn't."

In that instant, he loved her fiercely, almost as fiercely as he had once loved Arsinoe. "Don't worry, Briseis. We've bribed one of his men to do it. He'll poison the glass after Julius's taster sips from it."

"Of course." Her chin nodded against his chest. "I should never doubt your wisdom."

And at last, as the moon began to sink, Ptolemy fell into a deep and heavy sleep.

He awoke alone, groping at the warm depression on his right. Less pleasurable duties must have stolen Briseis from his bed. Much as he resented her for leaving, the blame lay with him. One word and he might have swept aside those duties, assigned another slave to dress him and heat his baths. And yet he liked to think of her as she bustled about the palace, to imagine his seed spilling down her leg as she aired out the small antechamber.

He walked to the window and cast the shutters open. The sun flooded his room in great yellow streaks—it was late, far later than he'd imagined. Pothinus should have woken him by now. That had been the plan—to rehearse the details of the plot one final time as the palace busied itself with feast preparations: what he would do, how he would react when Caesar fell ill. The eunuch should have arrived hours ago. Ptolemy cast about for explanations for Pothinus's delay—as a rule, the eunuch was punctual to a fault—and then his stomach dropped. What if they had been found out?

His door creaked open, and Ptolemy suppressed a shriek. He steadied his breath before he turned toward the intruder. Their plan had been discovered—the Romans had come to rip him from his chambers and drag him to the executioner's block. He thought of Berenice, wheedling for her life. Cleopatra, he knew, would be as hard-hearted as his father. He swallowed and spun around to face death.

Instead, he found his little brother, dressed in the rich royal purple of feast day, shuffling from foot to foot.

"I didn't mean to scare you," Ptolemarion murmured apologetically. With his long lashes and chestnut eyes, he looked a spitting image of Arsinoe as a child.

"Why aren't you at Cleopatra's celebrations?" The accusation came out harsher than Ptolemy intended. It wasn't his brother's fault that the eunuch hadn't shown. Pothinus must have decided there was no point in dredging up the plot yet again. And a morning meeting might draw unnecessary attention. His tutor was nothing if not cautious.

"It hasn't started yet..." The boy knit his brow in concern. What, Ptolemy wondered, did Ptolemarion have to worry about? Though only two years younger, his brother still inhabited some placid childhood of banquets and lessons, untainted by the harsh choices of rule. "I thought you might be ill. You slept so late this morning, even though you left the banquet early last night."

The feast had stretched on and on, with Julius and Cleopatra exchanging toasts in more and more obscene terms, his sister batting her eyes, nestling into the Roman's neck. Their flirtations had sickened him—there was only so much fawning he could endure—and so he had left, preferring to take his own comfort in Briseis's embrace.

"I'm quite well, Ptolemarion," he answered haughtily, but then, thinking better of it, "It's kind of you to worry."

His younger brother grinned mischievously; the expression made him resemble Arsinoe all the more. Ptolemy didn't want to think of Arsinoe—wherever she was—camped in the eastern delta or headed back to Alexandria. He didn't know or care. He swept all thought of her from his head.

"I don't much like the banquets either," Ptolemarion confided. "The Romans are dull. Once they've finished reciting the same two or three battle tales, they haven't a thing to say for themselves at all. And most of them hardly even *speak* Greek."

Ptolemy laughed; his brother had always been a bit of an odd study. Most boys of twelve would want nothing more than to soak in tales of valor from the source.

"They're soldiers, Ptolemarion, not scholars. What use do such men have for the tongue of Homer and Herodotus?"

"I guess you're right." The boy shrugged. His brother didn't want to fight; there was so little acrimony in him. Ptolemy tried to imagine what it would be like to look at the world with neither loathing nor disgust, to feel so little fury churning in one's gut. "Want to play a round of dice?"

Dice. A simple game, a child's game. Though he'd heard that Caesar had referenced it before he crossed the Rubicon. *The die is cast.* So it was then, and so now. Eager, chafing at the irony, Ptolemy hunted about for a set. Before he'd settled in the royal chambers, he'd had a whole chest of games, a finely crafted cedar box embossed with mother-of-pearl. But so much time had passed since he'd thought of playthings that he had no idea where it might have gone. Ptolemarion—delighted that, for once, his brother wanted to join—rushed back to the nursery to hunt down a pair.

As the two squatted over the Dionysus mosaic, Ptolemy raised the proffered dice to his lips. He breathed all his hopes into them, and they seemed to take on a fresh significance. His throw would answer all his questions: here he'd find the harbinger of things to come.

"Cast them, Ptolemy," his brother urged, impatient.

And so he did. Two cobra eyes gleamed. He would have studied them, transfixed by horror, but Ptolemarion was quick to snatch up the pair.

"Easy to beat that," his brother declared, triumphant. And already the dice spilled from his hand. A seven glinted up—but Ptolemy couldn't scrub away what he had seen. Even as they played the next round and the next, and even though he won as many as he lost, he couldn't shake the first vision from his mind: the black eyes staring up at him. His heart drummed in his ears.

The door screeched open once more. And as he turned, he

realized it hadn't been his heart pounding but approaching boots. Soldiers swarmed his chambers—more than he could count. A shriek pierced the air. His own. A pair of hands jolted against his shoulders—Ptolemarion, too, was ripped away. They didn't drag him from his apartments but back into his bedchamber. The Roman threw him roughly onto the mat.

The guard barely glanced at him before he turned to leave. The shame burned in his ears, but Ptolemy collected himself enough to speak.

"Wait," he commanded, or perhaps he squeaked. He couldn't tell the difference. "I am the king. What is the meaning of this?"

But the soldier—a worn and weary man with deep wrinkles about his eyes—merely shrugged. As if to say: *You know the meaning. Don't ask dull questions.*

"I command you tell me," he tried, this time in shaky Latin. And finally, once more, as the door was closing behind his tormenter, "Who betrayed me?"

At this, the Roman glanced back. "Never trust a whore. Not even your favorite," he said.

The door slammed. His heart cracked. He was alone.

SISTER

Alexandria had transformed itself for Cleopatra's celebrations. Long chains of laurel leaves draped over statues, sphinxes and deities alike; the heady smell of incense wafted along the breeze; figurines of Isis, ranging from rough wooden carvings, scarcely more than sticks, to polished bronze casts that seemed to gleam with the essence of divinity, were sold at every corner. As a child, perhaps five or six—six, it must have been, for Ptolemy was already a sniping, sucking thing at their mother's teat—Arsinoe had begged for a statuette, one to treasure among her sundry toys. Her mother had laughed and told her that icons of the gods were meant for purposes higher than as playthings. But years later, when her brother had asked for one, his request had been rewarded. As they always were.

Besides these customary changes, something else had shifted. The city was rife with a murkiness, a desperation, that she couldn't quite place. Even from within the sticky cloister of her litter, she sensed it—though now she realized the entire purpose of the litter, the escort, all the pomp and circumstance Cleopatra had awarded her, was to distract her from what was happening on these streets.

Her memories had faded with time, with the soft castle years and the hard desert months, but she could still recall each quarter of the city well enough. The synagogues that dotted the Jewish quarter, and the sphinxes that lined the Egyptian one, and the great marble facades where the Greeks, the high Macedonian noblemen and their coterie of slaves and concubines, made their homes. Here, among the native folk, the alleys were usually crowded with men sipping beers and talking shop, women with babes balanced on their hips squabbling over prices as their older children darted along the canal. In another life, she'd been one of them. Or dreamt she was, at least. She recalled how the sights and sounds and stinks attacked from every angle. No prayer of solitude.

And yet today the streets were subdued. A few wary locals looked on, but by and large, the boulevards had been ceded: a smattering of Roman soldiers, drunken and dreary, wreaked their havoc between the houses. At every turn, those bordered tunics announced their infestation. The festivities attracted some determined revelers, including a cluster of drinking, shrieking women on the rooftops, who resembled nothing so much as a clutch of Bacchae. These the Romans watched with particular interest. Arsinoe remembered, vaguely, that worship of Dionysus had once been banned in Rome, years ago, during the time of Mithradates. The last great scourge of the dynasty had seized upon the god's mantle, and once she had allowed herself to believe that her father took on the name for the same reason. But *New Dionysus* or no, the Piper had always been more concerned with making concessions to Rome than breaking free of it.

As their procession neared the royal quarter, she spotted a group of men—locals, not Romans—milling about the palace walls. The oldest was perhaps her age, maybe a few years older, but many were boys as young as ten or twelve. The sons, she imagined, of merchants and shopkeepers. One boy tossed a rock from hand to hand, nervously, as the others goaded him. He took a step back and hurled the stone at the palace gate. A guard cursed, and the children scattered.

She was glad, suddenly, that she'd left Alexander behind at the

Sun Gate and bid him find his own way back to the palace. She needed to sort out what to make of these events—the rock throwing, the Romans streaming through the streets—on her own. With her friend—she blushed, her lover—at her side, her mind would grow too cluttered with what *he* might think of all this. Perhaps he wouldn't care, she thought darkly. After all, he'd joined Rome's forces not so very long ago.

Her sister's festivities had transformed the palace too. Each of the cypress trees in the outer courtyard was bedecked with ribbons. As Arsinoe drew closer and descended from her litter, she noticed that these streamers didn't merely appear to glitter with jewels—small rubies and sapphires had been sewn into each one.

The royal courtyard was lined with two sets of soldiers: one group from Galatia, the other from Rome. Her innards knotted to see so many men of the Republic within the palace walls; even after her father's restoration, he hadn't paraded the Gabinian troops as his own. From the garden gate, Cleopatra entered, gliding so lightly over the central path that it appeared the dolphins of the mosaic carried her. She was dressed as the goddess Isis—the violet linen twisted between her breasts and the horned moon set glimmering on her head. Arsinoe paled at the remembrance of her own imitation— Cleopatra's pride, her bearing, would always render her the greater goddess, the perfect queen.

"My sweet," Cleopatra addressed her. "How tired you must be after your travels."

"It's been a long road." Arsinoe frowned, scanning the gathered men. She'd witnessed the strange quiet of the streets, the unrest simmering to the surface. But where was Julius Caesar, the great Roman general who stirred such turmoil?

"And solemn too." Cleopatra laughed. "What? No cutting remark about the Romans who now stretch their legs along our boulevards?"

Arsinoe started. Her sister—it seemed—hadn't lost the ability to read her very thoughts.

"You can't believe you can hide your judgments from me," Cleopatra said playfully, though a foreboding lingered beneath the lightness. "But come, let's not sully our reunion with such talk."

Arsinoe nodded; she could hardly trust herself to speak. Her anger formed a raw weight in her belly. And yet her sister acknowledged nothing. Impulsively, Cleopatra flung her arms around Arsinoe's neck.

"It is so good to have you home," the queen whispered in her ear. "Now let us go somewhere where we might speak in private. I have news."

They retired, not—as Arsinoe had expected—to the royal chambers but to the ones Cleopatra had occupied in childhood. Alone, though she removed her horned crown and wrapped a simple white mantle over her Isis gown, Cleopatra grew less familiar, not more. Her cheeks flushed crimson, and her eyes darted, bright and eager, across the room. At first, Arsinoe tried to follow the gaze, to make sense of it, but after her sister's pupils flashed from a Medusa-headed pillar to the spinning Fates to the lion mosaic arching across the floor, she gave up.

"Thank the gods you're here," Cleopatra exclaimed. Her eyes fixed on Arsinoe, as though registering her presence for the first time. "I've so much to tell you: you won't believe what has happened since my return."

Cleopatra launched into a strange tale about how Ptolemy had tried to poison Caesar. Her sister spoke so quickly and interrupted herself so often that Arsinoe had trouble piecing together the story. She supposed the details were of scant importance. What mattered was the message: not only had the queen yoked herself to Caesar, she had imprisoned Ptolemy for bristling against Rome's bonds. No wonder the streets seemed fitful; Alexandria had revolted over less provocation.

"But enough about Ptolemy!" Cleopatra interrupted herself. "I have news that concerns you. You are to be *crowned*."

That wasn't possible—Arsinoe *knew* it wasn't possible, even with Ptolemy sidelined. And she, for one, remembered the last time two women tried to rule. Berenice with her terrifying mother, Tryphaena, at her side. Neither had met a pretty end.

"Crowned?" she repeated dumbly.

"Yes, my dear. Have you gone deaf?" Cleopatra clapped her hands together with delight. "You are to be Queen of Cyprus, and little Ptolemarion its king."

Poor Ptolemarion. Though she rarely found it in herself to pity either of her brothers, her heart ached for the boy. Now Ptolemarion—so long impervious to the temptations of power—would be polluted like the rest of them.

"Cyprus, Arsinoe, *Cyprus*," Cleopatra repeated. "Julius will return it to us from Rome and bestow the island on you and Ptolemarion. My gods, Arsinoe, the very island whose loss shamed our father—look how we are restored!"

Had her sister lost her mind? Did Cleopatra not see how Rome's charity only made them look weak?

"It is a gift, then," Arsinoe started slowly, "from your lover."

"Yes, a gift, and what a gift indeed!"

"It is a *gift*, Cleopatra, and thus can be revoked as easily as bestowed."

"What nonsense! Caesar doesn't plan to revoke anything from you. It's all so much more than I'd dared imagine. I'd thought, of course, I knew—" Her speech cut off. "Arsinoe, what is it?"

"I don't want Rome's bread crumbs."

"Rome's bread crumbs?" Cleopatra scoffed. "Bread crumbs,

Arsinoe? Need I remind you, of all people, of the importance of Cyprus? Of how our father was shamed by Cato, the thief who dared give the king of Egypt an audience from his *chamber pot?* The stink lingers in my nose, even if you've forgotten it."

Her sister's voice grew shrill, wounded, as she continued.

"No, you don't remember that. You don't remember that at all, because you weren't there. You know *nothing* about bread crumbs from Rome, Arsinoe, nothing. You weren't forced to watch Father beg and plead and debase himself before the Senate as they mewled on about their gods, their pigheaded prophecies. Bowing and begging until his knees callused from the act, and still they denied him. That is what it is to beg for *bread crumbs* of Rome. And I've done none of it."

"I never said you begged," Arsinoe answered carefully.

Her sister glared at her, pulling at the edges of her mantle, her knuckles whitening in her clenched fists. "You may as well have. *Bread crumbs,* Arsinoe? You think this is charity? That I haven't worked my fingers to the bone fighting for us?"

"I think you've worked something to the bone," Arsinoe spat. She regretted the words almost as soon as she'd uttered them. Some cruelties couldn't be unspoken. Cleopatra squinted at her; the hurt hardened in her eyes.

"I see," her sister replied. "I see how it might look that way to you, you who've never had to shoulder the burdens that I have."

"Stop, Clea," Arsinoe pleaded. "I didn't mean—"

Cleopatra ignored her. "You who can choose to take whomever you please to your bed, no thought of Egypt, no thought of anyone but yourself. Alexander is handsome, pliable. I am sure his cock is suitable as well. Young boys' often are. But what does he bring you, Arsinoe? And what does he bring the double kingdom? *Nothing*. And yet you dare come here and lecture me when I've taken the most powerful man in the world as my lover, and I have bought us time. Time to grow strong again, and you scorn me for that. What other option do I have? What else would you have me do?"

"What would I have you do, Cleopatra?" Arsinoe echoed. "What would *I* have you do? When was the last time you sought my counsel? You've long listened to Apollodorus's poison. I'd have had you lead an army against Ptolemy rather than sneak back into the palace. I'd have you be brave and brash and bold rather than cow to Rome at the slightest prod."

"You're a fool, Arsinoe. Did you pay any heed to the histories we read as girls? Rome destroys every dynasty that stands in her way; challenging her only brings death." Her sister's eyebrows sunk over hooded eyes; her tongue flicked as a serpent's. It reminded Arsinoe of her vulture dreams, of soaring high above the river's bed, and then diving down, racing an eagle's wing. The eagle, of course, was Rome: had they no choice but to chase it?

As Cleopatra railed, Arsinoe saw her own future stretched darkly out before her: now that her sister had tied herself to Caesar, surely she would soon be forced into some other alliance. Perhaps it would not be so bleak, she told herself, to wed some petty client king. And then, in time, if Cleopatra had no offspring, and the years dragged on . . . she would be ready to sweep in and take the throne.

"You're right, Clea," Arsinoe replied quietly. "I should thank you."

But her softening only incensed her sister further. Cleopatra tore at her mantle so hard Arsinoe thought she might rip it in two.

"You don't mean that," her sister said.

Arsinoe choked back her pride. The scraps of power she'd gathered greedily outside Pelusium shriveled—they meant nothing here. No matter how her sister had sinned against her, she had no choice but to embrace Cleopatra's lead, accept what's done as done. As she always had.

"Thank you. I mean it, Cleopatra. Thank you for granting me Cyprus. And for seeing to Egypt's interests, no matter the price."

Her sister's blackened eyes brimmed with tears. Arsinoe couldn't say whether they were true or feigned.

"Do you mean that? Do you really?"

Her sister loved her, Arsinoe reassured herself; Cleopatra had acted as she thought best. What more could Arsinoe ask of her? Of anyone? She wrapped her arms around her sister's waist and stroked her wild hair.

"Of course I do."

But even if Arsinoe wanted to embrace Cleopatra's path, her courtship of Rome and of Caesar—and more than anything she *did*—she couldn't ignore the stirring of the populace. Whenever she ventured outside the palace, followed though she was by a narrow line of Caesar's men, she heard the murmurings. The words themselves eluded her, obfuscated by class and distance—and the people, subdued by the foreign army in their midst, didn't dare boo.

Still, she recognized the sentiment well enough. An undercurrent of fear coursed through them: Arsinoe saw it in their faces, beneath their laurel wreaths and forced smiles. She could taste their terror and their rage. Among them, she could no longer beat back her doubts; their fury became her own. Everywhere she looked, Roman soldiers swarmed, the selfsame soldiers she'd loathed for as long as she'd known to loathe anything. It was they—not the Galatians or the Upper Landers—who guarded her person as she went to accept their master's gifts. As the priest whispered the words and set the diadem upon her head—"Rise, queen of Cyprus"—the little boy kneeling at her side not so little now, the changing Ptolemarion, she wanted to cry out. The moment should have filled her with joy and rapture—this restoration of their rightful land. Instead, she felt empty, the bitter recipient of Rome's alms.

But she tucked away her misgivings and went about her days, watching as Cleopatra clasped Caesar's hand and whispered, giggling, in his ear, even as the Alexandrians hurled rocks against the gates. This solitary act of rebellion had begun simply enough, or so Ganymedes led her to believe. She didn't know how far to trust the eunuch now—he cited Ptolemy's watchfulness as the cause of his silence, but she wasn't fully convinced. Regardless, in his telling, the troubles had begun some weeks before her arrival, when a few street children—*Had Cerberus been among them? No, no, surely he would now be too old, Little Ajax too fearful*—started daring one another to cast a stone against the Roman guard. Each passing night their numbers swelled—no longer just children now but grown men who came to fling their indignities against the night. Did they yearn for Ptolemy's return to rule? Or merely to have drawn a better lot in life?

If Cleopatra noticed anything amiss, she hid it well. She looked happier and lovelier than Arsinoe had ever seen her. The queen's hair shone—a few loose curls springing from beneath her sparkling clasp, her eyes accentuated with rich kohl, her lips such a lush crimson that Arsinoe almost wondered whether some slave girl trailed her with a bowl of powders to freshen her face.

In truth, Arsinoe knew the glow emanated not from meticulously applied paint but from some deeply sown contentment. Each time Cleopatra cast a glance at her Roman consort, the Earth stilled on its rotation. Every smile, every whisper that passed between the couple seemed to hold some tantalizing secret that no one else could understand. Arsinoe certainly didn't. All she saw in Caesar was his faults: his balding pate and thickening paunch, the ugly belches he let out after he ate, and the accented Greek that sputtered from his lips.

But most of all, she hated his very Romanness, how he embodied the stoic, stubborn nature of his city. And yet this man had gifted her sister everything she longed for: Alexandria, Cyprus, the opportunity to rule alone. Her sister had retaken the royal apartments, banishing their brother, like a petulant child, to his boyhood chambers by the nursery. Arsinoe almost felt sorry for him. A prisoner of his old rooms and old routines.

Arsinoe, meanwhile, slipped into new ones. She drank, and heavily, as though each passing cup of wine might loosen the Roman fingers poised about her neck. The circumstances made it easy to indulge in quiet debauchery; Caesar's soldiers needed entertainment to keep them from wondering why their forces lingered in Alexandria while Pompey's sons were busy gathering the remnants of their father's army. Amid the sweet-voiced singers who serenaded the banquet hall and the rough-handed boxers who clashed in the colonnades, the courtesans who flirted with the Roman guards and the actors who flirted with the courtesans, her own antics went unnoticed. She would drink until her mind dulled, until the stones hammering against the ramparts dissipated.

One night, as the hour grew thin and her vision started to blur over the faces of the surrounding company, the reedy voice of a baby-faced eunuch wearing against her ears, Arsinoe felt herself fade. Her limbs were leaden, and she wanted nothing more than to sleep. She murmured some excuse to the men who sprawled over the nearby divans—at least half, she noted, were Roman and of so low a birth that the conversation shifted in and out of Greek. As she stood, her legs shaky as a fresh foal's, her sister beckoned to her. Reclining at Caesar's side, Cleopatra looked as full of vigor as she had at the start of the night, her wine virtually untouched.

"Stay," she urged. "The feast is still young."

"Yes," Caesar added, his voice slurred with drink. "Stay. Many of my men . . ." He trailed off as though he'd thought better of his words. Arsinoe saw Cleopatra squeeze his knee.

Arsinoe smiled and offered a second string of excuses. She bid the Roman good night and kissed her sister's cheek. Cleopatra's flesh was clammy beneath her lips. Its stickiness spun her back to childhood. She was six or so, and she'd sunk her hand into one of the garden ponds. To her surprise and delight, her fingers closed on some scaly creature, and she'd wrenched it out at once. The animal wriggled from her hand and flopped, gasping, on the grass. It would die, she realized, just as surely as she would die if she stayed too long beneath the waves—and she wanted to save it. Yet no matter how hard she tried, her grasp kept slipping. She couldn't get a hold until it stopped writhing, and—by then—it was too late. Even at six, she'd known the creature couldn't be revived, but she'd cradled it in her hands and placed it gently in the pool among its fellows. It had floated on top of the water, eyes wide and unblinking in condemnation.

Arsinoe's stomach churned violently at the image, and she stumbled between a few rows of divans, past the lavishly set tables, stepping over a soldier who'd fallen from his seat and didn't have the wherewithal to remove himself. Outside, the fresh air revived her, even as her sight blurred and the dolphins of the great courtyard appeared to dip freely along the path.

At first, the way was lined with oil lamps, but once she reached the Sisters' Courtyard, the torches grew sparse. In the dark, the purple pillars loomed like bloodstained teeth. Her dynasty's glory shined with false brightness, a fool's gold, and once that revelry was stripped away, what remained? Cleopatra had gathered every storied marker of their house—and forged fresh ones of her own— golden goblets and sapphire-encrusted platters, ivory-hewn tables and freshly stitched divans. Only the finest for their Roman guests.

The same would-be Stoics who mocked their father for his opulence, who made a show of eschewing all luxury. *Hypocrites.*

Arsinoe glanced up to the second story, to the rooms around the nursery that held Ptolemarion and the imprisoned Ptolemy. The windows were all dark—were her brothers asleep? Or simply wise enough not to draw attention to themselves? One of those chambers housed her mother too. To her relief, Arsinoe hadn't seen the woman since she'd returned to Alexandria. Under Cleopatra's rule, her mother kept herself hidden, tucked out of sight.

"Arsinoe."

She jumped and then steadied herself against a column. Only Ganymedes, crouched as still as a statue on the fountain's lip. With a nauseating certainty, she realized he had been watching her from the moment she'd entered the courtyard, no doubt smirking as she stumbled and murmured to herself.

"You're drunk," the eunuch said with a hint of disgust.

"You would be too," she told him, "if you had to while away each night among Romans."

The wine dulled her anger. Ganymedes couldn't begrudge her that. He gestured that she approach, and sickeningly, she complied. She squatted beside him. The water gurgled in her ears, and farther off, stones slammed against the outer walls.

"If I had to while away each night among Romans, I'd behave rather differently. I'd stay alert. I'd listen."

The words smarted. "I do listen. I do nothing *but* listen. What difference does that make? Rome's hold tightens on Alexandria, and Cleopatra embraces it. I can't convince her otherwise—I know what power she relies on now."

She remembered how cool, how clammy Cleopatra's skin had felt against her lips—despite the queen's outward health, her glinting hair, perhaps she'd made some dark trade: her inner fire for the Roman's love. Had her sister, as Caesar's soldiers whispered, seduced the older man by magic? Or had they all misread the signs and it was Caesar who pulled her sister's strings?

"Your people see that too, how she weaves herself more and more closely to Rome," Ganymedes went on quietly. "They rumble, angrily, against it."

"I hear them," she snapped. "Do you think I'm deaf?"

The eunuch leaned in to whisper in her ear: "They beg for a new dawn, a new day for Alexandria. A new *ruler*."

Ganymedes let the word settle between them. Arsinoe saw herself clothed as the goddess Isis, the double crown heavy on her head, men prostrate before her—the same guise she'd worn before her sister's armies outside Pelusium. Steely, she watched the Roman ships sail from the harbor, the frightened men turning tail. She'd pictured this all before, she realized. Not once but many times. The image would come in flashes, before she had time to banish it, and yet now, how quickly that forbidden vision coalesced. Her thoughts had already betrayed her sister. To imagine her own reign was to wish Cleopatra's death. Some rot fermented deep inside her that made her think such things. To dream of her father's murder and now her sister's.

"Arsinoe," Ganymedes interrupted before her mind could spiral deeper into the abyss. "Alexandria has lost faith in those who lead. Will you restore it?"

"Yes," she answered. She gripped the stone lip of the fountain to steady herself. "I will. By any means."

BROTHER

Confined to his childhood chambers, Ptolemy found himself condemned once more to wait. This time he awaited the arrival of Achillas's troops, though he wasn't sure what good that would bring. He and Pothinus had gambled in their attempt to poison Caesar, and they had failed. What hope did his army have against the trained Roman legions now patrolling Alexandria?

In his first few days of imprisonment, when he was still captive in his royal chambers, Ptolemy had tried to wheedle favor with the guards. Now that he was back in the rooms above the nursery, he no longer bothered. He wasn't even sure they understood Greek, and his Latin was shoddy at best. Instead, he spent his time poring over the scrolls that he'd left behind here—Polybius and Herodotus and more—and praying some visitor would come break the monotony.

None did. He had to assume Pothinus was being held somewhere as well. As for Theodotus, Ptolemy had overheard a slave in the courtyard recounting how the rhetorician had fled the city. Ptolemy knew better than to be surprised: courage had never been the man's strong suit. Even his mother and brother were lost to him. Neither dared appear at his door.

When he grew weary of reading through the long, lonely hours, he sought out sleep. That last escape of the imprisoned. Dreams might bring him a joke with Ariston, an embrace from the perfidious

Briseis—even a kiss from Arsinoe. No such waking pleasures were left for him.

"It's a pity to witness such despair in one so young."

Ptolemy started at the interruption. The voice sounded familiar, but it hardly matched the man who stood before him. Round and sleek, the intruder had the look of a well-fed tom. And then, slowly, Ptolemy recognized the face.

"Ganymedes—" The word caught in his throat. "How did you get in here?"

"I know my way about the palace," the eunuch replied with a self-satisfied smirk. "And a foul mood is no excuse for such a dismal greeting."

Ptolemy cleared the phlegm from his throat. It was a struggle to form words, as though his tongue and mind were unaccustomed to the exertion. And, in a way, they were; he was used to speaking only broken Latin to his guards.

"You look well, Ganymedes," he managed. "I scarcely recognized you."

"That's better." The eunuch smiled. "I suppose you know already why I've come, a smart boy like yourself."

Ptolemy couldn't begin to guess the eunuch's motives, but he could hardly blurt that out. Better to hold his tongue and listen.

Ganymedes gave him a quizzical look. "Perhaps not. I do hope you know, at the very least, what sort of trouble your Achillas has been stirring up."

His heart leapt at that news—confirmation that his general was still on the march—though he had no precise notion of where Achillas was or what other moves he made. This was the advantage of listening—the eunuch might reveal more flecks of truth.

"Caesar even sent out men—your men—to negotiate.

Dioscorides and Serapion were to beg Achillas to abandon his plan to enter Alexandria."

Betrayal, familiar and sour, in his mouth. He swallowed and said nothing.

"It's said Achillas killed them on the spot."

His stomach bottomed out. His general was right; they'd been traitors. He shouldn't mourn their deaths. But all he could see was how Alexandria had been shorn. His father's court ripped up by its roots. Ganymedes, meanwhile, appeared unmoved as he wandered about the room.

"These chambers," the eunuch mused, "such lovely decorations..."

Ptolemy didn't rise to the bait; he remained on the divan, feet planted on the onyx. Still it was hard to resist the urge to bat the eunuch's hand away as it reached out to caress certain items—the bronze statuette of Dionysus, the gold-framed mirror on his desk, an inkwell molded as a lotus blossom. These trinkets were all he had left; he didn't want the eunuch's prints on them.

"A scene of Theseus, I see." Ganymedes lingered over a terracotta vase by the window. The vessel, a gift from his mother, turned fragile in the eunuch's hand.

"Yes." He nodded. "Theseus."

"A brilliant tale. And informative too." Ganymedes shifted the vase from palm to palm, and Theseus trembled before the Minotaur, Ariadne's string clutched tightly in his fist. Theseus's terror echoed Ptolemy's, as though they both feared the shattering floor beneath. "Theseus learns thorny lessons. And what, pray tell, is the most important?"

Ptolemy shrugged and stared out the window. He had more important concerns than the eunuch's riddles, or a broken vase. He was no longer a child, and he was sick of playing at a child's games.

263

"Why don't you tell me?"

"Very well," the eunuch sighed. "The most important one he learns comes after he's conquered the Minotaur, after he's saved his fellow Athenians from their deaths. It comes when the god Dionysus asks to wed his brave Ariadne, without whose cunning he could never have slain the monstrous beast. And yet, despite his love, he relinquishes her to the god. Because there are times, Ptolemy, when we must sacrifice what we love for something greater."

What more could he sacrifice? He'd already lost everything—his kingdom, his friends, even his lover. What else remained to him?

"It wasn't enough," Ptolemy protested. "It wasn't enough to give her up, because he forgets to change the sails from black to white, and then his father jumps to his death."

"That should make the lesson doubly strong," the eunuch replied, grinning infuriatingly at Ptolemy's objection. "Because what Theseus should have done was forget all about his affection for Ariadne, but instead, distracted by it, he brought about his father's death as well."

For years Arsinoe had complained of how her tutor spoke in riddles. And Ptolemy shared in her frustrations now. This silk-clad eunuch spun stories that made no sense at all. He couldn't unravel the lesson beneath the tale. Better not to try.

"It must have been difficult," the eunuch continued, careless fingers wrapped around the Minotaur's neck, "to watch your sister and your wife choose another."

"I've never cared for Cleopatra," he answered flatly. If the eunuch had any gift of perception, he should have picked up on that.

"Ah, I see." Ganymedes paused. "I am glad, then, that the sight of your sister in Caesar's arms stirs no great jealousy, that the fleet of Romans running through Alexandria does not churn your fury, that the thought of some half-wolf Ptolemy ruling after Cleopatra doesn't make your blood boil."

The bait dangled; Ptolemy could not help but leap.

"No child of Cleopatra's shall ever rule," he snapped, "save one she bears to me."

"And how do you propose to ensure that?"

"I—there are ways . . ."

"So there are indeed," the eunuch whispered. "There is another path. You're lucky in your sisters: should you lose one, you could still see that a Ptolemy—with pure, unimpeachable blood—was born to rule."

Ptolemy stared at the eunuch in disbelief. It was a joke, some strange test to prove his disloyalty once and for all. The eunuch had teased this prospect before, and it had come to nothing. Only a trick to save Ganymedes's own skin. But what benefit could lying possibly bring the eunuch now?

"Times change, Ptolemy." Ganymedes gingerly restored the vase to the windowsill. "And Arsinoe must change with them."

Those words buoyed him, and the next day buoyed him further still. Caesar had demanded his presence in the Great Theater, and for the first time in ages, Ptolemy was permitted to leave his chambers. The fresh air filling his lungs and the breeze whipping through his hair—he reveled in the outdoors. Even the murmurs of the men around him brought a rush of joy. Weeks of isolation made him treasure every sign of life he encountered.

His eyes stung as he stared down at the empty stage—he worried the long days indoors had ruined them. As a boy, he had always been warned about what horrors might befall him if he didn't keep his body and mind active. Whenever his nurse, Ligea, had found out that he'd shirked some exercise, she'd chided him. *What sort of king will you make with no legs to walk on?* Or *How do you expect to rule with no mind to read?*

Three shadows crept onto the platform, and the crowd quieted.

Ptolemy squinted to make out the figures. Two Romans dragged some unfortunate from the wings. A round man reduced to shaking flesh. His left leg trailed behind him, a useless, broken thing. The prisoner had been beaten, clearly, and for what crime: thievery, murder, treason?

Righteous anger burned in his bones. It should be him sitting at the front of the royal box, doling out justice. But Caesar, perfidious Caesar—he refused to call him Julius now—had usurped that role, just as he'd usurped the palace and Cleopatra's bed. Below, the condemned wheezed, cupping his hands on his strong knee. And in that moment, Ptolemy recognized him. The wounded prisoner was a eunuch. His eunuch.

Stop. The word teased his lips, but he couldn't bring himself to speak it aloud. Besides, the Roman meant to frighten him with this display—nothing more. Not even Caesar would be so brazen as to kill his tutor. Achillas's arrival would further inflame the crowds against his sister, and such a direct threat—the murder of the king's tutor—would not go unanswered. His people would rise in defiance. Of course they would—they must. At this very moment he set the image clearly in his mind: a tumultuous crowd crashing into the great stadium.

But none came.

Phantom fingers tightened around his throat; this, he realized, was fear. His past brushes with the emotion had been no more than that—mere brushes. The time he'd nearly drowned himself in the sea, and again later, when he'd spotted Ganymedes riding on the beach. In each case, he'd thought he'd tasted terror, but that was nothing compared to the choking sensation that gripped him now.

And what sort of king did he make, in the end? A king who watched silently, frightened, as his tutor was judged before the mercy of a Roman, an enemy. That was no king at all.

Ptolemy tore away his gaze. A braver man, perhaps, wouldn't turn from Pothinus's shame, but he couldn't help himself. He looked around—anywhere but down—his eyes darting over the stands. The stadium was too quiet, more than half empty of men. During plays and celebrations, the risers overflowed, but now only the lower tiers bustled with life. Roman soldiers, he discerned from their white tunics hemmed in red. Alexandrians weren't welcome here. No one, he realized, would speak up for his eunuch.

Cleopatra least of all. The white diadem tied about her hair, she sat a row in front of him, near enough to smell, to touch. Not that he wanted to touch her—he never had. She disgusted him. Her smiles and simpers, her charms and caresses, her gold-stitched linens so fine that any commoner could see the curves beneath. His father had groped at divinity with grubby fingers, trying to spin it from his misplaced styling: Ptolemy the New Dionysus. And yet, for all his efforts, he'd failed. It was unfair that Cleopatra achieved the effect so readily, her tongue oversweet, her words too apt.

Ptolemy's eyes wandered to her consort. Seated at Cleopatra's left, Caesar looked somehow reduced, ordinary, his authority eclipsed by the queen's. His hand even rested on her belly, as if to confirm that he drew his strength from her. He appeared aged too. A far cry from the powerful man who'd summoned Ptolemy to Alexandria.

She's with child. Briseis's rumor, whispered in bed one night before she'd betrayed him. The thought of his slave sprung other unwelcome memories: the girl wrapped in his arms, her eyelashes kissing his cheek. Lies, he told himself harshly, every second of it. Why would those words be any different? But the claim refused to dissipate; it loomed as a great terror in his mind. If Cleopatra was carrying Caesar's babe, then his own cause was more desperate than he'd feared. It would ruin his only stratagem: to play to the Roman's deeper heartache, the heartache of a man who had never cradled a son in his arms.

Desperate, he needed now to catch Caesar's glance. To apologize. To make him see. *I didn't mean to kill you; I never wanted to,* he would whisper. He scoffed at himself. As though the Roman—mighty warrior that he was—would care about intent. That smiling man, the one who'd called him *son,* who'd cared for his opinions and ideas of rule, had been no more than another ruse. And he, a fool, had believed it.

Below, in the pit, Pothinus had fallen to his knees. That or he'd been pushed. Ptolemy wasn't sure; he hadn't seen. He'd been so eager to find distraction—to look anywhere but down.

"Please." The eunuch's voice floated up to him. His gaze did too, though it was Caesar Pothinus beseeched. "Please. Even in Alexandria, praises are sung of your magnanimity, of how you embraced Brutus when he repented for having backed Pompey. I beg you, Julius Caesar, the greatest of the Romans, the bravest of all men. Embrace me now. I have tried to serve my king, and if I have any fault, it is that I have loved him too well. But I see now that what I planned—"

"You mean my death," the Roman interrupted.

"Not—I wouldn't—I wouldn't say your death," the eunuch stammered.

"What would you say, then, Pothinus?" Caesar sneered, his voice drained of any warmth. Cleopatra sat silently, only acknowledging the goings-on with a slight inclination of her head. That, too, Ptolemy realized, was part of the theater. The attempt— *his* attempt—on Caesar's life was deemed Rome's business, not Cleopatra's. And so she had stepped aside and allowed the general to play at king. Another spectacle to raise Caesar in the eyes of his men.

Pothinus straightened his back, though he didn't try to stand. "I might say that I made a miscalculation."

The eunuch was hedging. And Ptolemy knew with crippling certainty that the last thing Pothinus should do was hedge. To have any chance with Caesar, he would have to speak plainly and openly.

"A miscalculation that nearly ended with my poisoning? That sounds a rather glib interpretation."

The eunuch didn't flinch. "A miscalculation based on misinformation about your intentions in Alexandria. In chaotic times, mistakes are often made."

Caesar chortled and shrugged, mugging at his men and pretending to weigh the eunuch's tale. "Indeed, you easterners are masters of deception, beguilers of the world. But we have a different sort of word for creatures of your sort: liars."

"My general, I would never dream of lying to you," Pothinus said, the picture of desperation. A few tears sprung to his eyes; his hands reached up toward Caesar. A suppliant. "I only tried, in my small way, to explain why I pressed such a course. King Ptolemy knew nothing of these plans. He has nothing but respect for your personage. Your valor is as well known as your honor."

The phantom hand about his neck squeezed tighter.

"My *valor?*" Caesar sneered. "That word is despoiled in your mouth. I know what little sway *honor* and *respect* hold here. I haven't forgotten your *gift.*"

The general stood; all about the stadium his soldiers shifted in their rows to do the same, but he lowered his palm to indicate they should stay seated.

"What sort of creature delivers a man the head of his onetime son-in-law, his former comrade in arms, his fellow citizen?" Though Caesar had spoken these last words softly, they echoed around the stalls, passed from one Roman to the next. The soldiers stirred, stomping their feet and jabbing spear butts against the marble. Ptolemy could already see his eunuch's dead body, neck parted from head.

"A son-in-law *once,* a comrade *erstwhile*." Despite the wrenching in his own stomach, Ptolemy recognized a lick of fire creep back into the eunuch's tongue. "But when we offered you our gift, he was most decidedly your enemy."

Caesar said nothing for a long moment, letting his men's anger boil into shouts. Then he lifted a palm to quiet them.

"So you defend your actions? You don't even admit the evil of what you did: stabbing a Roman *citizen* in the back, a guest claiming refuge on your soil." The general shook his head with disgust. "Thank you, for wiping any blot from my conscience. I, for one, am not afraid to look a man in his eyes as I order his death." Again, he paused as the soldiers' chants surged and ebbed. "Not that a *castratus* like yourself deserves such consideration."

The eunuch shrunk: the Latin name for what he was sounded, somehow, so much harsher than the Greek. And Caesar's revulsion was mirrored in the face of every soldier in the stands. They curled their lips and sneered their curses: *castratus, mendax, interfector.* Some stood, ignoring Caesar's pleas, and planted their palms on the shoulders of the men in front of them, ready to vault their bodies forward toward the pit and strangle the eunuch with their bare hands.

"I—I didn't—I misspoke," Pothinus stammered, his defiance stripped away, leaving only this halting husk behind. "I mean— there were reasons that Theodotus believed—you can ask the boy. It wasn't my idea. It was Theodotus's. I told him—I told them all— we should wait and see what you advised, how you thought we should proceed . . . " The breeze tugged at the eunuch's weak words; it didn't matter that they were true. Caesar silenced him with a raise of his palm.

"Enough. Enough begging. Guards, bring the traitor to the block."

Two men yanked the eunuch to his feet. Ptolemy swallowed back the bile in his throat. He could do nothing more; he ruled only in name, and soon not even in that. Cleopatra, though, tugged on Caesar's tunic, and her lover bent so she could whisper something in his ear.

"You have the most generous of souls, my love," the Roman cooed. Then he turned to face Ptolemy and continued. "Your sister worries for your soft heart. You've seen enough bloodshed for a child. My men will escort you back to your chambers."

Cleopatra cast a wicked smile at him. It wasn't enough for her to have his tutor murdered; she needed to belittle him too. And much as he wished to flee, to return to his old childhood rooms and lock the world away, he refused to leave. Watching was crucial. His one act of defiance. And of loyalty too. They couldn't steal it from him. Arsinoe had taught him that. Years ago, after hearing the tale— the bloodstained silver, the lifeless eyes—recounted half a thousand times, he'd asked her why she hadn't closed her eyes at Berenice's death. *I had to watch,* Arsinoe had told him. *I couldn't abandon her then.*

"My sister, the queen, is kind indeed," he replied. The words came easily, and measured. "But I would rather witness the judgment carried out."

His sister pursed her lips as though thinking of how she might persuade Caesar to force him out, but the Roman had already lost interest in the matter. Alone, shorn of advisors, Ptolemy was no longer even a threat worth contemplating. His people might rally their rages in the night, but they'd made no move to rescue him.

And so he watched. As his tutor blubbered and begged. As Julius Caesar denied his pleas. As the two guards dragged Pothinus forward. He winced as the eunuch was shoved to his knees, his neck slammed against the block. Above, the executioner lofted his axe into the air. Its sickle blade trembled a moment before it came crashing down.

The eunuch's headless body flailed before it collapsed to the stage. The bald pate spun across the sand until it stopped, dust smeared, some cubits before the royal box. Its empty eyes, a washed-out brown, stared up at him. At no one. At nothing. And only then did Ptolemy, retching, turn away.

SISTER

She tumbled through air and years. A lion, a snake, a vulture—her limbs sprouted and shrank at such a fevered rate that she could no longer keep track. Rose bushes swallowed their flowers into buds. Seasons pared back to childhood. Grass grew thick between her toes, and she was racing Alexander through the gardens, chasing the sun as it darted behind the clouds. Onward she ran, until she could no longer hear her friend's footfalls. She spun around to find him—and stumbled, falling, falling. The ground rushed up to meet her; her body wrecked on impact. Her lungs clogged with smoke. Gasping, she opened her eyes.

In the moonlight, Arsinoe could just barely discern the contours of her chamber: the scrolls stretched across her ebony table, the perfume vials straight as soldiers on her window ledge, the glint of lapis in Kaliope's eye. The muse of epics and adventures smiled, serene as ever, oblivious to the suffering of her charge. Somewhere a roar shattered the temporary peace. A heavy gate and a hundred guards separated the mob from the palace, but they could still make their anger known.

Did Ptolemy listen to the crowd, clamoring for his return? It would please him if he did—all her brother had ever wanted was to be loved. By her, by their father, by the soldiers who now sparred with the Roman centurions in the city's streets. Not that this was love, precisely, that sent men hurling at the gates. It was need, but she supposed that was near enough.

Arsinoe peeled away the coverlet and let the cool night wash over her. Catlike, she stretched her arms above her head and arched her back. The action outside called to her, drawing her across the room, and she flung open the panes to relish it: the strike of stone on stone. Her sentiments calcified alongside the rocks, harsher and bolder each passing day.

She closed her eyes and pictured the Alexandrian horde. In her mind, she walked through the crowd: Cerberus, bright-eyed and unscathed, shouting himself hoarse, and Little Ajax, his teeth full of pomegranate seeds. The dead lurked among them: the boy's cousin, Big Ajax, the one she'd killed. The ancient crone who'd tried to hawk her a scarab for protection, and the Jewish youth she'd overheard telling his fellows about her father's forces returning to the city. All the faces she'd encountered in her clawing, cloying days on the street. Though she'd grown tall and high chested, each of them remained as she remembered: frozen in their time and place.

The shouts sharpened against Arsinoe's ears. She could almost make out the words. Not their meaning, but their differentiations—short, staccato blasts punctuated by a few longer notes, the blaring of a trumpet. Curses cast against Rome's whores. There lay the crux of the matter, the one that ate away at her—whether Cleopatra counted in that number.

Whatever game her sister played, its outcome was murky. When Arsinoe had first returned, she'd thought she'd caught a wink in Cleopatra's smile—*Don't fret, my sweet, this is all a great show. I haven't truly fallen in love with the Roman general. I'm only using him to buy power and time.* But her doubts had since intensified. Perhaps her own tenderheartedness had misled her. Each morning she scanned the queen's face for some echo of her own fears: that the palace had already yielded to Rome and that Achillas was right to march on the city. No matter how hard she looked, she found none. The queen slept as peacefully as a child and woke untroubled; it was she, Arsinoe, who had to suffer for her sister's sins.

The air tasted strange on her tongue, a hint of smoke. Arsinoe gazed out over the sea. The light from Pharos was matched by another glow on the horizon. She leaned out the window to catch its genesis, the breeze teasing at her stray strands of hair. And there, by the docks, she saw it: the Alexandrian fleet, nearly a hundred galleys, swathed in flames. Her heart caught; the greatest defense against Caesar flaking to ash. A coward, the Roman had burned them in the dead of night, when he could wash his hands of the deed. He might claim that anyone had set the ships aflame. She had to tell Cleopatra. This, surely, would wake her sister from her love-sotted reveries.

Arsinoe stripped away her night tunic. Naked, she shivered in the winter air. The hair on her arms stood at attention and her nipples stiffened. She thought of Alexander. *Let me come to you in your chambers,* he'd whisper each time they met, in passing through the corridors or among the divans around the high table. After the news had come of his father's death, his mood had darkened and his pleas had grown more urgent. In her heart, she had softened—whatever hopes of legitimacy he clung to had died unrecognized with Dioscorides. But, still, she refused to yield to his advances. Alexandria had her conventions—the queen frowned on their relations, and so did Ganymedes. Her lover was a distraction; her head clouded at the very thought of him, and more than ever she needed her mind clear.

With care, she wrapped the next day's chiton around her body, pinned the fabric beneath her arms. The linen felt as smooth as water against her skin—a revelation, still, after long months of sand-roughened clothing. Not long ago, she would have gone to see her sister like this—dressed as simply as she wished. The pressing of time—the burning of the ships—outweighing all other concerns. But after her sojourn in the desert, she'd finally learned the lesson that first ill-fated Myrrine and later Ganymedes had taken such pains to teach her: what mattered as much as anything was that she *looked* like a princess, a Ptolemy.

And so she fetched her jewelry box, a pearl-encrusted trinket that Cleopatra had given her years ago, and fished out a few of her favorite bracelets. One by one, she slipped each over her hand and onto her wrists—the two intertwined snakes with emerald eyes, a vulture embossed in sapphire and pearl. She even smeared a bit of kohl around her eyes. She slung a mantle about her shoulders and slipped toward the door. With each step, the smoke thickened, as though the fires had spread along the shore, menacing the palace itself.

In her antechamber, Arsinoe could make out Eirene, curled on the small divan, her chest's steady rise and fall. The noise, the flames—nothing upset the maid's slumber. She couldn't remember when last she'd slept so soundly herself. As she descended into the Sisters' Courtyard—a misnomer now, Cleopatra had long since returned to the royal apartments—doubts pestered her. She saw herself through Ganymedes's eyes: a child clinging to some fantasy of sisterhood. How many times did Cleopatra have to betray her— betray Alexandria—before she could accept that her sister didn't see Rome as the enemy? The queen had *never* cared whether the Republic controlled Alexandria. But this treachery, the burning of their fleet, would force her sister to see reason at last, to recognize what horrors her alliance with Caesar wrought.

Amid her raging thoughts, Arsinoe kept her face smooth, implacable. Rome's soldiers lined the great courtyard. The palace didn't belong to her, or even to Cleopatra. It was Caesar's now. Outside the walls, these guards always traveled in clumps of three or four, as though to insulate themselves from the city and its depravities. In this way they contrasted starkly with the Gabinians, ever eager to weave themselves into Alexandria's fabric. These new men held themselves apart. And they stared—at her, in particular. She could tell that she, like Cleopatra, puzzled them: a noblewoman, not a courtesan, free to go and do as she pleased, to travel on her own and consort with strange men. Such behavior would be unheard of in Rome.

To her relief, these guards didn't try to prevent her entry into the royal courtyard, its violet columns tinted an ominous gray beneath the moon. Eagerly, she rushed onward until she barreled into a solid mass. Stumbling back to catch her footing, she found Apollodorus staring down at her, his square-jawed face set in a scowl.

"What are you doing here at this hour?" he demanded.

"Nothing that concerns you." She sidestepped out of his path in an attempt to hurry on, but Apollodorus placed a heavy hand on her shoulder. His palm pressed her down into her heels, forcing her to reckon with the sheer size of him. He wanted to render her small and meek. She loathed him for that.

"You've entered the royal courtyard; all matters here concern me."

Arsinoe pried his fingers off her.

"Yes," she replied, "I can see that your concern is a great boon to my sister and to Alexandria. What a wondrous job you've done, protecting her from Rome, shielding her ships from Caesar's flames."

"Those ships are no longer under your sister's control, as you are well aware. And Cleopatra knows they burn. She ordered it."

"I don't believe you."

Even if the galleys had fallen to Achillas, surely her sister would not have had them destroyed, the docks left exposed to an endless number of Roman ships. Arsinoe slipped by Apollodorus and walked toward the vaulted staircase to the royal chambers. She heard his footfalls pursuing her.

"Then you're a fool," he spat, voice trembling. "Cleopatra has chosen a path for Egypt and it is the *only* path. Without Caesar, your dynasty cannot stand."

"If that is true, then why not let me hear it from Cleopatra's lips? What danger do I pose, bearing what you tell me is old news?"

"You pose no danger other than nuisance. It falls to me to protect your sister's precious sleep, these few moments she has alone."

Arsinoe laughed.

"Do you believe that, Apollodorus? Do you pretend that she is alone? Perhaps we both cling to foolish fantasies."

She saw she'd hit a nerve. His face reddened and his lips sputtered. At his side his hand clenched into a fist. She wrapped her fingers around his whitened knuckles.

"I keep your secrets, Apollodorus. Allow me mine. Let me go to her."

She kept her gaze fixed at their enjoined hands, and when his fingers loosened, she knew she had won. Freed, she raced up the stairs two by two. Her nerves, until now almost numb, grew frayed. Everyone—Ganymedes, Apollodorus, even Alexander—thought her a child for believing that Cleopatra would heed any warning at all. And in her own heart, she knew she clung to wisps.

At the top of the steps, a pair of Roman soldiers guarded her sister's door. In her own way, Cleopatra was as much a prisoner as Ptolemy.

"Step aside. I must see my sister at once."

She steeled herself, readied her arguments, prepared to pitch her voice and demand admittance. But the two sentinels stepped aside wordlessly. Within, Cleopatra's native slave guided her to the dining lounge, the gold-encrusted chamber where the Piper had hosted his private rites. Here, she discovered her sister, bare elbows flush against the window ledge, eyes fixed on the flames. *She'd known.* Calm, unfazed, Cleopatra drank in the destruction. Arsinoe's throat tightened; she'd come on a fool's errand. Part of her longed to flee down the stairs, through the courtyard, and out the eastern gate.

Instead, she greeted her sister warmly. As the queen turned to face her, an apparition flickered: a crone aged twenty years, an adder clutched in her hand. Arsinoe nearly gasped at the lines that traced her sister's face, the dreary defeat in her eyes. But then she blinked—the hideous mirage vanished, the snake only a candle.

"You couldn't sleep either?" Cleopatra asked lightly. Arsinoe nodded; she couldn't muster words. "They are making quite a racket out there, my people."

My people, not *our*. Not so long ago Cleopatra had spoken to her in *we*'s, as though anything that belonged to her belonged to them both. Another lie—another intimacy—shed by the wayside. Once, Arsinoe might have collected them, these slights, but now they were far too commonplace to count.

"Come, watch the flames with me," her sister whispered, entranced, and Arsinoe obeyed. She took her place at Cleopatra's side and stared out the window. The dining lounge faced north and east, and so they could witness the ruin in its full, maddening glory. The conflagration had spread across the docks, and a fiery arm flexed its fingers westward along the shore. One blaze raged brighter than the rest, flickering its way toward the hulking library storehouses.

"You have to stop the fires—they'll swallow up the scrolls." Arsinoe pointed at the wooden edifices. She was reminded of a half-forgotten dream: the city was on fire and all the learning burned away.

Her sister looked on, unmoved. "Caesar has men guarding the flames—they'll put them out before they do more damage. They're only to wreck the ships."

"And you trust that?" she asked, unable to hold her tongue.

"Of course I do," Cleopatra retorted, staring at her with harsh, unblinking eyes. "To love someone is to trust him; he acts only in my best interests, and in Alexandria's."

"Love?" Arsinoe scoffed. Her rage boiled to the surface. Cleopatra no longer proffered Caesar as a means to an end—she presented him, and his *love,* as an end unto itself. "You place your faith in *love?* If that's what you sought, I wish you might have found it in a more convenient place."

"A lesser place, you mean."

"Yes," Arsinoe replied. "Since Rome stands as the pinnacle of greatness in your mind, then, yes, a lesser place."

"And what good, pray tell, Arsinoe, would that have done for me or Alexandria if I'd bedded some Judean king? Ptolemy would still be on the throne—and you and I would be battling desert winds."

"We had raised an army, Clea. We might have *fought*."

"We would have *lost*. What chance did our ragtag group of Arab tradesmen and Cypriot mercenaries ever stand against Achillas's troops? They were hardly worthy of the name *soldier*. If you wish to speak of soldiers—"

"Don't mention the ones that Caesar leads," Arsinoe snapped. "Those aren't yours. They never will be."

"How caught up you are in what belongs to whom. You sound like a wizened merchant scolding me for sampling too many of his wares. I know the Roman legions answer not to me but to Caesar. But Caesar..." Cleopatra paused, a rare blush creeping onto her cheeks. "Caesar answers to me; he is mine."

"No doubt Medea was just as sure of Jason in her day."

Cleopatra laughed. "What *furor,* what *bitterness*. Arsinoe, you are too young to have grown into such a cynic. Has your Alexander treated you that poorly? You might have a hundred other lovers, *better* ones, *useful* ones."

"Why? Would you whore me out to your lover's second-in-commands? I thought you'd already secured the Roman legions." She'd failed to keep the edge out of her voice.

"It would be less foolish, at least, than sleeping with the first boy who cast a mooning glance in your direction. Do you know how they mock you, Arsinoe—you, the daughter of the New Dionysus? Fucking some bastard boy?"

"I'm not—"

"Don't lie to me. Everyone knows what happened once I left the camp."

Her throat closed. It had been her moment then to keep the troops from revolting against their leaders, from scattering like so many grains of sand in the wind. And she had done it—she'd held them steady. Secure and armed and ready for Cleopatra's return. And this was how her sister repaid her, with recriminations about Alexander. *That* was what the queen remembered. Never her loyalty, never her strength, only her solitary breach.

Arsinoe fixed her eyes on the great fire licking at the storehouse walls.

"And do you know what they say about you?" Her words scarcely cut above a whisper.

"I know what they say about me, Arsinoe. I know everything that is said. But when you are queen, you must learn to ignore the naysayers. They know *nothing*." Cleopatra held her gaze for a long moment. "But I suppose, my dear, you will never be queen."

The words they had always been so careful not to speak suddenly divided them. Arsinoe couldn't—*didn't*—want to rule. She never had, she told herself, because to rule meant to wish her sister's death. But even when they were small and Cleopatra would babble on about when she was queen, she had never completed the thought. *When I am queen . . . and you are not.*

"You know, then, that they say you are a traitor." The recriminations poured forth from her lips. "That you've sold yourself to Caesar, Alexandria to Rome. And for what? A few days longer on the throne? A few more banquets? To revel as our father reveled, drunk and lustful and pathetic, a mere puppet suckling at the wolf's teat across the sea?"

Cleopatra's eye no longer twitched. It fixed on her in anger. Arsinoe recognized the hard, narrow look on her sister's face. A thousand times she'd seen it—aimed at their mother, or at Ptolemy, even at the Piper once or twice. But never before had it been directed at her. Whatever line they'd traced between them in the sand, she'd crossed it. That comparison to their father—more than any mockery about Rome or power—could never be unsaid.

"So I have become our father, you say, of no use to anyone. Will you rid yourself of me as you rid yourself of him?" Her sister's voice was glacial, merciless. Arsinoe bid herself to speak, but her tongue, so lithe a moment earlier, sank heavy and useless in her mouth. "Killing me won't prove as easy for you. I won't agree to do your dirty work."

Arsinoe had pictured this confrontation a thousand times over. The day her sister turned against her and the Piper's death sundered their bond completely. And what defense was left to her? On the nights when she couldn't sleep, it wasn't her father's ghost that haunted her but Egypt's, not yet dead but nearly so. Arsinoe didn't fear she'd overstepped in her flailing attempts to save her kingdom— she feared she hadn't done enough.

"Clea—" she tried to object.

"No, Arsinoe," Cleopatra said with crushing finality. "I won't listen to more of your evasions. Not now."

Below, the first of the storehouses went up in flames. Cleopatra didn't flinch—and Arsinoe couldn't remain another second with this impassive stranger. Instead, she slunk, a wounded animal, off into the darkness. For a brief, enfeebled moment, she slowed; she prayed that Cleopatra would call her back and beg forgiveness. That her sister would confess that her heart ached for the papyrus scrolls condemned to ash, that their city and its rich swaths of knowledge still held meaning for her, and then reveal the secrets of some larger game. Roughly, Arsinoe shoved those fantasies aside and brushed past the waiting guards.

As she descended the stairs, she felt the shades close in around her—all the men, and women too, who had died for her. *And up out of Erebus they came, flocking toward me now, the ghosts of the dead and gone.* She shook such thoughts away. She was no Odysseus; she'd made no sacrifices to part hell's gates—these were gloomy imaginings, nothing more. This silence, too, was natural. Even rebels, she supposed, had to sleep.

Deep within herself, some fragile thing—welded together by memory and longing—had shattered. She felt no pang, only an empty void where the love she'd shared with Cleopatra had once lived. Not just love, but all the hope and tenderness and expectation that she had clung to for her sister. Each breath, each step, ground the shards smaller and smaller until the break became irreparable. She couldn't fit the scrambled bits back together if she tried.

Ganymedes had been right, and Apollodorus too. Both had seen the truth that she had for so long denied: Cleopatra had tied herself, her fate, decisively to Rome's. She was too blinded by her need for soldiers—her *love* for Caesar was born of nothing more complex than that—and if the queen had to offer the double kingdom in exchange, sacrifice the library and the learning of their lands, she would. Alexandria would never place her trust in such a woman again, and neither would Arsinoe.

Regret began to nag at her: she'd played her turn poorly indeed. Cleopatra must already suspect her loyalties—she'd done little to conceal her rage. Arsinoe hurried toward the Sisters' Courtyard. She raced by her namesake's fountain and up the steps to her chambers. Within, she found her maid asleep on the divan, peaceful and snoring as though the world hadn't changed.

Arsinoe bent to whisper in the servant's ear, "Eirene." And then louder. "Eirene."

"What...?" The girl stirred, rubbing sandy slumber from her eyes. "My lady?"

"Find Ganymedes," Arsinoe commanded. "And be sure no one sees you. No one can know our business tonight."

Once the girl had gone, Arsinoe paced back and forth across the onyx. The stone lent her some stability; the rest of her had grown somehow unhinged. All the barriers she'd erected had crumbled, and the humors she'd bottled in her gut were free to roam her body as they pleased. Anxiety tightened in her lower back; euphoria pulsed through her veins. The lump in her throat swelled until she could scarcely swallow, and her lungs felt so shallow that she had to pant for breath. Her ears sharpened for the sounds of guards, soldiers come to trap her in her chambers. Everything fell to her now. She alone could rescue Alexandria from Rome. She would join her cause to Achillas and lead the disenchanted rebels against the palace. She would fight Caesar—no matter what the cost.

Where was Ganymedes? Ages had passed since she'd sent Eirene on her errand. Had she been betrayed? The thought stung—she'd felt a certain closeness to her maid. After all, they'd come of age together. Had Eirene turned against her? And why shouldn't she? What loyalty was owed Arsinoe, who cast off every natural bond—that of father and sister alike?

No. She wouldn't let her mind descend into idle conspiracy. If Eirene had deceived her, there was nothing she could do to save herself. As time pressed on, relentless, an uncanny calm fell upon her. The doubts faded from her mind, and her path stretched as straight and clear as the Nile on a bright winter's day. She would rebel against this proxy Roman rule, and she, the least likely heir to the New Dionysus, the second daughter of the second wife, would become queen. The twisting snakes that wound about her stomach devoured themselves, and she stared into the starless sky. Far off she could make out a breaking light, the thrashing of a new dawn. And she prayed to the gods of all things dark, to Hades and Apep and Erebus, to preserve the blackness of night a little longer.

The door cracked open and Ganymedes entered. Unlike Eirene, he had no sleep to rub from his eyes. In fact, with his fresh tunic and his satchel strapped to his side, he looked as though he had not been to bed at all.

"You called for me, my queen?"

Queen. She'd told him not to call her that—the title kindled too much torment. Arsinoe nearly admonished the eunuch for using it now, but then she realized: he knew, without even a word passing between them.

"I did summon you." She beckoned the eunuch closer—and then, noticing Eirene lurking behind, she motioned to the maid as well. The girl had served her faithfully, and she would know the truth soon enough. "We must leave the palace, tonight."

The eunuch nodded. She studied his narrow eyes, his thin jaw, searching for a hint of triumph. For years he'd poked and prodded her to cast off Cleopatra. Did he revel in his victory? If he did, he hid it well. His lips pursed, and then he let out a sigh.

"I feared this time might come," he said softly. "I hope you won't judge me too harshly for making the necessary preparations."

From the bag that hung at his hip, he unwound a spool of dull fabric. Only when its length was splayed between his hands did she recognize it as a tunic. Eirene sprung into action, her hands everywhere at once: unfastening the pins of Arsinoe's chiton, stripping the bracelets from her wrists, wiping the kohl she'd hastily applied from her eyes. Robbed of her royal accouterments, and nearly naked in the night's air, Arsinoe shivered. Mingled with the cold, another sentiment shuddered through her: a sense of freedom, levity. Shorn of the material markers of her birth, the very birth that had yoked her to Cleopatra, Arsinoe felt certain she might shear away her other sentiments. That her agonies might be discarded as easily as her jewels.

As Eirene slipped the rough-spun tunic over her head, the maid whispered in her ear: "I will come with you?"

The suggestion surprised her. Three, surely, would be spotted more easily than two—and she didn't think Eirene would be much use in a fight. As she turned over the idea in her mind, she caught a glimpse of her own reflection in the looking glass. She almost gasped at the sight. Dressed in the gray tunic—she recognized it now, the familiar garb of the palace slave, the same smock that Briseis and Eirene wore—she looked like one of them. She swallowed her vanity—so much the better. She'd draw little attention this way.

In the mirror, she saw Eirene's eyes wide with anticipation. The icy, empty part of her wanted to deny the maid's request—after all, her own dreams were tattered. But she did not succumb to the coldness that ran through her veins. She would not leave this girl to die, not as she'd left Myrrine all those years ago.

"Of course you will come with me, Eirene," she said, and in a fit of tenderness, she kissed the maid's brow.

* * *

This third smuggling felt little like the first. When she'd been a child of ten, the courts and corridors, plazas and fountains, had yet held a mystic quality. No matter how well she thought she knew the palace, it had always surprised her then—one wrong turn might lead into some long-forgotten garden of a great-great-uncle forgotten longer still. This time, she recognized the paths that Ganymedes chose: first twisting toward the library, then away through the practice fields. But when they'd reached the complex's walls, Arsinoe began to fear the eunuch had spun them into a trap—until Ganymedes ushered them down into a secret passageway she'd never seen before. Here the smell of smoke faded and the air grew stale.

"What is this place?" she whispered, stumbling on a rough patch of stone. "I've never even noticed it."

The eunuch's voice floated back to her. "It was built long ago, my dear, so that an embattled king might always escape these walls."

"And wouldn't this be precisely where Cleopatra would first think to look?"

"Do you really imagine your sister will look for you, Arsinoe?"

Arsinoe bit her lip and gave no answer. Instead, she listened to the footfalls cast behind her: Eirene's even step on the jagged stone. The girl's steadiness soothed her; it was a relief to have a companion besides Ganymedes. She had little hope for more—who knew if Alexander would follow her? She'd held him at arm's length, chiding him for addressing her in public and forbidding him from calling on her in private. She'd told herself she'd been protecting him, but now she saw she'd been merely cowing to Cleopatra's wishes. Her sister had shamed her for her relations with Alexander, and Arsinoe had been eager to hide them from the queen's sight. The humiliation gnawed at her.

At last they three emerged from the earth, reborn as Osiris would be at the end of days. Beneath the ground, Arsinoe had imagined they'd traveled stades upon stades—half a hundred, even—but she glanced up to find the imposing edifice of the Great Theater before her eyes. Outside the palace walls but close enough to see the action at the gates, the throngs around the western entrance. Now, and forever, she would be irrevocably on the other side.

The sight of the rebels, after so many nights of listening to their antics, made her blood tingle. As she drew closer, she saw they did more than heave stones. They'd built up great structures: spindly wooden cranes and sturdier-looking apparatuses with battering rams cradled between. Soon they would be able to send much larger pro-jectiles—even pitch and fire—against the palace gates. Achillas had done a far better job of organizing the city than she'd imagined. This looked to be a crowd not of idle dissenters but of well-ordered ones, prepared to tear down the walls themselves to free their king. And here, outside the citadel, she could discern the stinging insults, chanted in earnest unison: *Traitor, whore, handmaiden of Rome.*

In the end, Caesar was a Roman, and her sister had forgotten what Romans did best. They crushed empires: the Carthaginians and the Seleucids, the Achaean League and the Pontic Kingdom. Each one had fallen to Rome—and this Caesar was no different from the rest of his ilk. Already he'd burned boats and books: her dynasty's twin claims to greatness. He would reduce Egypt to a province, the Ptolemies remembered merely as another clan that fell to the She-Wolf.

All at once, as though on some unseen cue, the yells quieted to a murmur. Disheartened, she turned to squint up the main boulevard to find the cause. Had reinforcements already arrived from Rome? A different source emerged: Achillas, mounted on a great bay stallion.

"Do you smell that?" the general cried out as he cut through the throngs. As one, the crowd drew in its breath; she inhaled as well, searching out a hint of the smoke that had permeated her chambers. But here, among the hordes, all she could smell was the foul stench of unwashed flesh. "That, my friends, is *smoke*. Smoke from our ships, from our storehouses, from our *books*. That whore has burned them to dust."

A groan erupted from all sides.

"We will rebuild, and we will conquer. Cleopatra's treachery won't go unanswered." More shouts of agreement. The man at her side jostled for a better look. Achillas held up his hand to calm the masses. "Night after night you've steeled your resolve. I doubt the queen has slept a wink. Nor her Roman paramour."

"Nor should they!" one voice cried out.

"Nor should they," Achillas echoed. "My soldiers and I salute you—and it is with you in mind that we will storm the palace to free our king."

The general volleyed back and forth with ease. The body quickly rallied about the head, and Arsinoe steadied her gaze on Achillas's face. With each call-and-response, his eyes gleamed and his smile widened. He drank in the cheer as though he were a Ptolemy, not some lowly soldier who rallied for his king. Even if the commander succeeded in springing Ptolemy from the palace, Achillas would still wield the real power. The rebels—soldiers and citizens alike—cleaved to him.

"That's right!" a woman shrieked in her ear. Not any woman, she realized, dumbfounded, but Eirene. "They hold his sister too, the true queen!"

Arsinoe nearly stomped on the slave's foot—the girl might ruin everything. But then, slowly, surely, a cry rose up from among the gathered folk—they were changeable, and they latched on to her name. Stunned, she drank in their screams—their outpouring was intoxicating. Her star, she saw, had risen—these citizens loved not Ptolemy, not her puppet brother long controlled by his advisors. No, what they longed for was a queen, a true queen, the sort her sister had once promised she would be. Arsinoe forgot her rough-spun tunic, her naked wrists and face. She didn't need royal insignia to rule—she needed only to be bold.

She cut away from the eunuch and her maid and shouldered her way through the crowd, squeezing between the bodies of well-fattened men and knocking up against the knees and elbows of the starved. The stink was overwhelming; she'd grown unaccustomed to common folk, who bathed only for special occasions, whose skin was impregnated with a heady stench. But she bit her lip and pressed onward until she reached the circle that had formed around Achillas and his men.

There was no turning back, not now. She could never again be Cleopatra's little sister, her shadow begging and pleading, urging and nudging her toward the light. She'd become the light herself. Achillas had fallen silent, jaw agape in shock.

"Weep no more tears over Cleopatra's betrayals," she shouted up to him. "A new queen stands before you now."

Achillas and his cronies stared at her with blank eyes. She saw herself from their perspective: a serving girl raving as a lunatic. She straightened her back and stood tall. Her voice reverberated twice as loudly as before; perhaps—she allowed the thought to sweep her up—some god aided her, just as one had helped Odysseus: *Athena made him taller to all eyes, his build more massive now, and down from his brow she ran his curls like thick hyacinth clusters full of blooms.*

"For I am Arsinoe, escaped from Cleopatra's clutches, arrived here to lead you into battle."

A taut silence trembled, but then she heard a voice scream out her name. A second joined, and a third, and soon the air filled with chanting. Chanting, at last, for her.

For Arsinoe, the Sisterless God.

BROTHER

His days had settled into a pattern. At dawn, he'd wake to the grunting of the Romans at their drills: archery practice and spear tossing, cavalry rounds and foot races. The same paces Achillas had once put Ptolemy and his companions through. He'd lie in bed as long as he could stand it, listening to the thud of swords, the laughter of men not much older than himself. He'd imagine what his absent friends might say. How Kyrillos would mock the soldiers' groans; how Ariston would moon over some javelin throw.

In the afternoon, he was permitted to wander the royal gardens. The privilege, proferred after Pothinus's death, puzzled Ptolemy. He couldn't say what he'd done to earn it. Perhaps his stoic behavior in the stadium had impressed Caesar. Or, more likely, Cleopatra merely enjoyed granting and denying his freedoms on her capricious whims.

These walks did little to assuage his loneliness: the gardens were always empty when he arrived, bereft of life save flowers and rose-bushes. Did some crier clear the grounds before he entered? Or perhaps he met no one because no one wished to meet him. That was how the palace functioned: rats flee a sinking ship; moths flock about the flame. Like Icarus, high courtiers and lowly slaves alike would dart as close to Cleopatra as they dared. Some would flail or even die for their insolence. But if Cleopatra stood at the hot center, he was on some marooned and desolate island.

It was this aching solitude—more even than the circumscription of his days and steps—that taunted him. He scolded himself for caring. In every way that mattered, he'd always been alone. Even with Ptolemarion clamoring at his side, even with Pothinus—dead, headless Pothinus—breathing in his ear, even with Briseis sucking on his cock. He should never have mistaken any of *that* for real kinship.

His mother was the only one who'd ever loved him, and what sort of man—and at fourteen, he *was* a man—could rely on only the woman who'd birthed him? And where was she now? Cleopatra must keep her prisoner too. The queen had always hated their mother. Perhaps his sister had already ordered her dead. Ptolemy couldn't dwell on such questions—there was his own skin to worry about.

At night, at least, he had the rebels for company. He listened to their shouts with something akin to joy. He needed this sole scrap of evidence that he hadn't been forgotten, that somewhere outside the palace Achillas performed the duty his other councilors shirked: fighting to restore his throne.

Tugging the covers over his head, Ptolemy trapped himself in blackness. Though the heat was smothering beneath the blankets, he preferred it this way, cocooned from the sights and sounds of his old rooms. Even the Argonauts spun onto his walls mocked his current plight. Heracles and Nestor laughed at him from their swift-winged boat—and Jason, at the prow, laughed hardest of all. He was being childish, curled in his ball of self-pity—he saw that—but he didn't know how else to be. Somehow he had to draw the Roman to his chambers. Then, suddenly, he hit on a solution. He'd refuse to eat until Caesar came to treat with him, man-to-man. The Romans wouldn't be so barbaric—or so foolish—as to let him starve. Not when it would incite the mob.

And so Ptolemy left the next morning's eggs and bread and dates untouched, and skipped over the midday meal as well. At first, his hunger fortified him—he felt stronger, the master of his future. But as the day wore on, his stomach grew less cooperative. By the time the sun had crept from Dionysus's bare torso onto his inky beard, his hunger pangs twisted in earnest. No matter which way he sat, whether he stretched his stomach taut or curled inward on himself, the pain only stitched itself deeper. His resolve flickered—would his starving even accomplish anything? As far as he could tell, no one paid much attention to whether he ate. The servants who cleared his platters away never said a word about the untouched hunks of bread and cheese, the dates he'd left out to wither in the sun. No one even cared if he slept whole days away.

Did Arsinoe fret over him? Somewhere she must roam the grounds—at times he was certain he could feel her fitful presence. Ganymedes had told him that she might change, must change, but what sign was there that she would? When he learned the store-houses had burned—some twenty thousand scrolls, copies for the most part but some originals as well—his heart nearly burst with hope that she might break with the queen. Arsinoe had loved those books—perhaps even more than she loved Cleopatra. But it was a fool's faith. Days faded, and no news came. Perhaps her feint in his direction had no bite—merely another lie added to his ledger.

He tried to sleep, but his dreams were haunted: an eagle tore at his liver. When he woke next, his belly groaned in agony and his head pounded. He pressed the pillow over his ears, but that didn't drown out the pain. In fact, the thudding seemed to reverberate around him, through him—pulsing into his fingers and toes, echoing throughout the room. He couldn't hide from it, so he peeked out from beneath his covers to check for something else he might clamp over his head—and then he realized the banging wasn't coming from within. Someone was at the door.

So soon. His throat went dry. Months—he'd thought, when he'd dared think of it at all—would go by before Cleopatra gathered up the nerve to execute him. After all, the better part—or at least some part—of the populace rallied to his cause. And surely his sister hadn't forgotten the violence a royal killing could yield. The specifics escaped him, but on his better days he could recall precisely how many of his forefathers had been torn down by angry mobs after dispatching with a more popular relation. Some wife or uncle or sister. But, he supposed, none of that made much of a difference to the murdered regents.

"Enter," he shouted boldly—and regretted it at once. What a picture he'd make: still in bed, weak and moaning from hunger. He should have taken the time to dress before he was led off to his beheading; instead, he sprung up, half naked and nerves jumbled, and stared stubbornly at the door. At death. In whatever form it might take.

Caesar. Relief flooded his veins—his death, then, wouldn't come today. The general had a thousand soldiers under his command who might murder him instead. But perhaps this embrace of duty to its darkest ends divided men from boys. If the Piper had wielded the axe that severed Berenice's neck, would that have staved off the whispers of weakness?

The Roman ducked his head to enter, as though he were too tall to cross beneath the lintel otherwise. Despite his thinning hair and the web of wrinkles about his eyes, the general projected that same image of crude, almost colossal strength—his legs solid and forceful, his arms thick and sinewy with veins. His fingers looked powerful enough to crush a grown man's skull—perhaps they had. Ptolemy wouldn't have been surprised. He blinked away the image, the blood running from some soldier's eyes—and prayed that wouldn't be his own end. Surely his would be grander—the gods, at least, could grant him that. On a battlefield, not murdered in his chambers at the hands of a man he'd been foolish enough to call a friend.

"I trust you have everything you need," the general said lightly, like a solicitous innkeeper confirming his guest's comfort.

That was Caesar's game, then. The Roman imagined he could pretend to be amicable, that Ptolemy would be dull enough to buy the act. Anger flared alongside another hunger pang, but he tamed both back.

"I do," he answered flatly. "I've found my own servants to be nothing but hospitable."

The Roman ignored the gibe. He took a seat on one of the divans. "Will you take a drink of wine with me? There are some fine vintages in the cellars."

Was Caesar mocking him by recommending his own casks? He studied the general's face, but he couldn't catch even a hint of a smirk. Though Ptolemy—stomach empty of all but bile—had no desire to drink this early in the day, he didn't dare say no. Few insults were graver than a refusal to share wine with a guest—or was *he* the guest now, in his own palace? A prisoner was a type of guest, he supposed. The gods themselves might be forgiven for confusing the rules of hospitality under circumstances such as these.

"Come, sit." The Roman gestured to the divan next to his, a red one stitched with gold. As a child, Ptolemy had preferred that perch above all others—he'd scream and stomp his foot if Ptolemarion so much as glanced in its direction. What he wouldn't now give for such ordinary pleasures—a brothers' petty quarrel. Was Ptolemarion imprisoned too? Or had Cleopatra already begun to sink her talons into the boy, grooming him for faux rule . . .

Ptolemy forced a smile and settled onto the proffered couch. "It would be my honor to drink with you."

Lies he could conquer; his dignity was more difficult to muster. Dressed in his night things and stinking from weeks without a bath, he hardly felt like a king. But he *was,* and this Roman—no matter how magnificent on the battlefield—was merely one more man infatuated with his sister. Ptolemy had seen these symptoms a thousand times before—even their own father had fallen prey to Cleopatra's charms.

A few moments later, a slave entered with a pitcher of wine. As Ptolemy watched the milky liquid splash into his goblet, he was relieved to find it pale and honeyed. With any luck, it wouldn't spin his head too quickly.

"To Egypt, may she rise and prosper," Ptolemy proposed, lofting his glass high, daring the Roman to meet his toast and declare himself a hypocrite. After the damage he'd wrought, how could Caesar pretend to care a whit about the kingdom's fortune? After he'd burned the city's boats and books?

Unhesitating, the Roman raised his goblet in return, echoing the words agreeably, as though Ptolemy had proposed a cup to the god of wine or health or any such ordinary pledge. Caesar lacked even the decency to blush; instead he drained his wine noisily. Ptolemy, in contrast, took only the smallest sip of his own. He had to cling to his senses or he'd never stand a chance of convincing Caesar—to what? To let him go? To let him rule? His mind already throbbed with barbs.

As he watched the Roman twirl his goblet between his fingers and cast his gaze about the chamber and back again, Ptolemy realized, to his puzzlement, that Caesar was at a loss for words. The general was famed for his quick wit almost as much as for his prowess in war. Why, then, did the man lean forward on his divan, tongue-tied? Was he plagued by some inkling of remorse?

Ptolemy couldn't believe that any of the fellow feeling Caesar had lavished upon him had been genuine. And yet—the man did lack a son. Though the Piper had never taken any particular interest in him, Ptolemy knew most men prized male heirs. Romans most of all. He could hear the fled Theodotus's whisper in his ear: *Watch a man's motions—you'll learn more of his purpose from his sighs than his words.* More attuned to this imagined rhetoric tutor than he'd ever been to the real one, Ptolemy studied how the Roman planted his feet firmly on the floor, bracing himself against the onyx rather than relaxing onto the couch. But try as Ptolemy might to parse some definitive meaning from these signs, he failed. Such games always eluded him. Even little Ptolemarion could intuit feelings and impulses, actions and reactions, better than he.

At last, the Roman cleared his throat and looked Ptolemy directly in the eye. "I am grateful for this meeting," he began in steady Greek. "I would hate for us to be enemies, you and I."

Those phrases grated too, the suggestion that blame stained both their hands. It was Caesar's fault—not his—that they were foes. But Ptolemy swallowed away his anger and inclined his head in interest as though—he hoped—to say: *Very well, Julius, go on. I'll hear you out.*

"These past weeks haven't been easy for you, I know," Caesar continued. "They haven't been easy for Cleopatra either. She can hardly sleep for worry over this misunderstanding between you two."

Ptolemy, choking back his laughter, coughed instead, hard into his hand. So hard he nearly drew up blood, and he worried that perhaps he was ill, dying, that his wine was tainted with wolfsbane. *Nonsense.* Caesar wouldn't poison him in private. His, he suspected, would be a public execution.

"I might worry too," Ptolemy answered once he'd recovered his breath. "The city is in quite an uproar."

He thought he saw the general's upper lip twitch. Was that doubt? Anger? Madness?

"Do you think that will change your predicament? Will your beloved Alexandrians rescue you?"

Despite the tenor of the questions, Caesar sounded more curious than cruel. There was even a slight gleam of humor in his smile.

"They might," Ptolemy answered defiantly.

Sadly, slowly, Caesar shook his head. "I wouldn't pin your hopes on that, Ptolemy. The mob is a fickle beast. And for the moment, it seems, they are distracted by your sister Arsinoe."

The name took him by surprise—Arsinoe was among the last people he'd expected Caesar to mention. And how could *she* be distracting the mob? Before he had time to consider what to say, before he had time even to think, he stammered back, "Arsinoe? What's— what's she—?"

He cut himself off, but it was too late. His words couldn't be unsaid. He should have guarded his surprise, pretended that he'd already known all about Arsinoe's moves.

Shifting forward on the divan, the Roman screwed up his face, his eyebrows crowding over his aquiline nose. His mouth tightened into a scowl. "What game are you playing at?"

That reaction startled Ptolemy—more even than the revelation about Arsinoe. His mind spun over the possibilities. His sister had done something—something incendiary, even—though he had no idea what. And now the general suspected him of being in league with her? Some small, sour part of him wanted to laugh at the notion. And then he realized what tactic he had to follow, one that he'd already set on even before he'd recognized its wisdom. He needed to convince Caesar he was neither a conspirator nor a threat. That he was a mere boy longing for the Roman's approval. And then, perhaps, he could discover what Arsinoe had done—and what it meant for him.

"I'm not playing at any game," Ptolemy whined, making his voice sound as plaintive as he could.

The Roman's expression softened slightly.

"I do worry, though, to hear my people so upset," he went on, testing this new strategy. "Especially when I must worry that they'll turn their anger against my dear sister Cleopatra, even against you."

Caesar appeared to relax at these words: for the first time since he'd entered the chambers, the general leaned back on the couch. Before he spoke, he took another hearty swig of wine.

"The Alexandrians are quick to cast about their anger," Caesar began through purple teeth. "And so Arsinoe's escape will fan their fury, but not for long. Soon they'll recall the suffering rebellion brings. Their little ones starving, begging up at them with wide and hungry eyes..."

Arsinoe's escape—the syllables drummed in Ptolemy's head. Had he heard correctly? Or was his own hungry mind playing tricks on him? As the Roman carried on about wives and children and all the sundry cares that might remind the citizens of what they stood to lose, Ptolemy fixed his mind on that phrase. *Arsinoe's escape*. The words were slippery—too sweet to be true.

"I must bore you," Caesar said, his tone growing rough again. "You think you've had me fooled. Convinced me that you knew nothing about your sister's escape. Now answer me honestly: what do you know?"

Escape, again. Arsinoe *had* fled the palace. At last, she'd betrayed Cleopatra—just as Ganymedes promised she would. Ptolemy didn't know whether to laugh or weep. And he had known nothing—though it pained him, he knew he should admit that much. Spin his ignorance into a larger lie.

"I wanted to believe the best of you." Caesar sighed, resting the bridge of his nose between two fingers. "I wanted to think that you wouldn't have played a part in such antics. But I suppose Cleopatra—"

"I knew nothing," Ptolemy interrupted. "I knew nothing of Arsinoe's intentions. I was . . ." His voice trailed off. He squinted as though fighting tears. "I didn't want to say because I was ashamed. Ashamed that I hadn't been taken into her confidence."

This was new, he realized. This melding of lies and truth. New and tantalizing: how easily the words poured forth.

"It's been so difficult, Julius, when I've been all alone and with no one to trust. And to realize that even Arsinoe would betray us . . ." He let his voice trail off, as pitifully as he could manage.

"It surprised me, too, Ptolemy." The Roman softened, looking up from his fingers. "Arsinoe had always seemed so loyal to Cleopatra."

"And now the people are even angrier," Ptolemy said slowly, almost gasping. "And they will tear the very palace to the ground."

"Nonsense, my boy," Caesar replied. "They'll do no such thing. Besides—it's you they want, not Arsinoe."

Ptolemy made a show of wiping his eyes before looking up at Caesar. "Is it?"

"Of course. They worry about you even now. They obsess over your absence from public life. What sort of people would choose a female heir when they could have the male?"

"And not just the male," Ptolemy tested. "But both brother and sister. With me *and* Cleopatra on the throne, there will scarcely be a man alive who'd dare question us. That was what my father wanted. Even your Senate far off in Rome would be pleased."

"Yes, Ptolemy." Caesar smiled and the wrinkles smoothed about his mouth. "Not even my Senate would question that."

"Is there—" Ptolemy stalled, feigning nerves. As though he feared he'd already overstepped his bounds. Perhaps he had—perhaps he *should* be frightened. The vision of Pothinus, his eyes rolling in his skull, lodged itself vividly in his mind. But for once, no part of him quaked in fear. "Is there anything I might do?"

Caesar's mouth tightened—the general was trying to read between his words and work out whether he could be trusted. Ptolemy bristled at the irony—after all, it was the Roman who'd deceived *him*. He had treated Caesar with generosity and respect—and then Cleopatra had wormed her way into the man's bed. He hoped she suffered over Arsinoe's betrayal, and that bitterness would congeal around her heart, just as it had hardened around his.

Finally, the general spoke. "There is something you might do. As I told you, the people worry more for your health than for anything else. Perhaps if you might speak to them—"

"I'll go to them," Ptolemy replied too readily—the offer so tempting, he couldn't stop himself.

"It's not safe for you to leave the palace," Caesar answered. "But if you might address these men from within the gates, and assure them that you are well and that all you want is peace. That you are ruling at Cleopatra's side and have no desire to be vaunted as a symbol of war. Might you be able to do that, Ptolemy?"

"Yes." He nodded eagerly, childishly.

Naïveté was his best mask, the one that would hoodwink Caesar and the rest. They all thought him lost without his advisors and his champions. In his heart, Ptolemy had feared he might be lost as well. And yet somehow he wasn't—even with hunger clawing at his innards, he felt stronger and surer than before. The blood of Alexander the Great, the Conqueror, pulsed hot through his veins. This wasn't the victory he imagined—this victory of shadows and lies—but it was *his*. Cleopatra proved herself with trickery, and he would do the same.

"You know that all I want, Ptolemy," the Roman told him quietly, "and all your sister wants, is for you both to rule Egypt in peace."

"That's what I want too. That's all I've ever wanted. And if you of all men think—if you think there's even the slightest chance that my addressing the rebels might help in that endeavor..." Ptolemy bit his lip and glanced up at Caesar through his lashes, as he'd seen Cleopatra do. The sheer absurdity of it made him blush, but he aped her expression just the same.

"You have the instincts of a good king." Caesar shook his head sadly. "If only you'd been better taught how to face the trials that power brings."

The Roman's words played so naturally into his hand that he could hardly believe his ears.

"Perhaps you could teach me now?" Ptolemy implored, coating his voice with longing. His own simpering sickened him. The Roman's too. Even Caesar, this greatest of men, had been unmanned by Cleopatra. She'd seduced him into a shadow of his former self. Ptolemy hardly needed the advice of such a creature to overcome the obstacles in his path.

A true smile spread over Caesar's lips—his contentment seemed to warm the room. That, Ptolemy realized, was why men loved him, for that grin that reached his eyes and wiped away his years. "One day, my boy, but first you must come and speak to your people."

Ptolemy trailed Caesar out of his boyhood chambers, down the stairs, and into the courtyard where he'd once played. He followed, small and silent. He still wasn't sure which part of his act had charmed the older man. The wrong word might send him back to his rooms.

As the two neared the palace gates, he could feel the hatred surging from the very ground. He heard the voices too. "Ptolemy, the Father-Loving God," they cried out, demanding him—whether to king him or kill him, it was hard to say. At some earlier, lesser time he might have felt fear. But he had shed his cowardice. He would face his people as a man, as their king. And for now—only for now—he would tell them to keep the peace. To keep it until he could find a way to join them and take his rightful place at the head of the brewing rebellion. He held his face blank and solemn; he couldn't let Caesar suspect his treacherous thoughts.

SISTER

A messenger came, whaling at the door. Arsinoe sprung from her bath, an ordinary copper tub—a far cry from the golden ones in the palace, an ivory rim its only mark of luxury. The room she occupied belonged to the master of the house, a ferrety-looking man who'd greeted her that first night and then faded into the walls, fearful of drawing too near this half queen. Shivering, Arsinoe wrapped a shawl around her shoulders and called through the door: "What's happened?"

"My queen, my queen," the man shouted back. "Your brother speaks. He addresses the throngs from the western balcony."

She was inclined to rush out as she was—mad, undressed, reveling in the moment's heat—and hear what Ptolemy had to say. But she couldn't cave in to such impulses. She'd pulled off the serving-girl-turned-queen ploy once—she knew better than to test its power again. This time, she needed to present herself as a queen, a goddess trapped in human form. And so she bade Eirene fashion her in the Greek incarnation of Isis, crimson robes crossed between her breasts, a shining diadem on her head. The girl painted her eyes with kohl, her lips with kermes; she brushed her hair with oil and pinned its plaits to form a coronet.

In the courtyard, bedecked in pearls pilfered from her host's wife, Arsinoe felt at once radiant and exposed. Her skin prickled in the outside air, beneath the eyes of the half-hundred soldiers who crowded the courtyard, crammed into entryways and between the columns of the narrow colonnades. One man in particular caught her eye, the army's second-in-command—Laomedon, she believed, was his Greek moniker, though his crown of taut curls marked him as Egyptian. Unlike Achillas, a Rhodian imported to instruct her brothers in the ways of war, Laomedon had made a name for himself by working his way up through the ranks. She noticed the deference accorded him: the way the infantrymen gawked at her and then glanced at him for approval. Here, she thought, was a man whose support she might wish to win.

The streets thickened in chaos. The usual coterie of rebels joined by flocks of shopkeepers, artisans, and even noblemen in bright embroidered tunics—all were drawn by word of Ptolemy's appearance. By the time a path was cleared down the Boulevard Argeus and her litter arrived at the royal complex's western gates, her brother had long since vanished, whisked back into the palace by Caesar's men.

The crowd still murmured, thirsty for his words. From what she could gather from the echoes coursing through the throngs, Ptolemy had bid the masses to stay peaceful. Declared that Cleopatra was his queen and pledged his loyalty to her. The mood had shifted; an uncertainty wafted in the air. The same boys who'd hurled rocks and built up battering rams at Achillas's bequest milled about listlessly. A round-faced woman, baby swaddled against her chest, glared openly at Arsinoe's litter, another loan from her rodent-like host. Unlike Achillas's soldiers, who had fallen so easily beneath her spell, the mob viewed her as an upstart, a lesser sister with little claim. The diadem felt flimsy on her head, another pretense of queenship. Even shielded by the litter's walls, Arsinoe grew conscious of her body, her movements, her very breath—how each could be found wanting.

These commoners loved her brother, she realized. Or at least loved the idea of him. Neither she nor Cleopatra nor even their father had ever discovered anything particularly remarkable about the boy. Of her two younger siblings, she'd always preferred Ptolemarion—he had a sweetness to him she recognized. One that she'd long since shed herself but ached for nonetheless. And yet somehow it was Ptolemy—not Cleopatra, not herself—who had enchanted the plebes. Now the mob jockeyed against its masters, unsure whether to tear down the palace gates or subside into the doldrums of its day-to-day. Whatever her brother had said, whatever feeble plea he'd made for peace, she needed to manipulate those words, mold them to her will. It was not enough to stand alone—she needed to bind herself to him.

Her litter shuddered to a halt. Something, someone, blocked her path. Voices raised in argument—the sound of flesh smacking against flesh. The soldiers who escorted her vehicle would have no qualms resorting to violence in return. The scene played fitfully in her mind: her men striking down the troublemakers, the next day rebirthed as martyrs for her brother's cause. Her feint at rule tattered to shreds before it had even begun. Alexandria brought once and for all under Rome's heavy thumb. *No.* Already she'd sacrificed too much—given up Cleopatra and every bit of kindness that had lingered in her soul. She would not sit idle as this last dream was wrenched in two.

Instead, she cast aside the curtains and slipped out of the carrier. Not even the litter bearers seemed to notice the lightening of its load. Despite her finery, Arsinoe felt impossibly small. Though the crowd had cleared a narrow corridor to let her pass, she couldn't see over the surrounding helms and heads—could barely make out the portico from which Ptolemy had addressed the crowd. She glanced from the gold-twisted gates to the stretch of the Boulevard Argeus behind her. Among the sea of people, there was no high ground she might climb upon to speak. All at once, inspiration struck—she hoisted herself onto one of the litter's poles, ignoring the startled gasp of the slave at its helm, and then, as gracefully as she could manage, she scrambled up on top of the vehicle. Its roof was slightly arched and she teetered for a moment. By the time she found her balance and straightened herself to stand, a cluster of nearby men had turned to stare at her.

"I love my brother, the king," she yelled. "And I know him well. Those of you who know him as I do must sicken at this day's deceit. Not only has Caesar stolen our palace and burned our boats, occupied our city and set our scrolls to flame, he has gone so far as to threaten the king's life. My brother is fierce, he is the torch that burns through the night—he would never ask you to submit to Roman rule. Not unless he had no choice. This *meddler* has threatened the king's royal person, forcing King Ptolemy to speak words that aren't his, to beg for peace even as he yearns— as we all yearn—to shake these Roman shackles from our city. I know my brother; I love him as a husband, as Isis loves Serapis. He would never abandon you, his people. Not when you've shown him the depth of your loyalty."

A few men cried out in support, tentative at first. One youth, a scrubby boy of sixteen or so, who'd been weighing a rock from hand to hand, made up his mind and flung it at the palace gates. Its thud cracked the crowd wide open. They hurled their rocks and roared in solidarity. For a moment, Arsinoe luxuriated in their screams. But she couldn't delude herself for long. It wasn't her they wanted—it was Ptolemy.

In the days that followed, their love for her brother proved enough. Enough to cut off supplies to the palace and send Caesar and

Cleopatra fleeing to the western part of the city, which, Arsinoe supposed, they imagined would be easier to secure in a siege. Her return at the head of her own army to the palace complex should have been triumphant. But once she reached the royal chambers, still dewy with Cleopatra's effects, her gut ached for all she had sacrificed: she'd bartered one sun to circle a lesser one. Arsinoe found herself scouring through her sister's clothes, her perfumes, searching for some note, a sign that their sundered bond still held by a thread. Something that would let her pretend, even now, that Cleopatra wished to comfort her, to soothe away her disappointments as she always had before.

No. As her sister had *once,* but not in years. Cleopatra had long rejected her. The image of her sister she clung to was a mirage. Her *real* sister was the one who'd left her weeping on the docks, who'd abandoned her on the battlefield, who'd sold Alexandria to Rome. Time revealed everyone's true colors, and Cleopatra had shown hers. How could there be love lost when there'd been no love to begin with?

Arsinoe distracted herself by searching for any clue that might reveal her sister's plans. The decorations had shifted from their father's rule. Where once the satyrs of Dionysus had piped along the walls, Cleopatra had hung tapestries of bare-breasted Isis, her robes knotted between her breasts. In one depiction, the goddess clutched the baby Horus, suckling at her teat, as the rising Nile threatened to envelop them. Rumors had teemed that her sister was with child, but Arsinoe hadn't known whether to believe the talk. Now—dwarfed by depictions of the deity and her infant—its truth struck her as obvious. Cleopatra had cast herself as Isis, and a babe born of the world's most powerful man would seal that imagery. It would also bind Egypt to Rome for generations to come.

"Your Cleopatra has chosen a different sort of chains,"

Ganymedes called out from the threshold. "Ones that tie her to the greatest of the undying goddesses and the most poignant of prophecies."

The eunuch appeared small beneath the enormous ebony door-frame, his shoulders hunched. His droopy eyes looked pained, as though he, too, mourned a betrayal.

"She's hardly my Cleopatra anymore," Arsinoe replied.

"As you say," Ganymedes agreed. "And the less so the better. Achillas asks you to meet with him, to discuss what moves we should next make against your sister and Caesar."

"The general summons *me?*" Arsinoe asked. "How much he takes upon himself, this Achillas."

Her voice was laced with honey. From the eunuch's expression, she saw he shared her fears. The palace wasn't safe from whispers. Even here, within the royal chambers, she didn't trust that no one listened. Who were these servants who tended to her needs? To whom did they owe allegiance?

"I suppose we must go to him, then. He waits in the great atrium?"

The great atrium, Arsinoe left unsaid, *where I will sit upon the throne.* Ganymedes nodded, and the lump thickened in her throat. It was a tantalizing image: herself on the gold-carved seat, directing whole armies to do her bidding. Even as a child at her nursemaid's teat, she had known the price of rule, a price paid in blood. Not long ago, she would have been content to sit by Cleopatra's side and bask in her sister's sun. That warmth had filled and anchored her. It would have been enough—if only Cleopatra hadn't set her eyes and loins on Rome.

Once Arsinoe quit the royal chambers, the tales she spun to comfort herself chipped and cheapened. Nothing was as simple as she pretended, and already she was untangling the past and molding it to her desires. In her heart, she was no longer sure of what might have contented her. Perhaps her ambition had always burned as fiercely as Cleopatra's and as Ptolemy's, demanding not merely a few sticks to stoke its flames but whole forests, empires.

Scores of soldiers swarmed outside the atrium, summoned, no doubt, by Achillas. He meant to intimidate her—that much was evident. As the guards parted to clear a path for her, Arsinoe caught sight of the man himself. The general's breastplate was stained by blood, rusted with sweat, a far cry from the pristine one he'd preferred when strutting about the practice fields with Ptolemy. This war-worn version, she supposed, was meant to impress his ragtag band of Cicilians and Gabinians, Galatians and Syrians. Among this last set, she spotted a few familiar faces—men who'd once, a lifetime ago, belonged to her sister Berenice's first husband. How many rulers she'd seen rise and fall. She could only hope Caesar would prove no different from the rest.

Her entrance teased the eyes of the soldiers from their conversations and onto her. Their gazes lingered on her diadem and her richly styled gowns. Noticing the shift in mood, Achillas sprung into action. A few loping strides brought the general to her side, grasping her arm, guiding her toward the throne. She shrugged away his grip—she saw his game: he wanted to dictate how she was presented as queen.

"Your concern is touching," she murmured, "but quite unnecessary. I can walk well enough on my own. I've had years of practice."

The smile slipped from the general's face. "I intended no offense. I merely wanted to reassure my men that we are friends."

"Indeed," she answered, casting her gaze across those gathered. "And what a great number seem to need reassuring."

"Only to be expected in times of such uncertainty."

The title he omitted echoed in her ears: *My queen, my queen.* She couldn't trust this man—he was too hungry to remind her of how shaky her position was. *My queen, my queen.* Even unspoken, those words called treacheries to mind. Perhaps the nomenclature served the same purpose for every monarch. Even Cleopatra—vaunted Cleopatra—was coronated in murder and betrayal.

As Arsinoe neared the chair, its previous denizens offered themselves up to her: her father, Berenice, her father again, and then Cleopatra, Ptolemy. Each face bloomed and withered before her eyes. Perhaps that was the seat's true potency: its ability to make quick work of its occupants. She shunted her worries away and sat.

"These are troubled times." She addressed the room, glancing from Achillas to a set of Gabinians, crowded in one of the small archways, to Ganymedes, who stood in the other. The eunuch winked; she drew strength from that. "And your service to Egypt will be remembered by both me and my brother. You are the sword of the kingdom, we the soul. We have already cast the Rome lover from the palace, and soon we will wrest the whole city from the She-Wolf's clutches and cast her legions back into the sea."

A few of the younger men whooped gleefully—the sort quick to proclaim their keenness at any call to fight. The battle-tested soldiers watched her with wary eyes. They wouldn't be so quickly won.

"Now tell me, Achillas." She beckoned the general to her. "What did you wish to discuss?"

The man stared her down, an unfamiliar ferocity in his gaze.

"It would be best to speak of such matters without an audience." He dared her to call him on his impudence. He'd never meant to talk strategy before all these men—only to taunt her with their presence.

"Rest, enjoy the wonders of the palace. Soon the real fighting shall begin," she announced, her eyes fixed on the general. He gave her a thin-lipped smile.

The Galatians and a few others began to file out, but most

loitered until Achillas gave a curt nod of dismissal: another reminder of where the army's allegiances stood.

"What news do you have that requires such secrecy?" she asked before the general had a chance to speak, tugging the conversation to her terms.

"Not so much as I would like. Your sister and her consort"—Achillas refused to call Cleopatra by name—"have set up blockades along the Boulevard Aspendia. They only need to buy time. Caesar has already sent for reinforcements from Syria and Cicilia; until they arrive, he seems happy to hole up with his whore."

His tone dripped with disdain for Cleopatra. No doubt he felt the same way about Arsinoe. The general had never liked either of them, and her hatred of Achillas calcified as he spoke. He was, she realized, one of those men who loathed women regardless of their attributes, whose life was fixed by some deep hatred of the female sex. If she had the power to dismiss him, she would have done so at once. But the army owed its loyalty to this man, so she had to stomach his contempt as best she could.

"We must find a way to make that option less appealing, then. To flush Caesar out of his hole before he's ready to fight."

Achillas snorted. "You speak as though this were some simple matter. The city's southern and western edges are guarded by a wall, a marsh, and a canal. Caesar's men have already barricaded all the adjoining streets."

Condescension oozed from the man's pores. As though she were some child who knew nothing of strategy. She'd prove him wrong. One by one, she pored over relevant battles in her mind: Scipio's capture of Carthage and Alexander's of Tyre, even the long-off sacking of Ilium. She could model herself as Odysseus in this too, discerning the breaking points and weaknesses of those within, where they would hold and where they would break. And who would be better equipped to outwit Cleopatra than she? Who more familiar with her sister's faults and foibles?

The choice of location was clearly Caesar's; no Ptolemy would have forsaken the royal docks for the Harbor of Happy Return. It was far easier to launch ships from the eastern port adjacent to the palace, with its gentler tides and proximity to the Pharos lighthouse. The sunset side of the city had other disadvantages too, ones that Cleopatra, forever spirited away by their father, wouldn't have considered. Arsinoe closed her eyes to picture the broad boulevards and the winding alleyways, the canals and subterranean streams that pumped water throughout Alexandria. And then—she stumbled upon the answer. She could hardly contain her glee.

"Do you know what's particularly remarkable about this city, Achillas?" she asked. "It has a network of underground channels that supply water to every private home within its walls."

"I am aware," the commander muttered, "of Alexandria's great feats of plumbing."

"Did you also know that the city slopes downward from east to west, and that the fortress to which Cleopatra and Caesar have retreated actually stands on *lower* ground than the palace?"

"I don't see why—"

"It would be, I fear, rather easy to corrupt that water supply without affecting the palace complex and the surrounding quarters."

"To taint such a large amount of water would take a great deal of—" Achillas cut himself short, as though to mention poison, that most womanly of weapons, would mar whatever little honor he could claim.

"Yes, it would," Arsinoe said, smiling. "But we don't *need* poison. Who needs poison when we have a sea at our disposal?"

After a few feeble protests—rooted, Arsinoe suspected, more in his aversion to following a woman's plan than to contaminating the water—Achillas embraced the proposal readily enough. It was Ganymedes's plodding over maps, pointing out which cisterns should be pumped full of salt and which spared, his careful tracing of each aqueduct and its subsidiaries that occupied the afternoon. By the time the details had been settled, the hour had grown late. The moon played hide-away among a few rare clouds, but as it peeked through, she noticed it was full, a swollen orb tempting all Alexandria to pluck it from the sky. As a child, she'd been sure a full moon brought good luck, but that certainty had faded with age. Who could say what that sphere might portend.

A chill had crept into the air, and Arsinoe hurried past the soldiers who lined the colonnades, soldiers whose loyalties were opaque to her. As twisted as her own. Something felt wrong, changed and sinister, about the palace, dank even, though it hadn't rained in weeks. If anything, the clouds overhead marked the better omen, the riper one. The sentinel guarding the stairs that led to the royal apartments stepped aside to let her pass; she thought she caught a knowing grin twinkle on his lips, but perhaps her mind played tricks on her. The night was dark and rife with dark imaginings.

Other figures haunted her as well. Berenice begging on her knees, her head rolling across the floor. And her father's face: first, as it had been that day of her sister's execution, cold and hard and implacable, a face that had suffered a thousand insults at the hands of Rome. And then a fresher iteration: a weak man whose greedy hands reached out to her living sister, desperate to drain what little life he could for himself. Her toe struck hard against the edge of the step, and she cursed loudly at no one and nothing.

"You should watch more closely where you walk." A voice, teasing and familiar, had emerged from the darkness. A man followed: Alexander. Dressed the part of the Roman soldier in his red-pleated tunic, he blended easily among the Gabinians. Their remaining

314

legions now formed the backbone of the Egyptian army, the most formidable force fighting against Caesar. In a way, she supposed, these erstwhile Romans had the most to lose.

"What sort of welcome is that?" Alexander asked, slipping his helmet from his head and tossing back a few curls.

"What sort of welcome do you want?" she returned.

"A warmer one than this," he told her as he descended, closing the space between them. Between his height and his advantage on the steps, Arsinoe found herself level with his chest. He'd been riding that day; she could smell horse on him—the cloying odor of hay and manure mixed with his own uniquely Alexander scent. There was a comfort, a safety in that smell, but she refused to be sucked in by it. She felt weary, suddenly, and old. Too old to play these games. Rather than crane her neck to meet his eye she sidestepped, pushing past him up the stairs.

"Arsinoe," he cried after her. "Arsinoe."

She ignored his calls. She heard his footfalls following her, and these, too, she ignored. To run would show fear—or worse, some acceptance of his game. His hand clamped around her wrist. She stopped, staring at his fingers.

"Is that all, Arsinoe?" Alexander pressed against her back. His breath was a hot mist on her neck. She felt small and fragile—nothing like a queen at all.

"We are in the palace, Alexander. I am your queen. What more did you expect?" She thought of the royal chambers and the many trysts that had unfolded there. Of the great canopied bed that had so recently cradled her sister and her Roman lover. The bed of her father's death, her sister's lust. "You should leave. And address me by my title."

In one fluid motion, Alexander pushed her shoulder and spun her body to face him. His breath tasted of something sour, wine left to linger too long. What impudence, to come to her drunk and demanding. This new Alexander troubled and thrilled her in equal parts. As she looked into his gray-green eyes, familiar yet flecked with something brutish and untamed, she realized that she'd long imagined him as an extension of herself. Destined to be loyal to her cause—whatever cause it might be on that day—just as no part could ever turn against the whole. But *this* Alexander, even more so than the one who'd sought her out in the desert, operated on his own terms. He didn't retreat the moment she asked him to, shrinking from her harsh words, tail between his legs.

"Very well, my queen," he whispered in her ear. The hair rippled along her neck. "I did expect something more."

He kissed her long and hard, with a fierceness she hadn't anticipated. Even though they stood just outside her chambers, within eyesight of a half-dozen guards, his hands crept up her sides, stroking her throat, her breasts. As one, they stumbled up the remaining steps and into the royal rooms, scattering maids and soldiers in their wake. Before they'd even crossed the antechamber, he'd started clawing at her robes, sending pins spinning from her chiton. By the time they'd reached the bedroom, she was nearly naked, wearing only a thin sheath, translucent in the moonlight.

Alexander lifted her onto the bed and stared at her a long moment, drinking her body in. And then he loosened his belt and hoisted up her sheath. At once he was inside her, hard and fierce, rutting against her. She bit her lip to keep from crying out—she couldn't tell from pleasure or from pain. Where had he caught this wildness, this vigor? He no longer treated her gently, like she was some delicate, breakable thing. She reached her fingers into the hair at the back of his neck and tugged—she needed to hold on to some wisp of him before he vanished into lust. His thrusts grew faster until she felt him twitch between her legs. He collapsed and rolled off to the side, his arms draped loosely around her. He fell asleep so quickly that she wondered—briefly—if it all had been a dream.

As she watched his chest rise and fall, her mind wandered to her sister. Across the city, did Cleopatra, too, lie awake, watching Caesar's breaths? Or had she snuck from her lover's bed to wander the keep alone, as she so often did when she was troubled? Had she wept when she learned of Arsinoe's treachery, wept for the two innocent girls they had once been? For the children who'd traded confidences in the night? Or had she merely shrugged and turned back to her paramour and said: *It is nothing, Julius, merely news of a sister I once had.*

Cleopatra's voice grew serpent-like, hissing along the dusty desert roads, deeper and deeper into the sands. Soon the road disappeared altogether, and Arsinoe squirmed across the rough, uncertain earth. The dryness transformed her throat, that whole long mass of self, into scorched wasteland. She slithered forward, onward—the scent of blood teased her. And there it was, the only liquid, a crimson leak against the sand. She twisted over its thickening river until it pooled before a corpse. A peeling corpse dressed for war, a vulture helm atop his head. A corpse with a familiar, sneering face. And then the breeze grew stale; a taste of something else teased her tongue: smoke.

Arsinoe awoke violently—nearly bashing her head against Alexander's as she scrambled from the bed. Her mouth still choked with ash, and she rushed to the basin. Ignoring its dirtied waters, she scooped a handful into her mouth. It tasted foul—yesterday's washing—but she didn't care. She drank down every filthy drop until she was choking, sputtering. Alexander rushed to her side, his brow furrowed.

"What's the matter? Are you ill?"

His concern restored her senses. She forced herself to swallow, and though her mouth still felt dry, the taste of ash had dissipated. A dream, nothing more. She shouldn't make a scene—not before this new Alexander, unfamiliar and capricious.

"It's nothing. I was thirsty. I'm quite well," she said firmly.

"You're not well, Arsinoe. Come back to bed." He slid one arm behind her shoulders and the other under her thighs, scooping her up as easily as he might a child.

Gingerly, he laid her down on the bed and wrapped the coverlets around her frame, as though to cocoon her from the horrors of the world. Then he curled his arms about her and whispered, "Was it a night terror?"

Her whole body tensed at the question. It wasn't safe to lie with him. He drew his power from her secrets, from his knowledge of her past. Arsinoe wrested free of her blankets and his limbs—her life had no room in it for the leisure of whispering confidences in a lover's ear.

"Where are you going?" Alexander pleaded. Here she caught a glimpse of her old friend, the weary sadness in his eyes. "It's been weeks since we've spent a night together . . . I thought we might—"

"You should go," Arsinoe snapped. "Eirene needs to dress me for the day."

"Arsinoe." His voice strained. "What's the matter? I thought . . ."

She had to keep him at arm's length: every time he drew too close, she shoved him back, rough and unsettled, into his place.

"Last night," he started, "I thought—I hoped you would be glad to see me. I'd kept my distance—I wanted to come sooner, but—"

"I was pleased, Alexander." His whining needled her. "But my world doesn't revolve around such pleasures. We are at war. Don't

318

you see that? I am fighting my sister and allied with my brother, and there are a thousand other—"

A shriek cut through her words, sharp and piercing. It knocked away the years—she was a little girl again, watching her fire-bearded guard struck down. A death she'd foreseen—a death she could have stopped. She rushed toward the door.

"Arsinoe, wait," Alexander implored. "Let me go first, let me see what the matter is." *Please,* his eyes begged. *Let me do at least this much.*

"Fine," she answered. "Go."

She had wanted to be alone, and Alexander seemed so very anxious to be useful. This way they would both be satisfied. The shriek meant nothing, she assured herself. Perhaps one of the fussier maids had found a gorged rat while cleaning behind some tapestry. Arsinoe focused on more relevant concerns: Once the water supply was pumped with seawater, it would be easy to turn Achillas's mind from Ptolemy. The general owed much loyalty to the boy, but surely his loyalty wasn't limitless. Her brother's charms lay in his exterior—the fact that he was male, the heir by rights—but she had other advantages to offer. Besides, the longer Ptolemy was absent, the more the army would cleave to her. What other choice did they have? The men could hardly hope to be welcomed back by Cleopatra.

When Alexander returned, he was ashen, paler than she'd ever seen him. His expression frightened her—his trembling lips seemed to belong to some withered crone, not the boy who'd raced her through the gardens, not the soldier thrusting inside her at night.

"What's wrong?" she prompted when he failed to form words.

"He's dead," Alexander croaked. He cleared his throat and repeated the senseless claim. "Achillas is dead."

"Dead?" she repeated, as though her dumbness might breathe life into the man. And then, dumber still: "You cannot mean *dead*."

"I didn't believe it either." Alexander grew more confident as he spoke. "And then I went to his chambers, and I saw it, Arsinoe. He was lying stiff on the floor, drenched in his own blood."

Her heart beat against her breastbone; not the quickened pace of a rabbit but the steady thud of panic. The army had little cause to love her—and the tales of her arguments with the general had no doubt already spread. The palace walls seemed to close in around her—she and Ganymedes and Alexander surrounded by twenty thousand of the general's sworn soldiers.

"Caesar's men?" Arsinoe heard herself ask. A stupid question, unworthy of her. Who else could have wormed their way into the palace and committed such an act: sneaking into Achillas's chambers and stabbing the man in his sleep? And yet—the means didn't sound like Caesar's. He was too concerned with false honor to carry out assassinations; his knowledge of the palace was paltry at best.

"No," Alexander was telling her. "It wasn't Caesar's guards, nor Cleopatra's either . . ."

But that made no sense. If not their enemies . . .

"Of course it was Cleopatra's men. Don't talk nonsense, Alexander." An image flickered in Arsinoe's mind: Ganymedes glaring loathingly at the general. She tried to push the thought away: the eunuch took too much upon himself, she knew, but surely he would not be so foolish as to have done this.

"What will you do, Arsinoe? The men will soon hear what has happened. I ordered guards to seal the door, but something like this cannot be concealed for long." His eyes glinted with fear, with worry for her. But she wasn't afraid of soldiers. Not anymore.

"Of course." She pitched her voice deep. "Such a thing cannot—should not—be hidden. Such a tragic act as this. This death, instead, must compel us to action. Send for Ganymedes at once—and

Laomedon too. We must push forward with our plan, the plan that will prove our salvation: we must pump saltwater into the wells."

"The wells? But, Arsinoe—saltwater poisoning. It's a cruel way to—" Alexander cut his tender objections short. "Of course, my queen. So it will be done."

BROTHER

No matter how he tried, Ptolemy couldn't sleep. His stomach roiled, though the room remained still. It felt unnatural after so many weeks of shaking. Here, in the western fortress, he was walled off from the raucous rioters who shouted his name, raw with rage. He should be pleased—his speech had stirred aggressions rather than quieted them, and still Caesar didn't suspect his motives. He played the role of naïf well—perhaps too well. He feared it wasn't a role but his true self—he was the child the world had always cast him to be. In their escape from the palace, he'd only had a few guards watching him. He should have been able to shed them in the chaos. Instead, his courage flagged and he'd gone along with his captors, trailing Caesar and Cleopatra even in defeat.

His limbs chilled as he slipped from beneath his coverlet; the new hairs he sprouted up and down his arms, dark and thick, stood in salute. Nerves had stripped his appetite, and all childhood chubbiness had melted away. His body fit him strangely; his knees and elbows jutted out at angles. He was no longer sure how to fold them or manipulate their length. He laughed harshly at himself, at this, his misplaced vanity. Even with his newfound height, he knew he was no Adonis, no Ariston.

Groping at the unfamiliar walls, he made his way to the window. The moon had begun to shrink again, and the flames of Pharos barely penetrated the wooden shutters. He cast them open; in the light-house's glow, he could squint out the contours of the shore. There was, of course, nothing to see—only the sea lapping and lashing against the beach. He willed himself to hear the voices of the mob, to bask in their fury. They were the reason he lay awake at night, dreaming up ways to gain Caesar's trust, so he could join in their common cause: to rid the city of Cleopatra and Caesar both. Let the pair rot in Rome; they were dead to Alexandria.

His dream drew so near he could almost taste it. After years of listless hopes and prayers, of plotting with his mother and lusting in his bed, he could at least celebrate that Arsinoe had come to her senses. She would be in the palace now, perhaps even gazing out on this same scene—at Pharos's bright beacon. She'd been the first to explain the meaning of the fire to him; by the time he'd returned to Alexandria after his childhood exile, he'd forgotten it. Or perhaps he'd been too young to notice the lighthouse before his father's flight to Rome and his eldest sister's ill-fated rule. Either way, it had been Arsinoe who'd told him what it was and what it meant. *It lights the path for sailors, so that any Alexandrian can always find his way home. Even you.* And in that moment, curled into his sister's side, he'd first realized that *this,* this was home. That he belonged in the palace, and that he'd never belong anywhere else.

Ptolemy planted his elbows on the ledge and leaned out into the cool air. Far off across the bay, Pharos's flames flickered, drunken, dancing in the waves. Nothing but beach and sea spread out before him. He closed his eyes to listen, as though depriving himself of one sense might heighten the other, might let his ears travel to the other side of the bay.

"Don't abandon me," he whispered to the night. "Come and rise before your king."

He listened harder still, sharpening his ears to each cicada chirp and each crash of waves below. But there was nothing, no response. And what had he thought would happen, anyway? No one could hear him—not locked away in this half-abandoned fortress, hidden from the fray. The mob had already forgotten about him and embraced Arsinoe as queen. His sister had been reared in the palace; she knew its ways. She bore a strange, almost obsessive love for Alexandria— the city would sense that too. Or perhaps they'd abandoned her as well and returned, as he'd bid them, to Cleopatra. A knock sounded somewhere in the distance, but he dismissed it as some trick of his imagination.

He would be remembered—if he was remembered at all—as the boy who'd cowed to Caesar. No one would ever know that his speech had set the foundation for a rebellion. He shook his head. Those thoughts befitted the old Ptolemy; self-pity was beneath him now. He was wiser than that.

A throbbing in his ears. That knocking again. Who would bother him so late? The other Ptolemy, the scared and frightened boy, would have trembled at the noise, fearing that guards had come to murder him, that Cleopatra had ordered him dead. But *he* knew better. It was the dead of night, and a soldier wouldn't rap the wood so gently.

He walked to the door, flinging it open to whatever fiend might enter. In the lamplight, he saw the last thing he expected: a nymph, with smooth skin and ruby lips, and bright, bold eyes. No, not a nymph. *Arsinoe*. His thoughts had summoned her—impossible. He was descending into madness. He shut his eyes and counted slowly to ten as the swirls of reds and golds danced on his lids. When he opened them, the mirage had vanished. A woman stood before him, true. But it wasn't bright, bold Arsinoe. It was Briseis, sheepish and meek.

Briseis, who had betrayed him. Who had stolen his love-sotted whispers and spun them into treason. Who had slipped from his bed, his semen still dripping from her cunt, to sell his secrets to the highest bidder. And this, he realized, *this* was Caesar's version of a reward. How *daft* the Roman must think he was, for what sort of fool would embrace this creature after what she'd done. She was to blame for Pothinus's murder, for Theodotus's disappearance, for the fact that Arsinoe—not he—would free Alexandria from Rome's grasp.

"Get out," Ptolemy spat.

"My—my king," she stammered. Her lower lip trembled. She was dressed in the light linens of a goddess, and he could see the dark spots of her nipples beneath the flimsy fabric. The costume bore little resemblance to the rough-spun tunics she typically wore. Someone had arranged for her to be clothed and curled, coiffed and painted to perfection. But that wouldn't sway him.

"You don't understand—I had no choice—. You don't know what it's like . . . " Her lies were thick with tears. "I knew they'd never hurt you, but me—I'm—. Please listen."

"Don't tell me what to do. Have you forgotten your place so quickly?" He dug his nails into his palms.

"No, my king," Briseis answered breathily, falling to her knees. Desperate, she seized his hand in hers and pressed her lips to his palm. Her eyes, wide and frightened—but hardly innocent—pleaded up at him. And despite himself, that look stirred something inside him, something cruel.

"I told you to get out. I won't tell you again." He tore his hand from her grasp and stared at it. Her paint had smudged and left a mark, a traitor's mark, on his skin. He rubbed it roughly with his palm.

"No, my king, I beg you, please—" She crawled toward him. Her fingers traced his calves, his thighs. "I haven't forgotten my place."

He felt his cock hardening, the blood rushing from his head, his tunic tenting about his groin. This he'd missed. And the wounded part of him, the wounded boy, grew scabbed and coarse. He didn't have to trust her. He didn't even have to like her. He'd been a naïf to think he must marry his sweeter sentiments to his baser ones. He could fuck her, and he could hate her too.

Briseis's fingers—*that whore's fingers*—closed around him. Her lips followed, soft and wet and sweet. Almost at once, he felt himself tensing, ready to release. But, no—he wouldn't be won so easily by her, by *that whore*. He knotted his fingers in her hair, so carefully arranged, and pulled. *That whore.* She'd tricked him when he trusted her; he forced her mouth harder on his cock. Her head pushed back against his grasp, but he wouldn't let her catch her breath. *Let her choke, let her die.* He hated her as he hated the world, and every man who'd turned against him. He wanted her to cry, to weep, to beg. He wanted her to suffer as he'd suffered. To take on all his sundry humiliations as her own.

When he'd finished, he watched as she collapsed, gasping, to the onyx floor, her tears mixing with his milky seed. He spat. Not on her, but near enough. And when he told her to get out, Briseis—*that whore*—did his bidding. She scampered from his room and fled. Alone, he crept back to his bed and snuck beneath his blankets. And *he* did not weep.

Sheltered by the rooms Cleopatra had chosen as her makeshift apartments, the small courtyard lay quiet long after dawn had stretched over the horizon. Here, the barracks with their clomping guards felt distant—only the sputter of water broke the silence. The very sound set Ptolemy licking at his chalky lips. He stopped himself— it wouldn't help; after long days without fresh water, his tongue was dry and swollen in his mouth. A solitary fountain graced this private garden; a lone nymph, her rich colors faded in the sun, bubbled merrily into the stone basin. The salt didn't seem to bother her. His own throat was parched; saltwater belched from every spigot, and only Cleopatra, it seemed, had access to the untainted kind. The rest of them made do with beer and unwatered wine—stiff, strong stuff he could scarcely stomach on the best of days. And even that wouldn't last forever. So when Cleopatra had invited him to break his fast with her, he'd agreed. He would have agreed to nearly anything for a sip of pure water.

When he stepped inside, he was surprised to find his sister alone, reclining on a threadbare divan. For once, Caesar was nowhere to be found. Despite her dimmed surroundings—the faded murals of Ptolemy the Father-Loving's Persian wars had been stripped of their gold plate; the fort had seen happier days—she spared no expense with her own costume. Her ears dangled with heavy pearls, and her wrists were so laden with gold that Ptolemy was amazed she could lift her hands to eat.

Though the rest of their company, him included, had started to take on a sickly pallor, his sister's face glowed a radiant bronze. Her belly had just begun to round beneath her chiton, and the pregnancy had softened other parts of her as well, widening her hips and filling out her cheeks. In short, she looked the picture of good health. He hated her for that—but when she offered him a gold-encrusted goblet brimming with water, he grabbed it at once.

As he raised the glass to his lips, his hands quaked with anticipation. The water touched his tongue and his head spun. He'd wanted to take only a small sip—to pace himself—but his self-control faltered. The liquid tasted so sweet, so soothing. He tilted the goblet farther back and let the water rush down his throat until he'd drained the cup dry. He stared at its mirrored bottom longingly, as though he could will more liquid from its depths.

"Easy, my sweet," Cleopatra said, stopping his hand with hers as he reached for the pitcher. "We must make it last."

Her face smoothed into a mask of sympathy. Another mask belied by her mocking words. His fury swelled; the liquid sloshed about in his belly. He thought, suddenly, of Briseis as he'd last seen her, weeping at his door. She'd come to him again, after the complex soured with salt, to beg for water. He'd had none to give her, but he didn't tell her that. Instead, he smirked and slammed his door. *Let her throat parch with thirst.* Something had wrenched inside him the moment he'd spat on her, and no matter how he tried, he couldn't soothe it.

"Yes, we must be careful," he replied evenly, though what he wanted was to spit on Cleopatra as he'd spit on his whore. "I'll drink more slowly."

Cleopatra lifted the edges of her mouth, the sort of half smile she used to give their father. She squeezed his hand and then let it drop.

"Father and I used to share our morning meals together, when I took on the role of his consort. He liked to begin this way—discussing the great matters of rule before we were overwhelmed with the day's minutiae." She paused, testing his reaction. Ptolemy kept his face blank, his own mask. Behind it, he laughed: he couldn't picture the Piper proposing anything of the sort.

"I thought, perhaps, that you and I—as king and queen—might revive that tradition," his sister continued in her most honeyed tone.

Ptolemy forced a nod. He still didn't know what to make of Cleopatra or her lies. At least this time he could recognize that she was lying. Their father hadn't led some secret life in which he fretted over the plebeian matters of rule.

"Julius . . ." the queen mulled, eyeing her goblet as she swished its contents from side to side. A droplet escaped and arched through the air before settling, a spot of dew on the stone floor. He watched its wasted path with longing. "Julius seems to think that I should trust you. That you are loyal to me alone. That no part of your heart sings each time that cursed and rebellious army batters at my gates."

A lump swelled in his throat. He tried to soothe himself; what could Cleopatra do to him now? *Caesar* was convinced of his cause, and she didn't dare contradict the Roman. Not head-on. His sister could be bewitching—a sorceress who blinded men with her wit and words—but Caesar had armies.

She glanced up at him again, that same flirtatious smile darting over her lips. "I'm afraid that I'm not so easily fooled. Julius is too trusting—he forgives his own enemies when given half a chance. We don't see eye to eye on such matters. He hasn't lived through years of treachery . . ." Cleopatra let her voice drift off as she took another lingering sip of water. His throat felt so dry that the smallest flint could set it alight. "You've always taken Arsinoe's side, always been partial to her. I know you'd rather rule with her."

"That isn't true," he objected. "I want to rule with you, as your king, as I told Caesar—"

"Don't lie to me, Ptolemy." His sister sighed. "You aren't any good at it."

"I'm not *lying*—"

"Enough." She lifted her palm to silence him. "I didn't call you here to argue."

If she wanted him silent, he'd stay silent. He set his gaze on his hands, one thumb folded over the other. His nails had worn away these past few days, not from work but from his incessant chewing at them. The habit had become second nature; he didn't notice when he did it, but looking at his bitten fingers, he felt sick. As king, his body was sacrosanct, an extension of his divinity. He shouldn't treat it so carelessly.

"You are so alone, my sweet," Cleopatra said sadly. "I know how comforting it can be to cling to someone. Even if you know it's only a delusion. A dream of the person that you wish her to be."

Ptolemy let the words wash over him; they wouldn't penetrate.

"I, too, was taken in by our sister. I, too, believed that she loved me, that her loyalty lay with me, with us. That we would rebuild this great kingdom together. Her brazen act of betrayal forced me to recognize the cold truth: that Arsinoe cares for no one but herself."

He caught a glimmer of it now, his sister's appeal. Her voice was almost enchanting. He could listen to it for hours on end.

"Her treachery cut deep," Cleopatra went on, quaking. "I wept for days. But her treachery against you is more painful still. She murdered your most faithful friend."

His eyes snapped up to meet his sister's. "What do you mean?"

Cleopatra paled; the healthy glow drained from her cheeks, and her expression wilted. "Oh, my sweet..." Her voice caught in her throat. "I thought you knew."

A ruse, Ptolemy told himself. Another trick of Cleopatra's. He would not be drawn in. And yet—how could he say nothing? He had no other link to the world outside, no other means of uncovering the facts. His best bet—his only bet—was to hear his sister out and try to parse truth from the lies.

"What did you think I knew?" His heart beat a marching pace beneath his ribs.

"Achillas is dead."

The words knocked the wind from his lungs. That wasn't possible—it defied reason. And yet Cleopatra made it sound so very true. His strength ebbed from his limbs, pooling on the floor. One by one his advisors had been stripped away, and now he was left naked as hulled wheat. Even his mother was gone; he'd heard neither hair nor hide of her in weeks. Had Cleopatra brought her to the fort? Or had his sister murdered the woman before they'd fled? Did his brother lie dead too? No, Ptolemy reassured himself. Ptolemarion had his uses. More likely, Cleopatra had trundled the boy off somewhere, a new king lying in wait for the moment she despaired of Ptolemy.

"Arsinoe had him murdered," Cleopatra continued. "It is hard to recognize the truth about those we love. Her betrayals wound me too."

Water welled in his eyes. He blinked away the tears. Now more than ever, he had to stick to his plan. Heart steeled, he looked up at his sister.

"And for my part, I owe no loyalty to her. My allegiance is to you and you alone."

SISTER

In her dreams, she drowned. Salt choked her throat and nostrils as she thrashed against the willful waves. When she fell, her feathers melted by the sun, she'd transmuted into a woman once more—her flailing arms as useless as her wings.

Arsinoe woke, twisting against Alexander's limbs. Her thoughts spun toward her sister. Some stades west, licking at her wounds, Cleopatra, too, would wake in the arms of a lover. Did she suffer such dreams? Once, Arsinoe had believed they two shared every-thing, but that closeness had been a lie. She had no notion of what portents came to Cleopatra, whether her sister, too, flailed in the salty depths of the sea.

"Hush, my love, my queen," Alexander whispered, his breath hot against the back of her neck. *My love, my queen.* The same appella-tion Seleucus had bestowed on Berenice, in the half-forgotten past. Every time her own lover spoke those words, she thought of her sister's murdered husband, of how he'd tricked Berenice into mar-riage, tried to tame her into submission with sweet words and rough hands. Did Alexander remember? She imagined not—why should he be haunted by Berenice's fate? He hadn't watched as the queen wilted beneath Seleucus's gaze, bruised like a rotting peach, until she found the strength to cast off his hold. He hadn't watched as the axe kissed her sister's skin, before it slammed down to sever her bony neck.

Alexander's efforts to calm her grew more fervent, fingers curling into her hair. His other hand slid along her side, stroking the rise of her hip, the curve of her breast. All shyness shed. He'd grown accustomed to her body, the liberties he might exercise on it. Not so long ago, the brush of his thumb against her palm would have set her teeth on edge—what a child she'd been then. They were man and woman with each other now.

He pulled her close, molding her form into his. His tenderness was edged with something else, though—she could feel him harden against her back. Perhaps Ganymedes had been right to warn her against letting Alexander share her bed. *Other men will grow jealous,* the eunuch had told her. *They will hate you for choosing a favorite. Their longings can work to your advantage—but only if they know these yearnings have no hope of being rewarded.*

But she was *queen,* or so she demanded to be named. Her father had afforded himself all sorts of debaucheries; the legends of his perversions still haunted the satyr-decked colonnades. Surely she could allow herself this small pleasure. She would forgo decadence; she had no desire to drape herself in lapis lazuli and pearls, to plate yet another palace in Nubian gold. Alexander was her one indulgence. His steadiness tethered her, and though she hated to admit it, she knew she needed to be tethered. His arms kept her from crying out at night; they bound her to the ground, and his fingers brushed away the cloying cobwebs of her dreams.

"Another nightmare?" He kissed her lightly behind the ear.

"It doesn't matter. It was only a dream."

That lie—*It was only a dream*—had become her mantra, and she clung to it fiercely. To cross the threshold of morning, she needed to believe that her visions had no place in daylight.

Outside her window, the dawn was red, a smear of blood over the sea. The sight recalled her to her duties: the aftermath of Achillas's death put her in a precarious position. Much as she'd disliked the general, he had been her strongest link to the army, which now was cast into chaos. Rumors swirled that she had ordered the commander's murder, and she didn't know whether to embrace or jettison them.

She castigated herself for her complacency. Secure in the palace, sleeping in the royal chambers, she could too readily imagine she'd achieved some victory. A desert mirage that flaked if she gazed at it too long. It was high time to rise and face the horrors of the day. No—that construction, too, was wrong. Better to wrest control from the Fates and decide her horrors for herself. Her troops needed a battle to cleanse Achillas from their minds. To date, their confrontations had consisted of scant skirmishes—tussles with Caesar's forces as they tried to find fresh water. Here and there, the remnants of her navy sunk a stray Roman vessel, but more often than not both sides withdrew before real damage was done to either. A triumph would clear the stench of death.

The coverlets, Alexander's twining arms, the nascent sun pouring through the arched windows—it all stifled her. Arsinoe pried away her lover's fingers and stole out of bed.

"What's the matter?" Alexander asked, affronted. Despite his soldier's body, his battle-hardened arms and calloused hands, something of a child emerged each time she left him. His eyes held a longing for those forgotten days of youth when they'd truly belonged to each other. She wasn't his. She never would be. Not now that she was queen.

"Nothing, my sweet. Night is over and I must meet with Laomedon and Ganymedes." She forced a smile to her lips. His hand reached out to her, and he kneaded her fingers between his. "I wish I could linger here all day . . ."

The lie curdled between them. Though he had never admitted

as much, Alexander—she suspected—would be content with a simpler life, one she could never offer him. The sort that played out after the final lines in some Menander comedy, where after overcoming a myriad of obstacles, the youth wed the bride of his dreams. The vision formed an unspoken barrier: the two of them rearing children on some fertile patch of earth in the Marshes or the Upper Lands, far from the capital and her sins. In her heart, she knew she'd stolen something from Alexander. His love for her denied him all ordinary joys.

Outside, the morning proved unseasonably warm, so she shrugged off her sticky woolen mantle. This Emergence had proved strangely dry as well, and though she knew she would curse the drought come Harvest, the odd weather worked in her favor. The lack of rainfall made the salt poisoning of Cleopatra's garrison all the more devastating. She thought of her sister, belly heavy with child. Did thirst squeeze her throat? Did she cry out for water—pray for some splash of rain?

Here, in the great courtyard, the guards sweated through their winter tunics, leaving looping stains beneath their arms, below their necks. Even the dolphins skirting across the pebbled path looked wilted in the untimely heat. The city's vaunted winds, like so many of Alexandria's denizens, had fled, waiting for pleasanter days to return.

In the royal atrium, she came upon Ganymedes and Laomedon. A great cedar table now dominated the room, its surface spread with a dutifully inked drawing of Alexandria and its environs. The two were bent over it, pointing and muttering at one another. Arsinoe felt a flare of disappointment—she'd wanted to arrive first, to examine the squiggled shorelines and fiddle with the ship markers on her own rather than present some half-formed battle plan.

"My queen," the eunuch said first, invoking her proper title, his head bowed. In private, he still called her Arsinoe from time to time, but he was careful not to do so in front of anyone else.

It was Laomedon's reaction that she studied with more interest. Arsinoe wanted to like the man. His story was appealing yet reassuring: rumor held that he'd begun life so poor his mother had sold him as a slave, and after he'd managed to earn his freedom, he'd climbed the ranks of Egypt's army. His loyalties, though, were more difficult to parse. To be sure, he straightened at the sight of her, casting aside the slouch of an ordinary man and transforming himself into one worthy of command. Another costume that slid on and off his frame with ease—one, evidently, he didn't bother to employ in front of Ganymedes.

Laomedon greeted her: "My queen, you rise early." Did she catch a hint of accusation in his voice? Arsinoe shrugged away her paranoia—she'd seen what a millstone it could be, how Berenice had heaved at every slight.

"Any movement in the harbor?" she asked as she approached. She doubted it; Caesar hadn't made a play in days. And then her eyes fell to the map. Caesar's fire had destroyed most of the fleet, and she knew the place of each and every one of the vermillion remainders. But as she looked now, she counted only thirteen decked galleys and a handful of open ones. Yesterday, her four-banked ships had numbered seventeen.

"What happened?" The urgency mounted in her voice. "My fleet has shrunk from seventeen decked ships to thirteen. Where are the other four?"

Laomedon slumped at her admonishment but held her gaze.

"We had a defeat last night," he replied. "One ship was sunk, and one was captured; the other two were stripped of their men, and we have not yet accounted for them."

"Why am I only hearing of this now?" Arsinoe lowered her voice, glancing about to see who might be listening. To her relief, she counted only six sentinels, a pair at each of the archways. "Why didn't you tell me of the battle *before* it had been fought? Who ordered such a maneuver?"

Laomedon rested one elbow on the table; a small groan escaped his lips as he let his weight lean onto it. As Arsinoe examined him more carefully, she saw why he'd been so hunched when she arrived. He was injured—a bandage bulged beneath his tunic and he favored his right side.

"I did, my queen," Laomedon answered. "The men grew restless, and there was a single ship—a Rhodian one—docked some stades away from the rest. It seemed an easy target, and so we went after it." His hand cupped his side as though it hurt to speak, but she felt little sympathy.

"I will say this once and only once: every military decision goes through me. Ganymedes," she said firmly, shifting her gaze to the eunuch, "you will serve as commander in my absence. Laomedon, you may address the troops, but you are not to follow your *whims* as to when and whether to attack."

Even in her anger, she kept her face and voice steady. Implacable. Too often she'd seen her relatives spin off into madness—she'd watched it with her father and both her sisters. One skirmish, one mark on her ledger, nothing more. Better to focus on the needs she might fulfill rather than the failures of the past, and what she needed now, desperately, were ships. Ships would bolster her troops and their morale. The fire had cost them nearly a hundred galleys—an unthinkable number. Arsinoe leaned over the map and traced each line with her forefinger. The blue pawns—the greater part of the Roman fleet—clumped along the western harbor, whereas her own crimson crosses gathered at the royal docks. If he had any sense,

Caesar would soon attack Pharos—even a paltry understanding of the tides would tell him he'd have better luck docking his reinforcement there. For now, the island lay in her control, but for how long? She *needed* more ships. Her eyes drifted eastward along the Nile's seven mouths.

"Tell me, Ganymedes, what sort of galleys exact the customs duties at the river's maws?" She tried to picture them firmly in her mind, but she'd only ever traveled by two of the Nile's mouths and certainly had never been stopped by the tax ships while sailing on the royal barge. Those vessels would be large and imposing, though. If there was one matter her father had taken seriously, it was collecting tariffs.

"They are four-banks, my queen," Ganymedes responded. His eyes brightened and she ignored the great bags beneath them, the lines about his lips, and pictured him as the smooth-faced eunuch of her childhood, before the years had gnawed away at him. The illusion was passing; his whole body had succumbed now to age. The weight he'd shed in the desert had never fully returned, and his skin hung in pockets beneath his arms and chin.

"We will summon those vessels at once. That will bring our total up to twenty, but that still isn't enough to match Caesar's. We've been too smug to rely on our superiority on the sea—Rome's men might be landlocked, but they're not idiots. We need to build more galleys."

With great effort, Laomedon straightened himself, shifting his weight onto his hand rather than his elbow. "My queen, I mean no disrespect, but it's not such an easy matter—"

"War isn't an easy matter." Her temper snapped. "And easy or not, it must be done. We control the greater part of Alexandria; we have nearly all the city's factories at our disposal; we can build ships—and we will."

"Of course, my queen," the commander averred, but she could hear another objection rising in his voice. "There remains the problem of timber. Much was burned at the docks, and it would take days—maybe weeks—before we could secure an adequate amount of pine from Cyprus. Assuming such a shipment could even clear Caesar's galleys."

Pine made for the best warships—or better still, silver fir. That was what her forefathers had used, culled from the forests of northern Macedonia, but that would be even more difficult to acquire than Cypriot lumber. She dug her fingernails into her scalp as though that might root out the answer. What little wood there was about the palace was ebony, though—and then it struck her.

"We'll strip the whole city of cedar," she said quickly, eyes darting between the eunuch and the general, daring either to contradict her. "There's not much in the palace, but we do have some. This table, for instance, and the rest of the city is rife with it. The agora colonnades are covered with cedar—and the gymnasium, too. We'll strip every public building with a wooden roof—and offer private citizens three times the going rate of lumber if they allow us to strip their roofs and staircases as well."

When she paused, she saw that she'd won. A glinting smile had spread across Laomedon's face, and the eunuch only mustered a single objection: "Are you sure *three* times the going rate?"

Beneath that question, she heard a hint of pride.

"Yes, three times," Arsinoe answered. The hungry days she'd spent on the city streets still loomed, days when the slightest kindness from the palace was lauded as a gift from the gods. Besides, if she lost the Alexandrians, she'd lose the war. Their sympathies housed and fed her soldiers, and starved Caesar's of supplies.

"One more thing I must make clear," she said sharply. "The next time we fight, I will lead the battle myself."

Again, she braced herself for some protest, some complaint about her lack of military experience. Her time with Cleopatra's army—shadowing the force she now led up and down the Nile—hardly gave her standing. And the soldiers' respect for her was grudging at best. Yet neither man nor eunuch spoke a word against the plan. Laomedon appeared chastened by his losses; maybe he still imagined her the author of Achillas's death. So much the better. Let him hold back his objections and fear his captain's fate.

And then she settled on her answer: she would adopt the rumors surrounding Achillas's death. Better to embrace the proffered role of murderer than allow these men's malleable fears to cleave to a rival source. As for the eunuch? She studied Ganymedes's thin lips, his tired gaze. Did he fear her too? Was he even capable of that? *Fear,* Ganymedes had told her once, *is the luxury of those with something left to lose.*

The silence sharpened on her ears; no protests came. She would indeed lead these men to battle. Quiet, she realized, could herald victory as soundly as could trumpets.

Aboard the ship, *her* ship, Arsinoe felt fully sundered from the past. For three days, the factories of Alexandria had whirred to life, spewing forth galleys, one after another, until the docks crowded with twenty-two refurbished four-banked ships and five freshly minted fives. As she'd traveled from workshop to workshop, watching the men sawing planks and pounding away at hulls, she marveled at the speed at which her words were made flesh. And now, standing in the deckhouse of her galley—a galley that existed only because she'd spoken it so—she was almost dizzy with anticipation. Beneath her the world thrummed, in the men readying themselves to fight, in the contracting bodies of the sailors who lived and died at her will, in the sweat pouring down the naked backs that tugged and strained against four sets of oars. They moved as one, this hydra of humanity, and she could scarcely believe how smoothly the war galley pulled over the sea.

Farther up, near the prow, a pair of boys, too small and spindly to man their own oars, stoked the flames. Unlike the rowers, whose every move was precise and calculated, these two were lit by a wilder spark. They laughed and joked and danced back and forth as they prodded the embers, their mood utterly divorced from the fire's baneful purpose. At any moment Laomedon—who had emerged as some louder, bolder iteration of himself—would chide them for their foolery. She felt a sort of kinship with these boys. It would be their first sea fight, she suspected, just as it was hers.

She glanced up at the Pharos lighthouse, its flame an afterthought against the brightness of day. Once their galleys cleared the outskirts of the island, they would be able to see what sort of defense Caesar had planned. There were few surprises here—it was virtually impossible to keep one half of the city from discovering what the other half did. It didn't matter; they outnumbered the Romans now, both in men and ships. The gods—even Poseidon, that capricious sea deity—smiled on their cause.

"Arsinoe." A hand came to rest on the small of her back. *Alexander.*

With his featherweight breastplate and his vulture helm tucked under his left arm, he looked every bit the seafaring soldier. If he put on his helmet, she might not even recognize him. She shuddered. She stood as queen of Egypt, in the regalia of the goddess Isis. He shouldn't touch her and pretend that he exerted some ownership over her flesh. Annoyed, she pivoted away from him, putting cool air between her body and his reach.

"There's no one here but me." His eyes bored into her, lingering on her breasts. It wasn't *right* for him to look at her that way, not when she was in command.

"Not now, Alexander."

His face fell, but he collected himself quickly. "My apologies," he replied, chastened, and then almost tauntingly, "my queen."

One day perhaps all her hard looks and words would sunder something between them—perhaps that was what she wanted. Because what she *feared* more than anything else was how meek she felt in Alexander's embrace. If there were more men she could trust, she wouldn't have permitted him aboard her ship. But as it was, her standing was precarious. It was foolhardy enough of her to have insisted on seeing battle—the least she could do was to fill her galley with the few soldiers she knew she could rely on.

Footsteps sounded on the stairs, and she moved to put more distance between her and Alexander. His stance, his attitude, stank of familiarity. The last thing she needed was for some soldier to stumble upon them and send a fresh wave of rumors throughout the ship. And at that moment, Laomedon emerged from the deckhouse, eyes heavy and rheumy. The long nights of strategizing wore on him more than they did her. She felt brighter, fresher with each passing day.

"Laomedon," she greeted him, biting back a smile. She knew— she *knew*—that any battle, in particular any battle against Caesar, was cause not for joy but for fear. But it was hard to remember that with the boat tilting steadily beneath her bare feet, twisting around the tip of Pharos and turning westward along the island's northern shore. She sharpened her eyes for Caesar's fleet—hers was organized in a front line of twenty-two decked galleys, with the remainder forming the reserve. Her flagship was nestled near the middle of the first row, eighth from the starboard side.

"My queen." Laomedon dipped his head, giving a curt nod to Alexander. She felt her lover bristle at her side. "A scout has caught sight of one of Caesar's ships," the commander went on. "He does indeed mean to engage."

She squinted beyond the prow, trying to make out ships against the blue expanse. To the left, she caught sight of one bobbing on the waves. Once she saw the first, more bubbled up around it— each with the Colossus of Rhodes as its figurehead, nine titans lost in the sea.

"The Rhodians, I see," she said. "And Caesar leads them?"

"No, they're headed by their own commander, Eupranor."

"The same one who bested you?"

Laomedon nodded. "It will not happen again."

"Good." She paused. "I want to address the troops before we attack. Rally them to my call."

Alexander stiffened at her side; his hands clenched into fists. He alone had tried to convince her to wait behind, and she was sure he thought little of her addressing the legions.

"Of course, my queen," Laomedon replied quietly, the wind grasping at his words. "But remember whose men they are. They have followed Achillas for years, drinking in his heaping praise of Ptolemy, believing that your brother was their rightful king, that he was as brave and bold as their general claimed. They will not forget all that so easily. Especially not—"

"When they believe I am responsible for Achillas's death." Arsinoe completed the thought.

The sun snuck out from behind a cloud and Laomedon's irises glinted amber in the harsh light. They, too, accused her. Then the ray passed, and the look vanished with it.

"All the more reason I should speak to them," Arsinoe said firmly. "To help them recognize that my cause and that of my esteemed brother are wedded as one."

She didn't need Laomedon's approval any more than she needed Alexander's. She was queen, and she would do as she willed. Without another word, she abandoned the two men on the deck and picked her way toward the stairs. Fighting not to stagger at each pitch, she descended into the belly of the vessel. She wanted to pass among the rowers, to be seen and recognized by each man who'd fight and helm her ship. The steps grew slick with sweat and salt, the air dank with its stench. By the time she was walking between the banks of rowers—three men deep on either side—she could scarcely even smell the sea. Most had shed their tunics, and she watched the tendons writhe along their backs with each pull. They were great beasts of men, these sailors, far more awe-inspiring than their counterparts who fought on land. These creatures needed the strength not only to thrust a sword into weak flesh but also to carry the weight of an armored ship across the sea.

She'd never stood in the pit before, surrounded by this engine of efficiency. Between the stink and the rhythmic panting of their breaths, she could almost forget sky and waves alike, the wide world outside. She straightened as she passed by each bench, daring them to stare as she picked her way aft: she was a Ptolemy, their goddess and their queen. The very thought thrilled her. Locked away with child, Cleopatra couldn't compete with her now. Her sister carried Caesar's son, and the Roman would protect his seed, shielding its bearer from any hint of harm.

Arsinoe flushed with her own freedom. Cleopatra had scorned Alexander as *nothing, no one.* And yet by bedding *Dioscorides's by-blow,* Arsinoe had gained the upper hand. If she should someday carry Alexander's child, her lover could never dictate her away from dangers. He didn't enjoy that right; his only power came from his proximity to her. And that she could revoke as quickly as she'd bestowed it.

Arsinoe hoisted herself onto the rear deck and clambered between the two rudder men. The curved wood of the stern made it difficult to balance, but her action had the desired effect: gaping stares and whispers sparked from each bench. She glanced over their faces and soaked in their distinctions. Her sailors looked to represent the whole swath of mankind, from inky-black Nubians to sun-pinked Gauls, more savage than any creature who lived along the Nile. All drawn by coin, a fool's dream of glory. The same dream that had ripped Alexander from her side to join a Roman legion. Her dynasty's empire might have dwindled to nothing, but its reach still extended to these far-flung lands.

"My subjects, my soldiers," she cried. Ever since she was a girl, she'd had a taste for these speeches. A thousand times she'd read and recited the ones Odysseus and Agamemnon had given to the gathered Achaeans. "Today we make our first great strike against the Roman horde. Caesar has grown cocksure and lazy. He imagines that he can burn our ships in the night and that we will slink away in fear. *But he is wrong.* This very galley we now sail proves that much." For emphasis she stamped her foot against the freshly crafted planks. "Over the course of three days, Alexandria built twenty-seven warships—a number that would take an ordinary city years. And now we will use these galleys to show the Roman from what sort of metal we are forged. We will show him dogs of the sea can cut the throats of landlocked wolves and rip their bellies out."

The men were quiet, unmoved. The rowers pulled their oars in tune; the archers along the perimeter leaned on their bows. She glanced from bench to bench, holding each gaze she could catch, snatching at sand. Her eyes trailed over the first row, where hulking giants heaved, two by two, and then farther, to where the smallest oarsmen sat, five to a blade. The far-off men, the younger ones, stared at her in curiosity, but the behemoths nearest her paid little heed. They didn't interrupt; they didn't even seem to hear. Just another general giving another speech. It wasn't, she realized, at all like in the epics. They were bought hands, nothing more—what did they care for rousing speeches, for calls to bravery? They'd just as soon join another, more profitable war.

"His legions have grown sluggish. They've plundered the wealthiest cities from Spain to Asia. But they will not plunder Alexandria—they will not plunder your wives and your houses. Instead, we will beat these interlopers and you will return home with more gold and jewels, cloths and riches, than you could have imagined in your wildest dreams."

At these words, a ripple of interest went through the men. The talk of gold, of that most material type of glory, intrigued them. It wasn't the sort of speech she'd dreamt of giving, not one that rivaled those of Odysseus, but perhaps it would be the one that worked.

"He laughs at us, this interloper who *fucks* my sister. He believes that *we* will cower, when we have so much to lose from defeat, so much to gain from victory. Before the day is done, you might hold in your hand the wealth plundered from Greece and Macedonia. Caesar thinks that we will cower, but we will not *shrink*. Each of you is worth thirty Roman centurions, and you shall receive that weight in gold. And so I ask you: will we cower or will we fight?"

The silence tensed and cracked; a fearsome cry of *"Fight!"* echoed up and down the rowing lines. It buoyed her. They would sail forward and envelop the Rhodian fleet. This would be no mere standoff between two ill-matched armies—it would be a battle, and she would win.

BROTHER

The weather had finally cooled, and the winds whipped across the rooftop. Ptolemy wrapped his woolen mantle tightly about his shoulders. His kingly clothes had been abandoned at the palace, and the replacements scavenged from the fortress fit him poorly. These vestments had belonged to a much larger man—older, he told himself—and he was constantly tugging at the cloak to keep out the chill. But these small vexations faded to the background, eclipsed by his acute awareness of Cleopatra's movements. He wove meaning into each breath and knuckle clench of the woman reclining at his side. He had no other choice. To make out the antics of the dueling galleys down below, he'd have to squint and press his fingers into the doughy flesh beneath his eyes. He didn't want to betray how much he had riding on the outcome. So he studied his sister for hints instead.

Ptolemy reached for his wine, but the glass teetered against his numb fingers. Vigorously, he rubbed his palms together to bring life back into his hands. Cleopatra eased herself up to sit. The motion set the hairs along his arms on end. Suddenly, she swooped over him and took his fingers in hers. She cupped his hands to her mouth and blew hot breath into them.

"There," Cleopatra cooed. "That's better, no?"

Dumbly, Ptolemy stared at their overlapping fingers. One set, he knew, belonged to him, but he could hardly claim them as his own. The other, ring laden, at least he recognized. A new cameo had joined the coterie: the queen's profile set next to Caesar's in warm-hued sardonyx. He wondered how she'd managed to have it forged amidst the chaos, what artisan she'd persuaded and where she'd found the stone. Or perhaps the Roman had procured the jewel: another in an endless stream of gifts.

"It is better now that we are friends," his sister said as she released his hands. "It never did us any good to fight."

Suspicion still stretched between them—Ptolemy couldn't tell where the truth petered into lies. The queen had requested his presence here, in this makeshift watchtower she'd had erected on the roof. Two of the fort's most luxurious divans—so worn with scrapes that in the palace they would have long since been set to kindling— had been pilfered from the dining lounge and aligned head-to-head. In the old days, Ptolemy could remember Cleopatra reclining with their father this way as they held court over suppliants. He didn't know whether the similarities should comfort or terrify him.

Below, beyond the barren harbor and the cluttered houses of Pharos Island, the sea thickened with war galleys. They looked wrong, out of place: sleek, skinny ships with spindly prows—a stark contrast to round-bottomed merchant vessels with their brightly colored sails. Ptolemy did his best to keep his expression neutral, to conceal the churning of his innards. The queen sat so close that a stray thought might pass from his head to hers, and so he tried to keep his mind blank too.

Ptolemy scolded himself. One lick of intimacy, and he'd fallen under some iteration of his sister's spell—speechless and all nerves. He needed to build on the affections she offered and convince her that he was well and truly hers. Besides, beneath his sister's serene exterior, he caught a glimpse of her worries: her hands were clenched, rings biting into her raw skin.

"Which ship is Caesar on?" he asked, though he recognized the vessel at once, its horsehead prow an homage to the general's famed but absent Tenth Legion. *The Mounted Men.*

Cleopatra freed a finger from her fist and pointed out the galley. It lagged behind the second line of combat, its soldiers hastily constructing its enormous crow until the device's claw sprung outward, reaching over the waves to where it might tear at the enemy.

"I am glad to watch this battle with you," Ptolemy continued uneasily.

"Strange, isn't it?" Cleopatra replied with a smile. "That we two should find ourselves the watchers. The Olympians on high, above the fray. After all, it was our battle that spawned theirs."

Did Cleopatra feel that same nip of jealousy? Did she yearn for the glory that had been stolen from them? It should have been his fight, *their* fight: the first division had arisen between the two of them. Since their father's death, they'd stood opposed, a pair of clashing alternatives for Egypt. For months, they'd faced off outside Pelusium. And now, two of the strangest proxies carried on in their steads: Caesar bearing Cleopatra's banner and Arsinoe carrying his.

"But I suppose our battle was never much of one," his sister mused. "Never something that consumed lives."

There lay the difference, naturally, between wars that mattered and wars that didn't. The wars that would be sung of in years to come. Whether men were slaughtered. Nothing he'd done—nothing he'd ever done—had made a dent. With one nauseating exception: the murder of Pompey. And for all he knew, that would be his sole legacy: the ignoble assassination of his father's ally. Dark thoughts consumed him too frequently now; he had to stay strong and drive them from his mind. He would escape, he swore to himself. He would join Arsinoe and fight.

"Where were you?" Cleopatra asked. "When Achillas led troops against us—Arsinoe was forever trying to pick you out."

"I was with my men," Ptolemy answered defensively.

"We are friends now, little brother. You needn't lie to me."

He hedged. "Sometimes I was in Pelusium, if you didn't see me on the banks."

Cleopatra nodded, a glint of sympathy in her green-smudged eyes. As though she pitied him for all the years he'd been cut off from true power.

There, as here, he'd found himself severed from the battle, watching as others made their decisions to shadow, retreat, or fight. He fixed his focus on the harbor, his vigilance a paltry proxy for control: the four Rhodian ships had drawn even farther ahead of the first flank. Smaller and lighter than the traditional Roman galleys, the narrow two-banked crafts had surrounded a pair of Alexandrian quadriremes.

These, he realized with a jolt, he couldn't identify; not long ago he might have named every vessel in his father's fleet. When he squinted, he could make out two unfamiliar figureheads: an ashen Medusa with dusky snakes writhing from her head and a chestnut-haired Alexander in his purple cloak. The Gorgon reared upward as a Rhodian vessel plunged its ram into the hull—Ptolemy's stomach clenched, and he bit the inside of his cheek to keep from crying out. A moment later, another of Caesar's ships cut a fire bucket from its roost and the air became a whirl of rippling fog. His eyes weren't sharp enough to discern the men themselves, but he could imagine their actions: the desperate patching of boards and dousing of flames, the soldiers and rowers leaping into the sea to escape the licks.

"Good aim," Cleopatra remarked. "The Rhodians live up to their reputation."

"They do," he repeated dumbly and searched for some relevant tidbit to add. "It's a pity Ptolemarion isn't here to see. He loves this sort of thing."

That last was a lie. Their brother was no fan of fighting, but he doubted Cleopatra knew enough to correct him. The mention was a gamble—he didn't know how his sister would react to referencing their shared blood. But, to his relief, she smiled.

"It is a shame indeed."

The question that had long simmered in his mind bubbled to the surface: where *were* his mother and brother? He'd caught glimpses of Ptolemarion, but he hadn't seen his mother in weeks. Did she languish in some forgotten cell? He'd already broached the topic of Ptolemarion—he need only tug the subject a little further. But his courage flagged, and his tongue thickened in his mouth. The long hours of solitude had changed him, and at times he felt incapable of even ordinary speech.

Below, the Rhodian ships launched their offensive in earnest, casting and lowering their sails with ease as they weaved in and out of the wind. The Alexandrian galleys looked sluggish by comparison— too newly formed to have mastered their sea legs. With a pang, he recalled the burnt galleys, the flaming storerooms, the stink that had haunted Alexandria for days. Even these long weeks later, he still couldn't believe that Caesar had let the scrolls burn. He could picture Arsinoe, her eyes blinking away tears; he could hear the words she might choose. *And to think,* she would say, *that these books were ravaged by one who imagines himself among the greats.*

Did Cleopatra mourn the knowledge that she'd destroyed? He chanced another look at his sister. Chin resting on hooked thumbs, she'd broken off her assessment of him—instead, she gazed down at the harbor. The queen loved learning too—to a one, his siblings held interests that had passed him by. Arsinoe spent hours poring over the lines of Euripides and Sophocles; little Ptolemarion had his love of drawing. Cleopatra, though, preferred the practical to the esoteric. Her interest in the tragedies was limited to how she might deploy their quotations in argument.

Several of the Lycian ships, broader and hardier than their Rhodian counterparts, skirted into the fray. Creeping forward, they set their prows against a few undecked craft of the Egyptian navy. These he recognized—they must have survived Caesar's conflagration. Amidst the maneuvering ships, one of the new quadriremes drifted listlessly—its hull had been breached and it sunk so low that only its top row of oars could be seen above the waves.

The day drew on, and Caesar's ships struck the Alexandrian galleys again and again with growing ferocity. Here, a Rhodian ship dumped oil onto the fresh-hewn decks of one of Arsinoe's vessels—only to send a fire arrow piercing into its hull. The damaged boat kindled, an echo of the royal galleys burning at the docks. A thick Lycian craft sank its claw into another of the Egyptian ships—and a stream of red-tunicked Romans rushed to board. Seamlessly, the invaders seized control of the pilfered vessel, sending its ram cracking into another Alexandrian hull. The ship sputtered as Arsinoe's men rushed to plug the breach, but it was too late—the deck was already sloshing with water, and soon the soldiers were jumping ship, spilling into the sea. Another Roman victory.

Cleopatra relaxed into herself. Gone were the clutching knuckles of the battle's early haze. Each time she spotted another figure clambering onto a neighboring roof to watch, she'd point it out to Ptolemy with a grin, as though every newcomer represented another mark against Arsinoe's ledger. The sheer pleasure that his sister took in each triumph was maddening. He let himself sink his teeth into this new hatred. The pettiness that usually spurred his fury faded away. He could forget about Briseis and her betrayal, and instead find the locus of his rage here. He recognized the roots of Arsinoe's loathing: Cleopatra didn't care for Egypt or for the glories of the past; she looked toward the future, and her future was Rome.

As Caesar's Pontic ships skated around Pharos's northern tip, past the lighthouse and its colossal statue of Poseidon, Ptolemy glimpsed the first of the Alexandrian galleys turn tail, the rowers pawing in reverse. Soon another fled, and then a third, all three racing back toward the safety of the royal harbor. His heart sank, a heavy lump of regret in his stomach. Silently, he urged the boats to right themselves and cut their rams into Caesar's hulls.

As yet another of Arsinoe's vessels curled eastward toward the palace docks, Cleopatra grabbed his wrist. His first instinct was to recoil, but he forced himself still. Instead, he stared at the place where her fingers dug into his skin—the rings would leave dark marks in their wake.

"See. I promised it would work out. We've already sunk half of Arsinoe's pathetic navy, and the rest have begun to flee. Poor Julius," she gloated. "I know he was hoping for a bit more of a fight."

"Poor Julius," he croaked, the words thick in his throat. He wasn't even sure if they were comprehensible. It didn't matter—his eldest sister thought him dull and wanting. No doubt she'd count his slurring as more evidence of his stupidity.

Below, as the Alexandrian vessels retreated, a double line of archers appeared along the curve of the Great Harbor. To his surprise, several of Caesar's galleys had recused themselves from the sea battle, docking instead along the Heptastadion, the broad causeway that linked Pharos to the mainland. He could just make out the scarlet tide of Romans flowing onto the narrow strip—they clashed with the bright-hued Alexandrians, swords and spears aloft. A flurry of arrows loosed, plumes whizzing from the shore.

Cleopatra's grip on his arm slackened. Another moment and her hand dropped away entirely. His skin tingled in the breeze. The divan beside him creaked—the queen had straightened again. She looked more fearsome now, as though each sunken ship buttressed her innate savagery. The wind had torn her hair into disarray, and she brushed a few stray wisps behind her ear before she spoke.

"What a fool," Cleopatra murmured, "thinking she could face off against the greatest general who ever lived."

He wasn't sure if she spoke to him or to herself.

"Come, my brother, my king," she resumed in her usual tone. "We should go, prepare our celebration."

He couldn't leave. Already he'd let his power slip, allowed Arsinoe to claim his fight as hers. So much he'd already abandoned, but he would not abandon this perch. He owed that little to the Alexandrians who'd hollered for him at the palace gates: he should bear witness to their deaths.

"You go," he answered fiercely. "I want to watch Arsinoe burn."

He'd planned to say more to convince Cleopatra of his motivations, but he couldn't choke out another word. Though Caesar's men had dug new wells and fresh water was ladled out at meals, his body still felt the lack of it. His tongue prickled at the slightest hint of thirst, and his lips grew sandy in an instant.

"Very well, my brother," she replied. "What a taste you have for bloodshed."

Cleopatra offered him a smile, a snarl softened only by a slight curl of her lips. As his sister descended the steps into the fortress, she bid a pair of sentinels remain. He supposed they were there to ensure he didn't exercise too much of a taste for bloodshed. Once alone, or as alone as he might hope to be, Ptolemy scuttled to the northern edge of the roof. He heard one of the guards follow behind—perhaps the man thought he meant to jump. Instead, he slipped down to sit, swinging his legs over the ledge. Gazing down at the alleyway, he had the uncanny sense that his body was floating up into the ether. He ignored the vertigo and instead looked again to the Heptastadion.

The causeway churned: red tunics tussling against a mob of motley men, shorn even of uniform. From time to time a figure would detach, spinning into the bay. He could imagine the shrieks, even if he couldn't hear them. *Zeus, lord of hosts,* he began, but then he cut short his prayers. What good had they ever brought him?

By the time the sun had settled into the horizon and darkness had clotted the sky, the gods had failed him yet again. He'd watched as Caesar's men fought their way across the mole, as they streaked red through the streets of Pharos and slammed their battering rams against its tallest buildings. He could hear the crack of iron-headed poles against stone, even across the bay.

Cleopatra had been right: Rome was the only future. Arsinoe could never emerge victorious. She'd been a fool—they'd both been fools—to imagine that she, a girl unschooled in war, could take on the Republic's greatest general.

SISTER

Fury pulsed through her, from her fingertips to the beads of seawater dripping from her hair. Every object in the atrium taunted her—the tired tapestries of Ptolemy the Father-Loving's conquests she'd dragged from some forsaken lodge to cover her sister's Isis motifs, the blue-dotted maps stretched across the onyx floor, the terra-cotta inkwell perched by Ganymedes's divan. All begged for her violence. Arsinoe found her peace in stillness, bracing her seat against the harsh throne, rooting her feet in the onyx.

Once steadied, she eyed those who'd failed her. Ganymedes at least had the decency to shrink into his couch. Laomedon and Alexander, on the other hand, both stood unbent, awaiting her command. A tension shimmered between them. The eunuch's words bore fruit; some jealousy had bloomed. She'd tried to counter it, but their sideways glances at each other emboldened the shriek rising in her throat. What good had their straight-backed, tight-lipped one-upmanship done her in the fight for Pharos? They'd still lost to Caesar's forces, and badly.

"We need to retake the island at once," Arsinoe said as calmly as she could manage. "How will it be done?"

"My queen," Laomedon answered, inching closer as he spoke, "we haven't lost Pharos. We still control the northern coast and docks. We could launch a double attack from the causeway and the far end of the island."

Her general gestured to the map stretched at his feet. The cedar table—sacrificed to the euphoria of boat building, its remnants now rotting at the bottom of the sea—made its absence felt. Planning required hunkering now; their very preparations cut down to size. Laomedon sunk into a squat. A finger—nail bitten to cuticle—smoothed over the northern archway and tapped each of the three red pawns, spokes on a paltry triangle. To the right, at the royal harbor, clumped the greater part of her fleet. For once she didn't count the remaining vessels—the wounds, the freshly hewn hulls pierced by Roman rams, their gouged hearts swelling with the sea, were still too raw.

"Tell me, Laomedon," she asked. "Why will this work any better tomorrow than it did today?"

"We'll have more men," Alexander piped in. Still standing, he towered over the hunched commander. A smirk had spread across his lips, and his eyes twinkled as he looked to her. His stare was hard, greedy with possession. The eunuch's warnings itched at her ears: *Do not take his counsel; under no circumstances take him to your bed.*

"Where will you find these men?" Laomedon scoffed. His knees cracked as he stood, and his chin jutted upward with a confidence ill-suited to a man who'd overseen the sinking of so many of her ships.

"We'll recruit them from Pharos," Alexander replied assuredly. "Before the battle, Caesar sent heralds through the town, swearing to the villagers that his men wouldn't plunder. That's why the residents surrendered, craven though that was. But within hours the Romans broke their pledge. Caesar has razed buildings to dust; his men have taken jewels, crops, women, anything they wish."

On its face, the plan's foibles were plain. It was madness to imagine the same cowards who'd relinquished their homes to the Romans could transform into warriors overnight. But Arsinoe had little choice other than to entertain such madness.

"And you think they will fight now?" she asked, glancing to Ganymedes.

Hunched over, the eunuch balanced a slate on his lap, scribbling wildly. In the last few days, Arsinoe noticed, he'd developed an alarming passion for records. Her tutor had grown quiet, obsessive in his note taking, as though desperate to provide some document, some proof, of this glowing moment of their rule. The army's attitude toward him had soured. It was Ganymedes they blamed: for Achillas's death, for poor rations, for poor conditions. *You can't trust a eunuch,* they'd murmur behind his back. *He doesn't know what honor means.*

"I know they'll fight for us," Alexander answered. His voice had shifted, softened—and she worried her fears were writ squarely on her face. "Several have already approached me. I might summon them if it pleases you."

The three would-be soldiers Alexander dredged up did little to mollify her concerns. The tallest among them—a scrawny, pock-marked boy with flared nostrils—didn't dare meet her eye. And the other two—brothers, perhaps, their pudgy faces the same almond hue—barely reached as high as Alexander's shoulder. Not one was older than fifteen. Their families and homes had been plundered, and somehow—as darkness fell and the battle ebbed—they managed to cobble their desire for redress into fierce adolescent outrage, the sort she feared would fade with the first prick of iron at their flesh.

That night, guilt spit stones into her gut, the failures meted out, the boys she'd sent—and would send again—to slaughter. Alexander came, as she'd known he would, but she'd told Eirene not to let him enter. Angry, hurt, his voice battered against the walls, asking, then begging, wheedling—shouting—at her maid. In time, she heard the stomp of feet on the stairs, a stream of curses wafting into the night. But she felt no pang of regret. Not for that, at least. So much was *lost*—Pharos and the causeway—what little hope they had of defeating Caesar crumbled, glass returned to sand.

The next day, aboard her ship once more, Arsinoe felt her spirits rise. She'd slept for only a few fitful hours, waking in the misting half-light, but her mind had been clear, not a wisp of niggling dreams. *That,* she knew, was the most promising portent of all. That she'd shed herself of imaginings and omens, of the haunting search for meaning from the gods.

Stung by the previous night's rejection, Alexander kept a studied distance, scuttling along the railings whenever she and Laomedon drew too near. But he couldn't cure himself of looking, and even from across the deck, she felt his glances, the puppy ache in his eyes. At least he hadn't shirked his other duties: he'd managed to scrape together some hundred or so men from Pharos, and Arsinoe could only hope they proved more promising fighters than the ones she'd already met.

Something in the air, the clarity of light, felt fresher than it had the day before. Even the wind blew in their favor, and their fleet skimmed from the royal harbor quickly, already bending westward along the island's southern shore. As the Heptastadion neared, Arsinoe reformulated the plot, whispering beneath her breath, envisioning it richly in her mind: her ochre-oared ships parsing off in two rows, one set of vessels curling into Pharos's northern shore to buttress the three galleys that remained there, and the other—her own—seizing the mole from the sea. The plan had merit—she'd spent enough hours mulling over it to know that much—and by lining ships on either side, they ought to be able to take the causeway in a few short hours. After all, as she'd explained to Laomedon time and again, the Heptastadion's platform was narrow enough that archers would have trouble defending both sides at once.

Finished with her imagining, having watched the Alexandrians in her mind overthrow the Roman archers on the mole and seen the red tunics tilting into the sea, she opened her eyes. The causeway was upon them, and she had to hold back a gasp of horror. The arch that allowed vessels to pass from one side of the stone structure to the other had been blocked, stacked with boulders—pilfered, no doubt, from the Pharos towers that Caesar had ripped from their foundations.

Laomedon kept close to her, and she barely moved her lips as she spoke.

"Look," she murmured. Her new commander nodded; chestnut eyes narrowed to slits at the sight of the barricaded mole.

A rock whistled past her ear. She ducked and spun around to see where the stone had struck. Among the rowers below, a patch had cleared: in its midst lay a bald, barrel-chested man, his forehead dented grotesquely inward and his oar loosed into the air, crimson pooling around his corpse.

"Get below; it isn't safe," Laomedon hissed.

She opened her mouth to argue, but before she could speak, the commander had thrown his arms about her shoulders and yanked her down onto the deck. The cedar scraped against her chin. Another stone whooshed through the air—and a third, and then it was raining rocks—and the commander was shouting orders, telling the rowers to "Hold port" and "Pull starboard." But louder than all else was the taunting voice in her head: *Retreat, retreat, retreat.*

The taste of defeat, stale as last night's wine on her lips. Twice they had attacked the Roman troops, and twice they had failed. She should have realized—*someone* should have realized—

that Caesar would have marked each move a step ahead. He was a lauded master of strategy—had proven himself against all manner of foes, from Pompey's orderly soldiers to the barbarous Gauls.

Even as the ship cut through the sea, putting a half stade between its hull and the slinging stones, the rocks shrilled against her ears. *The wind, only the wind.* Not for the first time, she wished that she could fly as she did in her dreams—sail across the air to Pharos and see what passed on its northern shore. Had Ganymedes enjoyed any measure of success? Or did his men chafe too hard against him, precluding any hope of victory?

"What now, Laomedon?" She tucked her knees beneath her and pushed her way up to stand.

For the first time since he'd taken control of her forces, he looked nonplussed. Rather than weave some tale of how they'd work their way to victory, he stammered. His confidence, his surety, had been stripped away. Here, in the dull light of defeat, he looked lost and younger than his years. She could read his terrors behind his darting eyes: his wondering if his whole life, all the years he'd struggled and connived to claw his way from slave to soldier to commander— would it end here? She shook away the thoughts—it wasn't the time for empathy. She needed to plant her mind firmly in the here and now.

The men scuttled about the deck in disarray, like ants, queenless, swarming about a crushed mound. Even the rowers were no longer sure in their positions—a few had stood up from their benches to catch a better glimpse of what was happening, and the boat's balance was thrown as a result. Some looked to Laomedon for direction, but others seemed just as eager to fend for themselves, scanning for an escape, ready to abandon the cause as lost.

There were no answers—none that Laomedon or Alexander or even Ganymedes could offer. Any solution was one she'd have to provide herself. Her mind spun into action—the sea had failed them; their freshly hewn ships and newly crafted sailors were no match for Rome's.

"We need to dock and rush the causeway," she said quickly, before the thought had fully taken root. "We must seize Pharos by land."

Laomedon gaped, his lips pursing and fluttering like a fish.

"But my queen," he said, scrambling for dignity. "Our great advantage lies on the sea. We can't abandon that."

"There are only so many soldiers that Caesar can crowd onto that platform. We control the town to the east—we need to surround the Romans in order to retake Pharos; we've shown we can't do that from our ships."

Before the general could rain objections on her, she raced to the aft and hoisted herself onto the rear deck. Apart, above, she watched as the chaos settled—the rowers returned to their oars, the scurrying soldiers stilled. Their tough exteriors had fallen away; as they stared up at her, most eyes were heavy with fear and longing. *Some men were born to follow, others to lead.* Ganymedes's words, from years ago. As she glanced over these bodies, these empty minds that looked to her, she saw that Truth, that fickle goddess, would fail her here. What they needed was confidence, and Truth surely couldn't offer that.

"Good news, my soldiers!" she shouted as loudly as she could against the wind. "Ganymedes's reinforcements have broken Caesar's fortifications in the north."

For a flickering moment, she feared that Laomedon might speak out to contradict her—to admit they'd had no word from Ganymedes, that the eunuch might be defeated, dead—but then he firmed his jaw. He'd submit to her lies.

"All we must do now is join our force to theirs and overrun the causeway. The Romans can fling stones at our boats, but we have great battering rams and catapults of our own. We will break down their barricades and send them spinning into the sea."

The men roared in answer—they no longer sounded like a sprawling set of miscreants but some unified animal roused to fury. What an army needed was a plan, any plan—it yearned for one, just as desperately as a lost kit yearned for its mother. The specifics of the plan itself were immaterial.

Even Laomedon fell under that same spell—sorting men into battalions, arming the rowers with spears and swords, ensuring that each knew what role he would play in the assault. A boarding plank wobbled as it was lowered to the shore, and with each set of feet that clambered over it, she feared the cedar might tip on its edge, flipping her soldiers into the waves. For a lingering moment, she was nearly alone on deck, left only with a skeletal crew that might defend the vessel from a surprise attack. And then she stepped onto the makeshift bridge herself, weighed the unstable cedar beneath her sandaled feet, and leapt onto the muddied sand.

The men, cut into their embankments, parted to let her through. Their eyes were light, their spirits lifted—looking at them, she might almost believe her lies had already forged into fact. Near the head of her phalanx, she caught sight of Laomedon once more. He'd stepped aside and was arguing with Alexander.

"What troubles you two friends?" Arsinoe asked sharply. The pettiness between them had no place here—she couldn't march into battle walking on eggshells about their egos.

"My queen," Alexander said, head bent. Each time they'd met that morning, he'd treated her with exaggerated solemnity, as though he hoped his aloofness might wound her, send her hurtling into his arms. Now he dropped to his knees. "Allow me to lead the assault—the men of Pharos are behind me."

Her lover gestured toward a clump of poorly turned out soldiers, arms and legs sprouting from dull, ill-fitted breastplates.

"Look at them," Laomedon scoffed. "A ragtag set of commoners who've learned of battles on their father's knee. Caesar's troops could destroy them with a stiff glance."

Alexander had to tilt his head at an awkward angle to take in her reaction—already, she suspected, he must be regretting his stilted supplications. And, indeed, he clambered up to stand, a vain brush at his muddied shins, for what little good it did. In her eyes, he was reborn a child, a scrape-kneed boy who'd cried when he found a wounded dove behind a bush. His baritone ruined the effect.

"They might be commoners, and they might be inexperienced, but they know the island, and they know the peculiarities of the Heptastadion. Besides, my queen, they have more reason to fight ferociously than any other men in our army. Their homes were razed, their wives and daughters raped. They hold their own stakes in this battle. Let me lead them in vengeance."

Vengeance—that she understood intimately. The pulsing drive to destroy that ran through her own veins—her need to defeat Cleopatra not only so that Egypt might throw off the shackles of Rome but also for the satisfaction of the thing itself. To strike her sister, her sworn companion and nearest friend, the one who'd loved her from birth and cast her aside.

"Go then," she told Alexander. "Take them as the first to fight. Laomedon will need time to set his phalanxes in order."

His eyes brightened, and as though he could not help himself, he crept forward, closing the space between them. On instinct, Arsinoe sidestepped away. His smile faded; the dream slipped from his eye. But he kept steady otherwise—rejection washed easily off him now. He, too, had grown accustomed to tossing back his bitters.

As Alexander weaved his way back toward the men from Pharos, they stretched their spindled arms to him, pawing at his sides and shoulders, basking in his strength. Jealousy twitched in her gut. She wished she had embraced him, squeezed his arm and whispered some breath of encouragement. She recognized the dangers—Alexander might be walking to his death—but she no longer felt them. Her fears had subsided, alongside her hopes of victory. The worst had already come to pass: she had betrayed Cleopatra, and she had lived; she had lost and gained the palace, and she had lived; she had been defeated in battle by Julius Caesar himself, and yet she lived. And so, though she knew she should tremble now for her life, for Alexander's life, in those first heady moments of battle, she did not.

Instead, a splitting, swelling ecstasy throbbed in her chest. The blood coursed as a violent tide throughout her limbs, each heartbeat in time with the pitch and fall of the waves. Her body, its very functions, seemed to flow in concert with the growing and decaying of the earth, as though the essence of Gaia, Mother of All, had passed into her being. Without her uttering a command, the men were flooding toward the causeway. She moved to follow them, but then a hand held her back, clutching at her shoulder.

"You can't, my queen," Laomedon whispered.

She shrugged off his touch. She was beyond heeding fear.

"You're unarmed."

Her fingers crept and reached for a phantom weapon—a bone.

"Give me your knife," she said.

"My queen, it would be foolish . . ."

Her ecstasy darkened, tinged with fury. The roars coalesced; she drew her strength from the war cries of her men. Her glare silenced Laomedon's objections, and he loosed the knife strapped to his calf.

"Be careful, my queen. You'll do none of us any favors by getting caught or killed."

But the commander had already faded from her mind. She gripped the knife's ivory handle and then she committed to the swarm, the churning haze of battle, as she filed and shouted among her men.

At once, she was swept into a coterie of companions. A clump of four soldiers surrounded her, cheered and buoyed by her presence. By their accents, the peculiar way they spoke their *rhos*, and the stout swords they drew from their girdles, she pegged them as Galatians. If she walked on tiptoes, her eyes barely reached the shortest one's breast buckles—and so the world became a swirl of bronze armor, the steady marching step, the relentless press onward.

They advanced and her protectors fell away one by one: locked in combat with the wave of Roman men. The world around her opened, and she could see that the causeway was rife with bodies, some living, writhing—and others still and bloodied, at times knocked unceremoniously into the sea. To her left, one of the Galatians stumbled. The movement—so near, so ripe—caught her attention: a glint of silver on his hunched back sprouted into a sword tip, blossoming crimson. Her eyes darted to the perpetrator, a beak-nosed Roman who'd thrust his blade in up to the hilt. His pudgy fingers tightened as he twisted deeper into her soldier's gut.

Her body untethered from her mind, shrugging away that useless muscle of doubt and hesitation. She watched as her feet carried her toward the enemy soldier, as her blade sliced across the Roman's knuckles, a bright trail of blood glistening in its wake. His nostrils flared; his eyes widened beneath his helm. A deep, guttural noise— half growl, half roar—escaped her throat. The adversary drew back, leaving his weapon buried in her soldier's stomach. When she slashed her blade at him again, he ducked and his helmet teetered into the sea. As he bent to fetch a dagger bound by the leather strap about his ankle, Arsinoe—this wild thing, this spirit—leapt forward. She recognized the terror in the man's swampy face, the pleading on his lips. Her hand thrust forward and plunged the knife attached to it deep into his eye, until the butt of her fist pressed into the spurting socket.

The squeal that escaped those sun-blistered lips didn't sound human. Her wrist twisted the knife until it did. Until it contained hordes of humanity, all the voices that she'd ever heard, and all the ones who'd never begged for mercy begged for it now. Not with words, but with a keening, horrid cry. Then she buried her fingers into his greasy hair and jerked the blade out. A wretched squelching sound, a bloodied, ruined face. Still gripping the man's head, she brought the blade to his trembling throat and sliced him from ear to ear. The same technique Osteodora had once seen used to slaughter pigs in the square.

The head clutched in her hand turned to lead, and her fingers slipped from the hair. The corpse collapsed onto the causeway. And slowly, slowly, her mind sunk into her body once more. All at once, she was hoisted upward, onto the shoulders of a pair of unknown soldiers.

A cheer went up, her name chanted over and over again.

"*Arsinoe Haimadipsa.*" Arsinoe the Bloodthirsty.

From this perch, above the heads and shields of the fighting men, Arsinoe could make out the battle's contours. On her left, she saw the vessels of Caesar's armada; opposite were the remnants of her own. On both sides, the ships were manned by depleted crews. Most soldiers had abandoned their vessels to squish and slice and stab along the Heptastadion.

Hoisted up high as a mascot for her men—"the queen who

367

killed," she heard at least one chant proclaim—she had become a goddess, a vengeful one. And in her vulture eye, she wasn't carried—instead she soared among her soldiers, whispering encouragement and imbuing them with newfound strength. *Her shield of lightning dazzling, swirling around her, headlong on Athena swept through the Argive armies, driving soldiers harder, lashing the fighting-fury in each Achaean's heart—*

"Arsinoe!" Another cry rang out. "Fight, *kill,* for our warrior queen."

Ahead, the throngs of Romans had stilled, their relentless slashing ceased. Her men pushed onward, sending their adversaries crashing into the waves. At the far end of the causeway, one set of Romans turned, and then another, until nearly half were facing away from her troops, eyes fixed on the isle. And then she saw the reason: her second flank—Ganymedes's men—was pouring over Pharos's hill.

"Look," she shouted, pointing at the isle. "I told you we'd taken Pharos from the north. Now we must only graft our splintered body back into one."

A cacophony of cries—in Greek, in Aramaic, in Egyptian—answered her. "You did," they told her. "You said and so it came to pass." And so she had. She'd spoken their victory into being, like the native gods of old, and baptized it in blood. Caesar's men were desperate and surrounded—cut off from their ships and their formations, battling for survival.

Facing two fronts of Alexandrians, the Romans were trapped, and like all trapped animals, they thrashed their claws. At first, their fear seemed to inflame their spirits—they cut down the front lines of her legions, felling the poor Pharos boys one by one. But then a man charged from her line. At first, from his red tunic, she thought him some misplaced Roman, a spy—and then, with a gutting jab, she recognized him: *Alexander.* He'd lost his mind, plunging toward the enemy, a sword clutched in each hand. She wanted to cry out to stop him, to tell him he didn't have to die to prove himself—at least to say a prayer in his defense. But instead she watched, tongue-tied, as he rushed onward, slicing two men's throats with a single slash. The other blade he plunged, hilt deep, into a third Roman's bowels. As the first pair gasped and staggered, the final fell, into a moat of red-smocked blood. Body after body thudded to the mole's stone; those who still lived lost faith, hurling themselves into the water, choosing to battle the waves rather than her Alexandrians. Victory—so near she could smell it on the breeze.

From the corner of her eye, she noticed a glint of flame. Arsinoe twisted her neck to catch a better look: a Roman vessel, succumbed to pitch and now set ablaze. Its deck churned with familiar chaos, a thousand soldiers abandoning their oars while one barked orders from the horsehead prow. As she squinted at the bellower, she saw he wore the crimson cloak of a Roman general. The realization hit her as shock, an explosion: it was Caesar, trapped on his burning flagship. Another plank on the deck caught; the flames hissed and raced across the helm. He glanced down at the waves from his precarious perch, a bundle of scrolls clenched in his hand. And then he leapt.

A resounding splash, and Caesar—the famed leader—was thrashing in the water. One arm stretched over his head, he struggled to keep the documents clear of the waves as he swam toward his retreating ships. In his wake, his cloak swirled like a bloodstained banner. More than once, the current nearly gulped him down—only the bobbing glint of white papyrus marked his place. As he struggled, Arsinoe found a prayer form on her lips: *Let him drown, Poseidon, let him die.*

But the flimsy gods betrayed her. The flailing man clawed his way to the port side of the nearest galley, where a pair of sailors cast a rope overboard for him to seize. As she watched Caesar hoist himself up and flop onto the deck, casting about like a hooked fish, this man who'd fled his battle, left his soldiers to die, his flagship to burn, she saw another truth: despite all his lauded triumphs, he was a far greater coward than she.

BROTHER

Drunk on victory—his, Arsinoe's—Ptolemy sat among the defeated and pretended he was one of them. At Cleopatra's table, he had to hide his joy; he was still declared for that queen's side. And that side had lost. A dark pall was cast over the company, unmoved by the platters of heifer, milky fat gleaming against gold, the jugs of unwatered wine. He let the mood bleed into his stature: he hunched his shoulders and looked as downtrodden as he could manage.

To thwart the overwhelming sense of loss, Cleopatra had ordered the banquet lounge crowded with additional tables and divans, pouring out into the courtyard so that the whole of Caesar's legions might dine with their commander. But the men, as far as Ptolemy could tell, were as unaccustomed to the pomp and circumstance as they were to defeat. And rather than rejoice over the luxuries, the greater part of the Roman forces seemed to eye their garish environs with distrust.

A few heads turned and Ptolemy looked to see what drew their attention: a scrubby boy—all arms and legs, his tunic too small—picked his way between the divans. The child's hair had grown wild and kept slipping over his face, and it wasn't until the boy looked up that Ptolemy recognized him: Ptolemarion. Ptolemy had to fight the urge to run and embrace his brother. He feared if he did, he wouldn't be able to rein in his joy, and his mask of misery would fall away. Instead, he contented himself with studying the boy from a distance: he was alive; he looked healthy—well fed enough to have sprouted several inches. As his brother passed his divan, Ptolemy grinned at him but received only the slightest flicker of a smile in return.

When Ptolemarion had drawn nearer, Ptolemy saw the boy's eyes were ringed with dark circles, as though some horror ate away his nights. Even his brother—sweet, innocent Ptolemarion, who insisted on freeing rather than killing any mice caught in the nursery—had been polluted by Rome's shadow. The realization wrenched some pang of sympathy in Ptolemy's gut, a fraternal fellow feeling he hardly recognized.

At his right, Cleopatra gestured toward Ptolemarion, pointing out an empty divan where he might sit and listen to his elders speak. In stark contrast to the rest of the company, Cleopatra looked positively gay. She squeezed Ptolemarion's hand and kissed him on the cheek. The boy knew enough to bear the caresses, but once she released him, he shrank into his corner, newly watchful and unsure.

The queen appeared more animated with each passing course— all laughs and japes and jauntiness. Watching her, Ptolemy never might have guessed that Caesar's army had lost Pharos that very afternoon. From time to time, she'd reach over and take her paramour's hand, pressing his fingers to her rounded belly. They'd share a look, a smile then, of intimacy, as though no one else existed in the world. Some three or four months along, the pregnancy had softened her; in the flickering lamplight, she looked fresh and lithe and full of life.

Caesar couldn't long resist her charms, and as evening ebbed toward night, his mood lifted too. He drank freely of his cups and made bawdy jokes about bathing goddesses and sex-starved satyrs.

His soldiers, at least the ones in earshot, mimicked his humors, and soon the walls echoed with belches and guffaws.

Careful not to let the heightened spirits affect him, Ptolemy stayed watchful of his drink. The wells the Romans had dug within the fortress's walls continued to spout fresh water, and so he was liberal when he lightened his wine. Still, he took only rare sips, and even when he did raise the chalice to his lips, he barely allowed any liquid to pass. He'd been of no use in this first battle—but he was determined to change that. With all the drink pouring down Roman gullets, surely someone would let some useful tidbit slip. Perhaps he'd overhear some whisper of Caesar's next move. He wasn't sure how he'd relay such secrets to Arsinoe—that was a problem for tomorrow's Ptolemy to puzzle out.

As the night drew on, the party shed all circumspection. Jugs were finished and refreshed, and the stories grew wilder with each passing hour. One soldier boasted of how he took down sixteen Parthinians with only a broken spear in hand, and then another, blustering, tried to top that tale, singing of the time he'd sent fully *twenty-seven* Gauls shrieking to meet Chiron. Only Caesar and Cleopatra appeared untouched by this blustering, folding deeper into each other's eyes until at last his sister abandoned her divan and slipped beside Caesar onto his.

A barrel-chested officer, a stubborn burr at Caesar's side—Aulus Hirtius, Ptolemy thought he'd heard him called—launched into another tale, full of gloating and pantomime. The more entwined Caesar and Cleopatra grew, the more this Hirtius demanded his general's attention. Soon, with every other phrase, he'd turn to Caesar for affirmation, slapping the general's knee and knocking him on his back, urging the commander to confirm or deny some especially salacious detail. Though Caesar smiled gamely enough, he was far too taken with Cleopatra to pay Hirtius much mind. This indifference served only to incite the man, whose voice grew to ear-splitting levels as he carried on about the Battle of Bibracte.

Ptolemy began to worry that he wouldn't hear anything useful after all: the Roman soldiers were far more eager to discuss past victories than reveal any plans for future ones. Bored, he let his gaze flit past the zealous Hirtius and fall upon a great boulder of a man dozing on his couch. His nose blotched and purple from wine and his tongue lolling out of his mouth, he made a pathetic sight. Ptolemy didn't recognize him—he must be one of the foot soldiers Caesar rotated at his table. The scheme bolstered Caesar's reputation for humility; more crucially, the honor of eating side by side with the general boosted morale. The man's head nodded off to the left and he started to tip off his seat. Ptolemy choked back a laugh.

As the soldier tilted farther, he stirred, bracing his enormous feet against the floor and belching loudly to announce his wakefulness.

"It's true," the giant murmured, picking up on some long-abandoned conversation. He pounded on the table for emphasis, but the company ignored him.

Cleopatra had straightened at Caesar's side and took a forced interest in Hirtius's story, smiling at him winningly and hanging on his every word. "Now, Hirtius." Cleopatra reached across the table to take the man's hand in her own. The loquacious officer stared at her blankly. "You've been so modest about your role in all this excitement. Surely you are too humble."

"My role is merely to execute the general's plans. And I have been too busy with affairs abroad to play—" He cut himself off before he finished the thought and simply concluded, "Too busy, I'm afraid, to see my share of glory. We'll have to look to Julius for that."

"Ah, yes, of course," Cleopatra purred. "He's charged you with more important tasks. Such as plotting the arrival of our friend from Pergamum. He's been quite busy in Syria, I hear."

Ptolemy's ears pricked up—*our friend from Pergamum*. It wasn't the first time he'd heard that phrase, though he still didn't know to whom it referred. But the room's reaction to those words convinced him it must be someone important. A name to include in his imagined missives to Arsinoe. Ptolemy racked his mind for the name of Pergamum's ruler, to remember what soldiers he might have at his disposal—but nothing came to him. And this man had reached Syria, where Rome already had legions fresh from fighting the Parthians. From there, would the army travel by boat, clinging to the coasts to avoid the wintery sea, or would they come on foot?

"That's right. We can't all be as brave as Julius," the mauve-faced soldier slurred, more loudly than he had before. As Ptolemy turned to him, he couldn't help but think that the man, with his pinkish hue and sweat-slick skin, closely resembled the pig whose head he'd eagerly devoured. "You should have seen him out there. When he jumped from the battle on the causeway, I never saw anyone swim so fast! And how he's been *praised* for it. If I'd've known I'd be praised for it, I'd've jumped ship long ago."

As the roused colossus spoke, juices spritzing from his mouth, the surrounding divans quieted. A taut silence met the man's accusation. And then, loudly, boldly, Caesar guffawed and slapped his hand against his knee. A familiar jealousy nagged at Ptolemy. He would never know that luxury—to laugh off such an indictment as absurd. The general's bravery was robust, not easily tainted—not a cheap bauble like his own.

"I daresay," Caesar bellowed merrily. "If I'd known you'd hog all the wine, Titus, I'd have drunk some more myself."

Ptolemy tried to picture how he would have reacted in Caesar's place. If Ariston or Kyrillos, say, had insulted him publicly—without a second thought, he would have had them flogged for debasing their king. But Julius had accomplished far more with honey. Humor could serve as a weapon too—maybe it was sharper than an axe. This Titus certainly bristled beneath its strokes.

"I drank my due, no' a drop more. I'll fight the coward who says o'erwise." His words overran one another, spewing from his mouth along with flecks of wine and pork. "At least I've fought well enough to make my sons proud. Good thing you have no sons to be ashamed of your desertions."

Ptolemy glanced back to Caesar, expecting to find the general ready with another quip. But instead the Roman had swung his feet onto the floor; his lips had thinned to a grimace. His whole bearing had stiffened: the soldier had hit a nerve.

"Enough, Titus," Hirtius counseled, weaseling an arm beneath one of the soldier's enormous shoulders. "It's time for bed."

Titus tried to shrug away, batting drunkenly at his rescuer's hands. But after a few minutes, the sloshed centurion gave in. He allowed Hirtius to help him to his feet, and he slung his weight onto the smaller man's shoulders, causing his aide to stagger on his next step. Cleopatra, for once, was silent: even when Hirtius almost collapsed under Titus's heft in the courtyard, she did not so much as crack a smile. Ptolemy wished he could read her mood, but her cavernous eyes were as impenetrable as ever.

Once the two had wandered out of view, Cleopatra leaned back, urging Caesar to relax as well. The movement tightened the linen against her stomach. The baby had popped her belly button outward, Ptolemy noticed; it used to curve the other way. Once or twice, when they were young, they'd swum together naked. She and Arsinoe shared moon-shaped indentations, so unlike the knot of flesh that jutted from his own stomach. *Yours is more manly,* their mother had whispered then.

Did Cleopatra worry about her babe? Did she fear the Roman's seed was weak? She'd have reason to—all those years, all those lovers, and only one child, a girl at that. If the queen had doubts, she brushed over them now, all smiles and japes. The men who remained were less circumspect: a few coughed; others shifted uncomfortably on their divans. The moment opened up before Ptolemy—here, he saw, was an opportunity, a way to renew his bond with Caesar.

"I would have been proud to have you as a father," Ptolemy murmured. He paused, casting a glance at his sister's belly. "I'm jealous of my nephew for that. From the rooftop, I watched how bravely you fought. My only regret was that I couldn't be out there, fighting beside you."

Here, he looked up and met Caesar's dark eyes. There was a gleam to them, though he kept his lips tight and pursed.

"But you had a great father of your own."

"Not so great as you," Ptolemy answered. "He was a coward; there's no need to deny that among friends. If only I had been born to a man like you, a brave and honorable man to guide me on my path, I would never have ended up fighting my dear sister."

Cleopatra stared at him with venom. Whatever fellow feeling he'd built up with her was seared away. He'd mocked their father—he'd tried to tie himself to Caesar—and that would be enough to secure her hatred. But she stayed quiet. Her lover was too changeable on this subject, and she didn't dare involve herself. The realization made him giddy. And that was before Caesar reached out to clasp his hand.

"It warms my heart to hear you say that. I have, since my arrival, wanted nothing more than to guide you. None of us three," the general said, flicking a smile to Cleopatra. "None of us want to face more infighting, not now."

The Roman squeezed his fingers, and Ptolemy felt his stomach turn. He forced himself to wipe the general's fickleness from his mind. *Just for a little while longer,* he reminded himself.

"Me least of all," he declared as he met Caesar's gaze. "I want only to make peace."

Wide and sunken, his sister's eyes bored into him. All blush of pregnancy drained from her face, and she looked as she always had—a creature of destruction, not creation. In that moment, Ptolemy knew—beyond a shadow of a doubt—that she would bring the walls of Alexandria crashing down before she loosed her grip on rule.

His days receded into a rhythm and he feared that his self-flagellation before Caesar had made no impression. Then one morning he woke to pounding at his door. Ptolemy admitted a rangy Roman soldier and watched as the man wiped the sweat from his oily face with the back of his hand, as casually as if he were addressing some commoner in a brothel. But, no, this wasn't the moment for pride. Caesar had summoned him. The vessel didn't matter.

The central atrium, which the general had coopted for his negotiations, was shrunken and unimpressive. Flanked by two austere columns, Caesar bent over a table thick with maps. He looked like a scholar, an old man worn and haggard. Barren. The wonder wasn't that he hadn't sired more children but that he'd managed to plant his seed in Cleopatra at all.

But then Caesar glanced up from his work; a broad smile lit up his face, and the years slipped away.

"My boy," he said. "What a pleasure. I beg you, come and sit."

Ptolemy glanced around—the furnishing was sparse: a few benches dotted the far wall, a single silk divan. Caesar, though, seemed to revel in the atrium's simplicity; the general had little love of luxury. Even the couch was probably Cleopatra's idea—she was the one with the taste for opulence. With the Roman's stoic sensibilities in mind, Ptolemy bypassed the divan. Instead, he cleared a few inkpots from one of the benches and sat.

"Did you sleep well last night?" Caesar asked, running a finger across a darting riverbank. Ptolemy squinted to make out the map's details, but he didn't recognize the terrain. It wasn't the Nile—that much he knew—but some other stream twisting through some other land. Was Caesar going to embark on a new war? He prayed the Gauls or one of the Germanic tribes had grown restless, that even now they wound down—which river would it be, then, the Rhine?—making their way toward Rome. Or perhaps, at last, Pompey's sons had sent their fleet sailing back to Italy. Surely a threat to the Latin capital would be enough to tear Caesar away from Cleopatra, even from his unborn son.

"I did sleep, in time," Ptolemy replied. "And you, Julius, did you sleep well?"

"The older I get, the less sleep I seem to need. And last night, I fear, brought too many woes." Caesar gestured vaguely through the air, as though the woes, like wasps, swarmed about his head. Ptolemy noticed a certain strain in the Roman's tone, a thinness he hadn't heard before.

"Did the night bring bad tidings?" he probed, setting his voice at a mournful timbre. Perhaps the Gauls *had* attacked. The thought—precarious, titillating—solidified in his mind.

"Your people aren't content with Arsinoe, despite her recent victory. I can't say whether that is good news or poor. They rally for you in the streets. Can you not hear them?"

Ptolemy had heard nothing; since they'd arrived at this fortress, it had seemed as if the whole city had faded away.

"I hear them, yes," he lied and then, forcing a whine, "but I don't know why they want me."

Whatever game Caesar played, Ptolemy could see it only in bits and pieces. The Roman was pretending to be his friend, though he wasn't sure, precisely, why. He'd acquired some sort of power, but he couldn't figure out what move he'd made to earn it. Best to keep playing the fool.

"They are frightened, my boy," Caesar said softly as he approached Ptolemy's bench. The Roman towered over him; his eyes struck at the man's gut, at a level with Caesar's girdle. His own gut stung with revulsion, and he wanted nothing more than to stand and demand the general treat him as a king. But he let the feeling ebb. And Caesar, his knees cracking at the effort, sunk onto the bench beside him.

"After all," the Roman went on, "your citizens find themselves caught between two warring women. What man wouldn't be afraid?"

Did Caesar mean to trick him? To force him into revealing his true loyalties? The thought almost made him laugh—he wasn't sure if there were any *true* loyalties left to him. He wished—he planned, when he could think of planning—to join Arsinoe, but it was hardly loyalty that drove him there now; it was sheer pragmatism. At last he'd left that first attribute, that squalling, keening childishness behind.

"Queen Cleopatra is a great and wise ruler," Ptolemy said carefully. "The people have no reason to fear her."

Caesar clucked his tongue, as though he were urging a particularly skittish horse across a river.

"They have much to fear, my boy. You don't need me to tell you that. This kingdom has *always* needed both a queen and a king. Otherwise, the land descends into chaos."

This proposal echoed the one Caesar had made before—that Ptolemy might rule with Cleopatra. *In name.* For he knew it would never be in action. But he couldn't figure out why the general had called him here to extend that offer once more. He tried to read the answer in Caesar's face, in his close-lipped smile and his sunken eyes.

He tried—as best he could—to recall every story he'd ever heard about this man. But what good had his advisors' assiduous character study done? Pothinus was dead, and Achillas too; Theodotus had fled to parts unknown, no doubt to throw his weight behind a more promising student.

All of these councilors, Ptolemy saw, had feigned knowledge of the world and pretended they could see what sparked men's hearts, including Caesar's. But none of them had understood the Roman any better than Ptolemy did. As he studied the general, the Roman assessed him too—the old man's gaze twitched with tenderness. That Ptolemy could do: play the son, the pupil, to Caesar.

"How can I help?" He'd pitched his voice as high as a girl's. His stomach twisted; Caesar's eyes softened around their edges.

"It's that eunuch, you know, Ganymedes, who's causing all this trouble," the general went on. "Your sister wouldn't poison the wells with salt. It's cruel, unnatural."

Ptolemy nodded solemnly, though he wanted to roar with laughter. How little Caesar understood his family. The image of Arsinoe—eyes black and serious in her heart-shaped face, her gaze shifting as it did before she lit on a solution—rose in his mind, so solid he might reach out and touch her. The *unnatural*—part and parcel with the *immortal*—had never stopped the Ptolemies. He suspected she had come up with the idea, not Ganymedes. Indeed, he *hoped* she had. A twinge of admiration prickled in his chest.

"You're right," Ptolemy whined again. "Arsinoe would never think to do something so cruel. She's dull minded and weak willed. And Ganymedes has always manipulated her. I can't blame my people for their fears—I, too, am frightened of what that eunuch might do, what measures he might take to turn Alexandria against her true queen. I wish—"

Abruptly, he cut himself off, as though afraid to speak his mind. His heart thudded, but he ignored it. For a soaring moment, he watched from above: there he was laying the plans, priming each trap, watching each piece settle into place.

"You wish what, my dear boy?" His sister's—his wife's—lover prodded, an avuncular hand patting his knee.

"I wish that..." Sighing, Ptolemy let his voice trail off. It was thrilling, this teasing out of deception. How many times had he watched Cleopatra work such magic? The delicate sowing of seeds of love and regret in their father's mind as she poisoned the Piper against his own sons. He cleared his throat and thumped his chest— made a production of struggling to find his voice. "I wish that there was more that I could do, that I could find some way...some way to be more like you."

"Like me?" The general made a show of scoffing at the idea, throwing up his hands and then slapping at his thighs. But Ptolemy recognized subtler, more telling markers below the exaggerated ones: a slight smile on his lips and small puff in his chest. Even the most insincere forms of flattery could work wonders.

"What makes you say that?" Caesar asked.

Here, he knew, he had to tread with special care.

"You are a great general—everyone knows that. You aren't frightened when men chant your name. Indeed, you stand up and answer their chants with bravery. If I—If only I were able to inspire such loyalty..." Ptolemy gave a heavy sigh and leaned his head back against the wall. "Then we might have avoided all this bloodshed."

"You might avoid further bloodshed," the Roman answered, giving a gentle squeeze to his shoulder. "And I don't see why you should have to be any different than you are to do so. After all..."

This time it was Caesar who let his voice drift off: the man shifted forward, resting elbows on knees, and stared into the distance.

"Your sister, I suppose, won't thank me for this," the Roman murmured, almost to himself. He sunk his head into his hands, digging his knuckles deeply into his eyes. All this trouble—all this worry—all over Cleopatra. Even this lauded general—hailed as the greatest in a dozen generations—wasn't immune to a woman's charm. Perhaps men had indeed grown weaker and smaller since the age of heroes. Surely glorious Alexander, who'd conquered as far as the Indus, had never lost sleep over some sweet-smelling cunt. And he—Ptolemy—he, too, owed his fall to a woman, not even a queen, a *slave* who'd fucked her way into his trust.

"If you don't . . . You needn't tell me," Ptolemy nudged as gingerly as he could. "I don't want to seed dissent between you and my sister. Her temper is fearsome. No one knows that better than I."

Caesar laughed, loudly and heartily, to hide the truth: that he usually yielded to the queen.

"Your sister is a woman, and like all women, she will fret. It makes no matter. I've fretted too much over how to break the good news, which is that you will have the opportunity you seek. The chance to echo my example—as you've so kindly called it—and inspire men."

Ptolemy summoned the most innocent gaze he could muster and looked up at Caesar with his gentlest eyes. Those same eyes that had watched his hand strike Briseis across the face, that had watched as he forced himself into her mouth. These eyes he could still moisten with dewy naïveté.

"I—I will?" he stammered. "How can that be?"

"You will go to your people." Caesar gestured in the direction of the city. "You will go to those men who cry for you in the streets—and you will bring peace."

His heart throbbed and the swelling was so great that it threatened to burst through his ribs. But he didn't smile; he didn't whoop or leap for joy. At last he'd learned to mask his emotions and deploy them with care. Besides, his feelings were no longer the clear beacons they'd once been. A year ago, he would have been elated to join Arsinoe at an army's head. But it made no difference now which woman was by his side. What mattered was that he'd beaten Cleopatra at her own game. She'd won the first battle, and the second, by beguiling Caesar with her body. But he, he would win the war.

"You mean," Ptolemy said, forcing his voice to tremble in its highest register, "you mean you want me to leave the palace."

The Roman squinted at him, his head cocked to the left, unsure of what to make of the boy sitting at his side.

"Yes," Caesar pronounced slowly. "Of course you must ride out into the streets and address your men. You need to convince them that you are the king to *Cleopatra's* queen and end this foolish row between your sisters."

"But I thought—" Ptolemy said in the same small voice, the child's voice he hated. "I thought you wanted me to remain here, to stay with you."

A glint of something—revulsion, maybe—flickered over Caesar's face, but the man covered it with a hearty cough. He placed a firm hand on Ptolemy's shoulder and his tone grew stern, fatherly almost. "What we all want is peace, and to achieve that, you must lead your people. They won't accept me. I'm a Roman. But you, you can stop this bloodshed."

"I will." He nodded earnestly, wiping away his false tears. And then, as though overcome, Ptolemy flung himself to the floor. Kneeling and clutching Caesar's leg, he seized the Roman's hand and kissed it. "I can never express how dear you are to me."

Later, when he was alone in his room, shielded from prying eyes, Ptolemy waited for the relief to wash over him. Yet even as he pre-

pared his speech—even as he pictured his reunion with Arsinoe—
he felt only a strange, itching emptiness. And when night swept its
heavy cloak over the sky, no sleep came to him. Only the dark,
restless gnaw of regret.

SISTER

A day passed and then another. But no matter how much time stretched after the battle, Arsinoe was still flush with madness. She thought of being lofted above the throngs, of twisting her blade into the aghast Roman's eye, the squelch of muddied flesh. Under the light of day, the remembrances buoyed her, and at night, she did not give herself over to sleep. Instead, she welcomed Alexander into her bedroom, where they made loud and reckless love until the dawn.

Eagerly she leapt to face each morning, racing down the steps from the royal apartments and only slowing to a steady pace when she reached the public halls. There, she knew she needed to bear herself as stately as a queen. Laomedon and Alexander had made amends, and Arsinoe took pleasure in their company. Their threesome would wander the palace grounds for hours, discussing at which point they might strike the enemy next, from where Caesar might receive reinforcements. The general had dedicated himself to safeguarding his fortress, barricading the western half of the Canopic Way with boulders. The Romans, it seemed, had found another source of water, for her patrols no longer stumbled across defectors, throats bloated, begging for a drop. Cleopatra's name was left unspoken, though it simmered in the back of Arsinoe's mind. Her sister had wed herself to Rome and faded into it. She merited no mention.

On one such ramble, as their trio passed by the shrine to

Alexander—she always glanced at her lover here, wondering whether he still clung to that mawkish connection to his namesake—Arsinoe heard voices rising from beyond the palace walls. Abandoning Laomedon midsentence, shedding Alexander's cloying hands, she peeled off toward the western gate. The way a child might, she pressed her eye against an opening in the twined goldwork. A great crowd had gathered—but it didn't face the palace. She stared out over thousands upon thousands of sun-browned backs instead. They stretched as far as she could see, and even when she hooked a foot onto a low rung in the gate and hoisted herself higher, she could not make out the mob's end. The scene had all the makings of a riot, except that rioters faced their queen.

Near at hand, the shouts railed. At first the syllables remained disparate, harsh *taus* and *xis* biting at the air. Then the sounds melded together, one cleaving to the next, until they formed a word: *Ptolemaios*. Her heart lurched; her mind must be playing tricks on her. She sharpened her ears and willed herself to be corrected, anticipating the delight she'd feel when she laughed with Alexander over the odd imaginings that haunted her. But then, more clearly, she heard the same syllables again, followed by others even more grating. "*Ptolemaios Anax, Ptolemaios Theos.*" Ptolemy the King, Ptolemy the God.

"Open the gate," she shouted. Her sentinels stared at her in confusion. She'd shrieked before she'd had time to think—to consider how to approach her subjects, how to punish them for their betrayals. How *dare* they scream for him, that crass and stupid boy who'd never heeded his lessons, who'd fallen freely into Caesar's traps, who'd never fought when he could flee? Whatever sympathies she'd harbored toward the child—the pity she felt for him as a boy when he, wounded, puzzled over their father's misplaced love—evaporated like dew in Inundation's heat.

"Wait." Alexander was at her side, easing her fingers off the gold-plated iron, helping her find her feet. "What are you doing?"

"I will not stand by as the city turns her love to *him*." Roughly, she yanked her hand away. "Go on, open it," she commanded the stunned guards.

The men sprung so quickly into action that she and Alexander had to scuttle back, roaches fleeing from a sole. The gates groaned, the sentinels heaved, and then the plaza spread out before her: heads swathed in manes of brown and close-shorn stubbles of black, here and there punctuated by the flash of copper or even gold.

A few scattered faces glanced toward her—a boy, perhaps of eight or ten, who clutched a pomegranate in his grubby hand; a gaunt man with a wizened beard who smirked slightly to himself. But otherwise the loosing of the palace gate—an event by rights greeted with cheers—went unremarked. Their queen—the Lady of the Two Lands, the Horus Incarnate—stood near enough to touch, and the horde barely let out a sigh. Silence, here, cut more sharply than jeers.

Part of her wanted to dart into the crowd—to face the menace at once, alone, on her own two feet. But she was no longer a child; she couldn't run barefoot through the streets any more than she could sneak into Cleopatra's bed for comfort in the night. She looked back to the knot of guards behind her—despite her victory, despite how they'd raised her on their backs, these were not her men. They'd belonged to Achillas before, and now to Ptolemy. And for all she could guess, her brother was at this very moment galloping through Alexandria, pledging a peaceful rule with Cleopatra and smoldering her rebel dreams to ash.

"Draw up my litter and a fleet of carriages," she commanded. "We must greet my brother with an entourage befitting a king."

Time collapsed into a rush of preparations. As the procession was readied, Arsinoe returned to the royal chambers, allowing Eirene to paint her face—"Quickly, quickly"—and drape her in finery. The linen kissed her body at her breasts and hips, and hung off her shoulders in translucent waves. The diadem wafted on her head, but her wrists and ankles were weighed down with trinkets, emeralds and amethysts and pearls. A passing glance in the mirror jolted her senses—the reflection staring back looked twice the goddess Cleopatra ever had. The realization struck hard and echoed strange. After all these years obscured, she'd burst forth—and beautiful.

Ganymedes, Laomedon, Alexander—each in turn begged to ride with her. She refused all three; she wanted—no, needed—to face this threat alone. Her body jolted forward as the slaves hoisted the litter, and the carrier lulled into its singsong pace. There was no advice her lover or her commander might offer—even the eunuch would prove of little use. The question that faced her didn't concern strategies or battle plans—only Ptolemy. And who could understand her brother better than she?

"Ptolemaios Anax, Ptolemaios Soter." Ptolemy the King, Ptolemy the Savior. The chants grew louder as her litter rounded onto the Canopic Way, but she did not plug her ears. Instead, she tried to tease out the fount of their enthusiasm: What, precisely, had her brother promised them? How had he persuaded them of his greatness? In the days since she'd retaken Pharos, she'd scarcely spared a thought for Ptolemy. Her vanity—bolstered by her reincarnation as a fighter, a killer—had blinded her, she saw that now. She'd forgotten that her brother might have undergone his own transformations; she'd convinced herself that he would never be a real threat. That the sway she'd held over him in childhood persisted, immutable. As a boy, he'd worshipped her, loved her, even—despite her indifference, or perhaps because of it. But now he was nearly a man. And a man prepared to abandon such childish fancies.

No matter how far she stretched her neck out the vehicle's window, she still could not see what lay beyond the throngs. The Sema loomed in granite on her left, but she could discern only flashes of other landmarks: the pediment above the temple of Isis, the great goddess flanked by kneeling priests, and farther along, bearded, stern-faced Serapis, staring down from his own sacred house. It took all her self-control to withdraw back into the carriage—she needed at least to feign that she already knew what was going on. To preserve the mirage, for however little time remained, that she and Ptolemy had plotted together in whatever action he undertook.

The litter stumbled to a halt. The roar of the crowd dulled to a murmur. There was no point in delaying—whatever would come, would come. As she stepped from the carrier, the Alexandrian sun battered her face, blinding her as it washed her in light. A good omen, that—to appear kissed by the sun, by the gods. She embraced the portent, staring into the brightness, widening her eyes until they watered.

The sun slipped behind a wispy cloud and her sight cleared. As she stood on the step of the litter, her brother loomed over her, seated on a breathtaking stallion. It took her a moment to recognize the animal beneath the gold-plated bridle and gleaming saddle—Aethon, the charger their father had given Ptolemy, gray dapples glinting silver. Her brother, too, appeared transformed: far taller and broader than when she'd last seen him. Arsinoe's stomach bottomed out, and she spoke to ward off her worst fears: that he had come to curse her and affirm his faith in Cleopatra.

"How brave and cunning must have been your escape," she said. "How marvelous to see you here before me in the flesh."

To her surprise, the boy—still awkward, odd footed in his motions—flung one leg over his horse's back and dropped from his mount. The crowd crowed with glee—though Arsinoe still could not say why. Her brother approached, and their eyes met. And as she stared into their milky brown depths, she could read no hint of emotion. He'd learned to shield his thoughts. The same lesson she had learned when she had been the captive of another sister, cowering before the threat of other Romans.

"My dear Arsinoe," he said as he reached her and wrapped his arms about her waist. "My sister and my queen."

The roar was deafening. As though their union alone would crack Rome's will. Nothing, she realized darkly—not her slaying of that soldier, not her victory over Caesar's fleet—could have ever heartened her citizens as much as this: the joining of a brother-sister pair.

On foot, they two cut through the crowds, mimicking the path they would have taken to be blessed before Serapis. Amid the ringing cheers, Arsinoe felt few traces of joy. Relief, of course—that washed over her in heady waves, threatening to buckle her knees and send her sprawling to the stone. Her brother had changed, not merely in height but in the way he could look at her without a blush creeping into his cheeks. His very bearing had altered, as though his months as a prisoner had drained him of the frivolities and vanities of youth. He had an almost ragged look to him, the mistrustful gaze of a stray too often kicked away from meat.

She smiled and slipped her hand into his. His palm was clammy, a slippery eel despite the day's chill. Under her breath, she asked him questions—bland inquiries into his health, how their mother and Ptolemarion fared. At their mention, the boy's body bristled— the answers he gave were little more than grunts. Defeated, she let the conversation lapse. In time, she promised herself, she would rule his heart again.

To celebrate the reunion, one of the lesser banquet halls had been prepared: the crocodile-frescoed lounge off the royal courtyard.

Here their dwindled numbers were masked by the nearness of the walls. As they toasted Egypt and Alexandria, the Nile and the sea, the old gods and themselves, she detected something grittier in Ptolemy's gaze—a trace of his childhood crush, not forgotten but warped into something fiercer, crueler.

The night stretched on and the company grew rowdy. If Arsinoe squinted away the smallness of the room, she might even have mistaken the scene for one of her father's infamous feasts. The revelers drank heavily; Laomedon, staid enough under ordinary circumstances, pulled a camp follower into his lap, and Ganymedes's words had begun to slur, one into the next. And yet each time she glanced at her brother, a slave seemed to be refilling his goblet with water—he appeared to eschew the stronger stuff almost entirely. As for the eunuch, the drink had tempered his gloominess, and when he launched into yet another animated rendition of how his ships had seized the island's north shore, Arsinoe stood and slid next to her brother on his divan.

Ptolemy scooted to put some space between them. His discomfort—which he'd fought so hard to hide—grew palpable: his left leg bounced and he tapped his thumb against the cushion.

"Did you see the battle?" she asked.

A nod and a gleam, she suspected, of envy.

"I should have fought," he muttered, almost to himself. "I would have proved my mettle."

A violent surge of tenderness clutched at her. Even as he strained to shroud his emotions, his words revealed much more than he realized—at fourteen, he was yet a boy in so many ways, clinging to a boy's dream of glory. His head still spun with tales of yesteryear, myths of the gods battling the Titans, the Achaeans at the gate of Ilium. A child's vision of war, devoid of pain and the heavy weight of death. Ignoring Alexander's glares from across the room, where he caroused with his newfound Pharos friends, she wrapped her arms about her brother's neck and stroked his hair.

"And so you shall fight in the next," she whispered in his ear.

"Pergamum," he blurted out suddenly. "Caesar has a friend from Pergamum he's called upon for reinforcement. The man is marching here—he's rallying Roman allies in Syria, I think."

"Who? How many legions?" She tried to modulate her voice, but her questions still sounded like accusations.

The boy glanced about the lounge, as though the scattered soldiers might speak for him. Did he look, she wondered, for someone in particular—some ally he might discover in this transmuted hall, at once foreign and familiar?

Gathering every bit of tenderness she could muster, she leaned toward her brother, acutely aware of how her robe draped to reveal the top of her breasts. Playfully, she squeezed his knee.

"Come, Ptolemy, tell me: how many men?"

"I don't *know*," he demurred.

Already, though, calculations unspooled in her mind: the weather had grown cool; the winds whipped dangerously—wiser to avoid a sea voyage and travel on foot. Syria covered vast swaths of land, but the most likely genesis of any Roman reinforcements would be Antioch: from that city, a commander might call upon all the client kingdoms, from Pontus to Judea, for recruits. Besides, Antioch provided quick access to Egypt: seven days, as she counted, to reach Tyrus, plus another five to arrive in Raphia—and from there, only three days would bring this *friend* of Caesar's to the gates of Pelusium. The city with its mud brick walls would be a tempting target, wealthy and unprotected. Poor dead Achillas had drawn away all its battalions when he'd marched on Alexandria, and she herself had stripped the port of even its tariff ships. Perhaps her motley group could muster a fight for Alexandria, trap this army as it crossed the

Nile's muddy mouths—but Pelusium would fall. There was no denying that.

"I don't know," Ptolemy repeated, though she hadn't pressed the
point. The more he spoke, the shriller his voice grew. "Cleopatra
didn't tell me specifics—I was hardly her closest confidant. I only
overheard her at feasts, dangling it over my head: *Remember our friend
from Pergamum.*"

Such a slight thing on which to set a stratagem, Arsinoe mused.
And then, as from the ether: *Mithradates.* The name shot into her
mind, ricocheting about and tumbling her back to the day that
Berenice wed her second husband, the pretender who'd claimed
kinship to that great ruler of Pontus. But that name belonged
as well to the true son of Mithradates the Great: the Rome-
allied commander from Pergamum. Suddenly she'd pieced it all
together. What rumors had she heard of *this* Mithradates? How
many legions might he have?

"No one ever mentioned a name, a Mithradates?" she asked.

"I told you," Ptolemy snapped. "No one said anything else in front
of me."

The fury tightened in her breast, but she clenched her fists beneath the table and prayed for calm: she needed to soothe him,
entice him back under her spell.

"Of course, my sweet," she replied. "And what you've told me
helps more than I can say."

Ptolemy glared at her. "Don't patronize me, Arsinoe. You'll
regret it."

With those words, he slammed his glass roughly on the table and
stood. A few of the assembled men had quieted their conversations
and watched with interest.

"My brother," she whispered, grabbing hold of his hand and
pulling him down to sit. Almost as a reflex, Ptolemy tried at first

to twist his arm away but then relented. She cupped his chin in her hand, a gentle gesture—or so it would read. More to the point, it forced her brother to meet her eye. "Whatever you're holding against me, let it fade. Every man here must have faith in our allegiance. Now embrace me and show those gathered we are friends."

Ptolemy leaned toward her and kissed her squarely—boldly—on the lips. His mouth tasted foul, as though he'd spent weeks eating nothing but salted trout. Perhaps he had. Disgust bubbled in her stomach, and she had to fight the urge to recoil from his touch. His hand tightened on hers and then released. The moment passed, and he pulled away, grinning. "Look, now the whole world sees what great friends we are."

"Indeed, they will remember our goodwill," she replied, all smiles as she returned to her own divan. Summoning a nearby slave to ladle more wine, she lifted her glass—a wide-mouthed goblet depicting Theseus locked against the Minotaur, hand to horn. The monster looked pathetic, shrunken—no match for the naked Athenian and his sword.

"To my brother, Ptolemy. May his reign be long and fruitful," she cried out. The room fell quiet, and chalices rose to match hers.

"To the rule of Queen Arsinoe and King Ptolemy," Laomedon shouted. "May it be great and prosperous."

Others followed suit, stomping their feet against the floor. The tread of guards had never sounded so sweet against her ears. Ptolemy might hold the misplaced love of the citizens—but the army knew *her*. They'd fought with her and watched her kill a Roman in their midst. She could siphon off their trust yet, and as she beamed at her brother, she saw his flinching recognition of that fact.

The night dimmed; the soldiers drank. Ptolemy set aside his temperance and downed cup after cup. When he started nodding into his goblet, Arsinoe called for a servant to accompany him to his chambers—a Nubian beauty, one Eirene had suggested, with henna-reddened hair and inky, deep-set eyes.

Her own bed called to her. The hall felt somehow cramped and claustrophobic; despite the piquant scent of myrrh, the room had grown foul with other odors too, the stench of moist flesh and stale beer. She did a quick accounting of her men: Laomedon, his hand stretched halfway up his whore's tunic, was far too drunk to notice if she left. She searched out Ganymedes, but the eunuch—as far as she could tell—had already disappeared into the night. Alexander, too, had vanished. And she was glad of it; there was no move that could be made tonight against this Mithradates of Pergamum. For a little while longer that knowledge and its burden were hers alone to bear.

With each step toward the royal apartments, another worry descended: what to do when Pelusium fell, how much longer she could hold Alexandria, whether Ptolemy would prove more adversary than ally. By the time she'd latched the door behind her, she was ready to sink down to her knees and weep from the load. Instead, she pinched the delicate flesh under her arm. She'd fought for these responsibilities, and she had won. At the head of a cobbled army, she'd defeated Caesar, brought down a legionary with her own knife. She controlled the palace and the city both.

"Not even a greeting, then."

Arsinoe startled at the voice. She squinted—an oil lamp was lit on the anteroom table, and its meek glow revealed Alexander, lounging on a divan. He made no move to get up; languidly, he stretched and then folded his hands behind his head. His eyes glinted, and though Arsinoe knew it was only a trick of the light, she couldn't help but notice that they looked as cold as she'd ever seen them.

"Not tonight, Alexander," she told him softly. He had grown

greedy—three nights in a row they'd slept together, and they'd made love so many times she'd lost count.

"Why *not* tonight?" He swung his legs over the divan's edge to sit. "What night would be better? After all, soon you will be *wed*."

An echo of an argument they'd had years ago, a foolish fight between two children, about what it meant to wed and to love. The spat had begun over the question of which man Berenice would marry, though Arsinoe saw now that they had been quarreling over something else entirely. It felt a lifetime ago—back in the days when she'd clung fervently to her faith in her elder sister, her belief that Cleopatra's return would right the world of all its wrongs.

"You know why not tonight." She was tired, her voice quiet. Ptolemy's effortless capture of her people's hearts, his news of another force massing in Asia, had chipped away at her confidence. With a rush of self-pity, she suddenly felt small, inconsequential. A fragile pawn in this game of war with Rome. A dull realization washed over her: Even if she faced Caesar again and somehow emerged victorious, sooner or later Egypt would fall. Rome had too many allies; they would come and come and come. She was but one woman flailing her hands against an approaching storm. "Leave me. I want to be alone."

Her own disappointments loomed too large; she couldn't face Alexander's too—that child's dream that they might share a life. At times she could see it vividly, as though he'd painted it out before her: two pairs of hands clasped together at the Temple of Serapis, a milky-eyed babe suckling at her breast, a half-grown boy grinning as he threw a javelin.

"Stop," she commanded the vision that spun before her. How she longed to shriek, to claw Alexander's eyes. *Don't show me days that will never lie ahead.* She would wed Ptolemy, and she would take her brother to her bed. It was the only path—her children needed to be full-blooded kings, their lines and reigns unquestioned.

"No," Alexander objected as he stood. His resistance threw her, and she could only watch, frozen, as he approached. He trapped her against the door, his sinewy arms braced on either side of her own. For all the steadiness of his body, his eyes looked strange, unmoored. He was drunker than she'd realized, and his breath was hot against her neck. She could taste the stink of it, the lingering tang of wine, sickly sweet. "I want you, Arsinoe."

She was tired. Too tired to fight, to deny him—and she felt that first tingling of fear. In a visceral way she grew aware of their differences. He was a man; she a woman—she'd never felt more conscious of the realities that distinction entailed. All the power in the city— every man from Nubia to Pelusium prostrate before her—but in the here and now, in this room, she could not fight him off. Trembling, she was at his mercy—whatever he wanted, he could take. Her heart thudded in her chest. It was at once pleasant and terrifying, this letting go. She craned her neck and kissed him.

The world was here, in the flicker between them, in the meeting of their tongues. She reached her fingers up his neck and buried them in his hair. She needed him closer—for them to swallow one another whole. And then it ended: Alexander pulled away, and she stumbled forward into the gulf where his body had been. He looked down at her, his gaze rife with grief and longing.

"No, Arsinoe. I want all of you, and all to myself." She pressed her forehead into his chest.

"Alexander . . . you know that can never be."

Not this argument, not now. Not when she needed him so badly.

"Why? Your sister takes Caesar as her consort."

She looked up at him and smiled wanly.

"Well, I might take you as a *consort,* if you place your draughts wisely." Again, she ran her fingers about his neck, gripping the short hairs at his nape, pulling his face to hers.

"I'm serious, Arsinoe."

"As am I."

"Don't marry your brother. Wed me instead." The words had tumbled from his mouth.

She kissed him, hard and furious, to flush that false future from his mind. What they had now was the best she could ever hope to offer. She would make that be enough. Lacing his fingers with hers, she slipped his hand beneath her chiton and placed it squarely on her breast. At first he resisted, but already he was growing hard against her stomach. With her other hand, she fumbled to unpin her robes. She would join her limbs to his and entwine them in body and mind, and his foolish notions would be forgotten. But then Alexander stepped away.

"No," he whispered. "You were right. I should go."

Gently, he moved her to one side, so that she no longer blocked the door. Quiet as a ghost, he unbolted the latch. She closed her eyes; the hinges screeched, begging as she longed to do.

"Don't." All dignity abandoned. "Stay with me."

"I will," he said softly, "when I can play your brother's part. When I can be your husband and your king."

And so he left. She lay down, and though her body wilted with exhaustion, sleep refused to come. How could Alexander be so daft to imagine that he might one day rule? But, she supposed, who was she to question ambition's baleful pull? Her own had already excised her father, Cleopatra—now her lover too, her true and only friend.

Her skin burned, feverish, and she tore away the sheets, crumpling them into an angry heap. None of it would matter—not her betrayals nor her heartache—unless she could stave off Rome. The sacrifices she'd made, the people she'd wounded—they only had meaning if she *won*.

Late, with dawn menacing, Arsinoe sunk at last into a haunted sleep. A vulture, she tore at cobras and she-wolves both. She could no longer tell which was friend and which was foe.

BROTHER

His return had been the triumphant stuff of dreams: his subjects swarmed about his charger and soldiers shouted his name. Even Arsinoe, swathed in Cleopatra's robes, a goddess radiant among the throngs, had embraced him. It was everything he'd ever wanted, and yet somehow it was not enough.

Ptolemy felt that something inside him—his *ka,* his soul—had sundered, leaving two crippled, shadow selves vying in its place. On the surface, he rippled with newfound boldness: he swept into the atrium and ordered alignments for the regiments; he kissed his sister square on the lips. But beneath his chest puffing, he wondered how much truly had changed now that he had swapped one sister for the other. He found himself studying Arsinoe's moods and glances just as assiduously as he'd once studied Cleopatra's. The play remained the same—only the cast had shifted.

For the first time in his life, he was master of his own hours, and contrary to what his tutors might have expected, he found himself anxious to fill them. He didn't seek out idleness—that was the hobgoblin of reflection, a far too terrifying prospect. Instead, the moment he woke, he'd rush down to the atrium, where he'd check to see whether any of Caesar's pawns had shifted in the night. Skirmishes cropped up around Pharos, but each proved less decisive than the last. Both armies seemed to know intuitively that the real battle would begin only when Mithradates of Pergamum arrived, and so they contented themselves with halfhearted lovers' spats over small stretches of land and sea.

Having watched helplessly the clash over Pharos, Ptolemy threw himself into planning the battles that remained. He was determined to fight for Pelusium—to defeat Mithradates before he established a foothold in Egyptian soil. Arsinoe swore such a victory was impossible—that the city would fall and there was no point in wasting defenders on it, but he refused to accept defeat. Instead, he offered one plan after another, until the moon rose and set again, and even Laomedon—the most tireless of the entourage—begged him to let them all go to bed. There'd be time for bed, Ptolemy retorted, after they'd driven Caesar and Cleopatra and Mithradates into the sea.

He barely ate and he hardly slept. He felt no need; his obsessions sustained him.

And then Pelusium fell.

The despair that followed was all-consuming. The wall between his two selves crumbled, and the darkness enveloped both. He scarcely noticed that the preparations carried on without him, and it wasn't until he found himself aboard a barge sailing down the Nile that he registered how Arsinoe had taken up the slack. It was she who now insisted they face Mithradates of Pergamum before he drew any nearer to Alexandria. But as his sister flourished, Ptolemy sank deeper into malaise. He'd never been more acutely aware of how—despite his best efforts to embody the role—he was still merely playing at king.

Outside Sais, they disembarked with the greater part of their forces, freeing the fastest ships to bring fresh supplies to their rendezvous point. There, on dry land, his spirits started to revive. On Aethon's back he looked the part of king, with the cobra gleaming from his helmet. He urged the horse forward, into first a trot and then a canter. Another nudge and the stallion opened into a full gallop, hooves almost silent on the silt.

The troops disappeared behind him, but their presence tugged at him, even—especially—unseen. It was new, this sense of being yoked—to an army, to his men, even to Arsinoe. Under Cleopatra's watch, he'd been untethered, his mind spooling plots to secure his freedom. He'd dreamt of all this, certainly. But he hadn't realized there could be something more powerful than leading: belonging.

Afraid, suddenly, that his army would melt away, he spun Aethon around so roughly that the charger careened sideways, almost diagonal to the earth. Mud flew up into his face, a wet clump splattering on his cheek, before Aethon regained his balance. Once Ptolemy rubbed away the dirt, he saw—of course—that the procession remained: a solid line along the river's blue. He allowed himself to luxuriate in the anxious prancing of the coursers, the slow plod of the plow horses, the steady march of the foot soldiers. Each had its own majestic rhythm.

One horse and rider broke away, racing toward him. The pair looked smaller than the rest, and lighter too—unburdened by armor, they seemed to fly. Squinting, he recognized the sorrel mare his sister rode. His heart skittered. Every time he thought he'd found his footing with Arsinoe, it got mucked up somehow. He'd established himself, then Pelusium fell, and he'd faded into the background. It didn't help that Arsinoe's very scent spun his thoughts into perversity. And he was never certain whether to treat her with admiration or with disdain—which would strengthen his position and which would lead him to her bed. Already she was upon him, reining in her mare, a dusky smile on her lips.

"My brother and my king." She offered up the formal greeting, though there was no one about to hear it. And when he said nothing, merely pressed his parched lips together, she went on. "Did you mean to bring down Mithradates and his army all on your own? You ought to leave some glory to our men."

Her tone was teasing, but he recognized the admonishment too. Better, though, not to quarrel. To treat her with indifference rather than admit how her words writhed under his skin.

"You're right, dear sister," he answered, dry and stilted. "I meant to take the whole army on myself."

Arsinoe squinted at him thoughtfully. A stray lock of hair tumbled in front of her face, and she brushed it away as she might a noisome fly.

"When did you grow so cold, Ptolemy?"

He bristled at the question, at the unfairness of it, though he knew he should have long ago abandoned any sense of *fair*.

"I'm not cold," he answered slowly. "But I have changed—I'm no longer a boy. I'm stronger now."

Another tendril escaped her diadem and fell over her eye. This time, she tossed her head to rid herself of it.

"Of course you are," she soothed. "But you needn't always be so strong with me."

His cheeks burned—traitors that they were—and he looked away. Across the next branch of the river and beyond—toward Pelusium. That first site of defeat.

"Is that so?" Ptolemy forced a chuckle. "Rumors suggest otherwise."

This was the closest he'd come to mentioning Achillas. More than once, he'd weighed the advantages of naming his sister's murder, but he couldn't see how it would do him any good. Now that he poked at the subject, he studied Arsinoe's face for a reaction, a hint of remorse, even grief.

"And what about the rumors that trail you?" she asked softly in return. "Half the army whispers that you must share Cleopatra's dark magic. How else could you have convinced Caesar to let you go?"

Dark magic. Did Arsinoe mock him by giving him a woman's attributes?

"Embrace the rumors," his sister urged. "Fear and love are two sides of the same coin. Our soldiers will follow you all the more boldly into battle since they think there's a decent chance you'll smite Mithradates with a thunderbolt on sight."

A laugh escaped her lips. That hadn't changed—it still rang like music. He struggled to ignore the tingle in his gut and his groin. He tightened his fingers on his reins until the leather plowed furrows into his palms.

"You're right," he declared, more forcefully than necessary. "And no doubt they think you can turn fresh water into salt."

"And who's to say I can't?"

Arsinoe's eyes flicked back toward the line, which drew nearer, toy soldiers burgeoning into men. Did it even matter what they whispered—about either him or Arsinoe? They fought for gold, not for house or loyalty. He didn't live in the age of heroes but that of men.

Horses locked in stride, the two siblings—the two gods—rode as one, for the most part in easy silence. From time to time a third would interrupt their union: Laomedon bearing tidings about Mithradates's camp or Ganymedes advising on where to pitch their own. For a few stades, his sister's childhood friend—the ill-named Alexander—lingered in their company. The man's presence unnerved him—he'd heard the gossip that buzzed about the troops. He'd nearly believed it himself. But Arsinoe's manner toward the soldier was so icy that he could hardly imagine them as the inseparable children they once were, let alone sharing a bed.

When Ptolemy caught sight of the camp, he had to credit

Ganymedes with its placement. The location might have been snatched from Philo's treatise on tactics: flanked by the Nile on one side, a ridge on another, and a marsh on the third, it required guards only along its southern edge. And by the time he and Arsinoe arrived, the soldiers had barricaded this unprotected border and even erected a walled enclosure around a supply route to the nearby village.

Once the sky had darkened and the fortifications were complete, the soldiers grew restless. Wine casks were pried open and the men drank. Or rather the other men did. Ptolemy didn't trust himself to touch much of the liquid—better to keep his wits about him with Arsinoe near at hand; otherwise, he might betray the power she still held over him. With each hour, the men grew rowdier, crooning ribald verses about Caesar and his illicit relations with some Bithynian king. Unsteady clumps of girls emerged from the barricaded passageway to town; perhaps, Ptolemy thought, this was the real reason his army had been so devoted to its construction. Songs turned to moans and cries—the last fucks before the bloody dawn.

A familiar laugh. His sister was stumbling toward him. The moonlight settled on a brimming jug clutched between her palms. She bent over his lap and pressed the cool terra-cotta to his lips.

"Come, Brother," she urged, tilting the vessel forward. So near at hand, she smelled of wine, and of weakness too. "What? Do you think I mean to poison you on the eve of battle?"

Sighing, she drank deeply from the jug. A trickle dribbled down her chin. Ptolemy watched its ruby path slide along her throat and onto her chest.

"Come, celebrate!" She thrust the wine at him. "After all, who knows when we might revel again?"

Folding her legs gracefully beneath her, she sat beside him.

Something stirred inside him—something reckless, animalistic, in the face of looming death—and he drained the rest.

More wine came to them, though he wasn't sure of its provenance. As they shared this second chalice, she traced the light hairs along his arm to his shoulder. Once there, her fingers lingered, toying with the neckline of his tunic. He struggled to dismiss the yearning in his groin and convince himself that her touches were sisterly affection, nothing more. But with each passing instant, that grew more difficult: her fingers massaging his scalp, her lips kissing a drop of wine from his neck.

No one paid the two of them much mind. Ganymedes, more sober than the others, was busy helping Laomedon stumble back to the latter's tent. The only gaze Ptolemy caught was Alexander's. His sister's friend stood, brooding, some meters away, but Arsinoe took no notice. Soon after, Alexander stormed off, only to return, hustling a pretty whore in tow. For a fleeting moment, Ptolemy thought he detected a tightening in his sister's expression. But then it vanished. A trick of the light.

Here, licked in flame, her dark hair iridescent with the glow, Arsinoe was the same girl who'd soothed him as a boy, the same budding woman he'd watched at their father's funeral. She hadn't changed—she'd never deceived him, not in her heart. They'd always shared something, a special kinship, and now, at last, she too had embraced it. The division that had sprouted between them—the fault for that lay with Cleopatra and the poison she poured into every bond. Arsinoe took him by the hand and led him toward her tent. A wide, glorious future lay ahead.

The sound of trumpets bleated away the sweetest dream, and Ptolemy stirred. He sat bolt upright on the mat, and the tent spun. *Stupid,* he cursed himself. He shouldn't have drunk so much. Pieces of the night floated back to him: the men lining up their whores, Arsinoe's hands teasing at his chest. *Had* it all been a dream? Blinking rapidly, he forced the world into focus. Maps strewn over a table, an array of perfume bottles lined on a cedar chest, jewels strung from hanging lamps. It was Arsinoe's tent, not his.

A shadow passed over the canvas flap. He noticed his own nakedness, and his hand seized at the sheet. Should he cover up? He stopped himself; the impulse was childish.

"Rise, my king," a voice—not Arsinoe's—called out. It took him a moment to register that it belonged to Ganymedes. "The battle waits for no man."

He struggled to stand, eyes scanning the ground for his tunic. He grabbed the garment—sweat stained but otherwise untarnished.

"Now, my king." Ganymedes's tone had sharpened.

Ptolemy slipped the soiled tunic over his head, buckled the belt around his waist. Clumsily, he staggered out of the tent. The camp had become a hive of activity: men fastening their breastplates, sharpening their swords, and vaulting onto steeds.

"What—what happened?" he stammered. A charger shied as its master tried to hoist himself into the saddle, and Ptolemy tripped over a stray tent peg as he struggled to get out of the way.

"Caesar has launched an attack on the village. Arsinoe has sent men to defend it."

"Caesar?" he echoed, as though repeating the name would make sense out of it. But Caesar was far away, in Alexandria. His sluggish mind cast about for an explanation. "Where's my sister?"

"Where you should be," the eunuch said. "With Laomedon, finalizing plans for battle."

As the eunuch shuffled him toward the commander's tent, bellowing at men to clear a wider path for their king, Ptolemy couldn't help but notice that the camp, despite its activity, appeared in disarray. The scenes he encountered bordered on chaos; shouts and curses flew about in Greek and Aramaic and Egyptian, even a slip or two of Latin. How could this haphazard army face the rigid discipline of Rome's legions?

Outside Laomedon's tent, men had begun to gather. The canvas flap of the tent opened, and he thought he'd lost his last grip on sanity. He could have sworn that Cleopatra stood before him—brilliant in the cross-stitched regalia of the goddess Isis. After a moment, he realized it was Arsinoe, her eyes blackened with kohl, her lips painted red.

"Be brave, my brother," she whispered as she stepped past him. The soldiers scarcely paid him any heed—their eyes all fixed on his sister. No matter what he did, power ebbed from his grasp.

"My men," Arsinoe began, her voice a mix of honey and iron, "Caesar mutilates another of our villages. We must fight him for it, and we must win. My brother and I stand united. Together we will build a better Egypt, a richer Egypt—one that will never empty its coffers paying tribute to Rome. An Egypt that will reward you for your bravery. Fight for us, fight for Egypt. Fight for Alexandria!"

Cries rippled among the men—"*Ptolemaios Theos*" from some, "*Arsinoe Thea*" from others—their halfhearted loyalties still divided. The cheering and the clattering of the javelins grated on his ears.

An attendant clamped a gold-hammered breastplate across Ptolemy's chest and fastened the helmet on his head. As he staggered to mount Aethon, the armor felt off-kilter, as though the left side was forged from some heavier metal than the right. His nerves, the lingering wine in his veins—those must be to blame. He needed only to regain equilibrium.

But there was no time to settle into his seat. No sooner had Ptolemy climbed on his horse than Laomedon—in bloodstained armor aboard a great chestnut stallion—was motioning him to follow. The commander cleared a wide path, sending servants and whores scurrying before the charger's hooves. The lackadaisical soldiers of that morning emerged transformed: shy boys and bawdy crooners metamorphosed into straight-backed sentinels. Ahead stretched the thickest line of men, javelins hoisted against the Roman onslaught.

Or so he assumed. His view was blocked by his own soldiers' helms, so he couldn't actually see Caesar's army. He could hear the cadenced stomp of boots and the trot of hooves beyond, though, spears whooshing through the air.

The battle sank into a rhythm, a dance he'd never learned. His foot soldiers hurled their projectiles; the Romans sent spears and arrows soaring back. From time to time, a few of Caesar's men made a dash and engaged his infantry hand-to-hand. Then the front line would curve and sway, undulating with individuated battle. Once, a Roman soldier broke through, and Laomedon—before Ptolemy had even thought to draw his own weapon—loosed an arrow that pierced the gap between the man's breastplate and his helm. A teetering moment and the enemy stood frozen before tumbling back, blood spurting from his throat. And yet, despite all this, the war— his war—still felt removed, filled with soldiers acting on instinct, with precision and coordination he couldn't hope to understand. The emptiness welled in him again—the sense that he would never truly belong, let alone lead.

Behind him, he heard shouts and the clatter of swords on shields. He glanced back to see his men pouring out from the barricaded path that linked the camp to the village. Eyes wild, helms askew, they appeared an entirely different breed of beast from the soldiers who held the front line. One, bearded and barrel-chested, pointed and shrieked as shrilly as a girl. Ptolemy's gaze followed the man's finger. There, on the ridge, where several dozen Alexandrians had been posted as guards, stood at least a hundred centurions. Maybe more.

At the hill's crest, an enormous soldier with a single glinting eye—a scar of twisted flesh where the other had been—cradled a severed head in his hand. With precision, he spat in the dead man's mouth before hurling the gruesome relic aside. As it spun through the air, Ptolemy remembered Berenice, her head teetering across the onyx. He thought of Pompey, hair frayed and skin peeling. Of Pothinus, with his empty, dust-smeared eyes. Above, the Roman throng roared and charged, and all recollections faded.

Steadying his nerve, Ptolemy drew his sword. There weren't so very many of them, and they were on foot—he, at least, had Aethon. He could feel the horse's heart pounding against his knees, the thud of excitement joining man and beast. He kicked and his mount lurched forward. And—as though they heard his heart's cry—a handful of his cavalry joined in the charge.

"For Egypt!" he managed to shout.

Acting of its own instinct, his sword swung down and—by some crazed luck—met with shield. The clang shocked against his hand, a brutish pain ached in his shoulder, and he nearly dropped his blade. He readied himself to slice again, downward toward the infantryman. Something—a javelin?—clipped his arm before clattering away. He cried out and didn't bother to be ashamed—no one would hear it among the crashing and swooshing of steel and flesh. There was a beauty in it, battle, in its bedlam and its machinations, just as he'd known there would be. The stench of fear and excitement rising off flesh. He spun Aethon around to charge again.

Inches from his head, steel sliced into the figure on his right. He glanced at the unfortunate man: a boy, really, no older than himself. It hadn't been a clean hit, not quite a kill; his soldier gasped and garbled at his throat. "My king," Ptolemy thought he heard him utter. Then the moment passed; the boy was trampled beneath the thrashing of hooves.

The chaos turned ugly, brutal—the Romans came at him from all sides. Madly, he slashed his sword one way and then the next, not bothering to steer Aethon, only hoping the horse's reflexes would serve better than his own. A squeal pierced the air, and a sharp pain sent Ptolemy reeling backward. His knees clung to his horse and time slowed to a crawl. A choice dangled before him: give up and fall or cling to his mount. He could recall other moments when he'd been knocked from a horse, when his legs would loose themselves and he would accept the rushing ground. But this time, he refused. Violently, he flopped himself forward and clutched Aethon's mane between his fingers. His left shoulder screamed in agony; a quick glance confirmed an arrow lodged between his breastplate and his armor, bright crimson blooming in its wake. The sight of his own blood sickened him, and so he didn't look again. He sliced his blade forward—and this time he caught steel. His sword had locked with the axe of that same one-eyed Roman who'd spat in the dead man's face. Again, he slashed at his foe, heard the satisfying clack of metal against metal. Not so very different from fighting his friends in the practice fields.

Yet, unlike Kyrillos and Ariston, this opponent—old and one-eyed as he was—didn't tire. Rather, with each blow, his strikes hit harder, as though the man was invigorated by the fight. Meanwhile, Ptolemy's volleys began to flail—his good arm grew tired; his frame jolted with pain. The Roman struck against his side and then at his shield. The blow knocked him off-balance, and Ptolemy lost his grip on his sword. He lunged forward to seize the blade as it fell—he would not, could not, be unarmed.

But just then Aethon, usually so sure-footed, stumbled. For an endless stretch, Ptolemy's body was hurtling toward the ground.

With a crack, he landed on his wrist; his mouth filled with dust and blood. From here, among the dead and dying—men reduced to heaps of bone and skin, moaning for their mothers and begging for their ends—the battle was stripped of any meter, any hint of honor or beauty. His attacker, thankfully, had vanished, taking him for dead. And Ptolemy was sure he would die here as the Roman had left him: trampled and alone.

No, he thought. He was owed a better end than this, something grander. With a surge of strength, he pushed his head up and spat the dust from his lips, and then collapsed again into the dirt. He wanted to call out for help—but there was no one to hear him. These other men, these defeated creatures—they couldn't help him. They couldn't even help themselves.

Here, now, his battle grew small. Nothing existed beyond the crash of hooves, the stomp of boots. A voice came to him, quiet at first, and then louder and louder: *Go to the river.* There he would find his supply ships. At first, he winced at his cowardice—but, no, it wasn't cowardice to flee. Hadn't Hannibal abandoned many a battle, only to regroup and fight again? The duty of a king was to survive. From the depths of his mind, Polybius's words floated back to him: *If the leader escapes uninjured and safe, though a decisive defeat may have been sustained, fortune offers many opportunities for retrieving disasters . . . all the hopes of the soldiers depend upon their leaders.* And so his men depended on him; Arsinoë depended on him.

Gritting his teeth, Ptolemy wrenched the arrow from his shoulder. The blood sprayed forth, staining his armor and the cloth beneath. Belly down, he dragged himself across the sand. A strange memory flickered in his mind: he and Ptolemarion, playing at some foolish game, stomachs on the earth, pretending to be snakes. No, not snakes, spies. His heart ached for his little brother, poor Ptolemarion, who'd never been seduced by dreams of dynasty, who'd only wanted to be loved. He would be kinder, better, if he lived, he promised himself. He promised the gods as well—Serapis and Zeus, Dionysus and Isis, and all the others he could name.

Slipping under supply wagons and slinking between jousting men, he managed to reach the river's edge. There was no time to think. His boats floated in the midst of the Nile's stream, hurling fire and arrows into the fray. He filled his lungs with air and slithered into the water. The current came upon him, sudden and fast—dragging him downstream. His arms flailed against it, but his strength was ebbing from his veins. He prayed for some native deity to rescue him. "I'll build a thousand temples," he whispered to the water. He'd protect those Egyptian gods from Caesar's onslaught and from Cleopatra's love affair with Rome. "I promise, Ptah, I promise, Horus."

His armor—crafted with such care—weighed him down, the heavy hand of death. The harder he struggled to keep his mouth above the waterline, the deeper he sank. Desperate, he grappled with the brass hooks that bound his breastplate. Ripples lapped above his lips, into his eyes—and his gasping mouth sucked the water in. Even as it choked him, its taste was somehow sweet and nurturing, like a mother's milk. His fingers slipped; the metal refused to budge. He was dragged under, the current rushing overhead. His hands stretched toward the surface—vain with hope.

The stream stilled; his body rose. He felt himself lifted upward, light and airy—a god reborn. The water grew dark, the world scrubbed and faded. The pain in his shoulder eased to a dull throb and then away to nothing. He could swim now; he could swim forever. A heart-shaped face floated above him. She offered him a hand; silence swelled in his ears.

AUTHOR'S NOTE

At first blush, writing a sequel feels seductively simple. The characters have already been introduced; the world—insofar as it differs from our own—has already been established. In the case of historical fiction, the background research has largely been completed, questions about religion, worldview, and customs answered. And so, when I set out to write *The Drowning King*, I was quite surprised to encounter a whole different swath of issues.

Cleopatra's Shadows exists on relatively untrodden historical ground. The happenings described therein are scarcely touched upon by ancient sources, at least the ones that remain to us today; Strabo's *Geography* contains the longest continuous description of Berenice's reign, and it lasts all of six sentences. (We learn that Ptolemy the Piper fled to Rome, that his eldest daughter came to rule in Alexandria, and the names, fates, and supposed lineages of her two husbands. Berenice's own name, it so happens, is not deemed worthy of recording.) My imagination by and large filled in the plot details set around that shaky scaffold.

The events involved in *The Drowning King*, however, are squarely covered by Rome's historical records. Plutarch, Dio Cassius, Lucan, Suetonius, Appian, and—of course—Caesar all touch upon aspects of these happenings. And to make matters more interesting, the writers often contradict one another on the particulars. (For instance, Plutarch, Dio Cassius, and Caesar all indicate that Pompey arrived in Egypt at Pelusium, while Appian claims he sailed to Mount Casius, and Suetonius posits Alexandria.)

But a novel requires a certainty of events absent in purely historical accounts. And what emerges—for this writer at least—is a sort of "choose your own adventure" approach to detail. As I was researching the various interpretations of disputed events and chronologies, I often found myself asking the following questions: What version of events seems most plausible? Most interesting? Best suits these characters as I've imagined them? One of the trickiest moments came when I had to decide when—precisely—to have Arsinoe and Cleopatra leave Alexandria. In the end, I imagined the sisters departing *before* Ptolemy signs his decree ordering all excess grain to be routed to Alexandria (a decree that was inked on October 27, 50 BC, and that some historians believe was an attempt, as it is depicted in this novel, to starve Cleopatra out of Memphis). Other historians argue that Cleopatra would have fled at a subsequent date (sometime in 49 or even as late as 48 BC), but for the sake of the narrative, I stuck to the earlier time frame. In my mind, it was Cleopatra's fallout with the Gabinians that drove her from Alexandria, and it felt more plausible—in my envisioning of her character—that the queen would have left the city rather than slink behind in her brother's shadow.

In sussing out these competing particulars, I owe a debt of gratitude to a great many modern writers and historians, including— but not limited to—Adrian Goldsworthy (*Antony and Cleopatra; Caesar*) and Stacy Schiff (*Cleopatra*). To get a sense of how Arsinoe and Ptolemy's world looked, felt, and operated, I found the following books indispensable: the British Museum's *Cleopatra of Egypt;* the Metropolitan Museum of Art's *Pergamon and the Hellenistic Kingdoms of the Ancient World;* Judith McKenzie's *The Architecture of Alexandria and Egypt, 300 BC–AD 700;* Blanche Brown's *Ptolemaic Paintings and*

Mosaics and the Alexandrian Style; and Jean Bingen's *Hellenistic Egypt.* And I hold a special place in my heart for autodidact Edwyn Bevan, whose 1927 *The House of Ptolemy* still provides one of the best overviews of this bizarre, fascinating dynasty.

I also immersed myself in the classic texts studied during the Ptolemaic era to capture the narratives that shaped Ptolemy's and Arsinoe's worldviews. For the sake of linguistic consistency, I favored Robert Fagles's translations wherever possible, and as a result, our protagonists tend to recall various works in his words (the novel's epigraph from Sophocles as well as all the Homeric citations belong to Fagles). However, the translation of Euripides's *Electra* comes from Peter Vellacott, and words of Polybius that Ptolemy recalls in his final battle are Evelyn Shuckburgh's interpretation.

ACKNOWLEDGEMENTS

Enormous thanks to Judy Clain and Amanda Brower for their brilliant comments and meticulous notes, and to Alexis Hurley for believing in this project. To Madeline Felix, Caty Gordon, and Carena Liptak for workshopping early snippets of this book, and to Meghan Flaherty and Julia Holleman for reading more iterations of the manuscript than I dare name. To Ivan Lett and Julia Kardon for the hand-holding and industry information. To Victoria Frings, Kate Abbruzzese, Leah Franqui, Jordan Spoon, Melissa Majerol, and Jenny Nissel for dealing with my omnipresence in 2A with grace and equanimity. To Lauren Hallett and Erik Pearson for reminding me to take adventures. To my parents and the rest of my family for their unwavering support. To the team at Little, Brown for making this book a flesh-and-bound reality, and to Cath Burke and everyone at Sphere for their work on the UK edition.

I am also indebted to the Sangam House residency in Nrityagram, India, and all the wonderful writers I met there, for providing me with peace, quiet, and creative energies to finish this book.